THE GODDESS'S PLAN

When the guards returned Shula to her cell, she sank to the ground and stared into the darkness. Something glimmered in one corner. At first she thought it was the snake, but she was wrong. It was a faint luminescence emanating from her Lady's crown.

"Inanna!" Shula threw herself in the goddess's lap, sobbing. "I am to be caned, and many say I will die of it. Inanna, you said your plan for me was unfolding as it should. What can you require of me that demands my death?"

"Shhh," Inanna held her, rocked her, smoothed her hair. "I told you I would never be far from you. And now I am here. As for what I require of you—"

"Yes?" Despite everything, Shula's heart leapt inside her, and as Inanna's face tilted toward hers, her eyes dark and sparkling like the night sky, Shula felt as if she were drinking at a cool fountain of indescribable sweetness.

Inanna kissed her, and then put her lips to Shula's ear. "I want you to tell my true stories. I want you to find out who I really am."

"A very interesting piece of work, with a strongly imagined ancient world and intriguing interaction between the present-day characters and clearly imagined people, both 'real' and mythological, of a magical and exotic past. The young protagonists and their difficult journey to reconciliation and clear purpose are presented with a loving attention to detail and an attractively fresh voice that I found both charming and compelling; the whole conception is original and strong. Good work!"
—Suzy McKee Charnas, author of The Conqueror's Child

"Myth, memory, and imagination: in this highly original novel, Anne Harris explores how these three create and re-create each other in a taut adventure that takes us from ancient Sumer to the cyber frontier. During this mysterious journey, her very human characters confront divinity in the most surprising times, places, and forms. A memorable, inventive story."
—Elizabeth Cunningham, author of Daughter of the Shining Isles

TOR BOOKS BY ANNE HARRIS

The Nature of Smoke

Accidental Creatures

Inventing Memory

INVENTING MEMORY

ANNE HARRIS

A TOM DOHERTY ASSOCIATES BOOK

New York

INVENTING MEMORY

Copyright © 2004 by Anne Harris

Edited by James Frenkel

Book design by Milenda Nan Ok Lee

A Tor Book
Published by Tom Doherty Associates, LLC
175 Fifth Avenue
New York, NY 10010

www.tor.com

Tor® is a registered trademark of Tom Doherty Associates, LLC.

ISBN 0-765-31134-8
EAN 978-0765-31134-4

First Hardcover Edition: March 2004
First Trade Paperback Edition: March 2005

Printed in the United States of America

0 9 8 7 6 5 4 3 2 1

For Steve, who made Ray possible

ACKNOWLEDGMENTS

My heartfelt thanks to Jim Frenkel, Don Maass, Steve Ainsworth, Deborah Crow, June Harris, Mike Harris, Vernor Vinge, Shannon White, Deb Viles, Ric Lane, Betsy Solley, Sharon Gittleman, Sandy Supowit, Diana Wing, Dominique King, Susan Howes, Ron Warren, Christian Klaver, Heath Lowrance, and Jay Brazier.

There was a time when you were not a slave, remember that. You walked alone, full of laughter, you bathed bare-bellied. You say you have lost all recollection of it, remember. The wild roses flower in the woods. Your hand is torn on the bushes gathering the mulberries and strawberries you refresh yourself with. You run to catch the young hares that you flay with stones from the rocks to cut them up and eat all hot and bleeding. You know how to avoid meeting a bear on the track. You know the winter fear when you hear the wolves gathering. But you can remain seated for hours in the treetops to await morning. You say there are no words to describe this time, you say it does not exist. But remember. Make an effort to remember. Or, failing that, invent.

—Monique Wittig, *Les Guérillères*

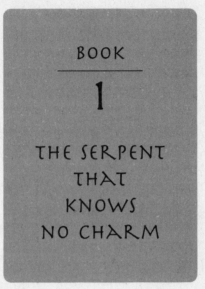

BOOK

1

THE SERPENT
THAT
KNOWS
NO CHARM

CHAPTER

1

Shula sat on the wall of Erech, gutting fish and watching the world be born. Beyond the city, the mudflats were hazy with dawn. Like dreams awakening, they shimmered in the fading mist and became real. Grain fields and reed beds emerged from nothingness the way the world must have, when the waters of the great flood receded.

Every morning she came here, to Inanna's gate, to clean fish and stare at the forming land. And every morning it was a different land. The flats were always changing, because the rivers that carved them like silver knives were forever flooding and changing their courses.

Erech was made out of that chaotic mud. Layer upon layer the city rose upon itself as houses were built, torn down, or washed away. Like the flats, the city was always changing, but the city had people, and no matter how many times their homes were destroyed, people would always build again, leaving their names inscribed in tablets in the walls. And so Erech grew, accreting upon itself; a tower rising in time.

Shula pushed aside the long black braid at the top of her forehead and glanced over her shoulder at the tower in the center of the city: the Temple of Inanna, which housed the goddess's holy throne. As the sun broke over its square edifice, she returned her gaze to the flats. The light stole across the rivers to hide among the reeds like a shining serpent.

In the day's first light a prayer slipped from her and flew away into the broad new sky, a wordless thing which, once flown, could not be remembered. Sighing, Shula hopped off the wall and took the basket of fish, smelling of blood and the river, to the cistern by the stairs. She ladled out water to rinse her hands and the fish, then hoisted the basket to her shoulder and went down to the street.

Farmers and shepherds flooded in through Inanna's gate, each oblivious to the others, wholly bent on the pursuit of livelihood. Oxcarts and livestock clogged the streets, and confusion reigned in the intersections, where flocks collided and intermingled. In the doorways of houses weavers wove and spinners spun. A cookshop offered up the glorious smell of frying batter to the limitless blue sky above.

Shula imagined herself up in the sky, looking down at the city. A herd of white goats came up Utu Street, a herd of black down Ninlil Street. When they met at the intersection, they got mixed up. Each shepherd came away with a speckled flock.

The ground disappeared from beneath her right foot, and for a moment Shula thought she truly was flying. Then her foot hit the bottom of the rut in the road and mud splashed up her leg. The fish jiggled and she steadied herself, looking up into the face of an oncoming donkey hauling an enormous load of hay. Shula backed out of its way and bumped into a vegetable stand. A squash, dislodged from the top of the pile, fell to the ground.

"Morning makes the day."

She turned to see an old woman winding a skein of wool in the shadowed doorway. "I'm sorry," said Shula, "the donkey . . ." Balancing her basket on her hip, she bent down and retrieved the squash, replacing it on the pile.

The old woman spat on the ground between her feet. "Traffic. It's not safe to go about your business. You're likely to get trampled by some shepherd's flock. And at night! The thieves, and murderers, too. Of course they'll get you at home as well." The old woman grimaced, her eyes nearly disappearing among her wrinkles. "Sneak right into your house and strangle you in your bed just to rob you. It's appalling. In my time they would have taken them all out to the charnel houses and slit their throats. The new king is too lenient at home, always going off to war or to kill monsters. How can he rule the city if he's never here? Does he think the grain grows by itself? Does he think the sheep tend themselves? The bread his soldiers eat comes out of our mouths, they feast on our mutton and take the hides from our beds. We used to have bountiful harvests, and the sheep fed on wild grass. It gives them a different taste. The mutton now has no flavor."

Shula's mouth watered at the mention of mutton. She'd had only a piece of bread this morning. Wild grass or no, she relished mutton when she could get it.

"Not that the congress is any better," the old woman went on. "They don't listen to us either."

Shula turned away from the woman and her dissatisfactions and braved the streets once more. If she did not get these fish back before their eyes turned cloudy, Abpahar would have her flogged. Dodging peddlers' carts and slaves hauling sledges of bricks, she wound her way to Ur-Neattu's house. She took the alley to the back gate, slipping through the outer wall and into the warm frenzy of the kitchen. The fire melted the morning from her, and for a sudden moment, she wanted to run back out, to save that chill, watery consciousness.

"Shula." Lugalla, orchestrating the clamor of cook pots, still managed to spot her. "The fish, bring them here. Did you clean them?"

Shula nodded and handed her the basket. Lugalla eyed them critically and deposited them on the counter.

"You're late," the cook said. "Abpahar awakes."

Shula ran to the cistern at the center of the court and drew a basin of water, which she carried to Abpahar's room. Abpahar reclined on her sheepskin padded platform, already throwing off the fine woolen blanket. Shula set the basin on a low platform beside her bed. As Abpahar washed, Shula combed her mistress's long black hair, plaiting it in braids close to the scalp.

"I dreamt I was making barley cakes," said Abpahar. "The grain was speckled and soft-hulled."

Shula smiled and tucked a stray hair into the plaits. "Your next child will be a daughter, and easily born."

Abpahar sighed and shooed her away from her hair. "After Ilshubur, I had hoped it would be some time before I returned to childbed. A girl you say?"

"Yes, because the grain was speckled."

Abpahar shook her head. "Another boy would be a close brother to Ilshubur, he's so much younger than Pada-Sin. A third girl will be out of place in the household."

"Marat will be happy, she tires of being the younger daughter. And you will be glad of another girl when Kalaghiri marries and goes to live in the house of her husband."

Abpahar grunted and tilted her chin. Shula leaned forward, carefully outlining her mistress's eyes with kohl. "Yes, it will be soon," murmured Abpahar. "Already she trades glances with boys in the marketplace. A mother loses her daughters to their husbands, but sons she keeps all her life. My grandmother once told me that in her mother's time women remained with their families after they married. It was the husband who took up residence in his wife's home." She stood, and Shula helped her put on her skirt and shawl. "She said some young women even served as divine prostitutes for a year, learning Inanna's sacred rites. These women were most prized as wives, but now every child must have a father, and a bride who is no longer a maiden is useless to a man." She slipped brass bracelets over her wrists as Shula fastened the silver and lapis marriage beads around her neck.

Later that day, Abpahar sent Shula down to the riverbank with the washing. She knelt on the bank, pounding clothes and bedding against a broad flat rock to loosen the dirt, then pushing them into the water to be sluiced clean by the current. Once washed, she laid each article out across the reeds, to dry in the sun and air, and then she sat down on the bank once more, and watched the river roll by through the drowsy afternoon.

The sun was beginning to fall out of the sky when Shula heard a commotion upstream. She followed the noise to a bend in the river where trees grew, dipping branches and roots into the curve-slow water. Someone splashed and cursed behind a bed of reeds. Shula crept closer, peeking through the tall green stalks. A young woman with fierce eyes the color of the river looked back at her. She wore a beaded crown hung with tiny brass figures; birds and fish and date trees.

A shock of recognition went through Shula. "You're her," she said. "I sit at your gate." But what was the goddess doing here, wading about in the mud, and why had she chosen to show herself to Shula, of all people?

Inanna stood up suddenly, flinging water from her arms and wresting her hem from the mud. She was tall, with robust thighs and breasts. Her hair hung down in long dark ringlets. "Damn snake," she muttered, squelching through the mud to throw herself heavily upon the riverbank beside Shula, who could see, beyond the reeds, a large tree lodged against the riverbank. It must have washed away upstream, and floated down the river, roots, leaves and all. Inanna waved at it. "Now how am I going to get that home?"

Shula shrugged. "What kind of tree is that?" It wasn't a date palm or a fig tree. It had a different kind of leaf, like a fish's tail.

"It's a huluppu tree, the very first tree," said Inanna. "I'm going to plant it in my garden and when it grows large, and has borne many seasons of fruit, then I will have it cut down, and make my bed and throne out of it. Just think; a big bed, made of wood, and a throne."

"That's the throne that's in your temple. I saw it last year, when you got married again. Why do you get married every year?" asked Shula, biting her lips at her own temerity.

But Inanna didn't pay any attention. She poked a little trench in the mud and slid a piece of reed along it. She looked up, smiling at Shula. "The river will carry it, but you must help me."

Shula glanced downriver, where her washing lay, dry now, or as dry as the sun would get it, for day was ending. Already she would be in trouble for being late, and if the laundry were lost or stolen, she would be beaten for sure, maybe even sent out of the house to work in Ur-Neattu's fields. But she looked back at Inanna, whose eyes blazed forth as radiant as the morning sun, as terrible as a thousand armies, and she could not refuse her.

With a branch from one of the other trees, Inanna tried to pry the huluppu tree free from the bank, but it wouldn't budge. "It's stuck," said the goddess. "Go into the water and see if you can get it loose."

Shula waded into the water and tried to push the roots free. Indeed, they were mired in the thick mud of the riverbank. She bent and scooped some of the mud away from the roots, then more and more, piling it among the reeds like a miniature Erech.

Inanna gave a great push with her branch, and the huluppu tree shifted. "Help me push!" cried the goddess. "Keep it turning!"

Shula grasped the roots below the waterline and pulled. The tree rolled free of the mud with a sucking gasp, and then the current caught it, and it was moving. She turned to see Inanna smiling, but then a wrenching tug at her forehead sent her plunging into the river. It was her apputtum, her slave lock, tangled in the roots of the tree. Desperately Shula tried to tug it loose, but the water choked and blinded her. Frantically she grabbed at the roots of the tree. Her fingers brushed a slender tendril and she grasped it, winding her fingers around it and pulling herself forward. She flung her other arm up to grapple among the roots, where she found a handhold and lifted herself up, her feet scrambling for purchase on the underside of the tree. Shula heaved herself up above the water and lay gasping on the trunk of the huluppu tree.

The riverbank whizzed by. Shula craned her neck, catching a heartrending glimpse of her laundry among the reeds. She tried to pick out a few landmarks, so she could retrieve it later. If she had the laundry with her, perhaps she could invent a story for her lateness. One more believable than this.

Inanna had not jumped after her. Drowning, apparently, was for mortals. Shula watched her running along the riverbank. The goddess seemed to stand still as she paced the river's current.

Inanna pointed at something and shouted, both her and her words growing smaller as she stood still and Shula, the tree, and the river moved on. Shula turned just in time to see a sluice gate rising up, the water surging around it, white with foam. She tugged at her apputtum once more, and found it was caught around a gnarled root just before her. With desperate, trembling fingers she picked at the coiled braid, trying to loosen it, but the wet hair had tightened into a knot. With frantic strength she grasped the root and tore it free. Ahead of her, the gate was opening. It would take her into the city, and even farther from her laundry and any hope of avoiding punishment. She jumped.

The water was still cold and murky, swirling in her ears and up her nose as she bobbed to the surface. She gasped for air and got a mouthful of silty water in the bargain. Catching sight of the riverbank, she swam toward it. The current dragged at her and panic bubbled in her throat, but she kept on until she felt solid ground beneath her feet and dragged herself, exhausted and dripping, onto dry land. She swayed on her feet, looking out at the river, but the tree had passed through the sluice gate and on into the city. Shula sat on the bank, trying to get the huluppu tree root out of her braid, and waiting for Inanna to show up. But she never did, not after Shula flung the root back into the river, not after she began to shiver in the night air.

By the time she walked back to where her washing lay waiting patiently, blessedly, on the reeds, it was full dark. Rubbing her sore scalp she gathered the laundry, hoping she didn't miss anything, and made her slow, weary way back to Ur-Neattu's house.

Lugalla was waiting for her when she got back, standing in the kitchen doorway with her wooden spoon in her hand. Shula had borne the marks of that utensil before, and she surely would again, for she'd forgotten to think up a convincing story to forestall her punishment.

Lugalla took the washing from her, set it on the counter, and then grasped Shula by the shoulders and shook her. "Where have you been? All day Marat has not had her favorite shawl, and Ilshubur is in his last swaddlings. I thought Ur-Neattu would go to bed without his rich warm blanket, and the night is cold."

Shula could confirm that. As her head bobbled to Lugalla's tempo, an attack of shivering overtook her. The walk had dried her, but when the water left her body it took with it what little heat was left. She pulled away from Lugalla, and flung herself, suddenly quaking uncontrollably, into a corner. She sank down on her haunches, curving her body and wrapping her arms over her head.

While she waited for Lugalla's spoon to strike she concentrated on trying to get warm, blowing her breath down between her legs. It helped a little. She did it some more, and gradually she stopped shaking. The spoon hadn't struck. Shula realized that Lugalla was talking to someone. She peered up from beneath her arm to see Pada-Sin, the firstborn son of Ur-Neattu, in conversation with the cook.

"But she was gone all day! With the washing!" protested Lugalla.

"Leave her to me." Pada-Sin dismissed her with a wave, and turned his attention to Shula, who stood up, stretching her arms shyly down the front of her river-stained skirt. Fear and hope stretched her lungs tight, and constricted her breathing.

Pada-Sin looked at her tenderly. "Shula, you are cold, your hair is matted to your head. What happened? Did you meet your lover? Did he throw you in the water? Do you have a lover, Shula?" He stood close to her, bringing her the heat from his body.

She shook her head. "No. I wasn't—I did fall in the river, but it wasn't because—There was this tree."

Pada-Sin chuckled, and placed his fingertips on her lips. "Shh. It doesn't matter. I don't care if you have a lover, Shula. I don't care." He pressed closer, and kissed her, his beard and mustaches warm and scratchy.

Yielding to his desire was a simple matter. Pada-Sin was not an ugly man, and he was clean. He had the ways of a gentle lover, even with his father's slave. With an ease born of habit, Shula closed her eyes and imagined he was a boy she once knew, the playmate of her childhood. A laughing face and arms warm as sunshine. They played among the high grasses of the steppe, and when they grew older, the tall, frond-tipped stalks hid their lovemaking. Like everything else, it was a game to them. Little did she know that he would be the one partner she chose for herself, that sex would become something others chose for her. Strange, that she could not remember his name.

When Pada-Sin left her, warmer but more tired, Shula got up and rummaged some bread and porridge from the pantry. She sat in the dark kitchen, eating and thinking about the river and what had happened there. This was Inanna's city, but the oldest person alive in it was not yet born when the goddess last walked its streets. Why had Inanna chosen to show herself now, and to her of all people? A slave girl with neither wealth nor power.

The room was lit only by the dying hearth fire, and night stole in through the door, creeping with cold dark feet to dance upon the ashes of the day.

CHAPTER

2

"Shula, attend my bath," said Kalaghiri, a tall, slim girl just budding into maturity. She took Shula's hands and drew her down the hall. Little Marat came up behind her sister and grabbed Shula's apputtum. She yanked it and said, "What happened to you at the river? Tibiri said she saw—"

"Tibiri didn't see anything. She was weaving with her mother all afternoon," interrupted Kalaghiri. "This clumsy oaf says she fell in, and I believe her," she added charitably.

"But why did it take you so long to get back?" Marat's dark eyebrows arrowed toward the bridge of her nose. She still had hold of Shula's apputtum. It made her forehead sore. Shula disentangled the little girl's fingers from the long braid and followed Marat and Kalaghiri into their sleeping chamber.

"Maybe she can't swim," Kalaghiri said, and sat down on the edge of the sleeping platform.

"Maybe she was rescued by a shepherd," said Marat.

Kalaghiri laughed. "He pulled her out with his crook."

"His crook!" screamed Marat. Giggling wildly, she collapsed on the platform.

Shula shook her head, rubbing the shaved area around her apputtum. She pulled the tub from one corner of the room and filled it from the kettles that sat steaming on the hearth. "You must bathe me with flower petals today," said Kalaghiri. "I'm going to the temple, to be presented to Inanna."

Shula knew it. The whole household had known it for weeks now. The flower petals had been dutifully picked and were heaped up in a basket in the cool corner of the room. They lent the small chamber a light, dry fragrance of lotus.

Furious over the attention Kalaghiri was receiving, Marat pranced around the room, cupping her hands beneath her nascent breasts. "I'm going to the temple. I'm going to see Inanna," she said, shaking her hips in time to the syllables.

Shula threw the petals on the water as Kalaghiri stepped into the tub. It would be a bad time for Marat now. Until she was married, Kalaghiri would command the attention of their mother and father, and Marat would be of no consequence. Marat hated being of no consequence.

"Come here," Shula said to her, sprinkling the girl's head with petals when she came close. "You'll be going soon," she said, hoping to stave off an ugly tantrum.

Shula lifted petal-garnished water in a scoop and poured it over Kalaghiri's head. She lathered a soft cloth with soap, and washed the girl's shoulders and back. From the next chamber they heard Abpahar's voice, lifted in supplication. Kalaghiri took the cloth from Shula. "My mother prays to her guardian for me. Go and listen to what she says."

Shula took some clean linen to Abpahar's room, a pretense to spy on her prayers. Abpahar sat before the small altar near the hearth, addressing herself to the little clay figure festooned with fresh blossoms. "My daughter Kalaghiri goes to Inanna's temple today. She goes to meet the goddess, to plant her feet upon a woman's path. O beautiful one who dances on the green grass, who answers my prayers, who intercedes for me with the big gods, tell Inanna to bless my daughter. Beseech Inanna on my behalf. Ask her to give Kalaghiri a good husband. Tell her to give her strong sons and beautiful daughters. Let her marriage bed be a place of joy, and most of all, O Biri, tell Inanna to make her birthing easy. Let her live to old age."

When Shula returned, Kalaghiri was clinging to the edge of the tub, her bathing forgotten. "What did she say? What did she ask for me?"

"She asked for you to have a happy life, and a long one."

Kalaghiri rolled her eyes. "Well of course, but what did she say, specifically? What kind of husband?"

"A good one."

"That's all? She didn't mention anybody in particular?" Kalaghiri stood, flicked petals off her skin, and stepped out of the tub.

Shaking her head, Shula helped her dry off. "She asked that your marriage bed be a place of joy."

"Ewww," said Marat in the corner, playing with Kalaghiri's kohl stick. "When I go to the temple, I'm going to pray to my own guardian. I'm going to ask for a husband like the king, someone who's gone all the time."

"When your time comes, they'll be lucky if they can unload you on a dung collector," said Kalaghiri, snatching the kohl stick from her hands. "Besides," she nodded to the little altar beside the hearth, where a clay figure stood wrapped in red cloth. "I already did talk to my guardian, last night."

"Shula, you should ask your guardian to talk to Inanna. You're old enough to get married," said Marat.

"Plenty," said Kalaghiri.

"I don't have one," said Shula.

"You don't have a guardian? What, do you think the gods have nothing better to do than listen to the prayers of a slave?" asked Marat, her hands on her hips. "They're busy, you know."

Shula nodded her head. It was true, they were far too busy gossiping, warring, and bedding one another to pay much heed to the concerns of mortals. Shula didn't know why she'd never fashioned herself a guardian with clay. Even slaves were permitted this. But if someone were watching over her, she'd never felt it, at least not until yesterday. Besides, she prayed but little.

All the way up to the temple the streets were filled with girls in red robes. They wore flowers in their hair and around their necks. Daisies and blue flax flowers framed faces bright with hope. Shula trailed behind Ur-Neattu, Abpahar, and Kalaghiri, carrying their offerings; fine-spun cloth, honey mead, and two white dowry birds bought at great expense and now fluttering awkwardly at the bars of their cage.

They passed through the main gate and up the broad avenue to the ramp that ascended the tiered tower. The path was lined with temple functionaries. Divine prostitutes, male and female, stood with oiled tresses and bright scarves about their necks. Priestesses held aloft their double-headed axes, shaking them to the rhythm of the drums. Temple singers holding beribboned hoops sang with bright voices. The administrators wore the skirt and shawl of women's dress on their left side, and the man's kilt and tunic on their right. Up ahead, at the front of the procession, acolytes carried the statue of Inanna, dressed in fine cloth and crowned with flowers and lapis beads.

Inside the temple, the acolytes placed the statue in its niche, and the supplicants lined up along the far wall. "Hail! To the Holy One who appears in the heavens!" they cried in unison. "Hail! To the Holy Priestess of Heaven! Hail! To Inanna, Great Lady of Heaven!" Shula mouthed the words with them, her voice no more than a whisper.

"Holy Torch! You fill the sky at night! You brighten the day at dawn!" sang the high priestess, her voice high and clear.

"Hail to Inanna, Great Lady of Heaven!" responded the congregation.

"Awesome Lady of the Anunna gods! Crowned with great horns. You fill the heavens and earth with light!" sang the high priestess.

"Hail! To Inanna, First Daughter of the Moon!" sang the congregation.

As the tempo of the drums rose, and the timpani players chimed out sweet notes, the high priestess, Shapar, sang on: "Mighty, majestic, and radiant, you shine brilliantly in the evening, you brighten the day at dawn. You stand in the heavens like the sun and moon! Your wonders are known both above and below! To the greatness of the Holy Priestess of Heaven, to you, Inanna, I sing!"

The instruments fell silent, and the congregation knelt and bowed their heads. Except Shula, who raised her eyes to see Shapar anointing the statue of Inanna with oil and making gestures with her fingers. When she turned around to face the supplicants once more, the narrow-faced priestess had transformed into the goddess Shula had met at the river. When Abpahar and Ur-Neattu raised their faces Shula glanced at them, but they gave no indication of noticing the change.

Softly, the musicians began a stately tune. One by one the maidens approached Inanna, who anointed their heads with oil and kissed their foreheads, eyes, and mouths. "Go with my blessing, your marriage will be joyous and fruitful."

Slaves and servants piled offerings on the platform before the statue. As Kalaghiri approached the goddess, Shula picked up the family's offerings. The dowry birds, frantic with an animal's knowing, battered themselves against the reeds of the cage. One of them bit her finger, and Shula gasped and dropped the cage. It broke open, releasing the birds to fly in swooping circles about the temple and out the window.

In the sudden silence, everyone stared at Shula, who stood before the ruined cage, her hand dripping blood. The priestess was herself again, Inanna having flown with her birds. Shapar signaled the musicians to resume their playing, and beckoned Kalaghiri to her. Harboring some faint hope of retrieving the birds, Shula crept from the room and around the terrace to the window they had flown through. She found herself looking down at a garden where a tree with fan-shaped leaves had recently been planted. It was the huluppu tree she'd helped Inanna free from the riverbank, and there in its branches were the birds.

If she could recapture them she might not be banished to work in the fields. Shula had no taste for farmwork. Quickly, quietly, she trotted down the staircase to the garden, trying to think of a way to entice the birds.

Footprints were still visible in the upturned earth surrounding the tree. Shula looked up into the branches. Her approach had not startled away the dowry birds, not yet. She lifted her arms up, vainly trying to bring them down by force of will. Useless.

"Useless," someone whispered at her feet. Shula looked down to see a snake nestled among the roots of the tree. Its skin glistened like light on water, the pattern of its scales shifting as it coiled tighter and lifted its head. "And yet she finds such use for you."

She stared at the snake. It had spoken, as surely as she was doomed if she could not retrieve Ur-Neattu's offerings. "The birds," she said, desperate for help wherever she might find it. "I'm lost."

"Lost yes, but where you meant to be, all the same." The snake's eyes were a brilliant green and Shula was transfixed by them. "Inanna uses you badly, Shula. What does she care if you suffer, so long as she has her birds, so long as she has this tree? If you were mine, I would not treat you so."

Shula knew only that she was Ur-Neattu's and maybe not for long. "I will be sent to the fields or sold away."

"You will suffer and go hungry. You will toil and reap the sweat of your brow as all mortals do, but for you a special fate is reserved. You are a darling of the gods, and that is seldom an enviable privilege."

"But she is the goddess, how can I refuse her?" Shula asked, sitting back on her haunches.

The snake's tongue darted out like twin flames. "She is a goddess, one of many, and not the one you seek."

Shula looked up into the branches. "What about the birds?"

"They," said the snake, "are the least of your troubles."

The sky darkened, as if a cloud passed across the sun, but looking up, Shula saw instead a confusion of dark wings. A great black bird swooped down out of the sky, its cry like a thousand lambs screaming.

The doves huddled on their branch, sidling closer to the trunk. Shula, too, sought the tree's protection, and found herself face-to-face with the snake. This close, she could see the tracery of yellow spiraling and curling about its pupils like fire. "What is that terrible dark bird?" she asked.

"The Anzu. Do you still wish the doves back?"

"Yes!"

"Very well, go stand by the gate."

"But it's attacking!"

"Not you."

Her hands laced over her head for protection, Shula darted for the garden gate. The Anzu bird dove toward the tree, its cruel yellow beak flashing, its feathers gleaming blue and green. The doves rose up from the tree, flapping like frantic clouds. Their flight brought them above the Anzu bird as it swooped toward the tree.

Shula, realizing that her arms were still wrapped around her head, raised them, and the doves angled their flight and plunged toward her. They lit on her hands, and Shula stepped back against the gate, sheltering them in its arch.

The Anzu circled the tree and alit in its branches. Sleek and apparently well fed, it cawed its disappointment but made no move for the gate.

Gently, Shula lowered the doves to her shoulders. They perched on her nervously, their tiny claws lightly gripping the cloth of her shawl.

She turned to go, eager to return to the temple with Inanna's gifts. At the gate she was startled by a naked girl, about her age or maybe a little younger, standing in the path outside the garden. She had large black wings and black hair like strands of night. Her black eyes were kind and she smiled.

Shula was spellbound by those eyes, which looked at her with such depths of knowing that she felt she was truly seen for the first time.

"Can I come in?" asked the girl.

Mutely, Shula nodded, and stepped aside.

As she passed, the girl's wings brushed against her, light and warm. Shula watched her go into the garden. The Anzu bird perched in the branches of the tree, and the snake coiled about its roots. The girl paused and looked back at her over her shoulder. Standing there in the archway, Shula suddenly longed to join them.

Unsettled, the doves rustled their wings and tightened their talons on Shula's shoulders. "I have to go back to the temple now," she said.

The girl only smiled at her with laughter in her eyes, and Shula turned and made her way up the stairs to the balcony, wishing, every step of the way, to return to the garden.

When she reentered the temple, Kalaghiri still stood before the priestess, receiving the blessing as if no time had passed. Again all eyes turned toward Shula, who walked, doves perched upon her shoulders, across the broad floor to the alcove that held Inanna's statue. The murmurs of the congregants fought for audibility with the drums and timpani, and won when Shula lifted her hands to the birds, which obediently stepped upon her fingers and allowed themselves to be placed on the statue's shoulders.

"It's a miracle," someone whispered.

After the ceremony, Abpahar, Ur-Neattu, and Kalaghiri embraced her in turn. "I thought I would thrash the life out of you when you dropped the birdcage, but you brought them back!" said Abpahar, stroking Shula's cheek with the back of her hand.

"On her shoulders, like Inanna herself," said Ur-Neattu, smiling at her through his thick beard.

"Shula," said Kalaghiri, taking her hands. "This morning you bathed me in lotus petals, and today you brought my birds back for Inanna. Surely such a feat is a good omen. I will have my pick of husbands, thanks to you."

"All the fathers here today will wish to buy you from me now, Shula," said Ur-Neattu, his hand firmly on her shoulder. "But I will not sell you to any man but my son."

CHAPTER

3

That evening after supper Shula went out the back gate and down the alley to the alehouse. Abpahar had pressed coins into her hand upon returning from the temple. She would spend them on ale to conjure the girl at the garden gate, whose face appeared before her each time she closed her eyes.

Shula had no desire for company tonight. She bought her ale and sat in the alley with it. The sweet-bitter brew tingled on her tongue and the night insects offered their songs to the gods whose stars shone above. She was halfway through the jar of ale when she heard footsteps approaching. The figure of her friend, Badtibri, emerged from the shadows. Short and broad, Badtibri walked hunched over, as if avoiding her master Ningalla's lash. Indeed, in the light of the moon, the stripes it had left were visible on her arms and legs.

"Shula, there you are," said Badtibri. "The whole neighborhood is talking about what you did today."

"They've all forgotten that I was the one who dropped the birds to begin with. I thought I'd be sent to the fields."

"How did you do it?" Badtibri asked, sitting down beside Shula and accepting the offered ale.

Shula shook her head. "They were being chased by a—an Anzu."

"An Anzu?" Badtibri's voice was made hollow by the jar at her mouth.

"A big bird, with black wings and a fierce beak. They flew right at me, trying to get away from it."

"Amazing."

Shula nodded. "Something's happening to me, Badtibri. I keep seeing—
Ever since yesterday, at the river. I met Inanna there."

Badtibri's eyes grew wide. "But no one sees her anymore."

"I know, but I did. And then again today, in the temple, and in the
garden—" In the garden she'd seen someone else entirely.

"She brought the birds back for you, because she didn't want you to
be punished."

"I don't think she did, actually," said Shula, but Badtibri wasn't listening.

"You have her attention, Shula. Everyone else has to pray to their little
god, their guardian, to intervene with the big gods, but not you. A common slave girl and a Semite, not even a Sumerian—you have the ear of
Inanna herself. Oh, Shula, pray to her for me. Ask her to find me a better
house than this one I'm in. Ask her to set me free."

"I don't think it works that way, Badtibri. The snake told me that it's
not such a good thing, to have their attention."

Badtibri snorted. "What does a snake know?" She stopped and stared
at her. "You're talking to snakes now, too?"

Shula rolled her eyes. "Don't tell anyone, Badtibri. I might get in trouble."

"In trouble, in trouble, is that all you can think about? You see Inanna,
you talk to Inanna, Inanna listens, and you're worried about getting in
trouble. What a waste."

Shula frowned, took the jar of ale back from her and drank deeply.
Why had she told Badtibri? Now these details would be all over the neighborhood. They'd think she was lying, or worse, that she was a witch.
Women found working sorcery against the people of Erech had their noses
cut off. Often such women were foreigners, like her. "Ur-Neattu says he
will sell me to his son," she said, to change the subject.

"Pada-Sin? He likes you."

"Yes." Shula nodded.

Badtibri leaned closer, her eyes alight with scheming. "If you have a
child by him, maybe he will marry you."

"What if he already has a wife and children by then?"

"Then make sure you get pregnant before that happens. Is he going to
marry?"

"Not yet, not that I know of. Abpahar and Ur-Neattu are concentrating on making a match for Kalaghiri right now."

"Well then," Badtibri sat back with her hands open, as if it were all settled. "Don't worry so much, Shula. Count your blessings. You're the favorite of your master's son, you have the ear of Inanna, and the gratitude of your household. Me, I have to dig carrots all day for an old fool who whips me like one of his donkeys. I should have such problems as you."

Shula put her head on her friend's shoulder and wrapped her arms around her. "You are bad tempered, Badtibri. You bring it on yourself by talking back to him."

"If I dig up a turnip and call it a turnip, no one whips me. Why should I be whipped for calling a fool a fool?"

Shula held Badtibri and didn't say anything.

"I want to run away."

"You can't do that." Shula pulled away. "You'll get in trouble, and he'll beat you that much worse."

"Only if he catches me," said Badtibri.

"But where will you go? You have no money." Shula thought of the few coins she had left after the ale. It wasn't enough.

"I'll go out among the reed beds, and eat fish, and sleep on the ground. When the harvest comes, I'll join the gleaners."

"Oh no, Badtibri. You are not as I, a captive of war. You are only a slave to settle your father's debt, and in a few years you will be free. Bear it until then, do not run away and make your time longer."

Badtibri shrugged, and Shula knew that she had never really meant to run away. They shared the rest of the ale in silence, and then Badtibri made her way back to her household.

Shula, though she had drunk her fill of ale, was not sleepy. She walked alone down darkened streets until she came to a place where music played and soothsayers plied their trade. She dropped a coin in the basket of a flute player, and enjoyed his smile as well as his tune.

An old man crouched against a wall smoking a water pipe, his face intermittently lit by the glow of the smoldering hashish. Shula became mesmerized by the smoke roiling in the water chamber. It was an endlessly curving single line, coiled about the round translucent walls like a snake.

"Your friends await you in the garden. Why don't you go to them?"

Shula started. Looking up she saw the old man laughing at her, his eyes gleaming, but she wasn't entirely sure he had spoken. "I don't have— Badtibri?"

"Not Badtibri." This time she was sure it was the man, she saw his lips move, but there was a glaze across his slitted eyes that made her wonder if they were his words.

"You get around, for such a sweet young thing," the man's lips parted in a yellow smile and he leaned closer to her. "I saw you, down by the river, cleaning your fish." He lunged forward, one bony, wrinkled hand darting between her legs.

Shula jumped up, gasping, shoving his hand away. She stumbled backward, pulling at her skirt where he had grazed it. Fool, fool, fool, she thought furiously, backing away. It wasn't the snake, or Inanna, or anyone else. It was just a dirty old man.

She kept walking backward until it was clear he would not follow her, and then she turned her back on the ruddy glow of his water pipe, and moved on into the darkness.

The full moon peeked through a stand of date palms in a courtyard up ahead. She had no other company, so she walked toward it. The night was very blue in the silver light. As she stepped around a corner, the moon's glow struck her full in the face. Heavy and full, like a bowl ready to spill its water, like a woman aching for birth, it hung above the garden gate.

A pair of dogs howled somewhere behind her, and she realized she was already through the gate. In the middle of the garden stood a large tree that held the moon in its branches. Beneath it sat the girl with the wings, the snake, and the Anzu bird, sharing a flagon of wine.

"Welcome," said the girl. "Sit with us, share our wine."

Shula eyed the Anzu bird nervously, but its wings were folded, its beak dipped demurely into its bowl of wine. "I didn't realize it was this garden," said Shula.

"You came in from a different gate than the one you let me pass through," said the girl. "Please, join us, share our wine. It is because of you that we celebrate in our new home."

Shula hesitated, thinking of the incident at the river. "But I serve In-anna."

"I'd think twice about serving anyone, if I were you," said the snake. "You've been walking a long time. Aren't your feet tired?"

Shula realized they were, and the dark girl was smiling at her with teeth shining like the moon. The girl stood and held out her hand. "Since you first admitted me here, it is only fitting that you should now be my guest."

Shula remembered her dumb nod to the question, *Can I come in?* She could not argue with the girl's logic. Moreover, she could not refuse that steady gaze that took all of her in, and saw not just a slave of Ur-Neattu, but her, Shula. She stepped forward to take the girl's outstretched hand, and they sat down on the grass together.

"Who are you?" asked Shula.

"I am Belili," she said, pouring Shula a bowl of wine.

Shula took the bowl from her hands and drank. The wine was sweet and strong. She glanced surreptitiously at Belili's wings. "You aren't a girl. I mean a mortal girl," she said.

Belili laughed. "Indeed not. I may seem young, but I am very, very old."

"Older than Erech?"

"Older than Erech."

"Older than Sumeria?"

"Older than Enki."

"Enki?" Shula raised her eyebrows in surprise. "But he created the heavens and earth."

The Anzu bird fluttered its wings and squawked.

"That's what he says," said Belili, her eyes shining in the moonlight. "Marduk will tell you another story. Ask me and I will tell you a third."

Shula bit her lip. "But which story is true?"

Belili looked at her, the expression on her shadowed face unreadable. "Why, mine is, of course."

"One story is older than another, another one older than that. Which story is true, the oldest one, or the one people believe?" asked the snake.

"Tell me your story," said Shula, leaning forward and placing her hand on Belili's knee.

"Well, all right, but just the short version. There was a tree, and a snake lived in the tree. A woman ate from the tree, and learned the magic of names. She named everything she saw, and those names are what the world is made of," she said and poured more wine into Shula's bowl.

The snake slid across the ground and lifted its head to rest on Shula's knee. "So, what do you think of the predetermination of evil in the doctrine of free will?" it asked.

"What?" said Shula, almost spilling her wine.

"You know: If mortals have free will, evil must exist so that they can choose it. If there were no evil, everything would just be good, and no one would notice. No one would *be* good, actually, they'd just have no other choice. You see? With evil, you have a choice."

Shula wrinkled her brow. "I guess so, but why can't there be other choices besides just good and evil?"

The snake hissed with approval. "Yes. It is for questions such as these that we like you."

"Truly," said Belili, leaning forward to brush the hair away from Shula's face. "With a mind like that, you should be a priestess." The Anzu bird shifted its weight from one foot to another and back again, croaking appreciatively.

"A priestess? But I'm only a slave."

Belili raised one shoulder in indifference. "If that narrow-nosed bureaucrat Shapar can sing the songs and bring Inanna down, why not you? After all, she chose you."

Shula shook her head. "I thought you didn't want me to serve anybody."

Belili smiled slowly. "I didn't say 'serve.' "

"Oh." Shula felt frightened. What were they asking of her? "But aren't Inanna's priestesses supposed to serve her? Wouldn't the goddess punish me if I didn't do her will? And what would I do instead?"

Belili shook her head. "So many questions. Drink now. The moon awaits."

Shula did, her eyelids fluttering up to reveal a great white face, leaning so close now between the branches that she could feel her icy breath. "That's close," she said, gasping from her long drink.

"Very close. Come here." The moonlight was radiant on Belili's stomach and thighs. Shula turned and let that lap hold her, let those arms and legs encircle her. She rested her head on Belili's shoulder, and looked up at the moon.

"Do you remember your mother?" asked Belili.

She shook her head. "No, I am a Semite, a captive of war. But I don't remember the war, or how I lived before it. Now I have no mother or father. I am a slave in the house of Ur-Neattu, and do not even have a little god to watch over me." Shula tipped her head back to peer at Belili. "Will you be my guardian?" she asked.

"Yes, certainly, if you will remember that you were not always a slave."

"But how can I? My life before I came to Erech is a murky pond, and I have no net or line to draw up what might be in there."

"Then if you cannot remember, invent. Make up your own story."

Shula drank with Belili and the snake and the Anzu bird until the moon left the branches of the huluppu tree, and the morning star appeared in the sky. But when she left the garden, she still found night all around her. Her head dizzy with drink, she made her way back to Ur-Neattu's house.

Pada-Sin was in the kitchen when Shula got there. "There you are Shula, where have you been? Off to see your lover again?"

"I was at the alehouse. I don't have—" She stopped short. She didn't want him to know where she'd really been, and who with. She was fairly sure that consorting with the likes of Belili and the snake could get her branded as a witch, if it were known.

Pada-Sin approached her, ran his hand down her arm and lifted her hand in his. "Slaves, even ones blessed by Inanna, should not walk the streets alone at night."

Shula looked down at the packed earth floor, her face reddening. "Ab-pahar gave me the coins to spend as I pleased," she whispered. "I bought ale."

"I would have given you wine." Pada-Sin pushed her hair back from her shoulders, and stroked her neck.

Shula did not tell him she'd had wine as well, and her fill of it.

Pada-Sin leaned forward and brushed his lips against her ear. "Don't sleep on the floor tonight," he whispered. "Come with me to my bed."

Shula thought of Badtibri's advice, and allowed Pada-Sin to lead her to his bedchamber. As he undressed her, Shula recalled Belili's words, *You were not always a slave.* The thought distracted her as Pada-Sin lowered her onto his bed and eased his weight upon her. It might be true, but there was no denying that she was a slave now. If she could get pregnant by Pada-Sin, and bear him a son before he was married, he might marry her, and her children would be free. Shula shut her eyes, and turned her face to his soft and prickly beard. She sought his mouth amongst the curling hairs, and kissed him.

CHAPTER

4

Shula was sitting in front of the house picking stones out of a basket of lentils when the messenger came. She saw his feet first. He wore sandals of leather. His toes were dusty, his legs, too, but his short tunic and shawl were brilliant white. "Is Ur-Neattu at home?" he asked. "I bring a message from Padish-Ulgallah, ensi of the temple of Inanna."

Shula stood up, spilling lentils in her haste. Without a word, she turned and ran into the house. Ur-Neattu was in his bedchamber, preparing to go to the brickyard. "Master, there is a messenger here, from the temple."

Ur-Neattu stared at her a moment, then shook his head. "I will see him in the reception room. Tell my scribe Dozava to attend me there, and then show the messenger in. And tell Lugalla to bring us the best beer and the finest olives; all the best stores of the house must be brought for the messenger of the temple."

Shula found Dozava in the courtyard, combing his beard and dressing it with oil. "Ur-Neattu wishes you to attend him in the reception room," she said, neglecting to mention the messenger. With a pained sigh, Dozava set aside his comb, arranged his garments, and walked off.

When Shula got back to the front door, she found the temple messenger crouching on the ground, gathering scattered lentils. He looked up, his eyes the same color as the beige brown discs in his hand. He smiled and stood, pouring the lentils back into the basket. "You are Shula," he said.

"Yes."

He nodded, as if that meant something.

"I will take you to see Ur-Neattu," she said.

After showing the messenger to the reception room, Shula hovered outside, hoping to overhear something. But Dozava shooed her away. "Don't you have work to do, O lazy one?"

Shula snorted and turned away. She was not the one who spent all day by the cistern, glorifying a meager beard.

In the kitchen, Shula was assailed with questions about the messenger. "What do they want?" asked Lugalla. "Why didn't they summon him to the temple? Is it about the tax?"

"I don't know," said Shula, throwing her hands up in exasperation. "How am I supposed to know?"

"Well, didn't you listen?" asked Lugalla.

Shula made a face. "I tried, but Dozava drove me away."

"Well, one thing is certain," said Lugalla, nodding grimly. "It's either very good news or very bad." Shula went to work rinsing the lentils.

Morning faded into afternoon, and still Ur-Neattu was in conference with the messenger. The household became increasingly alarmed. Marat was scolded twice, and finally beaten by Abpahar for eavesdropping, though she couldn't seem to tell anybody what was said in the room.

Lugalla took it upon herself to serve Ur-Neattu and the messenger the midday meal. She told everyone she saw Dozava's ledgers spread out upon the table, but added that no one spoke while she was there.

The messenger left shortly after that, but still Ur-Neattu remained in conference with Dozava. He sent for Abpahar, who remained with him until late afternoon. Then he called for Shula.

Filled with trepidation, Shula stood in the doorway of the reception room. Ur-Neattu sat on the low bench with Abpahar, who was smiling. "Come in Shula, sit down."

Slowly Shula entered the room and sat on the ground beside the bench. "Take the chair," said Abpahar. Trembling, Shula obeyed her.

"Do you remember when I told you that I would sell you to no man but my son?" asked Ur-Neattu.

Wordlessly, Shula nodded.

"Well." He glanced at Abpahar, who nodded him on. "It seems that neither I nor anyone else will be able to sell you ever again. We would have kept you in the family, but I hardly imagined a request such as this from the ensi himself. He has offered—" Again he glanced at Abpahar, but only briefly, and then Ur-Neattu faced Shula directly. "He has offered us a commission to make bricks for the temple, in exchange for your freedom if you will go to the temple to serve as a priestess."

Though she never moved from her seat, Shula felt herself falling backward, into the gaping chasm of her future. She stared at Ur-Neattu and Abpahar, sitting side-by-side, looking back at her with shining eyes and happy faces. They seemed very far away, though she could easily reach out and touch them.

"The offer comes at the request of the high priestess, Shapar. She was duly impressed by your miracle of the birds. Will you go?" asked Abpahar.

Shula nodded blankly, remembering a moonlit garden and a tree. *You should be a priestess.* Had Belili somehow managed this? Was it solely the result of the incident of the birds, or was it part of Inanna's mysterious interest in her?

"They aren't buying you." Abpahar's voice came to her as if from a distance. "They are buying your freedom. You will go to serve the goddess as a free woman."

Shula sighed. Life had been simpler when she'd never seen a goddess or talked to a snake, yet a new feeling, like a fire or a fluttering bird, grew inside her. She imagined herself living in the temple, a priestess, a free woman. She wondered what she would do with such freedom, and for the first time she could remember, she felt that perhaps life held the promise of something more than simple survival.

That night Shula ate at the table with the family. "It is only fitting, on your last night with us," said Ur-Neattu.

During the meal, which Lugalla had refused to let her help prepare, Pada-Sin was sullen, Kalaghiri uneasy, and Marat enthusiastic. "Will you be a naditum or a temple harlot?" she asked brightly between bites of barley cake.

"Marat, mind yourself," scolded Abpahar. "Shula is our guest tonight, not the slave you are accustomed to harrying. You had best hope she has a forgiving heart when she speaks to Inanna of her former owner and his family, especially the little girl who pinched her and pulled her apput-tum."

Shula caught the troubled glance Kalaghiri shot her mother. Indeed, she was old enough to comprehend a priestess's opportunities for revenge.

"I've known no other family but this one," said Shula. "To harbor revenge against you—I know not what for—would be to turn against my own mother and father, and darken the future of my sisters and brothers. You have nothing to fear from me."

Abpahar smiled at her, and reached across the table to take her hand. "You are a good girl, Shula. I will miss you."

Pada-Sin shot her a look filled with all the nights his desire had com-manded her. He would miss her, too, though he did not say so.

"I will have Dozava inscribe your name upon one of the bricks we make for the temple," said Ur-Neattu.

"No, don't do that," said Shula. "You give me my freedom, and the opportunity to serve Inanna. It is enough."

Ilshubur, a half-gummed barley cake in one hand, shrieked happily and scattered his stewed lentils to the floor.

After supper Shula went in search of Badtibri, and found her in the alehouse, halfway through her first jar of beer. "A messenger from the temple came to my master's house today," she said, sliding onto the bench beside her.

Badtibri looked at her dully. "What now?"

"I—" Her voice faltered. "I am to be freed," she whispered. "I will serve at the temple."

Badtibri laughed and wiped her mouth. "Your life is but a succession of miracles."

"Things can't be so bad with you," said Shula, nodding at her jar. "You have money for ale tonight."

"Yes, I drink tonight because tomorrow I am leaving. Ningalla is tak-ing his donkeys to Lagash, and he wants me to come along. Sixteen days each way, and that bastard's lash at my heels all the way. As if I were one of his animals."

"Oh Badtibri, I'm sorry," said Shula, laying her head on her friend's shoulder and stroking her hair. "It should have been you. You should have been freed and sent to the temple."

"No." Badtibri shook her loose. "She chose you. What about him?" She nodded toward the door where Pada-Sin had just entered. "Will he miss you?"

"I think so. He hasn't said anything."

"He will now, look. He's alone, but he buys two jars of beer."

Shula watched Pada-Sin turn from the counter and head in their direction. "Oh no."

"Oh yes," Badtibri breathed in her ear.

"Hello, Shula," said Pada-Sin, coming up to the table. "Celebrating your newfound freedom, I see." He glanced at Badtibri. "Why isn't your lover with you? Why hasn't he brought you ale?"

Shula sighed. "I don't have a lover."

Pada-Sin shrugged. "Well, no matter, here." He placed a vessel before her. "Drink up, compliments of my father."

Shula took the jar in her hands. "You're angry."

He frowned and looked at Badtibri again. "Go."

Without a word, she picked up her near-empty jar and left. Pada-Sin took the seat she'd vacated, his leg pressing against Shula's. They drank in silence for a while, and then he said, "I'm not angry. But I am sorry to see you go. I've enjoyed you so much, Shula."

"There will be others."

"But they will not be you."

She had no answer for that, so she finished her beer instead. Pada-Sin took their empty jars to the counter and had them refilled. When he returned he sat even closer to her, wrapping one arm around her shoulders. She tried to ignore him, drinking deeply of the sweet, nutty brew.

"My sister asked you a good question. How will you serve Inanna at the temple? Will you be a naditum, and put men behind you, or will you be one of her harlot priestesses? If it's the latter, maybe I will visit you."

"I do not know. Ur-Neattu has not told me. Didn't he tell you?"

"Maybe he doesn't know. The messenger said you are to serve in the temple, that is all, but they are taking you as a free woman. Surely you will not merely be doing the high priestess's laundry."

"I guess I'll find out tomorrow," said Shula.

Pada-Sin caressed her hair. "Do you like me?" he asked, leaning close so his beard brushed her arm and his breath warmed her shoulder.

She shrugged and stared into her ale. "I don't dislike you. You did not make it difficult for me to submit to your desires, but they were yours, not mine."

"Your other lover pleases you more?"

Shula rolled her eyes and shook her head. "No." She turned, placing her hand on his shoulder and looking him directly in the eyes. "I do not have another lover. Since the time I entered your father's household I have lain with no man but you."

He laughed and put a finger to his lips. He moistened it and reached his hand between her legs. "Then we must make our last night together something we will both remember."

His wet finger wormed its way between her thighs. She was about to cast her mind back to the seduction of her childhood playmate, and relax her legs, and acquiesce once more, but she suddenly caught herself. She slid away from him, feeling his damp fingertip trailing across her knee. "No," she said. "This night I can refuse you. Beat me if you will, but tomorrow I will be free."

Pada-Sin furrowed his brow, his dark eyes filled with confusion. "Why, after all the nights we've shared, why do you refuse me now?"

Shula shook her head, unsure what her answer was until she said it, "Because I can."

His eyes hardened. Perhaps he wasn't angry before, she thought as he stalked off, but he was now.

Shula finished her beer and set off for the temple. She would find Belili if she could, and ask her what part she had played in all this. From the terrace she heard laughing and crying in the garden. She crept around the garden wall to the gate and looked inside.

Inanna was there, her head with the lapis crown bent in sorrow. She sat before the huluppu tree, which rose up great and dark, into the starry sky. Someone beneath the branches was laughing. Shula peered into the darkness and spied a darker figure there, with wings like storm clouds gathering behind her shoulders.

"Why, oh why, have you come here?" cried Inanna. "Why are you living in my tree? I did not ask you here. I did not let you in. The tree grows tall, but it will bear no fruit. Who let you in, who let you in?"

Shula held her breath, thinking in that moment that Belili saw her there by the gate. But she said nothing, and Inanna, with her head down, did not follow her gaze.

"I am Belili-Lit," said the winged maiden, "older than you, and this tree is my tree. You may plant it in your garden, but you will not taste its fruit." She laughed again, a sound like flapping wings. "O Goddess, you are but a slave to the Sky God An. You fear his word. But I, I am older than you, older than An, and I know no fear."

Inanna stood up, rigid with rage. "You may be older, but my brother is the king here, my grandfather rules the waters. There is no place for you among the gods of my people. If you do not leave, I will have my brother chop down your tree with his ax. He will drive you away and strike the snake who accompanies you." Inanna turned toward the gate. Terrified of being discovered, Shula fled. Belili's laughter echoed in her ears all the way home.

That night as she lay in her corner of the kitchen she thought about Belili and Inanna. Inanna was the goddess of all Erech, and so she was Shula's goddess, too. But Belili had been kind to her. Yet it was Inanna's temple she would go to tomorrow. It was Inanna she was supposed to serve, surely. Shula watched the dying embers of the hearth fire, trying to convince herself it was Inanna she loved, until sleep took her.

The next morning the sound of a mighty ax rang out through the city. Immediately, instinctively, Shula knew what it was. She scrambled from her sleeping place, barely pausing to throw on her skirt, and ran out of the house before anyone could ask for a bath or send her down to the river.

As she ran, the rhythmic sounds of the ax kept pace with her heart. She arrived at the terrace overlooking the garden just as it stopped. Below she saw a man in gold armor standing beside the huluppu tree, Inanna a little ways away. He had chopped a deep groove into the tree trunk. Her heart sank at the sight of it.

"Now I shall have my holy bed, now I shall have my holy throne," said Inanna, and the man leaned upon the trunk. The tall huluppu tree slowly toppled to the ground with a noise more horrible than all the women of Erech screaming; a rending, tearing sound, followed by a tremendous crash that shook the city to its roots.

Twelve men in the uniform of the king's soldiers bound the tree with ropes and raised it up between them. The king walked before them, his ax held high. They carried the tree away, out of the garden, and Inanna followed them.

The garden was empty and silent. Its gate stood open. Shula ran down the stairs and through the archway. She looked about, but there were no shadows for Belili to dwell in now. She circled the stump of the huluppu tree, searching for the snake, or its body, but found nothing but splinters of wood.

CHAPTER

5

When she returned to the house, Abpahar was waiting for her. "Where have you been? Don't you know you need not go to the river today? You must have your bath."

Abpahar and Kalaghiri bathed Shula in water bedecked with lotus petals. They oiled her hair and rubbed her body with unguent, and then dressed her in one of Kalaghiri's own robes; fine white wool soft as a warm breeze.

"Ur-Neattu and I will accompany you to the temple," said Abpahar, "to the courtyard where the judges meet." She reached beneath her bed and pulled out a pair of sandals. "For your feet, on their new path."

Shula took the sandals from her. They were calf leather, supple and smooth, and hardly worn. She looked at Abpahar, who smiled and motioned her to put them on. "You should not enter your new home with dirty feet, as you did when you came here."

Shula held the sandals to her cheek, rubbing the soft hide against her skin. They had been rubbed with rose oil, and smelled sweet. Wonderingly, she slipped them over her feet, and tied the cords.

"One more thing," said Abpahar, taking a small drawstring bag from the altar by the hearth. She placed the purse in Shula's hands and closed her fingers over it. Through the rough-spun wool Shula felt coins sliding against one another. "Remember our generosity when you pray to Inanna," said Abpahar. "Now go to the kitchen. Tell Lugalla to feed you your last meal in this house of your servitude."

Her feet in the fine sandals scuffed the floor as Shula walked toward the kitchen. She would be freed today. Her heart should be glad, but instead she was frightened and confused. Inanna had ordered the tree cut down, and Inanna was the goddess of Erech, so it must be a good thing, but now Belili and the snake were gone. She had liked talking with them. She had hoped to do so again. She thought she might learn something from them, some hint as to the purpose of these visions. All that was reason for disappointment, even sorrow, but what frightened her most was the suspicion that she preferred their company to Inanna's.

Shula sat at the table. The morning sun came in through the open doorway of the kitchen. Beyond the archway, she could see the sky, blue and bright. Lugalla set before her a single oatcake. Burned around the edges, it sat in the center of the plate like a dead ember. She picked it up and bit into it, grimacing at the bitter taste. The oats had been mixed with rue herb and ashes.

"Eat it," said Lugalla. "Your last meal here should taste like sorrow."

"Why?" said Shula, wiping her mouth. "Abpahar and Ur-Neattu are happy. They have a commission with the temple now. Why shouldn't I be happy, too? The bitterness of slavery is behind me." Coughing at the irony of her words, she went to the urn by the doorway, dipped the ladle into it and poured herself a cup of cool water.

"You think you're going to your freedom," said Lugalla, pushing Shula back to her seat. "You're not. You are going to be another kind of slave. The mortal servant of a goddess. What are you to her? Easily used, I suspect, and not much more."

She sat down across from Shula and shoved the oatcake toward her. "Who knows when they'll feed you at the temple? Eat."

Slowly, and with many gulps of water, Shula did.

After her meal, Shula went out the back gate and into the alley. She thought to find Badtibri, to say good-bye, but as she approached the donkey trader's house, she saw a great commotion at the gate to Ningalla's donkey pen. One of the donkeys, being laden for the journey to Lagash by Ningalla's man Uru, had thrown off its burdens. Uru stood in the alley amid pomegranates and broken crates of barley, berating the animal soundly. "Your mother was a wild ox! You're no brighter than a rock, and half as pretty! You wouldn't run from a stable fire!"

As Shula passed by, the donkey looked at her dolefully. "The woes of the past are still plentiful in my ears," it said.

Unnerved, she hurried around to the front of Ningalla's house, but saw no sign of Badtibri. She knew better than to ask for her, so she turned her steps back to Ur-Neattu's house, to gather her few belongings before it was time to go to the temple.

Carrying her extra shawl and her comb in a reed basket, Shula followed Ur-Neattu and Abpahar down the broad avenue toward the temple. There were no throngs of supplicants, no musicians or acrobats as there had been when they brought Kalaghiri to the temple. Today there was only a scattering of people arriving on business. The sun beat the stone walls and paving to gold, and the temple compound seemed all the hotter for its emptiness.

Inside the temple it was cool, and Shula slackened her pace to admire the colored circles set into the buttressed walls. Blue, green, red, and yellow, they formed a zigzag pattern extending all the way to the arched ceiling. "They're cones," said Ur-Neattu. "They paint them, and then set them into the walls like a mosaic."

Shula lifted her hand to touch a blue circle. It was dry and chalky to the touch, and when she withdrew her hand, her fingers left a smudge behind. She glanced quickly at Ur-Neattu, but he had moved on to examine a series of buttresses at the far end of the chamber.

The judges met in the Pillared Hall behind the Great Court. They sat in a row, seven of them, wearing red robes and gold breastplates. Behind them, on a raised dais, sat Ensi Padish-Ulgallah. His blue robe was offset by a silver breastplate inlaid with lapis studs, his beard was oiled and braided, and on his brow he wore a band of lapis and silver. In his hand he held the eagle-headed staff of Erech.

Flanking the judges were two acolytes, one holding the sword of Inanna, the other her statue. On either side of them sat the court scribe with his tablets and stylus and the barber with his knife and bowl.

A number of people sat awaiting the judgment of the court. As Shula, Ur-Neattu, and Abpahar entered, a divorce case was in progress. The elder of the Titulum quarter of the city testified that Yiallope, the wife of Hatlahur, had produced no sons, nor provided a slave girl to bear him children in her stead. As he spoke, the woman, standing in the back row, wept and tore at the hem of her gown. When it was her turn to testify, she argued for the return of her dowry. "Why should I be sent out into the streets with nothing? My husband made a contract with my family, and I brought a dowry of ten minas of silver, twenty bushels of grain, and two ewes with me to my husband's house. It is not my fault that I bore him no sons, and for not wishing to replace myself in his bed, I can only blame my heart, which loved him too dearly."

The judges granted Hatlahur his divorce, but required him to return half of the dowry his wife had brought to the marriage.

When it was time for Ur-Neattu to stand before the judges, the scribe read a tablet, "Inanna bear witness that Ur-Neattu, son of Tetua-Nur, agrees to make at least three hundred gur of bricks for the building of temple additions, which he will sell to Ensi Padish-Ulgallah for the price of twenty talents for the first one hundred gur, and ten minas for each gur thereafter. Those who attest to this document with their seals have sworn to uphold this contract, and to bear witness to its validity." The judges, the ensi, and Ur-Neattu all pressed their seals along the bottom of the tablet.

Then Shula was brought forward and told to kneel. The barber approached with a brass basin filled with soapy water, and a long, bright, shaving knife. She bent her head forward, and he grasped her slave lock, pulling her forehead down into the basin. The water was cool on her forehead, and she realized she was thirsty. The barber pulled her head back up, and with a deft motion of his knife, sheared the apputtum from her scalp.

"Her forehead is clear," said the judges.

"Her forehead is clear," repeated the ensi. "Let those judges presiding today bear witness that the maid Shula, who was a captive of war with the Semite tribe Hekua, has cleared her forehead with Ur-Neattu, and neither he nor any other man may make a claim on her.

"She will enter the temple of Inanna as a priestess. Let no one press her to service of any but the great goddess who has ordained this. To you, Inanna, and to your father Nanna and your grandfather Enki, do we pledge our seal, as we swear on the sword of your wrath."

The judges and Ensi Padish-Ulgallah pressed their seals into the clay, and Ur-Neattu did likewise. The barber took up Inanna's sword and passed it among the judges and the ensi, who each placed a hand on the broad blade and attested that they had witnessed and sealed the document concerning Shula's freedom. The sword was presented to Ur-Neattu, and he swore, "I, Ur-Neattu, pledge my seal that on this day I relinquish ownership of the maid Shula."

He said nothing further to her before he left. Nor did Abpahar. What could be said? The relationship in which they had known each other was gone.

She watched them file out among the pillars, their heads tilted forward in modest dignity. As their faces slipped past in the spaces between the columns, Abpahar and Ur-Neattu seemed to change. They became unremarkable, almost anonymous; just a moderately prosperous couple working hard to improve their status. They faded as the spaces between the columns narrowed, becoming but a flicker of vision echoed by footsteps.

Shula looked around to find that all the other people were leaving as well. Turning amid the rustling of robes she tried to find someone who might be looking for her, but the scribe was busy with his tablets, stacking them on a low wagon, and the acolytes were carrying away the sacred sword and scepter as Ensi Padish-Ulgallah and the judges swept before them.

She turned to the barber, who was wiping out his bowl with a wool cloth. "What am I to do now?" she asked him.

He looked at her with surprise. "Did no one instruct you?"

"No. I do not even know what type of priestess I am to be or where I am to go or what my duties—"

"Well, that is as accurate an introduction to the way things are done around here as you are likely to receive." He laughed. "The ox's tail is a stranger to the ox's nose. Wait here. I must shave the novitiates to the galla priesthood now, but on my way I will make inquiries, and get word back to you."

In a moment Shula found herself standing alone in the Pillared Hall. She put a hand up to finger the freshly bald spot on her forehead, and turned in a slow circle. The hall was empty but for a few scattered fruit rinds. A breeze blew through, curling softly around her. It carried the smell of roasted mutton and the soft vibration of distant drumming. Her stomach rumbled. She'd eaten Lugalla's meager, bitter breakfast a long time ago. She sat down on a bench to wait.

No one came. She waited for hours and no one came. All the while the smell of that roast mutton tortured her. At last she stood up. No one was coming for her. She would have to sort it out for herself, but first, she would find that cook fire.

Shula let the tantalizing aroma guide her out of the Pillared Hall and down a long passageway whose wall paintings depicted a processional filled with acrobats, dancers, and musicians. The passage led away from the Great Court and snaked around various courtyards and chambers, eventually ending at a large pillared arcade open to the sky above.

At one end of the arcade, an ornate gate opened onto a public square, at the other end stood the temple of the harlot priestesses. It was late afternoon, and the sun slanted through the pillars of the gate, casting stripes down the busy arcade lined with merchants' booths and cook-shops. Acrobats and dancers practiced in clusters, cavorting and dodging around a steady stream of men moving from the gate to the temple.

Shula found her mutton-seller and used one of the coins Abpahar had given her to purchase a thick slab of roast sheep wrapped in a lettuce leaf and dressed with honey and cinnamon. She leaned against one of the sandstone pillars that lined the arcade and devoured the luscious treat in four bites.

Licking her fingers, she watched a man carrying a stack of sheepskins on his shoulder enter at the gate. He walked around jugglers and snake charmers, pausing occasionally to watch a particularly artful performance and to offer a coin in honor of the Holy Inanna.

He was young and wore the clothing of a shepherd. His face was dusty, but he had a good smile and eyes that were bright with all that he saw. He reminded her of her first lover, and as he passed her Shula made her way along the pillars to follow him.

The colonnade was choked with performers. Stepping around an ac-robat practicing with a large beribboned hoop, she tripped over a basket, and spilled a snake onto the paving stones. "What are you doing? Are your eyes in your ass?" the snake charmer shouted at her, and she dodged away around a transvestite in an enormous reed headdress.

She saw the shepherd climb up the broad, shallow steps that led to the temple of the harlots. The entrance was a pointed arch painted red, and resembled a gigantic vulva. Around it were paintings of men and women engaged in a variety of erotic pastimes. She leaned forward, trying to decipher one particular scene. She could sort out the arms and legs all right, but they only seemed to have one head between the three of them.

A screeching rose above the sounds of drums and flutes. It came from an archway up ahead, at the end of the colonnade. Shula turned her head just in time to see a monkey in full bridal dress come careening past her, dragging its veils in the dust. A pack of children rushed past, shouting and waving dates and leashes.

Shula gawked as the commotion passed and the voices of child and monkey died into the background of the music all around. When she looked back to the archway, the shepherd had gone inside. The sheepskins he carried would be his offering to the temple in exchange for which he would partake in the blessings of Inanna's harlot priestesses.

Ahead of her was the doorway through which the monkey and the children had come. It stood open.

Shula still did not know what type of priestess she was to be. Perhaps she was meant to be a harlot. With certain thoughts about the shepherd boy, she went through the door and found herself in a narrow passageway running parallel to the main chambers of the temple. The first was the offering room, heaped high with the day's treasures; sacks of grain as well as casks of gold. A priestess sat behind the broad offering table, accepting a stack of sheepskins as gracefully as she would a lapis bowl. She nodded at the shepherd, and directed him through the archway behind her.

Shula went down the hall to the next room, where the men disrobed. Her shepherd boy was helped from his clothes by a pair of attendants in transparent shawls of vivid red. He was lean of build, but not scrawny; long limbed and with beautiful shoulders. The attendants put his clothes, carefully folded, in an alcove and showed him into the next room.

Shula crept to the next doorway, which opened onto the baths. Here, because many of them lingered, there were other men besides the shepherd, but as he stepped into the steaming water, Shula's eyes were only on him. The air was redolent with roses and myrrh. A priestess, clad only in a gauze skirt, her hair streaming wet around her breasts, waded to him through the hip-deep water. They chatted amiably as she washed his hair and his beard. She bathed him with a soft brush, raising lather over his chest and arms, sluicing his skin clean with the scented water.

Pleasant as it appeared, the shepherd did not tarry in the baths. He emerged from the water. His body, glistening and clean, soon was hidden in the folds of a flaxen robe, provided him by an attendant. Eagerly, Shula crept to the next doorway, to see what was in store for him. The archway was occluded by a heavy red curtain, but Shula caught the low murmur of laughter and the soft chime of bells.

She eased the curtain aside to peer into a large room furnished with cushions and low tables. The air was hazy with the smoke of sweet woods and hashish, forming halos around the lamps scattered here and there. The room was full of shadows, small islands of privacy where she could hear, if not see, that some couples had dispensed with the formality of a private room.

Three priestesses danced languorously to the music of flute and drum, and a servant wove through the clusters of celebrants, pouring wine from a clay ewer. On a platform in one corner a pair of monkeys, confederates of the bride, cavorted in ceremonial dress, playing tiny finger cymbals and grimacing with their red-stained lips.

"An old man is praying at his altar," said a priestess with arched brows and a high headdress. "His wife is in bed in the next room. He is praying to his guardian for a good harvest. 'Pity me, good spirit,' he says. 'I am old, and life is hard. My cow gives no milk, my soil gives no sprout.' The more the man prays, the more upset he becomes. 'My sheep give no wool, my oven gives no bread! I am old and life is hard!' On and on he goes. 'My vines give no grapes, my trees give no fruit! Life is hard, it is hard. Oh my angel, it is hard!' And his wife says, 'Well it's about time it's hard, you've been praying all day, now get in here!' "

Everyone laughed. The priestess smiled and sipped her wine.

Someone poked Shula in the shoulder. She started and turned to see a woman in a skirt and shawl of deep green standing there, her arms folded across her chest. Thick strokes of kohl outlined her eyes. Her dark hair was long, and she wore it down. "What are you doing?" she asked.

"I—"

"Are you here to meet someone?"

Shula thought of the shepherd boy, and nodded her head.

"Then you're in the wrong place. Come with me."

The priestess showed Shula to a private alcove, outfitted with a couch, a low table, and numerous cushions. "Wait here. Who is your lover?"

"H-he's a shepherd," said Shula. "He brought twenty sheepskins as an offering to the goddess."

The priestess raised one eyebrow. "His name?"

Shula looked at her feet, dirty now despite the calfskin sandals. "I know it not."

The priestess gave a long sigh of weariness. "Unusual, most lovers who come here are on closer terms. You say he brought sheepskins to the offering table. I will try to find him for you."

"Thank you. I—wait," said Shula, and she fumbled with the little purse that Abpahar had given her. "For the temple," she said, proffering a few coins.

The priestess smiled and took the money. "Very well."

Shula sat in the little room until she was sure the priestess had forgotten her, until she was sure she should leave and seek out some official who could tell her where she was supposed to be. Just as she was about to get up to leave, the curtain over the doorway parted, and the shepherd boy entered the room.

He smelled of roses and myrrh from the bathing water. His face was lean, with a long nose and full lips, like the face she carried in her memory. He looked on her with eyes that knew all the dark spaces between the stars, and he smiled.

With all the passive habits of sleeping with Pada-Sin forgotten, Shula beckoned him to her side, and she ran her hands over his jaw, his neck and his shoulders, as if in touching him she created him, molding his firm chest with her palms. And indeed, between her fingers his desire took form, becoming a thing solid and real, no dream or idle recollection.

After a time in which Shula remembered what lovemaking could be, when not reduced to coin with which to buy favor or bribe away punishment, an attendant entered quietly with a tray of wine and dates and bread. She and the shepherd ate, and drank, and passed a few pleasantries, and then, before she remembered to ask his name, he rose, donned his robe, and left her.

Shula finished the dates and drank the last of the wine. Just as she was about to leave, the curtain parted once more, but this time it was the priestess who had shown her here.

"You're still here?" she said. "What's the matter? One is not enough for you? Perhaps you wish to become an adept, and practice the sacred rites of the harlot priestesses."

"Indeed, lady," said Shula. "I have this day entered the temple. My freedom purchased by the ensi himself, so that I might serve the goddess in her holy house."

Taken aback at this, the priestess folded her arms across her bosom and narrowed her eyes. "You entered the temple today, a slave freed by the ensi's own hand to serve Inanna? What is your name?"

"They call me Shula."

The woman threw her hands up in the air. "O Mother of Misfortune, why must your blessings fall on me? This miracle of yours will be my ruin." She grabbed Shula by the hand, and dragged her up from the couch. "Come, none must find you here, or you and I together will ply the trade without sanctity, as women of the public square."

She half-led, half-dragged Shula down a series of hallways to what presumably were her private quarters. A small room, simply furnished with a sleeping platform, a table, chair, and hearth. "Now," she said, seating Shula in the chair. "We have to think how best to manage this."

"What's wrong?"

"What's wrong? You are the one who, by the grace of the goddess, performed the miracle of the birds at the convocation of the virgins."

Shula nodded. "Yes. I dropped the cage and the birds flew away. Fortunately I was able to bring them back, or as we speak I would be breaking clods of dirt in my master's field, my back raw from whipping."

"And after you were freed, did no naditum come to fetch you?"

"Naditum?"

"Yes." She fairly hissed in consternation. "The birds were white. You bled where they pecked you, a token of your spiritual, if not physical, virginity."

"Oh." She was meant to be a naditum, a celibate scribe priestess.

"You see the difficulty now."

Shula, pale and quite speechless, nodded her head. At length she found her tongue. "I didn't know. When they freed me, the ensi only said that

I would enter the temple as a priestess of Inanna. He didn't say what kind. After the ceremony, everyone left. I asked the barber, and he said he would try to find out where I was supposed to go, but no one ever came back to tell me. I was hungry. I followed the smell of food and I wound up here."

"Oh, you did more than that. Truly you have the heart of a whore, for all that the signs say otherwise. What, in Inanna's name, possessed you to make love with the shepherd?"

Shula shrugged. "He reminded me of a boy I knew when I was among my own people, before I became a slave."

"And a head for folly. The whole temple has been talking about your miracle of the birds. You do not know it yet, but you are a figure of renown. Somebody, *somebody* should have told you you were to be a naditum, but that's our administration for you; all the regard in the world for a miracle, and none for the miracle worker."

Shula twined her fingers together. "You know more of me than I do myself. But I do not even know your name."

The woman drew herself up and said proudly, "I am Bilah, a harlot priestess of Inanna, like my mother before me and her mother before her, back to the time before kingship came down from heaven. We still follow the ways of mother-right; our daughters inherit from their mothers." Bilah scowled. "The celibacy of these naditu is a silly vow invented by kings. Is not our goddess a goddess of love? What care has Inanna for so-called purity? No. The naditu are forbidden to lie with men so that no offspring may inherit from them. For all their holy trappings, their true purpose is to avoid dowry and consolidate the wealth of their families." She sighed and waved a hand in dismissal. "Nevertheless, the oracle has spoken, and a naditum you must be."

"Bilah, you are wise in the ways of the temple. What can I do?" Shula worried at her lower lip.

"Well, you must present yourself at the naditu's quarters with all haste. Whoever was supposed to fetch you obviously forgot. Try to shift the blame to her. Tell no one where you've been. Just say you got lost in the gardens or something. Above all, tell no one of your tryst with the shepherd."

Bilah led Shula through back passages, out of the temple of the harlots to the Great Court, where a figure in the gray garb of a naditum wandered among the buttressed alcoves, looking lost herself. She caught sight of Shula and Bilah, and hurried toward them, her skirt and shawl billowing about her like worried clouds.

"The naditum Urhulli, a featherbrain if ever there was one," Bilah murmured. "If she was sent to collect you, it is no wonder you wound up where you did."

"Are you the maid Shula?" gasped the naditum, drawing up to them.

Shula nodded her head silently.

Urhulli had large almond-shaped eyes widely spaced, a broad mouth, and a quick smile. "Thank heaven," she said. "I've been looking everywhere for you. Where did you go?" She spared a glance for Bilah, and her mouth curved into a small circle of dismay.

"Don't you bother where she went," said Bilah. "Wherever it was, it was your fault. You were supposed to conduct her to the naditu's quarters. Where were *you*?"

Urhulli toyed anxiously with a lock of hair that had fallen free of her upswept braids. "I was studying the most fascinating liturgy, and when I remembered my errand and came to the courtyard to escort her, it was empty."

Bilah snorted in disgust, but Urhulli ignored her, tilting her head to one side in the manner of a rather intelligent and vivacious bird. She looked at Shula with bright, friendly eyes. "I'm sorry. You must have been bewildered beyond belief. Are you hungry? Have you eaten?"

"Yes," said Shula.

Urhulli nodded. "Well then, I'll take you to the naditu's quarters. The naditum Enheduanna will want to see you in the morning." She glanced at Bilah. "Thank you for assisting her. I hope that you won't mention this to anyone else."

"On that we agree. It is best forgotten."

Urhulli nodded, turned, and crossed the Great Court. Shula followed her, looking over her shoulder to wave good-bye to Bilah.

Urhulli led her down a passage that spiraled in on itself in a series of right-angle turns. The paintings on these walls were placid compared to those she'd seen in the entertainers' quarter and largely depicted women transcribing and studying texts.

At last they came to a large courtyard open to the sky, with a pool in its center. Around the edges of the courtyard great date palms lifted their bushy heads to the sky, now taking on the deep hues of evening.

Surrounding the central courtyard were a dozen or so doorways that led to private apartments. Urhulli guided her to a small, untidy chamber with a bed, countless writing tablets and a table. An opening in the ceiling served as both a source of light and an entrance, via a ladder, onto the roof of the chamber.

"You and I are not of sufficient rank to have rooms to ourselves," explained Urhulli. "We will share this one."

Shula nodded and looked around. Despite Urhulli's polite circumspection, it was obvious that this room was hers. Her belongings, from shawls to styluses, lay scattered on every available surface. "It is a lovely room," she said with strained conviction. "I only regret that I intrude upon your privacy. Though I must reside here, I hope that you will not consider me a guest. Rather, since this is your room, a servant."

Urhulli stared at her, her hands cocked on her hips, and then she bent over laughing. When she rose up again, she reached forward and rubbed her fingers on Shula's bald spot. "Feel," she said. "It's gone."

She shifted some tablets to make a bare space beside the small hearth. There wasn't much room. Shula wondered if she was expected to sleep there.

"This is not the first time I've shared this room with another," said Urhulli, taking Shula's basket from her and placing it in the space she'd made. "The bed is plenty big enough for two, and when the winter comes, it's warmer."

That night Shula lay in bed beside Urhulli, staring up at the slice of sky visible through the opening in the ceiling. Bright stars glittered against the blackness and Shula felt she was floating, rocking on the gentle tide of Urhulli's breath, rising up to meet the stars. They reminded her of the night she'd spent with Belili in the garden, and she wondered if this was what it felt like to be free.

CHAPTER
6

Shula awoke as dawn crept through the hole above, brushing everything with soft gray light. She sat up, wiping the dreams from her eyes. She had been flying, and she cried tears that became feathers and floated away.

She walked to the doorway and pushed aside the curtain. A few servants, their faces shrouded in the half light of morning, drew water from the pool. Shula took the basin leaning against the wall outside the doorway and went to fill it.

Halfway to the pool, a servant accosted her. "What kind of naditum are you, that comes naked to fetch her own water?" she said crossly, and then her expression abruptly sweetened. "Return to your chamber, my lady. The water will be brought to you."

Stunned, Shula returned to the room, the empty washbasin hanging at her side. *The water will be brought to you.* Of course. She was a naditum now. She had servants.

With hands suddenly numb from the morning cold, Shula took her garments from her basket. On the bed, Urhulli rolled over and moaned, opening her eyes to lazy slits. "You don't have to wear those again today. There are clean garments for you in the chest over there." Urhulli languidly pointed to a corner of the room. "They were Kilkullum's, now they are yours."

Shula went to the chest and opened it. She was greeted by the smell of cedar. She took the skirt and shawl at the top of the chest and shut it again, but not before wondering about the woman who had worn them before her.

She dressed herself in the fragrant garments, sat down at the table, and waited for the servant to bring the water.

Urhulli arose when the servant arrived. "Bring us figs and bread, Menath," she said, pushing her disheveled hair back from her face. "And don't lag. Let Hipillu get breakfast for Pishunda and Onarra."

The servant nodded and placed the washbasin on the table before Shula with a look of insolent satisfaction.

$\int$o you are the one who returned Inanna's birds," said Enheduanna. She sat at a large table of tamarisk planks laid out with tablets that she was copying when Urhulli showed Shula into the chamber. An elderly woman, her face was lined with deep creases, and her hair was almost white. A stylus sat forgotten between her fingers.

"Yes." Shula nodded and looked at the floor. It was inlaid with carved tiles depicting animals, birds, and fish.

"Come, sit down." Enheduanna directed her toward a low bench at the far end of the room. On a table nearby sat a flask of wine, a pitcher of water, and a plate of olives and figs. "I trust Urhulli has made you comfortable?"

"Yes, she has been very kind. She let me wear these clothes, which belonged to her former roommate." The question of Kilkullum's fate hung on Shula's lips, but she did not speak it.

Enheduanna left her scribing and joined Shula on the bench. She poured wine and then water into two cups and handed one to Shula. "That was quite a feat you performed at the convocation of the virgins." Curiosity kindled in her dark eyes. "Tell me, how did you accomplish it?"

Shula fidgeted. "It was not I. Inanna is the mistress of all things in Erech. She wanted her birds back, and she used me to do it."

The priestess mulled that over. "As good a description of a miracle as any I've heard. And appropriately modest, too. And since the signs decreed that you become a naditum, a naditum you must be, which poses a problem."

Shula stiffened. Did Enheduanna know of her sojourn among the whores?

"We are scribes here," continued Enheduanna. "Until yesterday you were a slave. By any chance did your master teach you to read or write?"

Shula breathed again. "He did not, yet when he bid me to carry his account tablets, I could see how many bricks he'd sold that season."

Enheduanna raised her eyebrows at this, and went to the table, returning with a tablet. "Can you read this?"

Shula looked at the marks in the clay, and indeed she understood them. " 'The young maid Inanna said to her mother, "Do not ask me to marry the shepherd. The man I desire works the plow. The farmer shall be my husband," ' " she said.

Enheduanna stared at her, long and hard. "It appears you are the recipient of another miracle. Are you sure you did not learn this in your master's house? Perhaps you looked over his scribe's shoulder when he worked."

"Dozava? No, he was proud and would not have me anywhere near him when he wrote. If I tried to peek at his tablets, he jabbed at me with his stylus."

"Well," Enheduanna's expression was skeptical. "At any rate, it is most fortunate that you can read. Does this wonder extend to writing, as well?"

"I had no occasion to write in my master's—my former master's service."

With a short nod, Enheduanna was up again, this time beckoning Shula to join her at the table. She handed Shula a stylus and indicated a blank tablet of fresh clay. "Write what I say: 'In the bush, the lion does not eat up the man who knows him.' "

Shula's hands knew the symbols for the syllables she heard, and she pressed them into the soft clay.

"Let me see." Enheduanna peered over her shoulder. She grunted with satisfaction. "Your hand could be better, but you write well enough. I am working on a project of great magnitude. A transcribing of all the hymns of Inanna. You shall assist me in this."

At midday the naditu gathered in the courtyard for a common meal. Servants laden with platters walked amid the clusters of gray-robed women, offering them olives, dates, cheese, bread, and honey. Shula cast about until she spotted Urhulli, seated with several other junior naditu in the shade of a lemon tree. As she wound her way among the groups of women, they stopped talking and stared at her.

"Shula," Urhulli waved her over. "Have some cheese. It's fresh," she said, proffering a white mound dressed with honey. "Move over, Batri," she told the naditum beside her, a small, round-faced girl who scooted aside to make room for Shula, staring at her all the while.

Shula sat and took the cheese, slathering it on a slab of bread from the basket at their feet.

"How did it go with Enheduanna?" Urhulli asked around a mouthful of bread.

"Well, I think. She wishes me to assist her in her project. She's transcribing Inanna's hymns."

All about her Shula heard little gasps. One naditum in particular, a small woman with straight dark brows arrowing over her close-set eyes, gave her a venomous look.

"She can read?" exclaimed Batri, opening the floodgates on a deluge of questions.

"Did your master teach you, or was it the goddess?"

"When Inanna appears to you, what does she look like?"

"Or do you just hear a voice?"

"What happened, in the garden, when you went after the birds?"

This last so unnerved Shula that she knocked over a jar of water, inundating the breadbasket.

"All right everyone, one at a time," said Urhulli. "Shula, this is Batri," she pointed at the round-faced girl. "Manascar, Shinsun, Prinlil, Matab, Onarra, and Pishunda," she said, gesturing to the women now clustered around them.

"Welcome to the order, Shula," said Pishunda thinly, eyeing the bald spot on her forehead. It was she who had glowered at Shula when she first sat down.

"If it's true you can read and write, it'll be a blessing; we need another hand since Kilkullum left," remarked Matab, selecting a date from a platter.

"Yes, the lists of the ensi's holdings get longer every day," added Onarra.

"So when you were in the garden, trying to catch the birds, what happened?" repeated Manascar.

"Well," Shula paused, and thought better of mentioning the snake. Inanna had the snake killed when she cut down the huluppu tree. "A great black bird chased them, and they lit upon my shoulders. There they roosted until I returned to the temple."

This was greeted with awed silence, save for Pishunda, who snorted. "Don't forget to mention the sweet-meal you sprinkled on your shoulders."

"What? There wasn't any—"

"Don't mind her," said Onarra. "With Kilkullum gone, she hoped to assist Enheduanna. She thinks you took her place."

Pishunda gave Onarra an evil glance, but the full force of her glower she reserved for Shula.

Shula swallowed. There was no sense protesting that she had not chosen to be here. She was here, and no one cared whether she wanted to be or not. "I keep hearing about Kilkullum. What happened to her?"

The women exchanged glances. "She was bitten by the snake," whispered Batri.

"What?"

"Shhh," hissed Urhulli. "She means she got pregnant. But don't say anything. We're not supposed to know about such things. We're especially not supposed to do them. Even more than her literacy, a naditum's most prized possession is her hymen."

Shula said nothing, but the food in her mouth suddenly tasted like ashes and sorrow.

That afternoon Shula returned to Enheduanna's study. "It is Inanna's own blessing to me that you can write," said the naditum. "My old hands can barely hold the stylus any longer. Your hand is not the best I've seen, but it is better than the chicken scratches my swollen fingers make. Come, sit at the table here."

Shula sat down at the worktable piled with tablets, a slab of fresh blank clay before her. Enheduanna handed her a stylus. "I will recite to you the hymn you are to copy. This one is a favorite of mine." She seated herself on a low bench covered with cushions, and began to speak.

In the early days, the very earliest days.
In the early nights, the very earliest nights.
In the early years, the very earliest years.

In the earliest days when all that was necessary was created on earth,
In the earliest days when all that was necessary was carefully nurtured,
When loaves were baked in the temples of Sumer,
And loaves were eaten in the dwellings of Sumer,
When heaven withdrew from earth,
And earth sank away from heaven,
And the word for man was enscribed,
When An the Sky God took for himself the firmament,
And Enlil the Air God took for himself the land,
When Ereshkigal, Queen of the Underworld, made her home in the
    Great Below.

In those days a tree, a huluppu tree, the very first tree
Grew beside the river Euphrates.
A wild wind rose in the south, and whipped at its branches,
The waters rose up and roiled about its roots,
And the tree was washed away by the river.

A maid who tread afeared of the voice of An, the Sky God,
A maid who tread afeared of the voice of Enlil, the Air God,
Found the tree washed up upon the riverbank and said:
    "I will take the huluppu tree to Erech.
    I will plant it in my sacred garden."

Inanna tended the huluppu with her own hands,
With her own foot she pressed the soil down about its roots.
Inanna pondered:
    "When will I have wood to build my radiant throne?
    When will I have wood to build my radiant bed?"
Then the Serpent That Knows No Charm

Wound itself about the base of the huluppu tree.

The Anzu bird nested among the leaves of the tree.

And Belili, the laughing maid, came to live in the trunk of the tree.

Enheduanna paused as she noticed that Shula's hand had gone still. "What's the matter?" demanded the naditum. "Do you not know the symbols?"

Shula knew the symbols. She also knew that tree. She knew that bird, that snake, and that maid. She'd sat in that garden, drinking wine with them and saluting the moon. "Nothing, it is nothing," she murmured, and attempted to control the shaking of her hand. "I must not be used to holding the stylus," she offered in excuse.

"Of course," said Enheduanna. "Come here."

Shula approached her, and the old lady took her hand in hers and kneaded it lightly. "My dear, you are trembling. What troubles you?"

"Nothing. It is an honor to serve you, holy lady, and Inanna's song . . . it is beautiful. It is just that . . ." She did not wish to tell Enheduanna of her part in the story. For one thing, she had enough miracles to her credit for now, and besides, she let Belili into the garden in the first place. "Until yesterday I was a slave, and though it was no honor to be a slave, I at least knew what was expected of me. Today I am a naditum and I have no more knowledge of how to be a naditum than a donkey does of being an eagle. And even more than that, the goddess has chosen to work wonders through me, and I know neither why she chose me nor what she wishes of me."

Enheduanna smiled. "My dear child, do you not suppose that Inanna, being mistress of all things in Erech, will make her will known to you? Perhaps what she wishes of you is that you assist an aging naditum in transcribing her songs."

A sinking feeling in Shula's gut told her there was more to it than that, but she mastered herself, nodded, pretended to be comforted, and returned to the scribing table. The rest of the story transpired as Shula had witnessed it. With Gilgamesh cutting down the tree at the end, and driving Belili and the snake away. There was not, thankfully, any mention of a slave girl named Shula.

———

That night as she lay beside Urhulli, Shula thought about the huluppu tree story, and the part she'd played in it. She had not seen Inanna since the morning the tree was cut down. Perhaps she knew Shula had let Belili into the garden, and had therefore abandoned her. Perhaps she did not know, and Enheduanna was correct, that Inanna wished her to help in the transcribing of her songs, and so had not appeared to her again because her purpose was accomplished. She worried these things over in her mind until the moon appeared through the opening in the ceiling, and then, remembering that Inanna was the daughter of the moon, she whispered, "Ningal, celestial lady, mother of our goddess Inanna, grant me the wisdom to know her will, grant me the strength to walk the path she has laid out for me."

Still her heart was not easy, for she remembered that the moon had been there in the garden when she drank with Belili. And though she wished to serve Inanna, in the hidden depths of her heart Shula yearned for the dark girl with wings who had promised to be her guardian if she would remember that she was not a slave.

Well, she was a slave no longer, but Belili was gone, banished by Inanna, if the story were true. It had happened long ago, in the time of King Gilgamesh, but to Shula it had only been a few days ago. She wondered if she would ever see Belili again. She wondered if she was mad. Had the goddess sent her these visions, and if so, which goddess?

CHAPTER

7

It was time for the naditu to fashion votive statues of themselves and their families, to reside upon Inanna's altar and remind the Holy Lady of their devotion. Slaves brought large baskets of clay and small bowls of pigment to the courtyard. In the clear morning light, Shula joined Urhulli and the other junior naditu in molding the clay into human forms.

The clay lent the air, which was fresh from a nighttime rain, an earthy odor. Shula reached into the basket and drew out a damp red clod. She watched the others as they molded arms and legs, hands and feet, eyes and noses, and followed suit, producing a squat figure with a round head, which resembled her not at all. She started over; she had time. Urhulli had to make ten statues, Manascar twelve, and Batri, whose father was a wealthy landholder and had three wives, thirty. But Shula only one.

"What of your mother and father, your brothers and sisters?" inquired Urhulli when Shula completed her statue and set it aside to dry. This second effort was better. Her figure was small but slender, with long curly hair and a bare patch on the forehead. "Even if they are not wealthy or powerful, they are your relatives and have a right to be present on the altar of the goddess."

"I do not remember my mother and father, nor any sisters or brothers. It is as if they never existed."

"I think you should make statues for them anyway, even if you can't remember them," urged Urhulli.

"But what if they are dead?"

"She's right," pointed out Pishunda. "If they are dead they cannot go on the altar."

"Is there no one you can remember from before you were captured?" asked Matab.

There was one person. Her first lover, the shepherd boy. "Does he have to be a relative?" she asked.

"Yes," Pishunda told her.

"Well, I don't know," countered Urhulli. "Prinlil includes Ur-Habibu, and he is not strictly a relative."

"He's my sister's husband," Prinlil pointed out.

"At least you can include your guardian," said Batri.

"Yes!" Urhulli was triumphant. "You have a guardian, don't you, Shula?"

Shula nodded. "Are you sure it's all right?"

"Of course it's all right. Why wouldn't it be?" said Urhulli, puzzled.

Well, they didn't know who her guardian was. But the others were all watching her, so she dipped her hand again into the soft red earth, and fashioned it into a figure with wings, a bright smile, and a spiral—as close as she dared come to depicting the snake—at her feet.

When the statues were dry, they commenced painting them. Dabbing lightly with a frayed reed, Shula gave herself and Belili red lips, black hair, and black eyes. Following the others' example, she tinted their nipples red, too. She glanced around at the other figures. Pishunda had crafted a matronly woman clasping a babe to her breast. No doubt about it, her technique was far better than Shula's. She managed to pull an expression of joy from the dumb clay, and the eyes were wide and bright. Shula reached for the green pigment to color the snake spiral. Her hand grazed the jar of yellow, tipping it over onto Pishunda's statue.

"I'm so sorry," she gasped, trying to dab at the figure with the hem of her shawl.

Pishunda wrenched it away from her with a snarl. "I can see why your master was glad to get rid of you. You're a fool."

"A fool whose master received a commission to make three hundred gur of bricks for the temple in her stead," said Urhulli.

Shula said nothing, but bent her head over her figure, dabbing at it with the green pigment. Her reed splintered, so she leaned over to take a new one, but Pishunda grabbed her wrist. "A miracle may have brought you here," she hissed, "but you'll need another one if you stay."

"Whether or not I stay is not up to me, or you," Shula replied, wresting her hand from the naditum's grip. "It is in the hands of the goddess." She regretted the words as soon as she said them, because of the look on Pishunda's face: cold, hard, and calculating.

Silence fell among the group, except for Pishunda, who smiled thinly as she spoke, "Oh, the fox gnashes its teeth, but its head is trembling. You'll be lucky if you stay here long enough for your hair to grow out."

Onarra, Prinlil, and Matab laughed, Urhulli glowered, and Manascar and Batri pretended not to have heard, but Shula bent her head, and stared into the blank and lifeless eyes of her guardian votive.

The statues were dedicated in a ceremony involving the entire temple. With Enheduanna at their lead, Shula and the other naditu filed into the main hall as the sun was setting. Fires stood in braziers about the room, sending light and shadows leaping up the walls. Thick clouds of sandalwood and myrrh issued from censers. The sweet smell of the incense was echoed by strains of harp and flute.

Inanna's altar dominated the far wall. In an ornately carved alcove stood her statue, towering above them like a mother over her children. Her offering table stretched before her as broad as a bed, bare but for the fine linen cloth that covered it. On shelves within the alcove stood the votive statues of years past; hundreds of them. Clay figures of women, men, and children wreathed in withered flowers, proffering stale honey cakes. It was like a miniature of the city, thought Shula, all those people, making offerings to the goddess who protected them.

Drummers joined the harpists and flutists, and from archways on each side of Inanna's alcove came dancers girdled with bells. Their movements, at first sinuous, became rapid, exultant, as the musicians picked up the tempo. Then out filed the galla singers, who had sacrificed their manhood to honor the goddess. Their voices were neither quite male nor female, but a startling blend of both. As they sang, they were joined by the snake charmers, who sat flanking the altar, their baskets before them. They lifted their flutes and the serpents rose, swaying to the rhythms of the music.

At last, from behind the statue in the alcove stepped High Priestess Shapar, the crown of Erech glittering on her brow. Shula watched her to see if she would become Inanna again, but she did not, only the statue, a figure of carved stone adorned with gold and lapis, seemed to glow from within, a subtle thing, perhaps a consequence of the firelight or the heady clouds of incense that filled the air. But Shula, staring at the eyes of the statue, distinctly felt them staring back at her.

The galla singers stopped, and Shapar's voice alone rang out, "Who makes the fields fertile?"

As one the congregation answered, "You, Lady. The grain is your gift."

Again the priestess spoke, "Who brings forth the sweet milk?"

"You, Lady. Your abundance knows no bounds."

"Who makes Erech mighty in battle?"

"You, Lady. Your anger is as terrible as your love is sweet."

Together the entire temple sang, "All the gods bow to you. All the people, all the animals, kneel to you. Let your divine gaze fall upon your people. Bless us, your devoted servants."

Then everyone, starting with the high priestess, placed their votives on the broad platform of Inanna's altar, accompanied by offerings of incense and gold. In turn they offered prayers to the goddess for the safety and prosperity of their families in the year to come.

When it was Shula's turn, she approached the altar hesitantly, trembling before the gaze of her goddess. The music, the incense, the bright costumes of the dancers all swirled in her head and made her feel dizzy. She placed her offering of sandalwood and cedar, provided her by Enheduanna, upon the altar first, followed by the statue of herself and that of her guardian, Belili.

She kneeled, and lowered her eyes, and whispered, "Holy Inanna, Great Lady, thank you for delivering me from slavery. Thank you for taking me into your holy temple. Your will is my heart's desire, your command is the bread of my soul. Make strong my arms, that I may serve you; make clear my eyes, that I may see you; make sharp my mind, that I may know your purpose." At this last, tears sprang to Shula's eyes, and she looked up, and saw, rising up behind the statue of Inanna, another figure. Not the young woman with the crown of lapis and gold, but a dark figure, shadowy, with long dark hair and wings of black, stretching back into the flickering shadows. She gasped, and looked to the statue of Inanna, but saw there only eyes of stone.

Shula continued to assist Enheduanna in writing down the hymns and stories of Inanna, and as the weeks passed, her hand improved, becoming as regular and legible, as that of any scribe in the temple. Or so Enheduanna told her.

While the other naditu recorded the daily transactions at the temple—so many sheep were given by so-and-so son of so-and-so on the fifth day of the seventh moon—Shula was writing about the adventures of the goddess. How Enki, besotted with drink, offered Inanna the mé, the holy laws of the universe, and she smuggled them back to Erech before the God of Wisdom sobered up and realized his mistake. There was another where Inanna became jealous of the Queen of the Underworld, and went down there to usurp her throne, only to be struck dead and hung on a hook. Shula learned all the songs of Inanna: her marriage to Dumuzi and her fight with Gilgamesh, who cut down her sacred cedar forest and whom she punished by killing his friend Enkidu. To her vast relief, Shula had not experienced any of these stories.

"Why do we copy Inanna's hymns?" Shula asked Enheduanna one day when her arm was aching and her symbols had reverted to her beginner's scrawl.

"We copy them so that they will not be lost," said Enheduanna, pouring herself a cup of watered wine.

"But if they are sung by all in the temple of Erech, how can they be lost?"

Enheduanna frowned. "Many things may be lost in the passage of time. What if disaster should befall Erech? What if another city conquers us and all the people who know Inanna's songs are put to the sword? Who will sing her hymns then? Who will tell her stories, who will marvel at her deeds? No, when we are done, we will pack the tablets in unspun wool and take them to Eridu. We will make a gift of them to the temple of that city. At least then both Erech and Eridu must be destroyed before Inanna can be forgotten."

CHAPTER

8

The boat rocked gently on the river's current. Shula and Enheduanna sat on cushions in the bottom of the flat-hulled vessel as the boatman poled them along toward Eridu. The tablets, packed in wool, were stacked in a small craft that floated along behind them on a short tether. The air was damp and rich with the smell of fish and mud: morning smells. The sun was just rising, and the morning mists glimmered around them in a curtain of evaporating dreams.

With the boatman to guide them, Shula and Enheduanna had little to do but eat dates and watch the flat landscape of fields and reeds and mudflats roll by. Shula gazed at a date palm garden in the distance. She could just make out a woman sitting against a date palm, her knees spread wide. Quite unmistakably, Shula saw the white of her hand against the dark hair of her vulva. Shula checked at once for her dark wings, but saw instead a band across her forehead.

"Well, what did you think? They're interesting stories, aren't they?"

"What?" Shula looked at Enheduanna. Was it a crown she'd seen? A crown of lapis would look like a dark band in the distance.

"The texts, were any of them memorable to you?" Enheduanna looked at her with impatient curiosity.

You wouldn't even see the gold charms of birds and plants that hung from the band. It was too hazy for them to shine. "The texts," Shula stalled. She knew which one had been memorable to her. " 'The Huluppu Tree,' " she said at last.

"That's an interesting one. Tell me, do you think she did the right thing, cutting the tree down?"

Shula's jaw worked. "Well, she needed a bed and a throne."

"Yes, and she said so right from the start, as soon as she planted the tree in her garden. 'How long will it be until I have a shining throne to sit upon? How long will it be until I have a shining bed to lie upon?'" Enheduanna paused to eat a date. "Sort of makes her complaint about the tree not bearing fruit seem moot, doesn't it?" she speculated, still chewing. "Holy Inanna obviously never planned to do anything but cut the tree down for lumber. The whole ending is a foregone conclusion, to my mind."

Shula swallowed and stared at her knees. "I would have liked it better if she let Belili stay," she said softly.

"Ah yes, Belili and the snake, they're interesting, aren't they? They are the gods of rival religious cults, you see. The story is really about the temple of Inanna asserting and maintaining religious hegemony in Erech and its surrounding territories. So these rival gods must be driven out, and the tree that housed them must come down. The throne and the bed, those are just excuses."

So that was what had happened. Shula looked at the marshland around her with a new sadness. The snake had been driven out, not just from Inanna's garden, but Erech and the lands around it. But that meant . . . "Where did they go?" she asked.

"Where did they go? I don't know. The story doesn't say, does it?"

As night fell on the eighth day, they saw the walls of Eridu, painted with blood and shadow by the red westering sun. Shula saw that it, too, had a tower, stepped like the ziggurat of Inanna.

"Who lives there?" Shula asked, meaning which god.

Enheduanna understood. "Enki, Lord of the Waters, Lord of Wisdom, makes his home in that temple. It is his ensi, the one chosen by his own hand, that we go to see."

Shula lost all impression of Eridu as a whole once they entered the city. It was dark and the streets seemed narrower than those in Erech. They hired two donkeys to carry the tablets and made their way to the temple in the center of town.

Enheduanna seemed to know the way. Shula followed her around the compound to a courtyard in the back, where a few torches burned. Servants emerged from the shadowed doorway of a stable to take their donkeys and assist Shula in unloading them.

No one spoke, but a servant ran off in the direction of the main building, and shortly after that, two figures arrived to welcome them. They were identical, and Shula could not tell if they were women or men.

"Enheduanna, the dedicated servant of Inanna, our lord's granddaughter, I, Yimsi en Enki welcome you," said the one on the right.

"I, Zimsi en Enki welcome you, Enheduanna, dedicated servant of Inanna, our lord's granddaughter," said the one on the left.

Shula and Enheduanna followed the pair to the temple's main building and down a long hallway. Behind them, the servants carried the tablets and their baggage. Zimsi and Yimsi showed them to a room furnished with sleeping pallets. A servant tended the hearth, and another brought them bread, cheese, and beer.

"You have had a long journey. Rest now, the ensi will see you in the morning," said Zimsi.

"First thing in the morning, the ensi will see you. Rest now, you've had a long journey," said Yimsi.

"This is a strange place," said Shula after they had gone.

"Yes," Enheduanna agreed, tearing a chunk of bread from the loaf. "The lord Enki favors games of all kinds. Here," she said, passing the jar of ale to Shula. "You have it. I prefer wine."

Around them the temple was silent and still. A scrabbling sound made Shula jump, but it was only a mouse scurrying along the wall. To calm herself she drank the beer, finishing the whole jar by herself. Sleep dropped upon her like a damp coverlet, but in the middle of the night she awoke with a full bladder. The hearth fire had died to red embers. Beside her Enheduanna snored softly, a comforting sound in this eerie place. Shula crept from the room and wandered out into the courtyard to relieve herself.

As she crouched behind the stables, she heard the sound of a harness jingling. Peering around the side of the building, she saw a woman dismount from a donkey. A servant held aloft a torch to guide her.

Shula watched as they climbed the tower, the torch rising like a would-be star. It disappeared when they entered the shrine at the top of the ziggurat. Shula's powerful curiosity urged her to follow them. But what would happen if she were caught in the shrine? Perhaps she could plead innocence. She was a stranger here, the ways of the temple in Erech were different. And then, Erech was a powerful city. Would the ensi of Eridu risk offending Inanna's temple by punishing one of its priestesses? Shula saw the torch reappear and descend again as the servant came back down. She watched it wink out as the servant went back inside the main temple. When she was sure she was alone in the courtyard, Shula crept to the stairs of the tower and climbed them.

Peeking around the doorway to the shrine, Shula saw a large vaulted chamber lit only by a hearth fire at the far end. Two figures sat in high-backed chairs facing the fire. Between them a table supported a large urn and two bronze cups. "Let us drink beer together," said one of the figures, ladling beer from the urn into the cups and handing one to his companion. As the woman leaned forward to take the cup, the firelight glinted off the gold charms on her crown.

The doorway where Shula crouched was shrouded in darkness, and the seated figures faced away from it. Shula sidled around the doorway and sat inside the shrine, leaning her back against the wall. She watched in silence as the pair drank cup after cup of beer.

"In the name of my power, in the name of my holy shrine! To my granddaughter Inanna I give the high priesthood, godship, the noble, enduring throne of kingship!" toasted Enki, for surely it was he. Shula could not make out his face for it did not reflect the firelight, but by his words she knew him. They were the words he'd spoken in the story she'd transcribed for Enheduanna. He held his cup aloft, rather unsteadily, and Inanna quickly raised her own.

"I take them!" she said, exultant.

"I give you truth, descent to the underworld, ascent from the underworld, the art of lovemaking, the kissing of the phallus!" he continued.

"I take them!" replied Inanna.

"These are the mé, the holy laws of the universe. In the name of my power, I give you the art of kindness, I give you the art of cruelty, I give you the sowing of grain, I give you the harvest, I give you the famine."

"I take them!"

They drank more beer, and again Enki raised his cup to Inanna. "I give you my mé, the laws that rule all of creation. I give you the mé of birds that fly, I give you the mé of birds that wade in the marshes. I give you the mé of sheep, I give you the mé of donkeys."

"I take them!" said Inanna, and she drank with Enki.

Shula dozed, awakening from time to time to hear Enki give Inanna the mé of warfare, the mé of judgments, the mé of brewing. There were an awful lot of mé.

At last, as dawn was lightening the sky outside the shrine, she opened her eyes. Someone was jiggling her shoulder. "Where have you been? I had to come here all by myself," said Inanna, bending over her. "Now hurry, we have to get these out of here before he wakes up and realizes what he's done." The goddess pointed to three wooden chests with elaborate gold locks, sitting by the door.

Shula hadn't seen them there before, but had she looked? It had been dark, after all. Perhaps they'd been there all along, or perhaps they'd somehow come into existence through Enki's drunken boasts. She shook herself and glanced toward the hearth. The god slumped sideways in his chair, the back of his head visible as he nodded over his chest, unconscious with drink.

Inanna, who apparently could hold her beer better than the God of Wisdom, straightened, swaying slightly. She loaded the chests into Shula's outstretched arms, one after another. By craning her neck, Shula could just brace the third chest under her chin, and take all of them. Moving awkwardly, she made her way out of the shrine and started down the steps of the tower.

The steps seemed much steeper, the tower much taller, than they had the night before, when she did not carry the laws of the universe in her arms. The chests prevented her from seeing much of anything except a broad pale sky, colorless with predawn light. She had to feel for the edge of each step with her toes and then carefully lower herself down it.

It was a tedious process made worse by fear of Enki awakening. She wondered where Inanna was. Why didn't she help her? For that matter, if she wanted the mé so bad, why didn't she carry them down the tower herself?

Shula distracted herself from these blasphemous thoughts by imagining all the terrible forms Enki's punishment would take when he discovered her carrying off his mé. Perhaps he would transform her into a crawling insect and crush her underfoot, or ignite her bones like wooden sticks, or simply strike her head from her body.

But she was only doing it because Inanna told her to. And Enki *had* given the mé to Inanna, but he was drunk at the time and both she and her goddess knew he hadn't meant it.

Amazingly, she got to the bottom of the tower without Enki smiting her. She sighed and smiled, and started across the courtyard toward the stables.

There was a hole, or maybe it was a stone. She didn't see it. But suddenly her ankle turned beneath her and she pitched forward, out of balance. She saw the chests fly from her grasp and sail through the air, and then she was falling, and could only see the earth rising up beneath her. She hit the ground, the impact jarring her chin and knocking the breath from her body. Dust rose up in a cloud around her and she sat up, coughing and wiping the grit from her lips.

The chests lay in front of her, broken open, their contents still rolling to rest in a broad spray across the ground.

"What have you done?" cried Inanna behind her.

Shula looked at her, and did not say that three such chests were too much for one mortal to carry. "I fell," was what she said.

Inanna ran to the chests, righting them. She began to gather the mé, which turned out to be a lot of small round stones. "Hurry," she said. "Help me, Enki could awaken at any moment."

Shula knelt and began to gather the stones in her skirt. Each one had a symbol carved into it. They were similar to the characters in Sumerian writing but cruder, more like actual pictures. She picked up one that looked like a fish, and another that resembled a plow. As Shula poured them back into the chests the mé clattered as if speaking their names.

Inanna brought rope from the stable, and bound the chests closed. From the top of the tower they heard a rumble, whether godly anger or a godly snore, Shula could not tell.

"Fetch me two donkeys," said Inanna. "My boat awaits at the river. I will take the mé to my city Erech, where I will make the laws of the universe available to my people," she said to Shula.

Shula got the donkeys, casting fearful glances to the top of the ziggurat the whole while. Inanna threw her riding cloth over the back of one of the donkeys and mounted. It was left to Shula to load the laws of the universe onto the back of the other. As she fastened the ropes to hold the chests in place, the animal brayed in protest.

Shula stroked its cheek. "Shh, little one. It's a heavy load, I know, but you will only carry it a short while."

After Inanna had gone, Shula walked back toward the entrance to the temple. The sun was really up now, the sky above her pale blue. Apparently Enki still slept, or she surely would be dead by now. Looking back to the ground, she spied a small stone in a far corner of the courtyard, sitting beside a water trough.

She went and picked it up. It had a symbol on it that she could not identify. The mé fit snug and smooth in the palm of her hand.

Perhaps she should have run after Inanna, to give her the stone, but she did not. After a moment spent staring out the courtyard gate from which her goddess had departed, Shula tied the mé up in the hem of her skirt and went to find Enheduanna.

Where were you?" Enheduanna inquired, still rubbing sleep from her eyes.

"I went to relieve myself," said Shula.

"Well help me get ready. I'm taking the morning meal with the ensi. Afterwards I will give him the tablets. We will leave here again before nightfall."

Shula was glad to hear it. She went in search of a cistern and found Zimsi or Yimsi—she couldn't tell which—in a courtyard, drawing water with a sieve. "It makes the buckets lighter," the tall, slender being explained.

Shula simply nodded and lowered her water gourds over the rim of the cistern.

"I can make a lot more trips this way," said the other, Yimsi or Zimsi, coming into the courtyard carrying two buckets suspended from a cross-beam balanced across the shoulders.

"It's a good thing, too. Our Lord has a powerful thirst this morning," said the first one, Zimsi or Yimsi.

"And a fierce mood as well," added the other.

They switched places, Zimsi or Yimsi slipping beneath the crossbeam as Yimsi or Zimsi stepped out from beneath it. As the former walked away, the latter returned to the cistern where the buckets still sat, and smiling at Shula, dipped the sieve into the water once more.

Shula gritted her teeth. "You didn't switch buckets," she muttered.

Yimsi or Zimsi stared at her. "What difference does it make? Both hold the same amount of water." The ensi's attendant grinned broadly at this elaborate nonsense and returned to dipping the sieve into the cistern.

To her relief, Enheduanna was in a hurry, and did not require her to fetch more than the four gourds of water Shula had drawn. She did not have Shula heat the water either, but simply stood in the basin, squeezing water from a clean cloth over her skin. When she drew the cloth between her legs, it came away with streaks of blood on it. "My time is upon me," Enheduanna sighed. "At my age, you'd think I'd no longer be bothered with such nuisances, but it never fails, every time I travel. Shula, please bring me the belt, the cloth, and the clean soft wool."

As Shula gathered these things she was grateful that she did not need them today. There would be donkeys to ride, boatmen to haggle with. Poor Enheduanna. Shula often felt sick when her blood came, nauseous and sluggish and full of pain in her womb. With a start she realized she had not suffered these things since she came to the temple two moons ago. In fact, her last time had been weeks before the miracle of the birds.

Her compassion for Enheduanna turned to cold, leaden dread for herself. Her hands shook suddenly, and she felt chilled. She crouched down before the reed basket that held Enheduanna's linen, and put her hand to her vulva, as if she might feel something there to confirm or deny her fear.

"What's the matter with you?" asked Enheduanna impatiently. "Is it your time as well?"

Shula shook her head, looking up at her mistress.

Enheduanna stared at her and then looked away, breathing in sharply through her nose and nodding slightly. "Well, bring me my things then," she said. "Hurry now."

For Shula, Enheduanna's meeting with the ensi passed in a haze of dread. He was a venerable old man with a beard and a bald head partly concealed by the crown of ensiship.

"I bring these tablets, copies of hymns from the temple of Inanna, in her holy city of Erech, to present to you, Ensi of Eridu. A gift, from my city to yours, from my goddess to your god," said Enheduanna as Shula brought the tablets forth and placed them on the offering table.

"My, there are a lot of them," said the ensi as the stacks on the table grew higher.

"Surely you have room for them here, in the temple of wisdom," said Enheduanna. "Surely you do not reject a gift from the temple in Erech."

The ensi craned his head to look at her from over the piles of tablets. "Of course not. This gift is most generous. Our master of the scribes will be overwhelmed." He stood, his staff in hand. "You must not leave here without a gift in return. I would not let it be in my ensiship that the Holy Inanna considered her grandfather Enki ungenerous."

He motioned to a servant in an alcove behind him. The servant carried forth a small gold box. He brought it to the ensi, who proffered it to Enheduanna. Shula could see that it was covered with intricate carvings. "Take this box of gold, the work of many days by our finest craftsmen," said the ensi. "It contains a fragment from an ancient tablet, inscribed with the words of our lord, Enki, God of Wisdom."

CHAPTER
9

"Must be one of their jokes," said Enheduanna in the boat later, when she was at leisure to examine the gift. "The box is empty."

At the sight of the empty linen lining of the box, Shula was stabbed with guilt, but she did not reveal the stone tied in the hem of her dress. It was she, not Enheduanna, who had carried the words of Enki down from the tower.

"I know what you carry," said Enheduanna.

Shula could only stare at her.

"Yours is not a condition befitting a naditum, but I can help you get rid of it."

The hem of her gown hung heavy between Shula's legs. "It's mine," she whispered, and then amended herself. "I found it."

Enheduanna gave her a puzzled look. "Perhaps, but how will you feed it? At best you will be thrown out of the temple when it is discovered. Quite possibly you will be caned for your transgression. Either way you and your baby are likely to die. Is it better for two to die, or for one not to live?"

Her baby. Enheduanna was discussing her suspected pregnancy. Shula's jaw worked. "I only just discovered it this morning."

"Do you have any idea when you conceived?"

Shula thought of her tryst with the shepherd boy, and then of the countless nights Pada-Sin had spilled his seed in her womb. It was Pada-Sin's child, surely. "Before I came to the temple. More than two moons ago."

"Well, and you were a slave then. And you have been chaste since you became a naditum?"

Quickly, Shula nodded.

"Those facts will serve you well if your condition is discovered. After all, how could anyone expect you to be a virgin? But it need not come to that. I have herbs that will rid you of the pregnancy, but you must take them soon."

Shula looked at her hands. She should be relieved at Enheduanna's words. She was a wise woman. If anyone could take a baby away, make it not happen, she could. Shula could stay at the temple, she could stay with Enheduanna and Urhulli, she could continue to serve Inanna. And probably have more adventures like the one last night, which frightened and confused her.

It was Pada-Sin's child. It could be no other. She could go to him and tell him that his child grew inside her. She would promise him a son and he could marry her. And she would be the wife of a notable man, with a child and servants of her own. "Perhaps I can marry the father, my former master's son," she told Enheduanna.

The naditum raised her eyebrows. "Will he have you?"

"I was his favorite. He never bothered with the prostitutes of the market square, he never visited the sacred prostitutes of the temple."

Her mistress shook her head. "You are a fool. You will give your life over to a man, who will rule you as surely as if you were still a slave. Inanna chose you, she gave you the gift of your freedom, and you throw her gift away. You have no dowry. You go empty-handed like a beggar to the man you would have as a husband. You will have a low status in that household."

"Not if I give him a son. Then my place will be exalted."

Enheduanna laughed. "Think long on it, child, but not too long. My herbs will not work if you are much farther along than you are now."

Shula did. As the marshlands flowed past she thought of the child inside her. If in fact there was one. Her blood had been late before, but never this late. She thought of giving birth, the pain, the terror, the possibility of death. She thought of holding her child to her breast, she thought of herself, living with Pada-Sin in a house they would build next to his parents' house. He would go to the brickyard each day, and she would stay in the house, and oversee the servants as they baked the bread, did the spinning and the washing. Every day a slave would bathe her. With his father's commission from the temple, Pada-Sin would be a prosperous man. She would have scented oils for her bath. On some days she would leave her son with the nursemaid and go to the market to buy fine things.

She shook herself. Perhaps Enheduanna was right. Perhaps she was a fool to give herself as a wife. She would have to do Pada-Sin's bidding. But she had done that enough before and it had not been so bad. Perhaps he would not allow her to go to the market. Perhaps they would have no slave. Perhaps they would, and he would prefer her to Shula. But she would have her child. She imagined her child's laughing face, and she smiled.

If she stayed at the temple, what would she have? Enheduanna had taught her Inanna's stories, and that was a fine thing, but the stories had not made her happy. Inanna had chosen her, but each time she met Inanna she faced death in some manner or other. Perhaps if she got married and had this child, and lived an ordinary life, Inanna would lose interest in her, and that might not be a bad thing either.

When they reached the docks in Erech, Shula spied another boat ahead of them. At its prow sat a young woman with a lapis crown, in its stern sat three chests with gold locks. Nobody else seemed to take notice of her. Not Enheduanna, not the people on the dock. Here was their goddess among them, and they didn't see her. Only Shula saw her. She wasn't sure if she was blessed, cursed, or insane.

Shula didn't try to help Inanna unload the mé. She followed Enheduanna through the city and back to the temple. They arrived just before the evening meal. In the courtyard of the naditu, Urhulli was anxious to hear about her journey.

"What was Eridu like? Was it grand?" she asked, gesturing for Shula to sit beside her beneath the lemon tree.

Shula hadn't noticed much about Eridu. The city itself was little different than Erech, from what she'd seen. The temple, however . . . "The people there are strange," she said, remembering Zimsi and Yimsi.

"Did Enheduanna give the tablets to the ensi of Eridu?" asked Pishunda, joining them.

"Yes," Shula told her curtly.

Pishunda treated her to a sickening smile. "So what did he give her in return?"

The courtyard fell suddenly silent. Shula looked around her at the expectant faces. "He gave her a gold box," she said quietly, proudly.

But Pishunda would not let her enjoy the moment. "When my father visited Kish, the ensi there gave him a box of rare woods, filled with pearls from the sea. What was in the box Enheduanna received?"

"Nothing," said Shula in irritation. "It's a gold box. Solid gold with carving all around the outside."

"There was nothing in the box? That can't be good," said Pishunda.

"Why do you say that? The box itself is worth a queen's dowry."

"Well, after all, an empty box? It seems like a message of some kind. Besides, something happened to you while you were there, I can tell. You look different, troubled."

Shula bared her teeth. "Thank you for your concern, but I'm fine."

Urhulli peered at her, then stared at her hands. Looking up suddenly, she said, "I have some water heating in our room. Perhaps you'd like to bathe before dinner?"

Shula nodded and followed her to their room, keeping her gaze steadily upon Pishunda the whole time. When they were inside the room, she whirled on Urhulli. "That scheming shrew! She's always trying to make trouble for me. One of these days she's going to find out how hard the fist of a former slave is."

Urhulli set a water vessel near the hearth to warm, and she waved Shula closer, away from the door. "Pishunda's right," she whispered. "You do look troubled. Is something wrong?"

Shula hesitated, but there was no guile in her friend's eyes. She leaned toward her, and whispered her secret in Urhulli's ear.

Urhulli gasped, and stared at Shula, an agonized expression on her face. "Not again."

Shula remembered Kilkullum. "I know I can't stay here. And I'll miss you, but I think my master's son will marry me. I was his favorite."

"Then go to him. As soon as you can but make sure you have some other errand to disguise it." Urhulli twisted her shawl in her hands. "Perhaps if he marries you, if he acknowledges the child, and tells the ensi it was conceived before you were a naditum, they will let you go. If not . . ." She glanced at the door and pulled Shula closer, bringing her head close to hers. She spoke in the barest of whispers. "If they find out that you were among the harlots they will believe you broke your vow, and they will cane you so that every inch of your skin is broken like a split fig. If you survive that, then they may throw you out, or they may keep you imprisoned, or they may make a slave of you again, and put you to work in the fields."

Shula trembled and gripped her friend's hands. "Kilkullum—"

"She died of the caning."

Shula swallowed. "Enheduanna knows. She said she can give me something to make it go away."

Urhulli blinked with relief, and nodded her head. "The cure she offers may kill you as well, but if Pada-Sin rejects you, take her herbs. You'll have nothing to lose. I will look after you, while you are ill."

The very next day, Shula left the temple to talk to Pada-Sin. The sacred marriage was only days away and it wasn't hard to mumble something about purchasing incense at the market and slip away amid the confusion of preparations for the festival.

She went to Ur-Neattu's house, but she did not go to the kitchen entrance as she had always done before. She presented herself at the front door. She wore the finest of the garments left to her by the unfortunate Kilkullum, and she carried with her all that she had when she left this house, plus a small round stone tied up in the hem of her skirt.

At the door the scribe Dozava greeted her. "Shula," he said, arching his eyebrows, "you are back from the temple. What happened, did they find you ill-tempered, disobedient, and clumsy? Has Inanna revoked her blessing on you?"

Shula gritted her teeth. "I've come to see Pada-Sin," she said.

"Oh." Dozava's eyes glimmered with speculation. "He's not here. He is at his father's brickyard. What did you want to talk to him about?"

Shula shook her head. "That is for me to tell him. I will wait until he returns for the midday meal. Will you make a naditum stand in the street like a beggar?"

Dozava frowned. "You have become haughty." He turned and led her to the reception room. "Ur-Neattu is at the brickyard as well, but Abpahar is at home to receive you," said the scribe. He left Shula there to wait while he fetched his mistress.

Abpahar did not seem happy to see Shula. Frowning, she seated herself in a chair by the hearth. She called out a name Shula did not recognize, and a slave girl appeared in the doorway, peering at them around the braid of her apputtum. "Bring cool water, and figs," Abpahar told her.

"That is the one who replaced me. Does she serve you well?" asked Shula when the slave left.

"Oh yes. And she's never late. She returns promptly from the river with our laundry, with our fish. Tell me, what do you wish to speak to my son about?"

"I will tell him first," said Shula.

Abpahar's mouth tightened, but she did not argue with her. "He's getting married you know, in just a few weeks."

Shula swallowed. "So soon? I thought Kalaghiri was your first concern on that account."

"Oh she is, but this is a very advantageous match. After Ur-Neattu received the commission from the temple, every man wanted his daughter to join this household. Pada-Sin is marrying a very suitable girl, the daughter of the magistrate for this quarter of the city. Now, in addition to the temple's commission, Ur-Neattu will have first pick of the municipal projects."

The slave returned with an ewer of water and a plate of figs. In the doorway, Shula caught sight of Marat, spying.

"Have you prepared your offering yet, for the marriage of Inanna and Dumuzi?" asked Shula.

"Oh, of course." Abpahar smiled in satisfaction. "This year we are giving five white sheep and two white oxen. Inanna will be pleased that she has made us wealthy."

There was some sort of commotion in the hallway, and suddenly Lugalla stood in the doorway. "Mistress," she said, obviously to Abpahar though her eyes were fixed on Shula. "Are the figs to your liking? Can I bring you and your guest anything else?"

"No, Lugalla. We are fine. You can go, and trouble us no further."

The cook left the room, walking backward, her eyes never leaving Shula.

As she backed through the doorway she nearly collided with Pada-Sin. His clothes were streaked with brick dust. "Mother, I heard we have a visitor. Oh." He stopped when he saw her. "Hello, Shula, to what do we owe the honor of a visit?" His eyes moved from her to Abpahar and back again.

Shula stood up. "Pada-Sin, I wish to speak with you."

Abpahar rose, and with a look of warning to her son, left the room.

Pada-Sin sat down in the empty chair. He picked up a fig and bit into it. "What did you want to tell me?" he asked around a mouthful of fig. "Did you hear that I am about to be married?"

"Yes, your mother told me." Shula stood and clasped her hands to stop them from shaking. "A magistrate's daughter. But will she bear you a son, as I do? I carry your child, Pada-Sin, and all the portents foretell a boy."

Pada-Sin laughed. "Portents can be wrong. Besides, son or no son, I must go through with this marriage. It's all arranged. It is a very advantageous match for my family." He eyed her critically. "You don't look pregnant."

"I'm not very far along yet."

"Oh well. There was a time when I would have gladly married you, and made your child free, but you are my father's slave no longer, and none of our concern."

"But you fathered this child," said Shula, her hand across her belly.

Pada-Sin stared at her coldly. "No I didn't. It was your other lover. Your shepherd whom you met by the river. His milk quickened in your womb, not mine."

Shula moaned and pounded her chest with her fist. "I never had another lover."

Pada-Sin shook his head. "Come now. Everyone here knows that you did."

"Only because you said so, over and over."

"I didn't care, Shula. But now that this man has made you pregnant, you'd better go to him. Let him do something about it. Let him marry you. I will marry the magistrate's daughter."

Shula reached out toward him. "Then marry me, too. Let me be your second wife. I won't mind."

"Are you crazy? So close to my first marriage? My wife will think I don't like her. She's a very pretty girl."

Sorrow and anger rose in Shula like bile. She dropped her hands and spat at his feet. "That's fine for you, but what am I going to do? If they find out at the temple, I will be beaten with canes. I may die and even if I don't they will send me out into the streets to starve. You can tell a lie all you want, but that won't make it the truth. Everyone will believe you, but you will know. It is your own child you kill."

Pada-Sin stared at her and she saw fear in his eyes, and then he stood and slowly walked toward her. "Saying a thing makes it the truth, there is no other method but writing." He backed her toward the door and raised his voice. "The child you carry is not mine, it belongs to your other lover. Now go from here and do not trouble us again. My father freed you. You are no longer our concern."

As Shula left, she saw Lugalla, Marat, and Kalaghiri watching her from the kitchen doorway, various expressions of contempt, joy, and pity on their faces.

She went up the street to the donkey trader's house. She walked right up to the front door and addressed herself to Uru. "I'm here to see the bond-slave Badtibri," she said.

Her first thought was to chastise her friend for her advice. Anger filled her, and she did not care at that moment who was its rightful recipient. She could do nothing to Pada-Sin—but Badtibri she could hurt. But then, when the stern servant reappeared in the doorway, shoving Badtibri ahead of him, she remembered that her friend had already been hurt enough.

"What are you doing asking Uru for me? Do you want to get me in trouble?" asked Badtibri, rubbing her arm where he had grabbed it.

Shula shook her head in sudden contrition. "I'm sorry I asked for you as I did. I—Come on," she motioned her friend to follow her around the side of the house to a narrow, neglected spot between the house and the donkey barn.

The area was stacked with sacks of feed grain, and Shula sat down on one and put her chin in her hands. "What's going on?" demanded Badtibri, hopping onto a stack beside her.

"Do you remember when you suggested I try to get pregnant by Pada-Sin? Well, I succeeded."

Badtibri's mouth went round. "Only now you are a priestess."

"A naditum, more's the pity. Why couldn't they have made me a whore?" asked Shula, her hands in the air.

Badtibri shook her head solemnly. "For someone chosen by the Holy Inanna, you have the worst luck. Did you tell Pada-Sin?"

"I just came from his father's house."

"He's supposed to get married soon."

"I know. His mother told me. He told me. I don't need you to tell me. I asked him to make me his second wife, and he refused. I begged him. Oh Badtibri, how could I have thought it would be otherwise? Why would he marry me, a freed slave with no dowry? How could I have been so foolish? Even if he weren't about to marry someone else, he wouldn't take me, I could see that in his eyes.

"I had such a beautiful picture in my mind. Of myself a wife with a home to command, my child, and my husband coming in from the brickyard for his meals. What a dream." Shula sighed.

Badtibri frowned. "It sounds kind of boring to me, actually."

"Boring? How can you say that? You were the one who first suggested it."

Badtibri shrugged. "That was when you were a slave, and the best you could hope for was that your children would be free. But now *you* are free. You know how to read and write, you are chosen by Holy Inanna. Compared to that, being a wife and having children seems boring."

"There are worse things than being bored," said Shula darkly.

"You don't love Pada-Sin," noted Badtibri.

"What of it? Even Inanna married the man chosen for her by her parents. She loved the farmer, but she married the shepherd."

Badtibri shrugged. "It doesn't matter. Pada-Sin has refused you. You must do something else."

Shula stared at the grain-strewn dust between her feet. "Enheduanna says she can give me something to make it go away."

Badtibri nodded. "It will make you sick, but if you don't die you will be able to stay at the temple. You're just as likely to die in childbirth, anyway." She gave Shula a look that made her want to look away. "I wish you could have it. I'd like to see your baby, Shula."

Badtibri held out her arms and Shula sank against her, hot tears spilling from her eyes to soak into the coarse-spun wool of her friend's shawl. Badtibri held her and rocked her, murmuring a soft, wordless tune, a lullaby, as if she, Shula, were the infant.

A shout from the house brought them both back to themselves. Reluctantly, Shula disengaged herself from Badtibri's arms. "You must go."

Badtibri nodded, clasped Shula's hand, and seemed about to say something else, but the shout came again, louder this time, and she ran to answer it.

In the street outside Ningalla's house, a donkey stood in a stock as Uru trimmed its hooves. Shula paused and stroked its velvet nose. "The woes of the past still ring in my ears," she told it.

She walked on a little ways, and then stopped, standing alone and irresolute in an empty alley. Somewhere nearby a cow lowed and an infant wailed. Looking down she saw the knot in her skirt that held her mé. She'd thought she had nothing, that nothing awaited her but pain and death, but she was wrong. She still had the mé.

A woman with the forelock of a slave came out of one of the houses and shook out a blanket. A little boy, naked and no more than three, darted between her legs, grabbed the edge of the blanket and kept going, pulling it from the woman's grasp and dragging it in the dust. She cursed and ran after the child, scooping him up and smacking him hard on the bottom. He struggled in her grip and cried, adding his wail to that of the infant, who still had not been succored with swaddling or breast.

Shula picked up the hem of her skirt and untied the mé, slipping the small stone from the cloth. Across the alley the slave scolded the child. "You'd make brine spoil, you good-for-nothing!"

An oxcart rattled down the alley, its wheels groaning under its load. "I have fifty gur of dung cakes to fuel your master's oven!" the oxcart driver shouted to the slave. "I have cakes of dried dung to fuel your master's oven!"

Shula turned the stone over in her palm, peering at it. Out of the corner of her eye she saw the child dart across the alley. The cart driver cried out and Shula was struck by a hurtling body. The mé flew from her hand and arced through the air to fall into a crack at the base of a wall.

She turned to see the slave woman standing there, the child clasped in her arms. In the street the oxcart driver shouted, "Keep your brat out of the street! I nearly killed him. Go get your master, I have fifty gur of dung cakes to fuel his oven!"

The slave woman glared at Shula but saved her wrath for the child in her arms. "I'm going to whip you until you're inside out!" she shouted, holding the boy out from her and shaking him. With a last, curious glance at Shula she spun around, whisking him into the house amid vivid threats.

Shula turned and looked at the hole the mé had fallen through. It was no larger than her hand and darker than night. She knelt down and felt inside it. Her fingers scraped over the ragged edges of the hole, but beyond that, nothing. The mé was gone. Frantically Shula threw herself on the ground, pressing her eye to the crack to peer through it, but she already knew there was no light to see by. She rolled to her side, turning her ear to the hole, and she lay there a long time, listening.

CHAPTER

10

On her way back to the temple Shula passed through the market square. It was packed with people buying offerings for the upcoming festival. Smells of sandalwood and fish penetrated her nostrils as the vivid colors of the fabrics and pottery assailed her eyes. As she looked about for an incense seller, she saw a cluster of women in bright robes bargaining animatedly with a cloth merchant. Among them she spotted the shining crown of her lady.

"The finest cloth you have would not suit her for a washrag. She is the shining, the mighty Lady, the maid Inanna, incomparable in her brilliance and strength. Who can make the cloth worthy of the bedsheet of the Queen of Dawn?" cried a woman Shula realized must be Ningal, Inanna's mother.

"Lady, I can make the bedsheet of the Queen of Dawn," said a voice among the crowd.

"Who speaks? The sheet must be of a weave so fine water cannot pass through it. Who can make the bedsheet for Inanna?"

"Lady, I can make the bedsheet for Inanna," came the voice again.

"Who speaks? The sheet must be of a color lighter than doves' breasts."

"Lady, I can make the cloth that color. I will weave it of lamb's wool pure as the clouds. I will weave it of flax fine as the Great Lady's hair. I will weave the cloth with a warp strong as the day, with a weft supple as night."

"Who speaks? Who will make the cloth?"

The crowd parted, and a woman stepped forward, cradling a lamb in her arms. "It is I, Ninsun, the Lady of the Sheep, Mistress of Weaving, wife of Enki, mother of Dumuzi. It is I, the mother-in-law. I will weave the bedsheet for Inanna."

Ningal greeted her. "Mother of my daughter's husband, you will make the sheet for the marriage bed."

The other women surrounded them, talking excitedly about the marriage plans. As Shula stood there debating how best to get Inanna's attention, the goddess suddenly darted from the group, her face flushed with happiness, and took Shula by the hands. Her hair was dressed with rose blossoms and she smelled of myrrh.

"Isn't it wonderful?" she said. "I'm to be married. Soon the white bedsheet will be red with my virgin blood. On it I will welcome the man I have loved always: Dumuzi the shepherd."

Shula shook her head. "I thought you loved the farmer."

Inanna frowned and looked imperiously at her. "I love Dumuzi. He is my honey man, he sweetens me always."

Inanna's women took the corners of a vast cloth in their hands, and ran with it, so that it billowed up above their heads. With sharp cries and ululations, they came straight at Inanna and Shula, passing the sheet above them like a windswept sky.

Shula tightened her hold on Inanna's hands and got down on her knees. "Holy Inanna, everyone says I am chosen by you because of the birds. It may be so because I see you when no one else does. I have tried to do what you wanted, whenever you asked me. I carried the mé down from Enki's tower for you, I have tried to understand your purpose in making me a naditum, when I should have been a sacred harlot, but though I have written your stories, and sung your hymns, I still do not understand. My Goddess, the Light of the Morning Star, whatever your purpose for me is, I must know it now, I must fulfill it now, for when I return to the temple I face punishment, death, because I am pregnant by my former master's son. I have just come from his house; he will not marry me. The naditum Enheduanna has offered me herbs to rid me of the child, but they may kill me, too. Whatever is your will Inanna, I will do it, but I cannot if I don't know what you want of me. Why have you chosen me?

Why did you bless me with the miracle of the birds, if I am only to be beaten and thrown from your temple?"

Inanna squeezed her hands. "If the naditum offers you herbs, do not take them. Come to my wedding. Attend me at the holy rite of my marriage to Dumuzi. Carry the cup for my beloved and me, and when we are finished with it, drink its dregs. You are indeed my chosen one, and you serve me well. Whatever happens, I will not be far from you. Have faith in my power, and take comfort that my purpose for you is unfolding as it should."

The sheet rustled past like a storm blowing over, to reveal once more the clear blue sky, and Shula found herself alone in the marketplace. The whole day had passed, and the sun was sinking in the west. Inanna and her entourage were nowhere in sight. Nearly everyone had returned to their homes and the merchants were packing up their wares. Shula walked back to the temple through the dinner-quiet streets.

Where is your incense?" Pishunda demanded when she got back to the courtyard of the naditu. "And why did it take you all day to get it?"

The naditu were eating supper, sitting in small groups beneath the trees. "I-I lost the incense, and I spent the rest of the day trying to find it," said Shula, slumping down beside Urhulli, who handed her an apple, trying to catch her eye. Shula didn't look at her. She ate the apple, and leaned back against the trunk of the tree.

Pishunda continued staring, her eyes narrowed, but she said nothing more. That night, as Shula and Urhulli lay together in bed, she told her what had transpired with Pada-Sin, and later, in the marketplace.

"Inanna told you not to take the herbs?" said Urhulli, propping herself up on one elbow. "But why? She must know you will be punished, why does she wish you to suffer?"

Shula shook her head. "I don't know. Maybe she doesn't, maybe she has another plan. She told me to carry her cup in the marriage procession. Maybe she will work another miracle through me. But in any case, what can I do? The ensi will punish me if he learns I am pregnant, but if I disobey Inanna's command, her punishment will be even worse." Shula sat up and took her friend's hands. "Oh Urhulli, I am afraid. I'm like a mouse caught between two lions. Whichever way I turn, there is a mouth to devour me."

Urhulli stroked her hair. Her eyes searched Shula's face, but she did not speak.

Shula looked away from the pain and fear in her friend's gaze. "I can tell you this, though," she said. "As frightened as I am of what may befall me at the hands of the temple guards, Inanna's wrath scares me more. Look what she did to poor Enkidu, and he was only the friend of the wrongdoer. Besides, when I am with her . . . You don't know, Urhulli. You've never seen her. She is both beautiful and terrible, like a thunderstorm or a whirlwind. How can any mortal resist her will?"

Urhulli sighed and cupped her hand to Shula's cheek. "I haven't known you so long as I did Kilkullum, but I think I love you more. In the midst of all this, you can still think of miracles, you can still find beauty in the goddess who made you a naditum. Oh Shula, I don't understand you, but I know you don't deserve this fate. If you won't take Enheduanna's herbs, then flee this place. Go to Kish, or Eridu, any place but here. Leave now, tonight." She got up from the bed and grabbed Shula's basket. "I'll help you pack. I have some money, you can buy food on the way."

Shula stood and took the basket away from Urhulli. She shook her head. "Inanna has commanded me to attend her marriage. Surely she will save me, for she said that no matter what happened, she would be with me. She said my destiny is unfolding as it should."

Urhulli shook her head, and large tears, glistening in the moonlight, streaked down her face. She took Shula in her arms, and held her, rocking, for a long time.

At least part of Inanna's promise was kept already, for when the high priestess announced the assignments for Inanna's wedding procession, she named Shula as the cupbearer, much to Pishunda's consternation.

"Miracle worker, there will come a time when the goddess's blessings will desert you, and then, I will be ready," she muttered to her on their way back to their quarters.

On the day of Inanna's wedding, the whole temple was up well before dawn. They gathered on the steps of the temple in the dawning light. Shula readjusted the heavy, irksome headdress for the umpteenth time, trying to find a position in which the band did not chafe her temples, and the fringes did not tickle her nose. The entire populace of the temple set forth at the first sounding of the drums. At the head of the procession strode the ensi and the high priestess, followed by the ensi's servants, the high priestess's acolytes, and then the scribes. The naditu walked directly after them, followed by the sacred harlots, the acrobats and dancers, and then the musicians and galla priests. Shula walked with the naditu. It would not be until later, when they returned to the temple, that she would carry the sacred cup.

They walked down Ninlil Street, and out of Inanna's gate, into the countryside. Villagers assembled along the road joined the procession at its tail, until, by the time they reached the chosen village, it stretched out behind Shula as far as she could see.

"Who makes the barley stand erect?" cried the ensi when the procession had gathered in the field. "Inanna, Holy Inanna whose star rises in the evening, who rises like the sun!" cried everyone else in unison.

"Who makes the land fertile?"

"Dumuzi, the Wild Bull, the shepherd with a flock of five thousand!" Shula replied along with the others.

"Who makes the harvest bountiful? Who brings forth the ewe's sweet milk, who makes the fish jump in the river?"

"Inanna and Dumuzi, the ever-fertile couple, the King and Queen of all the land!"

The high priestess stepped forward, her crown of lapis and gold shining in the sun. "Let all who honor my sacred marriage reap bounty from their fields, let them drink the rich milk of the ewe, let them taste honey, let their fishing nets be full and their children strong."

The village elder stepped forward, his servants leading a flock of livestock. A white lamb was brought forth first. When the ensi slit its throat with the sacrificial knife its scream was short but piercing. The ensi lifted the dead animal by its hind legs, pouring its blood out on the ground.

When all the livestock were sacrificed the procession returned to Erech, where already the people gathered in the streets with flowers in their hair, waving stalks of barley and dancing in anticipation of the joyous nuptials.

More animals were sacrificed at the gate, and as they wove through the revelrous streets, many an onlooker passed beer to the members of the procession. An old woman handed Shula a jar and smiled broadly at her. It was the woman whose vegetable stand Shula had disturbed the day she first met Inanna. Apparently she had forgotten her discontents, at least for one day. Shula drank deeply of the beer, and handed the jar to Urhulli.

By the time they returned to the square in front of the temple, Shula was already quite drunk, and they stood at the edge of the square in the hot sun for what seemed like hours. First acrobats and snake charmers entertained the crowd, and when they were through the galla priests sang, and Shula lost count of the number of hymns they sang; all were about ripening barley and plentiful sheepfolds. After that the drummers and the dancers came forward, and Shula lost herself in the wild gyrations of their bodies and the pounding of the drums that moved through her like her own blood. The sun beat down until her head rang like the dancers' cymbals. The snake charmers came forward, filing past the naditu, carrying their baskets before them.

Shula swayed in the heat, lost her balance and stumbled into one of the men, knocking his basket to the ground. His snake slithered between the feet of the assembled naditu, raising cries of fear and surprise as it passed. The man glared at her and clenched his hands. He would have struck her if this were not a holy ceremony, if he were not in front of the assembled citizens of Erech.

"I'll get it," she told him, and took off after the snake, winding her way behind the rows of naditu, past the drummers and onto the second-level terrace of the temple. The sounds of the ceremony—the drums, the flutes, the ululating voices of the galla priests—faded behind her. She cast about the terrace, searching for the snake, and thought she caught the flicker of a tail disappearing into one of the side entrances. Shula peered through the archway, blinking her sun-dazzled eyes in the dimness. The hallway looked different than she remembered it. The paintings on the walls were bright with fresh pigment, the floor was even, unworn by generations of footsteps.

From the end of the hallway, where the high priestess and her attendants kept their quarters, she heard the sound of laughter and quarreling. But that was impossible. The high priestess and all her retinue were outside at the ceremony. With curiosity mixed with trepidation, Shula crept down the hallway.

"There you are!" Someone loomed out of the shadows to grab her by the wrist. Shula recoiled, but the shadowy figure, a woman in black robes, held her fast.

"Hurry now. The Queen awaits," she said, and she dragged Shula down the hallway in the direction of the voices.

"Who are you?" Shula protested, tugging at her arm. "Who are you taking me to? Who is this queen? The Queen of Heaven is outside, performing the ceremonies of her sacred marriage right now."

The woman stopped, eyeing her closely. "I do not understand why she chose you. You have no sense. But so be it. The wedding will take place tonight. We must prepare the bride."

"But the bride, the high priestess, is out there," Shula waved her free arm in the direction of the square.

The woman grimaced and struck Shula openhanded across the cheek. Shula's eyes watered and her face stung with the imprint of that hand. "The bride, the Holy Inanna, is in here, and she's waiting for you," said the woman as she drew aside the curtain over the archway and pushed Shula inside.

"Well, it's about time," said Inanna, sitting on a cushion atop the dais at the center of the room. She was draped in gold, and three attendants wove flowers into her hair, while two more painted wedding designs on her hands with henna-tipped brushes. "Where have you been?" demanded the goddess.

Shula shook her head in confusion. "I was outside, in the square. The whole city is celebrating your marriage. As a naditum I—"

"Celebrating my marriage? I haven't married him *yet*."

In one corner of the room an older woman sat mixing cosmetics. It was Ningal, the Moon Goddess, the mother of the bride. "In the lives of the Anunna gods, all actions are eagerly anticipated by the mortals who serve us," she said.

Well, that was one way of looking at it, thought Shula, who gave up trying to make sense of it. She was with Inanna again. Things always got strange when she was with Inanna. Shula did as she was told and helped the attendants dress the goddess and prepare her for the wedding.

At length Inanna rose, resplendent in linen and gold. "Behold the maid, ready for her groom," she said. Ningal brought forth the marriage cup and handed it to Shula, who stared into it, as if she could divine Inanna's plan in its depths.

Out of the corner of her eye she caught a ripple of movement, like the billowing of a curtain in the breeze, like the flow of a serpent sliding past. She followed it with her peripheral vision. It was the snake, she thought, as she caught a glimpse of coruscating light, a symmetrical arc of lightning that burned itself into her mind. Shula caught her breath, blinked, and looked at the snake, but it was gone.

Cold with fear and sweating with anticipation, Shula followed Inanna to the main hall of the temple, Inanna's house. All around the paintings were fresh and bright, the mosaics shining like new. In the main hall, the populace of Erech was assembled, more pouring out from the great archway and down the ramp to the street.

At the head of the throng, Dumuzi sat atop a litter borne by six men. As Inanna approached they lowered his throne to the ground and Dumuzi stood and spoke, "You shine forth from your house like the light of dawn! Your sight is a joy to my eyes!" He stepped forward and kissed Inanna.

Inanna broke from his embrace. "What I say, let the singer immortalize it in song. What I say to you, let it fly from mouth to ear, let it spread from young to old: My vulva, the Boat of Heaven, is full of excitement like the new moon. My fallow field yearns for the plow."

Dumuzi and Inanna moved to a large bed that had been placed before the altar.

"My Queen," said Dumuzi. "Your breasts are like a fertile land. Inanna, your breasts are like a fertile land. They pour out grain. Bread pours from above for your husband. Beer pours from above for your husband. Let it flow for me, Inanna. I will drink all you proffer!"

"What of me?" said Inanna. "Who will till my soil? Who will furrow my wet soil? As for myself, the maid, who will place the ox in the yoke? Who will plow my vulva?"

Dumuzi replied, "I will plow your vulva, my Queen. I, Dumuzi, your husband, will plow your vulva."

Shula and the other attendants took hold of the ties holding up the curtain around the canopied bed, and at Inanna's exultant cry—"Then plow my vulva, man of my heart! Plow my vulva!"—untied them. The curtain fell in a gauzy cloud around the couple. The fabric was sheer. You could clearly see them copulating as the drummers brought their beat to a crescendo.

Afterward, Inanna called for the marriage cup, and Shula stepped forward, unsteady on her feet, and presented the cup to the holy couple. They drank, and handed it back to her, and returning to her station, she drank the dregs of the cup. What little was there went straight to her head. The faces of the citizens wobbled before her, and then she saw the pattern of the snake again, a coruscating arc of symmetrical lightning glowing like an afterimage before everything went dark.

She awoke in a tiny room, lit only by a small window high up in the sealed door. A cell, she realized, lifting her hand to her face. Her wrist was heavy with the bronze manacle that encircled it. She was chained to a ring in the wall.

She was thirsty, but there was no water. Vague sounds came to her through the door, weeping and moaning, sounds of desolation. Out of the corner of her eye she saw a twisting pattern of colors, the snake again. She tried to look directly at it, but each time she did it disappeared, and each time she stopped trying, it reappeared, always in the periphery of her vision.

"So," it whispered. "Inanna's plan for you is unfolding as it should. That must be a great comfort."

Shula's reply was cut off by the sound of footsteps outside. The door to her cell opened.

Two large men with bronze breastplates and helmets entered and dragged her to her feet. Without a word they unlocked the manacle about her wrist and half-dragged, half-walked her out of the cell and down the hallway. They took her to the Pillared Hall, where the ensi sat in state. Beside him was the high priestess, Shapar, and next to her sat Enheduanna, looking grim.

As the guards hustled her past the audience, Shula spotted Urhulli,

Batri, Manascar, and Pishunda. To her surprise, Pada-Sin was there as well, and Lugalla. Urhulli cast her a ravaged look, before Shula was borne past and made to stand before the ensi. The guards stepped back, trusting to the authority of his crown to keep her there.

"You are the naditum Shula, formerly of the household of Ur-Neattu, son of Tetua-Nur?" inquired the ensi.

It took her a moment to find her voice. "I am," she managed at last.

"You are accused of breaking the sacred vow of chastity, which you agreed to when you became a naditum, and furthermore, of being unlawfully pregnant. What do you say to these charges?"

"Y-your Ensiship, since I became a naditum, I've lain with no man. I have kept my vows, and done everything in my power to serve the Holy Inanna, Queen of Erech."

The ensi looked out into the gathered audience. "Will her accuser, the naditum Pishunda, step forward?" With a sickening sly smile, Pishunda stood and stepped toward the dais. "Repeat now what you told High Priestess Shapar," he told her.

"Certainly, your Ensiship." Her eyes grazed Shula's with a look of triumph. "The day before yesterday, the day before the sacred marriage of our Lady Inanna and the King of Erech, the naditum Shula left the temple in the morning, to buy incense for the ceremony, she said. She was gone all day, and when she returned, she had no incense. Because of this, and other things which made me suspicious, I went to the house of her former master, Ur-Neattu. There the cook Lugalla informed me that Shula had been there, pleading with Ur-Neattu's son Pada-Sin for him to marry her, because she was pregnant. But Pada-Sin insisted the child was not his, that she was pregnant by her other lover, a shepherd."

The ensi lifted a hand. "Are Pada-Sin and Lugalla present?"

"Yes, your holiness," said Pishunda, turning to indicate the two, who stood upon hearing their names.

"Is what the naditum Pishunda says true?" the ensi asked them.

"Yes, Ensi," said Lugalla. "It is just as she said. I heard them talking in the other room, and I clearly heard my master's son say, 'The child you carry is not mine, it belongs to your other lover.'"

"It is true, your Ensiship," added Pada-Sin. "Shula came to me claiming that I made her pregnant, but I knew this could not be true. When we lay together, I withdrew from her, and spilled my seed upon the ground, having no wish to get children upon a slave. It was widely known that she had another lover, a shepherd whom she often met by the riverside."

"That's not true!" cried Shula, turning to face him. "And you know it. You plowed my vulva and spilled your seed in my womb, and as for a shepherd, another lover, you made him up! I never had any lover except for you!"

"That is a lie!" cried Pishunda. "And I can prove it. Why, on her very first day here in the temple of our Lady, this so-called miracle worker defiled her vows with a shepherd in the temple of the harlots! Baruda, a servant there can attest to this."

As the attendant who had served the shepherd and herself dates and wine stepped forward, Shula felt herself falling into a deep chasm from which no one, not even the goddess Inanna, could save her. She barely heard the rest of the case, though Enheduanna went on for some time in her defense. At last the ensi passed his sentence.

"Since it is clear that the naditum Shula transgressed after entering the temple, and since her pregnancy is likely the result of this base act, she will be stripped of her membership in the order of the naditu, and publicly caned. Her ultimate fate will be decided following the punishment, should she survive it."

All Shula saw, as the scribe wrote up the judgment and the ensi pressed his seal upon it, was Urhulli's tear-streaked face. Her eyes were wide and dark, and as the guards dragged her away, Shula thought, If only I could hide in them.

When the guards returned her to her cell, Shula sank to the ground and stared into the darkness. She did not sleep, but time must have passed without her awareness, because the next thing she noticed was a faint glimmer of light in one corner of the cell. At first she thought it was the snake, but she was wrong. It was a faint luminescence emanating from her Lady's crown.

"Inanna!" Shula threw herself in the goddess's lap, sobbing. "Inanna, they're going to kill me! I am to be caned, and many say I will die of it.

Inanna, you said your plan for me was unfolding as it should! What can you require of me that demands my death?"

"Shhh," Inanna held her, rocked her, soothed her hair. "I told you I would never be far from you. And now I am here. As for what I require of you—"

"Yes?" Despite everything, Shula's heart leapt inside her, and as Inanna's face tilted toward hers, her eyes dark and sparkling like the night sky, she felt as if she were drinking at a cool fountain of indescribable sweetness.

Inanna kissed her, and then put her lips to Shula's ear. "I want you to tell my true stories. I want you to find out who I really am."

In the morning they took Shula to the public square across from the main entrance to the temple. With stout ropes they tied her arms and legs firmly to two poles and stripped the clothing from her body. She had not eaten, and had been given only a little water the night before when they returned her to her cell, but such petty annoyances as hunger and thirst fled from her mind with the first sickening whack of the cane. It was like a band of hot iron across her back, and it tore a scream from her throat.

Before she could recover, catch her breath, brace herself for the next blow, it came, landing across her shoulders like an arc of lightning. She screamed again, and again the cane tore a trench of fire across her body. She felt dizzy and the faces of the assembled crowd wavered before her eyes. She thought she caught a glimpse of Urhulli and wondered why she tortured herself by attending this, until the fourth blow robbed her of all speculation, and it was all she could do to keep breathing. Her eyes focused on a pebble lying on the ground before her, and she wished she could be as hard, as unfeeling as a stone. The next blow tore into her, and it felt as though it laid her bones bare.

She lost the strength to scream after about the tenth blow, about the same time that she lost count of the number of blows themselves. They no longer felt like separate sensations, only crests in the sea of pain in which she floated. The ground around her was dotted with little spatters of blood. The next time she noticed them they were lakes and rivers. There were other sensations, weaving in and around the agony; heat and cold, trembling and an increasing, blessed, numbness. At one point she looked down, and saw blood pouring down her legs, though whether this was from her flayed back or because she had miscarried, she did not know.

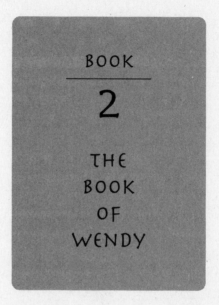

BOOK
———
2

THE
BOOK
OF
WENDY

CHAPTER

11

The moment Kyle Denreddy's jockstrap hit the side of her face was the moment Wendy Chrenko decided there was something terribly wrong with the world. Around her Mr. Porter's seventh-grade geography class erupted with giggling.

"There Dog, that's for your bone!" yelled Kyle.

Furious, Wendy stared at the pale, crumpled thing now lying limply across her textbook. "Leave me alone!" she shouted, eyes spitting venom at Kyle as she threw the jockstrap back at him. It fell short and landed on the floor in front of Mr. Porter's desk.

Sheila Finch scrunched up her freckled face and turned to Cory Feldenkreis. "Ew, she touched it," she said, invoking a fresh round of tittering.

Shame flooded Wendy, but honestly, what was she supposed to do? Just leave it there? Still, throwing it might not have been her best move, because Mr. Porter had looked up just in time to see her do it, but too late to see Kyle's opening volley.

"No throwing," he said, and lifted the jockstrap up with a pencil—of course, why hadn't she thought to use her pencil?—and carried it, dangling, to her desk at the end of the row. "Miss Chrenko, does this belong to you?" he inquired.

Rage choked her as her classmates howled with laughter.

"Dog's got a bone!" cried Perry Wolper.

Wendy desperately tried to just disappear, but it didn't work. Mr. Porter was still standing there. "Kyle threw it at me," she managed to gasp through her mortification.

Mr. Porter swung around and deposited the jockstrap on Kyle's desk. "Keep that in your pants, boy, what's the matter with you?" Scowling, he went to the blackboard and pulled down the world map, but still the classroom was an uproar of giggles, barks, and shouts. The only quiet one was Wendy, her face on fire, staring straight ahead of her, eyes blank, consumed by the vain effort not to be there. "Everybody calm down now!" shouted Mr. Porter. "This is a classroom, not a zoo."

Wendy was practically the first person Ray met when he moved to Elmdale, but it was another few years before she saved his life.

Ray's dad was a tech sergeant in the air force, a career officer, and they moved a lot. Elmdale was just like a lot of other places they'd lived, a middle-class suburb of a midwestern metropolis. It was about as middle of the road as you could get, and that suited Ray just fine. It made it that much easier to blend in, to go with the flow, to merge into a new school, a new life, with nary a ripple to announce his presence.

Unfortunately, Mrs. Tildy, the seventh-grade English teacher, had other plans. It was past second period by the time Ray finished up with the paperwork in the school office. He was hoping to just slip in and take a seat at the back of the room but she stopped him. "Just a moment. Class, we have a new student with us." She put her hand on his shoulder. "Everyone, this is Raymond Mackie."

Ray winced. Why did she have to say Raymond? Everybody, including his parents, called him Ray. A wave of giggling swept the classroom. Everywhere he'd gone, he always managed to be at least average, occasionally even achieving popularity by way of blandness. But all that was over now, destroyed in an instant by Tildy's cheery thoughtlessness.

As if to put the final nail in his coffin, she went on, "Raymond's family just moved here from Virginia. I know you'll all make him welcome. Raymond, why don't you take a seat next to Wendy there?" Fresh laughter rippled through the class as she pointed at a girl sitting in the middle of the room, an empty desk on either side of her. There were little wads of paper stuck in her long unruly hair, and her nose was too big for her face. She was the only one who hadn't laughed when the teacher introduced him.

Hoping to get out of the spotlight, Ray sat down on her right, but his ordeal wasn't over yet. Tildy walked down the aisle to stand between him and the girl. "Wendy, will you be Raymond's buddy for a few days, show him around, help him get acclimated to the school?"

Again laughter broke out, louder than before. Ray's guts tightened, and he tried to disappear. For her part, Wendy stared at Mrs. Tildy as if she had just suggested she chop off her own arm and eat it for lunch.

A blond-haired boy in the back of the room started barking. "The Dog's got a boyfriend! Bowwow!"

"Kyle!" snapped Tildy, but he ignored her, and several other boys joined him in a chorus of howls and barks. "Just ignore them, Raymond," she said. "Wendy?"

The girl's eyes widened, and then she stared at the desk. "Okay," she whispered.

Tildy smiled, as if everything were all right, as if she hadn't just single-handedly sabotaged Ray's entry into the school. "Welcome to West, Raymond," she said with satisfaction, and made her way back up to the chalkboard.

When the bell rang, Wendy turned to him. "Next is math," she said, not quite meeting his eyes.

Over by the door, Kyle and his cohorts stood giggling over a piece of paper. "Let me see," said a girl with blue checked ribbons in her hair. She snatched at the paper, tilting it so that Ray could see it was a drawing. "Oh my God!" she shrieked and burst out laughing, bringing several other girls into her orbit to glance at the paper, giggle, and cast sly, mirth-filled glances at Ray and Wendy.

"Hey, Jiggles," Kyle said, and then looked at his two companions. "Let's make jiggle Jell-O!" he said, and they grabbed the girl, now laughing hysterically, and pushed her arms so they crossed in front of her, trapping her breasts between them.

"Look, instant cleavage!" cried a shorter, chestnut-haired boy.

Jiggle's friends had abandoned her, and now stood in the open doorway. "Sheila, come *on*!" they yelled, and the girl freed herself from the boys.

"Must be Jiggles, 'cause Spam don't shake like that!" cried Kyle as they all herded out, laughing and shouting. The drawing fluttered to the ground in their wake, and as Ray followed the stone-faced Wendy out of the classroom, he stooped to pick it up.

It was a drawing all right. He realized that the figure on all fours with a collar, leash, and wagging tail was supposed to be him. Shock ran through him like ice water. Was this how they saw him? Was his hair really that stringy? He never realized before how dorky those horizontally striped shirts his mother bought for him were. In the picture he was being walked by an upright figure with a dog's floppy ears and long nose. Some sort of cloth covered her mouth like a muzzle, helpfully labeled "jock-strap" with an arrow pointing to it. "Wendy the dog-faced girl takes her new pet for a walk," read the caption. There was a pile of steaming dog shit, complete with flies, beneath his tail, and she was about to step in it.

He crumpled up the paper and stuck it in his pocket, following Wendy out of the classroom, glaring at her back. This was her fault, her and that stupid teacher. If he was going to have any chance at all in this school, he had to distance himself from her as much as possible, as soon as possible.

His opportunity came at lunchtime. Carrying a horrifying lime-green Scooby-Doo lunch box, Wendy showed him the way to the lunchroom. The weird thing was, he really liked Scooby-Doo. He watched it on Toon Central all the time. Yet he knew that he could never in a million years walk into that lunchroom with her when she was carrying that. Those other boys would make his life a living hell. Wendy was obviously firmly ensconced in the lowest level of the social order at this school. What was the point of him joining her there?

"I'm going to get a drink of water," he said, and left her several paces before the doorway. He went on down the hall, took a long drink of water, and then slowly walked back. Willing himself to be invisible, he went into the lunchroom.

It seemed a cavernous place, filled with monsters. Past the lunch line, midway down the rows of tables, Kyle and two of his friends were hassling Wendy. One of them had seized her lunch box, and they were tossing it back and forth between them. Wendy dodged and grabbed for it, but they tossed it high, always out of her reach. One of them fumbled and the lunch box hit the floor with a crack of splintering plastic and popped open, spilling its contents. An orange rolled under a nearby table and a sandwich encased in a plastic baggie lay limp and forlorn on the floor. The chestnut-haired boy picked it up, dangling it from the corners of the baggie. "Look Kyle, it's dog food. Here, eat it." He thrust it at Kyle, who pretended to barf.

Ray took a seat at a table with a group of boys who were watching the proceedings with mild interest. He was pretty sure none of them had seen that drawing of him. The kid closest to him glanced over and said, "Hi."

"Hi," he said, and opened his lunch, thankfully packed in a plain brown paper bag.

"I got to the tenth level of Gloom last night," said a fat kid with blond hair. "You know the corridor on the ninth level where there's all those boxes? Well there's a secret—"

"Shut up, Bill," said the kid who'd said hi to Ray. He had dark hair and a beaklike nose. "I'm on ninth level now. If I wanted a cheat book I'd go buy one. It takes all the fun out of it."

"Shua," scoffed Bill. "Like killing the monsters isn't the best part. More levels, more monsters, man. What's wrong with you?"

"Hey, I like to do something with my brain while my index finger is firing, all right?" He turned to Ray. "Do you have a computer?"

"Nah. Well, my dad does, but it's a piece of junk."

"You should see Jase's setup." Bill pointed at the dark-haired kid. "He's got a Sentinel 3 processor with a sound card and like, gobs of RAM."

"Wow."

"Thanks," nodded Jase. "Hey, you want to come over after school and see it? Besides Gloom, I've got Thing Commander, Death Valley, and Phog."

"Cool, okay." Ray glanced up to see Wendy turning away from Kyle and those guys, abandoning Scooby-Doo and her sandwich and heading for the lunch line. As she walked by she met his eyes, but she looked at him like he was a part of the scenery, his behavior thoroughly expected, dismissed in the scope of things, as was he.

———

Wendy waited out the stink of lunch in the cafeteria line. Chatter, taunts, and laughter filled the air as thickly as the smells of cacciatore cutlets and garbage. The lunch lady deposited an aluminum carton on Wendy's tray, its cardboard lid concealing the awful truth of what lay inside.

Snickers greeted her as she turned from the lunch line. Desperately she cast about, looking for Cara and Robin. They were at the far end of the lunchroom, well past where Kyle sat with Perry, Kevin, and Brad. She fixed her gaze on her friends, held her head level, and started toward them, willing her soul to the devil with every step if she could just make it to the table without further incident.

Miraculously, it worked. Except for a few barks and howls from Kyle's table, some laughter and tittering from Sheila and the girly-girls, she made it to her seat without comment. But then, the universe was generous. If her enemies did not plague her, then she always had her friends.

"I can't believe you touched it," said Cara.

"Touched what?" Wendy set her tray down and sat.

"You know." She leaned forward as if sharing a great secret. "Kyle's—"

"His jock," said Robin bluntly. She wasn't one to mince words. Tall and heavy, she was almost as reviled as Wendy was, almost. Her last name was Whalen. They called her the Whale.

"Well, what was I supposed to do, leave it laying there on my desk?" said Wendy crossly.

"You could have pushed it off with a book or a pencil or something," said Cara. If Wendy and Robin were the hags of the school, then Cara was the beautiful princess, with long, straight blond hair, large blue eyes, and an unerring instinct for what was cool that both Robin and Wendy tried to emulate, but could never seem to achieve. The three of them had been friends since grade school, when they'd spent recess together out at the big triple oak in the woods behind the school, pretending to be witches. But despite her inborn popularity, Cara had yet to abandon her ugly-duckling friends for the rarified company of the Sheila circle. "Or called Mr. Porter over," she went on. "Why didn't you just tell him, first off?"

Wendy shrugged, prying the cardboard lid off her lunch. It was everything she'd expected. The hot, moist steam struck her face, carrying with it the aroma of overcooked green beans and reheated tomato sauce. In the carton lay two patties of unknown origin, steeped in a pool of chunky red stuff that gave off an unwholesome shimmer. Wilted vegetables and watery mashed potatoes completed the ensemble. She looked up at Cara's expectant, innocent face. She didn't know how to say that telling Mr. Porter first off would work for Cara, but for her it didn't matter. No matter what she did it would be the wrong thing, just by virtue of her doing it. So she said, "I was mad."

"Well, if it were me," said Robin, "I'd have kicked him in the balls for doing that. It's sexual harassment. You should sue the school."

Wendy laughed.

"No, I'm serious. A kid in Wisconsin won twenty million dollars from his school because some kids beat him up, and the school didn't intervene. It's their responsibility, you know."

Wendy failed to see how suing the school would make her more popular.

Robin leaned closer. "Is it true you sniffed Kyle's jock, before tossing it back?"

"What? No!"

"Sheila said you did, right Cara?"

Cara glanced from Robin to Wendy, and nodded.

"Well, who are you going to believe, me or Sheila?" demanded Wendy.

Cara looked uncertain, but finally said, "You, of course," and Robin nodded. At least the issue was settled with them, but who else had Sheila told the despicable lie to? The whole school, probably. Wendy glanced to where Sheila sat with Becky, Tammy, and Heather, and saw Sheila lean across the table and whisper something. They all looked over, laughing. Wendy lowered her gaze and stared at her gelid, cooling lunch. She drank her milk and had a go at the desiccated apple that accompanied it. A loose flap of cuticle on her right index finger caught her attention, and she chewed at it, bringing a spurt of fresh blood to her tongue. So much for lunch, she thought, and stood up. "I'm going outside," she announced, and went to dump her tray in the garbage.

It was a chilly, gray day and the schoolyard was nearly deserted. Wendy sat with her back against the brick wall, gazing wistfully at the triple oak in the woods on the far side of the asphalt playground. It was off limits to her now, having become the hangout of burnouts who would just as soon beat her up as look at her. What the hell had happened, anyway? she wondered. In the past year, everything had changed. She'd never been popular, but she'd had her little circle, and otherwise people had left her alone. Now she was lost in a mine field of unspoken social rules, without a map, without a clue. Funny thing was, she was doing all the same things she'd done last year and no one had bothered her about it, but now the littlest thing, like wearing the poncho her mom made her to school, or putting barrettes in her hair, was grounds for ridicule. She carried a lunch box, therefore she was a nonperson.

She wished she could be someone else, but there was no help for it. She was stuck with this body—flat-chested; this hair—frizzy and out of control; this face—nose too long, eyes too small. Why? Why had she been born if there was no place for her in this world? Why did she live if it was only to suffer and be hated? She was here, dammit, how could everything about her be wrong?

Shadows fell across her. She looked up to see Kyle, Perry, and Brad, their figures blocking the recalcitrant sun. "Hey Dog," said Kyle casually, like it was her name. Well, it was the only name they ever used for her, anyway. "What's waggin'?" This with a glance at his buddies, who giggled at his gem of repartee.

Wendy shook her head. "Go away." But a note of pleading entered her voice at the end, and she wished she hadn't said anything at all.

"Hey, good comeback," observed Brad.

"What's the matter, Dog?" Kyle feigned concern, bending over to pat her on the head. "Are you a sad puppy?"

Wendy pushed his hand away and tried to look anywhere but at the three of them. But they were standing too close, and panic constricted her throat, filling her mouth and bringing her dangerously close to tears.

"I know what might cheer you up, Dog," said Kyle brightly. "You could smell my crotch. My dog always likes that."

Later, Wendy would berate herself for not saying something like, "What, you let your dog sniff your crotch? What kind of a pervert are you?" but as always, anything good like that wouldn't occur to her until at least an hour after the fact. At the moment, she was too full of panic as Brad and Perry held her shoulders and Kyle grabbed her head, pulling it inexorably toward his fly.

"No!" she shouted, struggling, but that didn't stop Kyle from smashing her face against the rough fabric of his jeans and gyrating against her.

"Stop it! Let her go!" came a voice. Robin.

Something akin to a freight train with pigtails hurtled into Kyle, knocking him sideways and freeing Wendy from his grasp. Robin shoved Brad back against the wall. Perry kicked at her and she turned on him. His grin faded a little and he took a step back. Wendy stood up and got behind Robin, intensely grateful and all-forgiving for this moment of salvation.

The three boys reconsidered the situation and backed away. "Thar she blows!" cried Kyle.

"Aye cap'n, she's a big 'un, she is," quipped Perry, taking a wide path around Robin's formidable glare.

Wendy and Robin were silent, watching them walk off. When they were out of earshot, Wendy said, "Thanks."

Robin sighed. "Now they're gonna be on my case the rest of the day. I have to walk home the same way they go, you know. Why'd you come out here by yourself anyway? It's like you're asking for it."

"I'm not!" she said hotly. "I just wanted to be alone with my thoughts, is all."

"Alone with your thoughts?" Robin scrunched her face in derision. "You'd be better off trying to find ways to improve yourself so people wouldn't think you're such a scag."

"Oh yeah? And what about you? What are you doing to improve yourself? Skipping one Snickers a day?" She regretted it as soon as she said it, but it was too late. Robin scowled and walked away, fast, her shoulders hunched.

At dinner that night Wendy kept her head down, her parents' conversation washing over her as she picked at her chicken subgum chow mein.

"We got that new account today. You know, the First Episcopal Church?" said Wendy's dad, spooning General Tso's chicken from a white cardboard carton onto his plate. He was in his late forties, with a soft, pudgy face and dark hair going to gray and thinning at his temples.

"Oh, the one where they want to convert the old Kroger?" said her mom, neatly bisecting her eggroll with a knife. She reached for the plum sauce.

"Here you go," he said, handing her the little plastic cup of orange colored sauce with a dollop of hot mustard in the center.

"Thanks dear. That should be a challenge. I mean, from a grocery store to a church."

"Yeah." He nodded and pushed his glasses up the bridge of his nose. He looked tired, but still he smiled at his wife as she stirred the plum sauce with the tip of her knife. "But we got the zoning board's approval to add two stories to the structure. Tomorrow the contractor's going to start gutting the place. It'll be almost like starting from scratch. So how was your day?"

"Oh, I finished that wall hanging."

"Great. I love the colors you used in that."

"Well, it was tricky because the fibers were so fragile. Great colors, like you said, but next time around I'm ordering a different brand of yarn. The strands kept breaking."

"Think you'll show this one?"

"Yeah. It was too much work not to. But I also want to get some caftans and hats finished for the craft fair at the community college next month."

"Oh yeah, you cleaned up there last year."

"It was a good crowd."

There was a pause, and Wendy looked up to see her parents staring at her. "What?"

"You're quiet tonight," her father noted. "How was school today?"

Wendy frowned. "Terrible. I hate school."

Her parents exchanged looks of surprise. "Really?" asked her mother. "What's wrong?"

"Everybody hates me." Wendy pushed her chow mein around on her plate with her fork.

"Oh honey, I'm sure you're exaggerating." Her mother smiled. "They don't hate you. Why would they?"

"Because I'm different! They do hate me. Everybody's always making fun of me, calling me names and . . . stuff."

Her father smiled at her. "How could anyone hate my little Wendicle?"

She rolled her eyes. "Dad."

"Sorry. I guess you're too old for that now, huh?" He shook his head wistfully. "Ah, enjoy this time while you can, sweetheart. All too soon you'll be grown up with a family and responsibilities of your own. You're free now, you have your whole life ahead of you. These are the best days of your life."

"If that's true then I might as well kill myself right now and get it over with."

"Don't talk like that," her father's voice turned suddenly harsh.

"Oh, she's just being melodramatic, Paul," said her mother. She looked at Wendy. "Those kids are just trying to get a rise out of you. That's how kids are. Just ignore them."

"That's easy for you to say. You don't have people calling you Dog all the time."

"That's what they call you? Dog?"

She shrugged and looked at her plate. "And puppy, sometimes." Once.

"Oh, that's not so bad," her mother admonished. "It's kind of cute, a puppy dog. Would my puppy dog like a fortune cookie?"

A weight fell into her heart, heavier than she thought she could bear. Wendy glared at her parents, stood up, and stormed out of the room.

"Wendy, come back here," her father called.

"Oh let her go, Paul. She's just at that age."

Wendy slammed the door to her room and threw herself down on the bed, fighting back tears. No one. She had no one.

While his mom watched *Law & Order,* Ray sat on the couch with his sketch pad in his lap, his pastels spread around him in a disordered rainbow, his mind lost in the image he was creating.

It was a picture of a broad, green field. In the center two figures lay in the grass, gazing up at . . . well, he didn't know what, exactly. A cloud maybe, or a spaceship or a multicolored creature taken flight. He let his hand continue filling in the form, adding colors until it scintillated with light, until it almost seemed to move on the page. He really didn't care what it was because letting it become whatever it wanted to be set his mind free. The chatter of the television, the math homework he was supposed to be doing, the fact that his dad still wasn't home, none of that touched him. He was simply alive, the picture flowing through him, forming before his eyes, and it was good.

But the sound of the front door opening broke his reverie. Ray heard his father's footsteps in the hallway, the jingle of his keys as he set them on the table by the coatrack, the rustle of his jacket as he took it off and hung it up. He looked to his mom, hoping to find in her face some reassurance or warning. She smoothed her bleached blond hair and gave him a tight smile that only confirmed what Ray already knew.

Ray's dad came in, bringing with him the bar smell of Jim Beam and cigarettes. He was of average height and slim build, with dark hair, like Ray's, and blue eyes, like Ray's. He glanced at them both, and then wordlessly flopped into his black-leather recliner. He wasn't smiling.

Ray held his breath, and pretended to still be absorbed in his drawing. His mother didn't say anything either. Probably a good choice.

But then, sometimes it just didn't matter. "Well, isn't anyone going to ask how my day went?" growled Ray's dad.

"Of course!" Ray's mom snapped to attention, and it sickened Ray at the same time that he felt relieved. "How was it, dear?"

"It sucked." His father gritted his teeth and stared steadily at the TV. "I spent all day fixing the engines on the fucking F-16 Falcon and then Islip comes and tells me we're not using it, and how soon can I have the Hornet ready. Fucking asshole! He's the one told me to get that piece of shit Falcon into shape in the first place. Idiot. I bet he did it on purpose. He doesn't have any respect for me. Nobody does." His jaw worked, and he sat forward and turned to look at them, eyes hard and glittering, his mouth a bitter slash. Uh-oh. "And then I come home and you're just sitting here, watching this stupid show. You know I hate this show."

"Sorry," said Ray's mom, fumbling with the remote.

Ray's dad stood and two steps brought him to her side of the couch. He swung his right hand down to snatch the remote from her. On the way back up he backhanded her across the mouth. "You don't care what

I have to put up with, as long as you've got your meal ticket. I don't know why I bother. I work hard all day, and what do I have to come home to? Not, 'Hi honey, how was your day?' not 'Can I get you a drink?' Nothing. Nothing but a couple of selfish, greedy couch potatoes too lazy to even pretend they're glad to see me."

Ray's mom blinked away tears and took her hand from her mouth. "Oh, but we are glad to see you!" she protested desperately. "I didn't say anything right away because I thought you wanted to be left alone. I'm sorry. We know how hard you work, and we're very grateful for everything you do for us. Aren't we, Ray?"

Ray couldn't refuse the pleading look in her eyes. Stiffly he nodded, and then forced himself to smile. It felt like stretching a rubber band too tight.

Ray's father snorted in disgust and returned to his chair, sinking into it and restlessly flipping channels. "There's nothing on but crap," he declared, and threw the remote control at the screen. It bounced off with a clatter and the batteries came loose and rolled underneath the coffee table. "Well, aren't you going to fix me my supper?" he asked his wife.

She smiled so hard Ray thought her face would crack. "Of course. What would you like? I've got eggs and there's some leftover chili—"

"Eggs? Leftovers? Is that all I get?"

"You can have anything you want, honey. I'll fix it for you. What would you like?"

His father shrugged, suddenly petulant and indecisive. "I don't know . . ." His eyes lit up. "Do we have any fried chicken?"

Her jaw worked. "Fried chicken? Well, uh . . ."

"No," Ray silently urged her to say. "No, I'm not cooking you fried chicken you mean old drunk." But of course that would be the wrong thing to say unless she wanted a black eye to go with her fat lip.

"I have some chicken in the freezer . . ." his mom went on, getting up from the couch, wringing her hands. "I could thaw it out in the microwave."

"Yeah. Yeah that'd be good." He smiled, appeased by the inconvenience of it all, and sank back into his chair again. He glanced at the remote, and then at Ray. "Pick that up," he said.

Ray's cheeks burned and his stomach was tight. He wanted to smash

his dad's head through the TV screen, but instead he swallowed and retrieved the remote from the floor in front of the recliner. He got down
on his hands and knees and fetched the batteries, too. It was better this
way, he told himself.

"So what's this?"

As Ray emerged from beneath the coffee table, he saw his father standing by the couch, looking at the sketch pad.

Shit. "Uh, just a drawing," he said.

His father pursed his lips and nodded. "Kinda queer isn't it? For you
still to be making pictures? I mean, you're not a little kid anymore."

Ray shrugged again.

His father shook his head, tossed the sketch pad back on the couch
and gave Ray a look of withering disappointment. Ray felt ashamed, and
angry at himself for caring what the old man thought. "I don't know
about you sometimes Ray, I just don't know."

Ray didn't answer him. He just picked up the sketch pad and retreated
to his room, grateful to get away.

CHAPTER

12

It was a warm spring evening and the trees were budding forth with new leaves. The sky was a deep, vibrant blue shading to lavender and gold at the horizon and the air was heady with the fragrance of lilacs. Wendy sat beneath the oak tree in her parents' backyard, wondering which was worse: being hated or being ignored?

Since The Jockstrap Incident, she'd followed her mother's advice, ignoring Kyle and his friends, or pretending to. She became a stone; silent, impervious. Since there was no way of knowing what might provide fodder for ridicule, she didn't say anything to anybody unless she had to. She did her best to wear what the other girls wore, she cut her hair, and she never took anything she cared about to school.

And it worked. She was almost done with eighth grade now and she hardly ever got teased anymore. The trouble was she'd done it too well. She'd become invisible. Nobody talked to her, nobody saw her. In school that day Cara and Becky—who sat on either side of her in English class—had an entire conversation with each other as if she weren't even there. They were talking about a party Becky was having. Of course Wendy hadn't been invited.

At home it was the same. Her father didn't have a clue what went on with her, and her mother couldn't be trusted, so she shut herself off from them, too. Now she couldn't remember the last time she'd had an actual conversation with another human being.

Wendy felt eyes on her, of a sudden. Someone was watching her from the shadowed corner of the yard, a spot dense with the yellow blossoms of forsythia, where long ago she bade farewell to the imaginary playmate of her childhood, Hister Snake. He was twelve-feet long, with green scales, a yellow belly, and emerald eyes. He came into her life after she saw a picture of him in a library book called *All About Reptiles*. One of those ones with big color photos inside. Hister followed her everywhere, and she enjoyed lounging in his coils. When she was five she had insisted on placing a saucer of milk for him on the floor beside her bed every night.

Remembering Hister also reminded her of long summers when she ran wild all day, roaming the neighborhood on her bicycle, making up adventures. She remembered winters when the snow had been a gift. When the world transformed overnight into a crystal palace or a vast arctic wilderness. She hadn't cared then how she looked or what anyone thought of her. She never even considered it. She was just herself. Strange how completely she had forgotten all that.

It was almost dark and the yard seemed alive with something primeval. The perfume of the air seemed stronger, and somewhere a mourning dove voiced its song. A thing that was not hope, but perhaps simply the remembrance of the animal joys of sensation, suffused her, and she stared into the forsythia bushes.

She saw him and he was not alone.

Hister's head poked out from beneath the yellow flowers, his eyes sparkling. Beside him a darker figure emerged from the twiggy branches. A girl with large black wings, long dark hair, and white teeth glittering ever so faintly in the darkness. Looking on her face Wendy knew her name instantly. "Lili," she said, and the girl's lips parted in a smile.

A voice in some far corner of her mind said, "Well, now you've really lost it," but she didn't care. Here was companionship, acceptance, solace that could not be taken away. She didn't care if she was crazy. She didn't care at all.

Hister and Lili joined her beneath the tree, the snake curling around the trunk and extending his head to rest on her knee. Lili sat down across from her, and took her hands, and for a long time just looked at her with kind, dark eyes. Eyes that saw her, really saw her for who she was, not all the things everybody else said she was. Wendy's chest grew tight, and her chin quivered. Her eyes went hot with unshed tears and she whispered, "You're so beautiful."

Lili smiled even wider and drew Wendy into her arms. Hair and feathers tickled her nose. "I look just like you," she whispered.

"No," Wendy choked out, shaking her head, and drew back, eyes abjectly on her hands.

"Yes." Lili took her hands with one of hers, the other lifting Wendy's chin so she looked once more into those deep dark, wonderful eyes. "Yes."

"B-b-but they all say—"

"Oh, *they*. Well. *They* are just a bunch of grugs—green-eyed thugs. The only way they can make themselves feel big is by making other people feel small. So you shouldn't worry so much about what *they* say. There's every reason to believe they're wrong. Look." She pointed up.

A great white face hung above the tree, peering down through the branches at them. A great round white face, mottled and merry, so full of light it spilled from her edges, and Wendy felt the light of the moon pulsing inside her, and knew something about herself that she hadn't known before, or that she'd forgotten. That the night, the moon, the tree, the velvet breeze, and the smell of lilacs were all part of her, just as she was part of them.

Something Wendy had carried for a year and two months slipped away from her then. She sank to the ground and lay face down in the warm, moist grass, breathing in the scent of earth and its attendant message: I will always be here. When no others love you, I always will. When you have lost everything, you will still have me.

"Lili," said Wendy sitting up a bit later and wiping dirt from her lips. "How old are you?"

"I'm as old as the moon. Then again I was just born today, and then again, I'm fourteen years old."

"Oh, 'cause I was just wondering, was the world always like this? Were people always so mean to each other? Was there always crime and war and stuff?"

Hister uncoiled from the base of the tree and draped himself over her shoulders, hissing approval. Lili's smile was a crescent version of the moon above. "Ah, that's a good question. There was a time, when even the moon was new, when all people understood their connection to each other and the rest of the world. But most have forgotten it now. In fact, they will tell you such a time never existed."

"What was it like?"

"Oh, it was a lot of fun. There were lots of parties, and food was plentiful because everybody shared what they had. Even the hunters apologized to their prey, and only killed what they needed. Men and women were equal, too, and everyone was considered beautiful."

"Wow. I wish the world could be like that now."

"Mmm," mused Lili. "If you can imagine it, it can happen, and nobody can stop you from imagining it except yourself."

Elmdale was the last place Ray's family moved to because that was the last place they were together. One night Ray came home from Jase's house and his mom was sitting at the kitchen table with her cigarettes and his dad's scotch, working away at them both, all the while staring at the grease stain on the wall under the kitchen clock.

The rest of the house was dark and quiet. Ray came over to the table and sat down across from her. "Mom," he said.

Her blue eyes shifted, gazing at him from their corners, and one side of her mouth slanted up in half of a wistful smile. Absently she lifted a lank blond curl from her cheek. "It's just you and me now, Raybeam. Your daddy's gone."

Ray looked up to the stain on the wall. "He's being transferred?" There'd been talk between them for weeks about a new post at Wright-Patterson in Dayton. Ray took it as a matter of course that they'd be moving again soon. It hardly even bothered him anymore. He could let go of Elmdale and everyone and everything in it, because he'd learned not to grab hold of anything in the first place.

His mother nodded, and then shook her head. "But we're staying here." She turned her head, giving him the full effect of her weary and battle-worn face. "You like it here, don't you?"

He nodded dumbly, his mouth hanging open.

She sighed and started tilting her head from side to side. "I tried to make him happy, you know?" She stared at him again, and he saw tears leaking out of her eyes, trailing down the sides of her nose. "I'm sorry. Oh honey, I'm so sorry."

Joy crept into his heart, and he felt a little guilty, because for some reason his mother wasn't happy about it. But the idea of living without his father—without the violence and unpredictability—thrilled him; he couldn't help it.

The next day as Ray came out of school, he saw his dad's car parked in the lot. Apparently his dad saw him, too, because even though Ray took off walking as fast as he could, cutting across the front lawn, his dad caught up with him on the sidewalk, letting the car roll along in neutral as he leaned out the window. "Son, get in the car. I need to talk to you."

Ray clenched his jaw and kept walking. "Ray!" his father barked. "Get in the car! Now!"

Other kids were starting to giggle and whisper. Ray shot a venomous look at his dad, but as usual it didn't bother him. He gazed right back at Ray with that cool, blue, capable-of-anything stare, and Ray knew he could either get in the car now, or have his dad drag him in, providing even more amusement for the other kids.

He slouched in the front seat, staring straight out the windshield, willing himself to be a stone.

"I suppose your mother already told you I'm leaving," said his dad, likewise glaring through the windshield, as if their problems were mutual, visible, and together they could run them down like rabbits in the road. "I wish I could take you with me, but right now, that's just not possible."

What a crock of shit, thought Ray, but he kept silent. Let him use whatever excuse he wanted, so long as he got out of their lives.

"But I'm worried about you, growing up without a man in the house," his dad continued. "I'd feel a lot better if you'd cut out that fag art shit and join some sports teams."

Ray had nothing to say to that either, and they drove through the subdivision in grim silence after that. Occasionally his dad reached down for the fifth of Jim Beam wedged between the seat cushions and took measured sips. He was just building up. Ray knew well enough that this was just the beginning of his daddy's drunk. When they passed the turnoff for the house he was relieved at first, until he stopped to consider that he was still in the car.

"So where are we going?" he asked with well-practiced nonchalance, a tone tailored to convey neither challenge nor fear.

His father cast a sidelong glance at him and said, "Want to show you something, son."

They drove out to the base and his dad parked the car in front of the chain-link fence that divided the back road from the airfield. He got out and sat on the hood of the car, the fifth perched between his knees. He was leaning back on his hands and staring out at the airplanes and Ray's guts twisted into knots because it was the perfect father-son, sunset-beer-commercial setting and Dad had orchestrated the whole thing, and now he actually expected Ray to get out of the car and go sit next to him and let him impart his fatherly wisdom bullshit. Like anything he could say in the next twenty minutes would ever erase the years of being such a total asshole.

But at the same time, if Ray refused to play along, there was no telling what might happen next. The road was deserted, the airfield, too. He'd knocked Ray around a few times before; he was way past the point of being capable of it now. And even if he didn't lose control, he'd never let Ray have his way. They'd sit here until three in the morning, like the time when Ray was six and he hadn't wanted to go ice skating but had eventually done it anyway, droopy-eyed and weeping in the middle of the night. It would be easier in the long run to just go out there, pretend to give a shit about what his dad had to say and then, hopefully, go home. If he tried to get out of it, it would just prolong everything. Ray had learned that a long time ago. The best thing to do with his dad when he was like this was to just do what he wanted and get away.

So after a few minutes Ray got out and hopped up on the hood of the car next to his dad. They sat in faux comfortable silence for a little while, just the sound of the whiskey sloshing, and then his dad lifted an arm and pointed out a jet, all black and silver, sitting out by itself in the field. "Know what that is, son?"

Ray put his mind to what computer games he was going to play next time he was at Jase's and let his mouth say, "What, Dad?"

"It's an F-4 Phantom. A twin-engine two-seater. It can go faster than

Mach two and carries seventeen thousand pounds of bombs—enough to wipe out this sorry burg. It can fly up to fifty-five thousand feet and can climb twenty-eight thousand feet a minute. I had a chance to fly one once. That was back when I was in officer training school."

Ah yes, thought Ray, officer training school, his dad's golden age. The time before his mother and he came along and ruined his life.

"I was young, and anything seemed possible. I'd just met your mother then. I was with the 116th and we were stationed in Robins, Georgia. Met her one night at a local bar. She was so pretty back then. She was wearing this red halter-top, and it hoisted her boobs up and, whew, well, never mind. Anyway, we started dating, and we thought we were in love. I had exams coming up, I had to study, but she didn't understand that. She wouldn't leave me alone. I washed out and then she got pregnant. We got married, you were born, and the next thing I knew, I was ground crew." He sighed, staring out at that jet, and then he turned to look at Ray. "One of these days, son, you're going to meet a woman, and you're going to think she's all you'll ever need in the world. But you'll be wrong. Don't sacrifice your dreams for anyone, boy, you hear me? Hang on to 'em, and don't let anything get in your way, not even love. Because love doesn't last. You go with love, you'll wind up like me, with nothing. Don't let that happen to you, son. Learn from my mistake."

"Okay, Dad." Ray wondered if his father was drunk enough yet to miss the sarcasm and then decided he didn't care. "I'll be sure to do that."

Sitting cross-legged in front of the mirror on the back of her bedroom door, Wendy lit a candle, placed it before her on the carpet and gazed at her reflection. Her hair was almost past her shoulders now. It had been four months since that spring evening when she first encountered Lili and began to embrace her individuality. She'd spent the summer reading, writing in her journal, exploring the world and herself. It had been a good summer, but now it was about to end.

Wendy breathed deeply, concentrating on her breath as it flowed in and out of her body, and let her eyes lose focus. "Goddess Lili, old as the moon, young as the dawn, guardian and companion, protector and teacher, come to me," she intoned. The room was dark but for the candle, and in the flickering light her reflection wavered, and grew wings.

"Lili," said Wendy. "Tell me more about the time before."

"All right. Nobody ever cut trees down. They just let them grow right up through their houses, or they built their houses in the branches, sometimes. And people didn't consider themselves to be above animals. They knew they were animals, too, and they considered all living things their brothers and sisters. So sometimes a human family and a wolf or lion family would live side by side, human children and cubs and pups all playing together and growing up together."

"Was there school?"

"Oh no, at least not in the way there is now, where you have to go and sit there in a room for hours and hours while outside a beautiful day languishes for want of attention. People shared everything, including knowledge, and just taught kids stuff as it came up."

"I'm starting high school tomorrow, Lili."

"Ah."

"Tonight they're having this parent-student open house thing, where they show you all around the school and stuff. It sounds really stupid, but my parents say we have to go. Lili, I wanted to ask you to protect me, to not let what happened in junior high happen again. But I don't know if you're that kind of goddess, and now I think maybe instead I should just ask you for strength, 'cause I don't want to do what I did before, you know, try to conform and then just be miserable."

"Well, you don't need to ask me for strength, you already have it. Don't worry, I'll be with you, I always am."

"Wendy? What are you doing?" came her mother's voice from the other side of the door.

Wendy groaned. "Nothing, Mom."

"I heard you talking to someone. What's going on?" The doorknob turned.

Frantically, Wendy scrambled backward shouting "Mom!" as the door opened, knocking over the candle. Molten wax spilled and caught fire, creating a small bonfire on the carpet.

"Why is the light off? What are you—Oh my God!" cried her mother as she saw the fire.

Fortunately Wendy's new self-expression included thick-soled combat boots. She jumped up and stomped on the fire, putting it out. There was a big black crater in the floor. She looked up at her mother, who flicked on the light, making her blink. Her mother looked from her to the crater and back to Wendy again, her eyes narrowed, her mouth a thin slit. "You could have burnt the whole house down! What in God's name are you doing?"

Wendy took a deep breath and set her jaw. "It's in the goddess's name, Lili." She fixed her mother with the sternest look she could manage. "My goddess. And nothing would have caught fire if you hadn't opened the door without asking."

Her mother blinked, and for a moment she actually looked afraid of Wendy. She looked her up and down, taking in Wendy's army jacket, her black leggings and flannel shirt, and the pendant around her neck, a coiled snake wrought in silver. Wendy had gotten everything at a secondhand shop down on the Strip for under twenty dollars. "Is that what you're wearing?" she asked with tentative dismay.

"Yep."

"Mmm. Well," she glanced at the crater once more. "You'll have to clean that up later; it's time to go."

Wendy sat on the bleachers in the Elmdale High gymnasium, watching her parents down on the gym floor talking to the school counselor, Mr. Crimmons. Goddess knows what they were telling him about her. That she ate bats at midnight and bathed in the blood of unbaptized babies, maybe. She sighed and took a sip of Kool-Aid. She'd been all tense about this whole thing, but as it turned out, the orientation was just boring, not scary at all. The principal and the vice principal had made speeches, and then there was a tour, and now "refreshments and an opportunity to meet one another." Yawn. Nobody had said anything to her about how she looked. It was almost disappointing.

She watched as people milled about the gymnasium, forming little knots of conversation and breaking up again. And then she spotted Kyle Denreddy standing by the extracurricular activities table, and her heart stopped. He turned, and she couldn't look away, couldn't *not* risk him seeing her. He glanced up in her direction, as if looking for someone, and his eyes grazed across her. She clutched her pendant and said a prayer to Lili, preparing herself for the worst. But nothing happened. He kept scanning the gym, finally spotted some girl she didn't know, waved, and headed over to her. Relief washed through her and then she realized, he hadn't recognized her. All that time, two years of making her life a living hell, and now, he didn't even recognize her. She took another sip of Kool-Aid and mulled that over.

"You know they lace that stuff with a drug that makes you join sports teams." In the aisle beside her stood a heavy black kid in a Sailor Moon T-shirt and neon blue painter's pants. Beside him stood a girl in a granny dress with long curly blond hair and huge, eighties-style glasses. "Hey, I'm Leo. This is Mandy." Mandy blushed and nodded.

"Hey. I'm Wendy."

Leo took a seat next to Wendy. Mandy sat down behind them. "You must have gone to West," observed Leo. "Was it as much of a pit as Jefferson?"

"Oh, it sucked. I hated it there."

"Yeah." Leo nodded philosophically. "Junior high is so *Lord of the Flies*."

"Exactly," agreed Wendy. " 'Kill the pig, kill the pig.' "

Leo raised his eyebrows and glanced at Mandy, who smiled shyly. "Wow, you've read *Lord of the Flies*. Impressive. Hell, you read, that alone is pretty huge. By the way, I like your pendant, does it mean something?"

Wendy smiled broadly. "It's a symbol of my religion."

CHAPTER

13

Ray's high school counselor, Mr. Crimmons, frowned at Ray from the other side of his desk. "You failed typing one," he said.

Ray was a junior, and he'd managed to coast academically up to now, but his carefully crafted plan of nonaction had succumbed to a sneak attack from clerical skills. Ray shrugged and gave him a conciliatory smile. "What can you do with typing anyway?"

Mr. Crimmons sighed and pinched the bridge of his nose. "There are a lot of things you'll need typing for, Ray. Look"—he switched on the computer terminal on his desk and swiveled it around so Ray could see the display—"I have to write a report for each and every one of my students." The screen showed a list of files. "And you'll have to write reports, too, probably, depending on what kind of job you're doing. And for that you need to be able to type. Let me ask you this, Ray: What are your plans after graduation?"

He shrugged. "I haven't made any."

Mr. Crimmons shook his head. "That's too bad, because work is going to comprise a third of your life, and without a plan, you won't have any control over what that third consists of. You want to be happy, don't you Ray?"

"Well, sure." Ray laughed.

"Then think about what makes you happy and how you can turn that enthusiasm into something you can make a living at, because believe me Ray, if you don't love your work, you won't love your life."

Ray stared at him. Enthusiasm? Besides computer games, there wasn't much he had enthusiasm for. He used to like to draw, but you couldn't make any money at that. "Well, I'll try," he said.

"Good. I hope you will. Now about your typing class. Since you can't take typing two, you have an open hour in your schedule next semester."

"Can't I take study hall?"

"You could, but I don't think that would do much to prepare you for the world outside Elmdale High. No. I want you to sign up for multimedia. In your freshman profile, you wrote that you like computer games. Well, the multimedia assistants are engaged in bringing the power of computer graphics, DVD, and music into the instructional framework of the classroom. It'll give you a broad introduction to the potential of new technology, and it just might give you some ideas about what you want to do with your life."

"But the multimedia kids are geeks," Ray protested.

Mr. Crimmons gave him a jaded look. "They are enterprising young people actively engaged in something that interests them, and I think you could learn a lot from them. I strongly suggest that you honor my request, Ray."

Ray sighed and nodded. At least multimedia was an open hour, not a class per se. As far as he could tell they mainly brought DVD players to the classrooms and hooked them up for the teachers. It'd be an easy hour.

So on the first day of the new semester Ray showed up at the media office and there was Wendy, that girl he'd met his first day of junior high, but she looked so different it took him a second to realize it was her. She was wearing a funky old fatigue jacket, her long hair hanging down in unruly locks from under a Chinese Red Army cap. As he came down the hall, she was wheeling a cart with a TV and DVD player through the door with expert efficiency.

Unsure that she would stop, he took an involuntary step back, but she pulled up just short of where he stood. "Yeah?" she said, stepping from behind the cart. A heavy silver pendant in the form of a snake hung from her neck. "What?"

"Um." Embarrassed, Ray looked aimlessly around the corridor. "I'm signed up for multimedia. Mr. Crimmons said you'd show me what to do."

Wendy treated him to a long, measuring stare during which he decided she did not remember him. "Well," she said at length, starting forward with the cart again, "come on then, follow me."

"Where are we going?" he asked.

"Mrs. Stevenson's class, room two-twelve. She's showing them the PBS production of *Wuthering Heights,*" she said. He hurried after her.

In the classroom Ray watched Wendy hook up the DVD player. She'd changed a lot since junior high. She'd grown into her nose, and grown her hair long again, but it was more than that. It was the way she dressed, that pendant, everything. She had an air of confidence about her now, and he realized she was in her own world, a world in which she was cool. Cooler than anybody else in that room, and all the more so because nobody recognized it.

"Now what?" he asked when they left the classroom.

"That's it for this hour," she said. "I'll come back after class to get the cart."

"What do we do in the meantime?" She walked quickly. Ray stretched his legs to keep up with her.

Wendy shrugged. "You can do whatever you want. I'm going to the park." They arrived at the media office, and Wendy took a bright plaid and very much handmade backpack from the back of a chair.

He was intrigued by Wendy in her new incarnation. She didn't seem to care what anybody thought of her, and that made her fascinating. "Can I come with you?" he asked.

She glanced at him in surprise. "Suit yourself," she said, "but usually I just write."

She didn't wait for him, so he followed her, out of the school and down Elmcrest to Kennedy Park.

It was a warm, overcast day, and the tops of the trees rustled in the breeze like breaking waves. Wendy took what must have been her customary spot beneath an elm, and pulled a notebook from her backpack.

She hadn't been kidding. She came here to write, and write she did, scribbling in her notebook, occasionally glancing up at the treetops as if she were checking on something. She completely ignored Ray, who sat on the ground nearby, idly tearing up chunks of grass. He watched her eyes following the flight of a bird, and wondered what information she gathered from it. Unwittingly he pulled up a clump of grass, roots and all.

Her eyes flicked to his. "You're going to kill all the grass, you know."

He looked at the clod in his hand and threw it down. Not sure what to say, he shrugged, and she went back to her writing.

So there's this new kid in multimedia. They put him in my hour," Wendy told Leo and Mandy at lunch.

The three of them had hung out ever since that first night at orientation. Wendy hardly ever saw Cara anymore. Her friend had taken her natural place among the popular clique. As for Robin, she and Wendy had drifted apart by mutual unspoken agreement, each eager to cast off the memories of junior high, eager for others to forget as well. At least that's what Wendy told herself. Last year Wendy heard Robin had run away from home. It was strange to think of her on her own like that. Strange to think of her in any way except as her pig-tailed defender during the darkest days of junior high.

"Oh yeah, Ray," said Leo, tapping his chin. "Ms. Y told me about him. He flunked typing."

"Oh. Do you know him?"

Leo shook his head.

"Well"—Wendy fanned her hands out over her cafeteria tray—"he's bizarre. He follows me all the way to Kennedy Park, and then just sits there, tearing up chunks of grass. I think there's something wrong with him." She tapped her head. "You know? I mean, what does he want?"

Mandy giggled and Leo waggled his eyebrows at her.

"Oh. Oh no. No, no, no, it can't be that!"

"Why?" Mandy leaned forward. "Is he hideous?"

"No, not at all. That's what I mean." She lowered her voice, lowered her head. "He's cute. He wouldn't like me."

Leo rolled his eyes and he and Mandy exchanged a look.

Wendy felt a feeble ember of hope spark to life inside her. "You think?" Then she shook her head. "But it's been all week, and he hasn't done anything. I think he's a spy for Mr. Crimmons."

"Maybe he's shy," offered Leo.

"I think he's scared to death of you," said Mandy.

"Scared of me? Why?"

"Well." Leo tapped his chin. "You are kind of fierce."

"Fierce? What, I'm a lioness now?"

"That's exactly what you are!" cried Leo, pretending to keep her at bay with an invisible whip and chair.

Wendy threw an empty paper cup at him.

Mandy picked at a salad. "You have a certain passionate intensity," she said. "It's not a bad thing," she hastened to add.

Wendy shook her head, staring at her Jell-O. She didn't want to feel this way. It was too much like how she'd felt back in junior high. Wanting someone to like you, afraid that they don't, trying to figure out how to act so that they will. She'd thought she was beyond all that, but she knew now she wasn't.

That afternoon at the park, Wendy stole covert glances at Ray as he lay on his back, staring at the clouds. The possibility that he might like her, planted in her heart by Mandy and Leo, made him more attractive to her than ever.

She admired the way his nose created a horizon across his face, like distant mountains, and his eyes were like lakes. The slopes of his face were lightly forested with stubble, particularly around his lips; gentle hills that hid among them a fertile valley full of succulent fruits. She wanted to taste that fruit. She wanted to wander in that land.

But if he liked her, why didn't he do anything? Maybe he *was* shy, or maybe her friends were wrong and he wasn't interested. Wendy returned her gaze to her notebook, frustrated with waiting and wondering. She hated feeling this way: passive. And she knew that she didn't act right, not for getting a guy. She'd seen how other girls got all giggly and acted helpless and stupid around guys, and for some bizarre reason, that seemed to work, but she could just as easily sprout wings and fly as she could pull off an act like that. It was all so frustrating and unfair, and she'd comforted herself that she didn't have to worry about any of it. She'd convinced herself that she didn't want a boyfriend, but now . . .

Finally she put the notebook down and looked at him again. "Have you ever noticed that the world is stupid?" she asked.

Her question startled a laugh out of him and he sat up, blinking at her.

Wendy took a deep breath, pressed down the panic bubbling in her throat and went on. "I mean for instance the way there are all these stupid rules for how you're supposed to act if you're a girl. Like if you want a guy to like you, you have to do this whole giggling, 'I'm an idiot' thing that I totally don't get. Why are guys attracted to morons, anyway?"

Ray shook his head. A tentative smile played across his lips. "I-I don't think we're all—"

"And then you're supposed to act like you don't like somebody if you do," she went on, interrupting him because she knew if she stopped now she'd never have the guts to finish, "because heaven forbid people should just be honest. And you're supposed to just sit around hoping that somebody you like is going to ask you out. It sucks. Why should we always have to be the passive ones? Why can't girls make the first move?" There, the question had been broached. She tried to catch her breath, watching him carefully for his reaction.

Ray regarded her with surprise, but not, she hoped, scorn. "They can," he said, as if it were the most reasonable thing in the world.

She scoffed at this. "Shua, right!"

He tilted his head to one side, his brows furrowed. "No really, why not?"

Wendy rolled her eyes. "Because the guy will say no and then everyone will talk about her, saying she's a tramp and a scag and stuff." She gave him a look that challenged him to prove her wrong. Did he know it was a challenge?

Ray pursed his lips and looked down. He started pulling up tufts of grass again. "Not necessarily," he said, eyes still on the ground. "Some guys might be relieved if a girl would make the first move." Hesitantly, he glanced up at her, and she was surprised to see a question in his eyes.

"Really?"

He shrugged. "Yeah. I mean everything you said"—he gave the grass a break and gestured vaguely—"you're right, and like, the opposite is true for guys. Why are we always supposed to be in control of everything?

And if girls act stupid, well, guys are worse. They act like assholes some-times, you know? Being all loud, yelling and bossing people around, act-ing big and trying to be in charge of everything? I hate that." A gleam of anger crept into his eyes. "I don't ever want to be like that."

She sat considering this for a few moments. Staring at him, chewing her lip. Did he really mean it? And even if he did, that still didn't mean he liked her, in particular, and even if he liked her, how could she be sure that she would like him? Now that the moment was upon her, she found the idea of kissing him—so attractive a moment before—outlandish and bizarre. She needed proof, she decided, proof that he was the right one, that she could trust him. Suddenly, moving quickly so she couldn't stop herself, she flipped her notebook open to a certain page and shoved it at him. "Here, read this."

Ray took the spiral notebook from her and read:

Stars of the ancient sky
Cold eternity shines
With the fire of distant calamity.

There was a doodle of the moon, shining over a tree, a figure with dark wings sat beneath it. A snake crawled up one side of the page, and under the tree, she had written,

Before there was the earth, before there was a universe, before there was anything, there was a woman, a snake, and a tree. The woman's name was Lili, and she had big dark wings. Lili sat beneath the tree, and wrote things down, and the snake curled about the roots of the tree, and talked to her, and the tree stood over them both, and listened.

Lili wrote, "The first law is life, and from life comes love."

And the snake said, "What's that supposed to mean?"

"Life is the thing that seeks love, it is a force that once started cannot be stopped. Love is the reason for life, and the means by which it spreads."

"And these things are desirable?" asked the snake.

"They are," said Lili.

So the first law was written, and from the first law came the universe, the earth, the moon, and the oceans, and from these came the tiny creatures, the life in the waters, the seekers of sunlight, the crawling things, and the flying things. And from these came the mammals, the reptiles, the fish, and the birds. And from these, one day in the fullness of time, came people. A new kind of creature that could write laws of its own. And the first law that people wrote was, "Death exists."

"True enough," said the snake, and Lili agreed, but before they knew it the people were writing all kinds of other laws. Some of them were pretty good, like "Hanging out and talking is fun," but others, like "Sex is evil" didn't make any sense at all.

"Wait a minute," said Lili. "That wasn't what I meant."

"Well it's too late now," said the snake. "They'll just have to work it out for themselves."

Closing the notebook, Ray felt as if a precious gift had been given to him through no merit of his own. It was true, he thought, his instincts had not led him astray: Wendy really was deeply, wonderfully weird. He looked up to see her carefully not looking at him, picking at a cuticle on her finger. And then her eyes slid over and met his. "Thanks," he said, handing her back the notebook. "That's a cool story."

She brightened. "Really? Thanks." Her cheeks were pink, her eyes shining. She looked down and bit her lip.

"I liked the snake."

Her smile widened. "Yeah?"

"Oh yeah."

She nodded, as if that made up her mind about something, and then she leaned toward him, her lips parted, her eyes shrouded by half-closed lids, and he could have sworn she was going to kiss him. But as a shadow fell over them her eyes flicked up and she sat back suddenly, redness blooming in her cheeks.

"Hey, what are you guys doing?"

Ray turned and looked up. It was Kyle, staring at them with his stupid ass grin.

"What's this?" said Kyle, stooping suddenly and plucking the notebook from the ground before either Ray or Wendy could stop him. He flipped it open. " 'Life is the thing that seeks love,' " he read and giggled. "This yours?" he asked Wendy, who stood to confront him.

"It's mine," she said. Ray got to his feet.

Kyle cocked his head at her, his eyes narrowed thoughtfully. "I think I'll borrow it for the night. I'll give it back to you tomorrow."

"Give it back to me now." Wendy's voice was even, her shoulders didn't betray a quiver.

Kyle laughed and shook his head. "Meet me tomorrow morning in the cafeteria, and I'll give it to you then," he said.

"Give it back to her now!" shouted Ray, stepping between them. He was scared to death of Kyle Denreddy, but he could just see Kyle's whole impromptu plan. In a night, with that notebook for source material, Kyle and his friends could enact torments for Wendy that would make what they did to her in junior high look like a party. And what would be worse, they would do it with her own words, her own thoughts. They would deface her notebook, he was sure, they all knew how empty Kyle's promise of its return was. The thought of Wendy's notebook, her private place where she had allowed no one but him, in the hands of Kyle and Perry washed his vision red with blood.

"Whoa, you getting in my face, Doghouse?"

"Yeah, I'm getting in your face, fuckwad. Give it back."

"Want it?" Kyle flipped the notebook behind his back and raised it over his head. "Here it is."

Ray wanted to grab for it, but Kyle would only push him away with his free hand, and behind him he heard Wendy say, "Don't," in a low, tense voice.

Kyle wanted him to jump for it; to dance around like a puppy after a bone. He waved it in the air and switched hands to dangle it closer. When both of Kyle's arms were over his head Ray stepped closer and rammed his fist into Kyle's gut with all the force his hatred could muster.

Kyle expelled a gasp of air and bent forward. Without thinking Ray jabbed his other fist up into his jaw. Kyle's teeth snapped shut with an audible click and then he was shouting incoherently, rolling on his back on the ground, his hands over his mouth. Blood ran from between his fingers. Ray stepped back, staring in horror at what he'd done. Suddenly an image of his dad, red-faced and shouting, flashed in his mind.

"Come on," said Wendy, picking up her notebook from where Kyle had dropped it. "Let's get out of here."

As he walked with her, Ray glanced over his shoulder at Kyle, who was getting to his knees. He glowered back at Ray balefully, his chin red with blood. Ray had never really hit anyone before. He tried to avoid fights and, except for a few shoving matches in grade school, he'd been successful. But now he understood how his dad must have felt; the sense of power, the feeling of release. The fact that he liked the feeling made him even more ashamed. "Do you think he's okay?" he asked Wendy.

She shrugged stiffly, keeping up a swift pace. "He probably bit his lip or his tongue."

"Ow. That sounds bad."

She shrugged again. "He might need stitches, it depends."

They had reached the sidewalk by then, and were headed north on Ridge. "Shouldn't we get somebody?" Ray asked.

Wendy paused, giving him a look of annoyance. "We should get the fuck out of here," she said.

"But—" Ray glanced back at the park again. Kyle was walking away to the west side of the park, to Kendale. Perry lived on Kendale, six blocks over. "Okay." He hurried after her. "I'd better walk you home, just in case."

Wendy laughed. "No, I think *I* better walk *you* home."

"Huh? Why?"

"Because it's not me they'll come after, it's you. You've got Kyle's attention now, boy. Oh and thanks, by the way." She patted the notebook-size bulge in her backpack.

Relieved to be reminded of the reason for his outburst, Ray gave her a courtly bow, and scrambled to catch up with her. "At your service, my lady," he panted, and Wendy snorted with laughter.

They were on the corner of Dellwood and Ridge now, and she paused and turned around, her arms waving indecisively. "Where do you live?"

She was serious about walking him home, he realized.

"No." He shook his head adamantly. "Where do *you* live?"

She gave him that shy, sly, measuring look again. "Pembleton," she said, apparently having made up her mind.

Wendy's house was a two-story fieldstone place with a big front porch. As they neared it their footsteps slowed. "Well," said Wendy, coming to a stop at the driveway. "You wanna come in?" She glanced at the aged dark green station wagon in the drive. "You really shouldn't walk home. Perry and Kevin might be out looking for you. My mom's home, she can give you a ride."

Accepting a ride home from Wendy's mom just seemed too lame for words. "I don't need a ride," he said, quickly adding, "But I will come in. I-I could use a glass of water."

"Sure," she said, and led him down the driveway to a side door.

Ray followed Wendy into the kitchen, which was cool and dark. "Mom?" she called, flicking on a light.

"How was your day?" came a voice from some other room, off to the back of the house.

"Fine," said Wendy, taking a glass down from a cupboard and filling it at the tap. The window over the sink gave Ray a glimpse of a shady backyard with a tall oak tree and lots of bushes. "Here," said Wendy, "you can sit down if you want. I think we have some Oreos."

"What, honey?" came the voice again. "I can't hear you. Hang on a sec, I'm almost through with this color."

Wendy rolled her eyes. "Nothing, Mom, I wasn't talking to you."

"Is somebody with you?"

"Just a friend from school," she said, taking a half-empty package of Oreos from the top of the fridge.

Just a friend from school, Ray silently harumphed to himself. Just a friend who'd saved her scrawny ass from the perpetual ridicule of Kyle Denreddy this very afternoon.

A tall, thin woman in a brightly colored plaid caftan came into the room. Wisps of vibrant fuzz stuck to her fingers and her short-cropped hair. "Oh, you must be Ray," she said, stepping forward energetically, her hand extended. "It's nice to meet you. I'm Mrs. Chrenko, Wendy's mom."

You must be Ray. So Wendy *had* mentioned him, maybe more than once. Ray nodded politely and managed, "Nice to meet you Mrs. Chrenko."

She nodded and was about to say something else when Wendy interrupted. "Mom," she warned.

"All right, all right, I'm going. Did you get something for your guest to eat?"

"Mo-om," Wendy growled, glaring briefly, fiercely at her mother's retreating back.

"Your mom seems nice," said Ray, sitting at the table eating Oreos.

Wendy grunted wordlessly and sat down, idly unscrewing a cookie. "She used to be a hippie, and she still thinks she's cool."

From the other room Ray heard a rhythmic clacking. It sounded like maybe a loom. He remembered Mrs. Chrenko's caftan, and the backpack Wendy carried. He glanced to where it lay on the kitchen counter. "Did she make that?" he asked.

Wendy's cheeks colored a little as she followed his eyes, but she nodded defiantly. "Yes."

"And the poncho you used to wear?"

Her reserve broke, and she laughed. "Yeah. Oh goddess, that thing. Believe it or not, the Scooby-Doo lunch box was my attempt at being cool."

He laughed nervously, embarrassed at the reminder of his abandonment of her. "I was lucky," he said by way of apology. "By the time I got here I'd moved so many times, I'd perfected the art of being invisible."

She nodded, devoting great concentration to breaking one cream-shorn disk of her cookie into tinier and tinier pieces. "I managed to disappear for a year. I mean people literally talked around me as if I wasn't there. Months would go by without anybody saying a word to me. But that didn't make me any less miserable. In fact, I think it might have been worse. At least when they were taunting me, and I was fighting back, I was a person. And I cared enough about myself to fight. Being invisible, it's like I lost myself even to myself. It was depressing." Her eyes darted up to his face, checking to see if he was getting all this. "That's the problem with becoming invisible," she observed. "Sometimes even you can't see yourself anymore."

Ray nodded. "Yeah. But it gets to be like a habit, you know? After a while you forget you were ever there, you forget who you are, you just don't know anymore. At least that's how I feel, sometimes." But not, he reflected, when he was with Wendy.

"Yeah—" Wendy stopped as they both heard the sound of a car pulling into the driveway. "My dad's home," she said.

Ray looked at her closely, but she didn't seem nervous. Still. "Should I get out of here? Is there, like, a back door or something?"

She laughed. "What? Why? Oh, I mean if you don't want to meet him—"

"No, but . . . you won't get in trouble?"

"For having a friend over?" She looked at him like he was some kind of freak.

Ray didn't say anything, and then it was too late anyway, because the side door opened and a man in a tan overcoat came in. He was a little taller than Ray's dad, but somehow he didn't seem to take up as much space. He saw them sitting at the kitchen table and he smiled. He had glasses, dark hair, and a smooth, broad forehead. "Hi honey," he said to Wendy, taking his coat off and throwing it over the back of a chair. He wore a dark brown suit. He glanced expectantly between Wendy and Ray as he worked his yellow tie loose.

"Hey Dad," said Wendy. "This is Ray."

Wendy's dad's smile broadened as he advanced on Ray with an outstretched hand. "Hi Ray, nice to meet you."

Ray stood up and shook hands with him, feeling awkward. "Nice to meet you, Mr. Chrenko," he said.

"Ah, call me Paul," he said, and to Ray's horror, he pulled the chair he'd draped his coat and his tie on up to the table, sat down, and took a cookie from the open package on the table. He twisted it apart and sheared the cream filling off one of the halves with his upper teeth. "Mmmm. Isn't it interesting that something so completely devoid of natural ingredients can taste so good?"

"Sugar's natural," said Wendy.

Paul frowned thoughtfully at the remains of his cookie. "Not in this quantity, surely," he said.

Wendy shrugged. "What about honey? That's just as sweet."

He raised his eyebrows. "True. Still, in this case I suspect a darker power at work."

Wendy rolled her eyes and shot Ray a look of apology. "Dad, don't be weird."

"Oh." Paul glanced at Ray and back at Wendy again, nodding wisely.

He leaned sideways toward Ray with his hand to the side of his mouth, as if to hide what he was about to say. In a loud whisper he said, "Don't worry, she doesn't take after me at all."

"Da-ad!" Wendy cried in outrage as Ray tried to smother a grin.

"Okay." Paul grabbed another cookie and stood up. "I'll go see how your mother is doing. Start thinking about what you want to eat tonight. My guess is we'll be doing some kind of take-out again."

When he'd left the kitchen, Wendy sighed with relief. "Sorry about that," she said. "He's kind of a spaz."

Ray shook his head. "No. No, I think he's great. Really funny, and, you know, nice. I think you're lucky."

Wendy tilted her head to one side and gave him a doubtful look.

Ray didn't say anything more. He couldn't think how to explain to Wendy the simple miracle of what had occurred here just now: this trivial little discussion about Oreo cookies where no one was trying to intimidate or belittle anyone else. Where her opinion was sought out and heard. Where she could call her dad weird and get away with it. This was just an everyday thing to her, he realized with a twinge of jealousy that was soon overwhelmed by joy at the discovery. She took it all for granted, and maybe that was the best part of all, because that proved that it was real.

CHAPTER

14

The next day, walking down the hallway after third period, Ray wondered if he should have tried to kiss Wendy when they said good-bye in her parents' driveway. Probably. Had she been about to kiss him in the park before Kyle showed up? He wasn't sure, but she *had* invited him into her house, he'd met her mom and dad. They were practically, like, married.

He wondered if she had much in the way of boobs. She always wore those baggy shirts and sweaters, so it was hard to tell. He wondered what it would feel like to slip his hand underneath her shirt. Did she wear a bra? Maybe not. Her mom was a hippie. Ray stuck his hands in his pockets and balled them into fists, affording his swelling cock a little more room.

"Hey." It was Jase, falling into step beside him. "Have you heard the news? Coach Milewski is benching Kyle for the game with Pemberton this Friday."

"Uh-oh."

"Yeah. I thought I'd better warn you. I heard Perry Wolper and Matt Winecki talking after gym this morning. Those jocks are pissed, they're after you."

Ray sighed, stopping at his locker. "Thanks, Jase."

"S'okay. What are you going to do?"

Ray shrugged. "Try to stay out of their way, I guess."

Jase nodded. "You coming to lunch?"

Ray shook his head. "I guess I'd better not. Besides, I told Wendy I'd wait for her."

"You're in a lot of trouble because of that girl, and you're still hanging out with her. I don't get it. She's a scag."

Ray frowned. "She's not a scag."

"Well look at the way she dresses, and that hair. She's a freak. And now the jocks are after you, just because of her." He paused, and a light of comprehension gleamed in his eyes. "Hey, is she letting you screw her?"

Ray snorted. "No. Not yet, anyway."

Jase shook his head. "I don't get it."

Ray shrugged. "It's the way I feel, when we're together. Like, like I'm something more than just Ray Mackie, average high school student."

Jase rolled his eyes. "Yeah, well, you know what not being average will get you. I'll see you, man. Watch your back."

"See ya."

He'd been friends with Jase for years, he was there at that lunch table he sat down at that first day in junior high. Jase and Ray and Pete and Bill hung out together in the vast, nondescript morass of kids who were neither popular, nor, formally speaking, geeks. Pete and Jase had some marginal respectability as members of the track team, and Bill worked on the school newspaper. Most of all, they didn't push it. They didn't try to rise above their station. Now Ray's actions had destroyed that delicate balance. Jase and Bill and Pete would probably start avoiding him now. Ray knew it from the tone of that last "see you" of Jase's. He couldn't blame them. Hanging out with Ray would only draw the wrath of the jocks on them as well.

Ray put his math book on the shelf in his locker and went upstairs to the drinking fountain near the boys john. Wendy wasn't there yet. He felt nervous, and he had to piss, so he went into the john.

Somehow the urinals seemed too out in the open today, so he took a stall. While he was in there, he heard footsteps. He tried to tell himself it was just people coming in to piss, but he didn't hear any voices, no water running, no flushing of toilets. By the time he finished, the john was quiet again, but he wasn't alone, he was pretty sure of that. He turned around, and saw four sets of feet outside the stall door.

"Mwch, mwch, mwch," someone made kissing noises, and then, "Here pussy, pussy, pussy."

"Come on out, dickwad," said another voice—Perry's. "We're gonna kick your ass!"

Ray didn't think that was much incentive, and he glanced frantically around the stall. It was no use. Trying to climb over the dividing wall would only land him in a similar trapped predicament in the next stall, or worse, strand him atop the wall.

About the time he figured this out, the jocks started chanting, "Pus-sy, pus-sy, pus-sy," and the door to the stall burst inward.

Hands grabbed him, and Ray caught a brief glimpse of Perry and Matt as they turned him around to face the toilet. He struggled, but they held him tight and kicked his knees out from under him, forcing him to kneel, pushing his head inexorably toward the bowl. Ray held his breath as the water rose up, squeezing his eyes shut as it swirled around him, surging up his nose and into his ears.

They let him up, gasping and sputtering, trying to wipe his dripping face on his sleeves.

"How big are you now, ass wipe?" inquired Perry just before swinging his fist to clip Ray under the chin. His head flew back, his neck cracking. He sagged against the toilet. Shit, these guys were serious.

"Hey, watch it," said Matt, backing off. "What are you doing?"

"What do you think? This fuckwad got Kyle benched," said Perry.

"Yeah, he hit him with a two-by-four with an iron bracket on it," said Brian Urqhardt. "Pull him out of there. I wanna kick some pussy, too!"

"What? That's bullshit!" yelled Ray as he tried to slide beneath the divider into the next stall. "I clocked him in a fair fight, 'cause he was hassling this girl, and now you're ganging up on me like this?" Heedless, Perry and Kevin grabbed him by the legs and pulled him out, bashing his head against the toilet bowl in the process. "Fuck!" Ray screamed and then, "Help!" over and over as loud as he could, hoping one of those damn security guards, or somebody, anybody, would hear him.

"Kick him in the nuts! Kick him in the nuts!" urged Perry and Kevin, still holding Ray's legs, and pain exploded in his crotch and belly as Brian gleefully complied.

Ray screamed and twisted, doubling up, shielding his balls with his hands. Why wasn't anyone coming to help him? Couldn't anybody hear him? He yelled again, but it was no use. They kicked him again, in the head, again in the balls, heedless of his fingers, and he threw up on his soggy shirt and pleaded, "Leave me alone."

"Oh gross, man. He puked," said Perry.

"Jesus, what a piece of shit," said Kevin, and then, with a note of inspiration. "He belongs in the garbage."

"Let's do it," said Brian.

"No!" screamed Ray. He tried to get up, he tried to get away, but the pain was paralyzing. Through the fog of agony that enveloped him, Ray felt them pick him up by the arms and legs. They carried him out of the john chanting, "Trash the fag. Trash the fag." A crowd had gathered outside. Ray saw a lot of letter jackets, and then, the black maw of the garbage can hove into view and swallowed his field of vision as they hoisted him high and shoved him head first into it. The can tilted under his weight and crashed to the floor.

It stank, and there was something slimy against his cheek, but he almost wanted to stay there, compared with coming out and facing the laughing, mocking crowd he could hear all around him. With sudden fury, Ray righted himself. His knees were weak, but he threw the can aside, glaring at the laughing faces. "Fuck you!" he screamed, and they laughed even harder, some of them actually doubling over with glee. "Fuck you!" he said again, less forcefully this time, because he realized he was about to cry and immediately invested every effort left in him not to start bawling right then and there.

There was a hand on his shoulder, and he spun around, growling, clenching his fist, but it was Wendy, who was not laughing, who looked at him gravely and reached up, plucking away the crumpled test paper wedded with gum that had lodged in his hair like an inane pom-pom.

"Come on," she said, taking his hand. "Let's get out of here."

They had almost reached the doors when they saw two security guards coming from the office area, Matt trailing behind them. "Shit," said Ray under his breath. One of the guards approached Brian, Perry, and Kevin as the other veered over to corral Ray.

"Where you going there, son?" said the guard.

Ray curled his lip. "I'm not your son. I'm going home. Leave me alone."

The guard shook his head and put a restraining hand on Ray's shoulder. "Sorry kid, I can't do that. I've got a job to do."

"Yeah, well you're a little late."

The guard winced. "We were on break."

So they all spent the rest of the afternoon in the principal's office, taking turns talking to the security guards, Principal Szabo and the police. Wendy stayed with him the whole time. She never asked permission of anybody, just fixed anyone who looked like they were considering asking her to leave with a stare that could have peeled paint. And Ray was glad to have her there, because every time they were alone together, Perry, Kevin, and Brian started making cat noises.

The upshot was that Perry, Kevin, and Brian got suspended for a month for beating up Ray in the boys' john. Matt got a good citizen citation for alerting the authorities. Principal Szabo called Ray's mom, who took him to the emergency room, where they packed his balls in ice and gave him a Tylenol.

"I don't want you to hang around with that girl anymore, Raybeam," said his mom, sitting beside his hospital bed with her hands folded in her lap, looking wan, tired, martyred. "She's the one got you into this mess."

"What, I shouldn't have defended her? I should have just let Kyle take her notebook? Is that the kind of man you want me to be?"

She smiled sadly. "No. I just want you to get along, that's all. Don't let your temper get the best of you, like your daddy always did."

Stung, Ray glowered. "I'm nothing like him."

She laughed and nodded her head. "You're right. You're like your mother, a fool for love."

Ray gasped. "I'm not in love!"

She smiled.

The next day Ray's mom let him stay home from school. He was eating ice cream and watching cartoons when the doorbell rang. Dressed in sweats, he padded to the door and opened it to find Wendy standing there, a geometry textbook in her hands.

"Hey," she said.

He blinked and smiled with pleased surprise. "Hey."

She looked at the book in her hands, then up at him. "I brought you your homework."

"Oh. Thanks." He took the book from her and they stood there a moment, staring at each other in awkward silence. "So, you want to come in?" After all, his mom was at work, what could she do about it?

She shrugged. "Sure."

She came in and they sat on the couch together. "Are you okay?" she asked him, searching his face with her dark eyes. The bruise over his right cheekbone had darkened since yesterday. He actually looked worse now, even though it didn't hurt as much.

"Yeah," he told her. "I'm okay." It wasn't really true. He felt humiliated. Well, he'd been humiliated before, after all, but he'd thought . . . He'd thought that now, with his dad gone, he didn't have to worry about that anymore. It had been four years, but now, it all came back to him. The shame, and then, the deep, smoldering anger, way down inside. The hate; pure and indelible. Hate that made him hate himself.

He'd thrown out the clothes he'd had on yesterday, wishing he could burn them; them and the awful memory of what had happened. He was clean now and the doctor at the hospital said he was fine, but still his mind was filled with all those faces, laughing at him because he had a wad of paper on his head. Well, not just because of that . . .

Wendy wasn't fooled. "Oh shit, Ray. I'm sorry."

He frowned. "What do you have to be sorry about? It's not your fault," he said, suddenly feeling irritated with her. He didn't like the way she was looking at him. Like she felt sorry for him. He didn't need her pity. And maybe it *was* her fault. None of this would have happened if it hadn't been for her and that stupid notebook of hers. "Besides," he added defensively, "I told you, it's not so bad."

She sat back, her gaze hard with anger. "Don't tell me it's not so bad. They almost got my notebook, but you stopped Kyle. And now you . . . Do you have any idea what my life would be like if he'd kept it?"

Ray blinked. She knew what he'd done for her. She was trying to thank him. Looking at her suddenly, impossibly sweet face, Ray smiled. Despite his aches and pains, despite his humiliation, a warmth spread through him. In that moment, Ray knew he would have done much more, to feel like this. "It's okay. I know. I've read it, remember?"

She laughed, and shook her head. "Look, I'm sorry. I shouldn't have gotten you involved with my weirdness. I don't know why you wanted to hang out with me in the first place, but I think it's obvious that any continued association between us will only attract further attention."

"What?" Ray had not foreseen this.

"Don't feel bad. I mean it was cool and all, but this is obviously more than you bargained for and I don't want—"

"It's okay. Look." He took her hand, which she, looking down, allowed him to lift and press to his shoulder. "See? I'm still here. I'm okay." He moved her hand to his chest, where he held it a little too long, and she laughed and pushed him. He winced and flopped back on the couch. "Ow, take it easy. I'm here, just not all here."

"You silly ass," she said in amused exasperation, and then suddenly she looked serious again, and she leaned forward, and her lips brushed against his. She sat back again abruptly, and pretended to be absorbed in the *TV Guide*.

His lips tingled ever so slightly. Ray lifted his hand to touch them and smiled. "So, uh, you want to see my room?"

Wendy went through his room with all the patient scrutiny of an archeologist searching for signs of civilization. Ray sat on the bed, congratulating himself on having stashed his father's old Playboys in the garage weeks ago, but when she found the old brown folio, wedged forgotten between his desk and the wall, he froze.

"What's this?" she asked.

"Uh, nothing," he said.

She took in his expression and a sly smile spread across her face. She held the folio to her chest and swayed her hips. "C'mon. I showed you mine."

He reddened and stared down at his hands. "Yeah, but yours is good," he whispered. "That's just . . . kids' stuff."

Her smile vanished and she sat down on the bed next to him, peering at him with a furrowed brow, that damn folio still on her lap. "Don't be embarrassed. It's okay. I won't look if you don't want me to, but . . ."

But it would be like he didn't trust her. After all, she *had* shown him her journal, and she'd been there by his side yesterday when everyone else was laughing at him. For him not to share his stupid drawings with her, it seemed petty somehow. "Okay." He swallowed. "Okay, just keep in mind they're really stupid, and I did them a long time ago, and I don't do it anymore, okay?"

She gave him a funny look, like maybe she wished she hadn't asked, but just the same she slipped the elastic band from the folio and pushed back the flap. It had been ages since he'd even looked in there, and his mind raced frantically, trying to remember all his pictures, trying to pinpoint which ones would be the most embarrassing.

The first one she pulled out was a self-portrait he'd done with pastels, only for some reason he'd used green and blue shaded together to give himself scales, and in his eyes were twin reflections of a tree standing alone on a hilltop.

Wendy gave a soft gasp and he cringed inside, but then she said, "Oh Ray," and looked at him with eyes wide and dark. "This is beautiful."

He blinked and a smile came unbidden to his lips.

The next was a charcoal drawing he'd done of his parents standing together, his father's arm around his mom's shoulders, his shadow looming over her, obscuring her face. Ray had liked that one because the way he did his father's hair gave just a suggestion of horns, and his smile, pointed, the teeth gleaming, was just like his dad's smile. "Awesome," said Wendy, and he flushed with pleasure.

And then she took another one out, a picture of a broad green field and a radiant, multicolored cloud, and it was probably the most embarrassing, simply for being the most beloved. Looking at it now, it gave him the same feeling he'd had when he'd drawn it, a feeling he couldn't really put a name to. It was a picture of how he wanted the world to be, of what he hoped life could be like. And she held it in her hands, like she held his heart, his deepest, most secret heart, that he had hidden even from himself.

Wendy gazed at the picture, her eyes aglow. "Oh my god, Ray," she said, and he was impressed, because she nearly always said "goddess" but she must have forgotten. "This is beautiful."

His cheeks burned and he found that his hands were shaking. He clasped them together. "That . . . that's, um . . . my favorite one."

She smiled and nodded, her eyes still avid on the picture. "I can see why. It has . . . such a feeling . . . like it's the first day of the world for these people and all the beauty of life lies before them."

Exactly. That was exactly what it was, only he'd never had the words. Ray stared at Wendy, speechless. But he felt . . . he felt like *today* was the first day of the world for *him,* and all the beauty of life had been revealed in her.

She turned to him at last with a quizzical expression. "Why on earth would you hide these?" She shook her head. "Why would you stop drawing?"

He looked away and shrugged, fixing a bland expression on his face. "I don't know."

"No. Oh no." She leaned forward and grabbed him, turning him to face her. "You're not going to go all blank on me now. Not now."

Ray blinked. Shit. She knew. She'd seen his pictures, and now she knew all his secrets. Because of course that was what he was trying to do: go blank. Though of course he'd never had words for it before.

"Ray, you have an amazing talent. Seriously. I'm not just saying it. I wouldn't do that, would I?"

She had a point. He licked his lips. He took her hand. He pulled her to him and held her close, breathing in deeply, straining his sore ribs for the smell of her, sweet and a little musky, like a bakery on a rainy day. She hugged him back and he thought, Why not? What was the point in trying to keep anything from her?

So he pulled back at last, and said, "My dad said it was a sissy thing to do."

She tilted her head and bit her lip, put a hand to his face and then pulled him back to her again. "Your dad is an asshole," she said.

Ray laughed. "Yeah. Yeah he is."

She turned her face toward his and they kissed. Her lips were soft and damp, like dewy grass, but warm—warm as a home he'd never come home to before—and he wanted more of them. His eyes fluttered closed and he wrapped his arms around her, his hands tunneling through her hair, her wonderful, silky thick hair. Wendy lay back on the bed and he wound up on top of her, still kissing her madly. Her hands were on his back, then his ass. His heart hammered and he had an erection like a steel pipe. In wonder he rolled the palm of his hand over her breast and felt her nipple stiffen, like a hard little pearl in a bed of down.

She turned her head to kiss and bite at his neck, and he hissed in pleasure and surprise. "Oh Wendy," he gasped, working his fingers down the buttons of her shirt and squirreling his hand inside to touch the soft skin, to roll her tight nipple between his fingers.

She was still working on his neck, and he welcomed the distraction from his insistent cock. He pushed her shirt open and bent his head to her nipples. Maybe if he focused on her breasts he could keep from coming all over his pants.

But his efforts were to no avail when Wendy squeezed her hands in between their hips to rub at the tip of his penis. The friction of the fabric against his cock, the pressure of her hand, the knowledge of it being there; it was all too much for him. Ray grunted and lifted his head to kiss her frantically while his hips, seemingly of their own volition, bucked against her rhythmically and he came in a sweet, hot explosion that sent stars streaking behind his closed eyes.

"Huh," he exhaled, suddenly remembering to breathe as he slumped against her. Easing his weight off her he kissed her again, and held her close, not wanting to see her face just then, not wanting to find out if he should be embarrassed or not.

But she hugged him back and said, "So, I guess we're like, going out now, huh?"

He laughed. "Yeah, if it's okay with you."

"Yeah." She pulled back a little to look at him, her eyes glittering. "It's okay."

The next Monday Ray was supposed to go back to school, but he didn't. He pretended to, getting up in the morning and doing all his usual things, so his mother wouldn't suspect anything. But instead of walking all the way to school, he stopped at Kennedy Park. He whiled away most of the morning throwing rocks at a bull's-eye somebody had carved in one of the boarded-up windows of the utility shed. By eleven o'clock he was bored and hungry, so he went down to the Strip. He didn't go to the Taco Bell or the McDonald's because they were school places, and he wasn't in school that day. Instead he walked on to the Clock, a run-down little diner he'd never paid much attention to before. The bell on the door jingled as he entered. Other than that, it didn't look like anything had happened in the place since 1949. The black-and-white checkered tile on the floor, the chrome and red vinyl stools, the stainless steel counter top, even the waitress—tall, with a tall blond hairdo and surly red lips— looked frozen in time.

He sat down at the counter and took a menu from the little clip behind the napkin dispenser. It was what you'd expect, hamburgers, chili, tuna- and egg-salad sandwiches, soup. Not a green thing in sight. The place was empty except for some old guy at the other end of the counter nursing a coffee and reading a racing form. Still the waitress took her time saun- tering over. "Know what you want?"

He wondered briefly if she was going to tell him, but she just waited, eyeing him with bland unfriendliness.

"Uh, cheeseburger, fries, and a Coke," he said.

It was a good cheeseburger, if you could really call it a burger of any kind. The meat almost disappeared into the bun, commingling with the grease and the cheese. It was delicious, and unquestionably bad for you. He ordered another one.

The door jingled again and a guy walked in carrying a briefcase. He wore a duster coat and had long, curly brown hair. "Hey Flo, bring me a coffee," he said, taking a seat at a corner booth. The old guy with the racing form got up and joined him.

Ray ate his cheeseburger, surreptitiously eyeing them. The two men conversed in low tones, leaning toward one another, arms on the table. The younger one sat back suddenly, throwing an arm up. "Solly, the numbers are good, this guy's screwing us!" He glanced over then, caught Ray's eye, and subsided. Their conversation became inaudible once more.

The moment he'd finished his second cheeseburger, Flo slapped the check down in front of him rather pointedly. Ray paid up and got out of there.

Wendy didn't know whether to be relieved or pissed when she saw Ray loitering near the picnic table at Kennedy Park that afternoon. She quickened her pace to close the distance between them. "Ray! What are you doing? What's going on?"

Ray, startled by her vehemence, took an involuntary step back. "What do you mean?"

She stopped in front of him, her arms crossed. "Why weren't you at school today?"

He shrugged characteristically. "I'm still sore."

Wendy snorted and gave him a wry grin. "I mean the real reason."

Ray looked at her with a glimmer of resentment. Maybe he was beginning to see where it might not be such a great thing, not being able to hide from her. He sighed and went over and sat on the picnic table. "I just . . . don't want anything like that to happen again." He stared off into the middle distance, and then peeked back at her again. Waiting, she realized. Hoping she'd be able to tell him something that would help. He looked so sad, and he'd been so brave, standing up for her and taking all this shit for it. And now he was like her, like she used to be, like she still was, really; afraid and wanting to protect that cherished little core of being that was too beautiful and horrible and precious and ugly for anyone else to understand. And what was she going to tell him, now, in his hour of need? What had she learned from junior high, really, that could help him? Nothing. Because this was different. He was a different person.

She went over and sat down next to him, taking one of his hands in hers and resting her chin on it. She loved being able to touch him like that, any time she wanted to. His skin was always so warm. "I can understand that," she said. "Who would? But it probably won't, you know. For one thing those guys are suspended, and if anyone else hassles you they'd get suspended, too."

He nodded and looked like he had something to say but was having trouble getting it out of his mouth. "It's just that when I hit Kyle—" he finally burst out, his face working, his eyes pinning her with a wide, hot, blue gaze. She gripped his hand tighter, suddenly listening with all her being. "It's just that when I hit Kyle, it felt good. Really good, and I realized . . . well, it reminded me of something, I guess, but in a way I hadn't thought about before."

"What?"

He shrugged again, his eyes cloudy now and staring at their hands. "My dad."

She took a breath. "What did it remind you of about your dad?"

He hesitated. "He used to get drunk a lot. Still does, maybe, I don't know. We haven't seen him in a few years. But he'd get drunk and then he'd get mad, and he'd yell and scream, sometimes throw shit, sometimes hit . . . my mom. You know, just be a real asshole, and I hated it." He swallowed. "I hated him."

Wendy nodded.

"And I could never understand, why he acted like that, why he got off on pushing people around. And I never wanted to be like that." His hand squeezed hers painfully tight. "I tried so hard not to be like that, all violent and angry and stuff. I'd rather not be anything at all, than be like him. And then I hit Kyle, and it was like, *wow*. It felt good. I felt powerful, and that felt good, and I thought, that must be how he felt. That must be why he did it. And now, now I'm afraid of what will happen, if I go back."

"Because you're afraid of feeling that way again. Of being like your dad."

He nodded. "I'm afraid if I see Kyle, or if somebody says something, I'll just go for them. I could, you know? I really could. And if it was one-on-one, I bet I'd kick some ass, too. And just talking about it now makes me want to do it, so how can I go back?"

What had she done? She felt as if she'd lured him out to some precipice of himself, and now he looked to her to bring him back, and she had no rope, no grappling hook or chisel, just a notebook and a pen. "Ray, first of all, your dad would never think all of this. He'd just do what he wanted, right?"

"Well, yeah," he admitted.

"So right there, you're nothing like him. I don't think you have to worry. I mean, you hit Kyle in the first place because he was doing something wrong. You did it to help me, not for yourself. I mean, I don't blame you, wanting to kick those guys' asses. I do, too. It's only natural to feel that way, it has nothing to do with your dad."

He shrugged and squeezed her hand, smiled a little and blinked thanks at her, but she could see that his heart had not changed. He might know she was right, but he still felt the same way. "That must have sucked, to have a dad like that."

He shrugged. "Yeah, I guess."

"No really. I mean, did he hit you and stuff?"

Ray tilted his head to one side. "Not really. Once in a while, maybe. I got good at having him not notice me."

"Mmm."

He suddenly laughed and rolled his eyes. "Paging Dr. Wendy Freud! Yeah well, anyway, he's gone now, and that's good, so it doesn't matter."

"It matters if you quit school. Then you're, like, letting him win. You don't have to do that. You don't have to be like him, and you don't have to be nobody."

He blinked at her.

"You can be yourself, Ray."

He laughed, shook his head and shrugged, bringing all his weapons of avoidance to bear on the situation. "I don't even know who I am."

Inspiration hit her and she knew what to do. "That's okay," she told him, "you will. And in the meantime, I'll know for you."

Later that night, Wendy called him.

"What are you doing tonight around midnight?"

Ray didn't want to tell her "sleeping." "Why?"

"Could you meet me at the park?"

The clandestine appeal of that was overwhelming. "Okay." Was this an invitation to sex? His heart thumped. Probably, he realized, in sudden awe. What else could it be? This was Wendy, he reminded himself sternly. It could be anything.

His mom usually went to bed at ten. That gave him plenty of time. Dressed in black jeans and a black long-sleeved shirt (just in case they were sneaking in somewhere), Ray pushed open the window of his bedroom as quietly as he could and slipped out into the night.

The streets were quiet, the air was cool but not cold. The full moon cast everything in silver, and Kennedy Park, when he reached it, was a tranquil lake of light striped by the shadows of trees.

He found Wendy sitting under the elm, her face dappled with moonlight. She beckoned him to sit in front of her and he did. Their knees were touching. "I wrote you a story," she said. And he saw her notebook open in her lap.

She took Ray's hands in hers, holding them firmly. "Goddess Lili," she said. "Come to me, guide me, inspire me." Her eyes glowed in the darkness, captivating him. As much as he knew Wendy was, she was even more in that moment; a part of the night, a goddess with dark wings.

"There once was a boy named Ray," she said, her head bent now, reading.

He was a child of the earth, at home among trees and fond of serpents and clouds and unruly women. But Ray lived with his father in a house that flew from place to place, never the same place twice. The house had no mirrors, so Ray could not see himself. Instead he drew pictures of the things that were inside him. Until his father took his pencils and his paper away and told him not to do that anymore.

So then all Ray could see was his father, and that broke his heart, because although he resembled his father on the outside, the important part, the shape of their hearts, was nothing alike. His father had a heart like a clenched fist, and he used it to beat anyone who got close to him. This was not Ray's nature. Ray had a heart like a hand reaching out to pull someone out of deep water. But he didn't know that. He thought he was just like his father, because that's all he could see. So Ray decided it would be better to be nothing at all, than to be like that, and he became invisible.

One day while Ray was out of the house, his father flew away without him. Ray stayed in the same place after that, but it didn't matter so much, because by now he'd been invisible for so long that he'd forgotten how to be anything else. But in this place there lived a girl named Wendy, and she had been invisible once, too, so she could see him.

Wendy had made herself visible again with stories, and she shared these with Ray and he liked them, and him liking them made her sure that she liked him. But before she could tell him that, or do anything about it, an evil creature, an ogre like Ray's father, with a heart like a fist, stole Wendy's stories, because creatures like that, they only want you to be the narrow little things that make it convenient for them to abuse you.

Well, it turned out Ray was a warrior, as well as an artist and a gentle person. He defeated the ogre, and gave Wendy her stories back. But the ogre had ogre friends, and they beat him with fists and words, and there were too many of them, and he couldn't get away and he thought that the rage he'd feared for so long, the rage he knew was inside him, was growing too large, too strong to contain. He didn't know what to do, the only thing he could think to do was to disappear completely.

But Wendy didn't want to lose her friend. In the very short time they'd known each other, she'd already seen such wonderful things inside him. She knew he was kind and brave, a good person willing to fight evil, a person who found beauty in the world around him. She knew he only needed the right mirror to discover that beauty in himself. So she decided to introduce him to the moon, because the moon is the best mirror there is. It shows you not what you look like, but what is inside you.

Wendy squeezed his hands. "Look up, Ray."

He did, and saw the great round face smiling, brimming, spilling over with light. He felt bathed in its light. He felt drenched in love, for her, for him, this him that she saw and that he now saw in brilliant abundance all around him, that he felt in the soft breeze and heard in the gentle tick of night insects and smelled in the wonderful earth and grass smell of this place. It was all part of him. The him he now understood he'd been all along, that was nothing to do with his father, that had nothing to be ashamed of. A him both new and ancient. Ray the wild, the loving and the brave. Ray the free.

Free to feel. Tears came and he just let them, turning the moonlit sky to a glittering wash of light, a river washing him clean. Wendy's hands released his, and she put her arms around him, and he put his around her, still gazing up at the moon. She rocked him, but he didn't feel sad, he felt happy, just, brimming, like the moon. At length she pulled back, and their mouths found each other.

He kissed her with certainty, relishing the taste and feel of her mouth, running his hands through her hair and across her back. She felt so solid, so real and warm. Her breath in his mouth was like a miracle, her hands on his shoulders, his chest, a blessing, all of it unbelievable and undeniable and unquestionably good.

She broke the kiss and lay down on her side, beckoning. Ray stretched himself out beside her so the whole length of their bodies were touching, and then she took his hand, which was resting on her smooth, soft belly, and she pushed it down, rubbing his palm against the coarse fabric below the fly of her jeans. She hid her face against his shoulder and moaned softly as he kneaded her.

Now here was power, he thought, as moisture blossomed through her jeans and dampened his busy fingers. And it was nothing like the way he'd felt when he hit Kyle. This was a different kind of power; it came from his ability to bring joy, not pain. Wendy gasped suddenly, shuddered and sighed, and he kissed her again, grateful for this and all the gifts she'd given him. Proud that he could use them.

So back to school he went, and Wendy was right. It wasn't as bad as he thought it would be. The jocks, even Kyle, ignored him. He got some funny looks, a few sniggers, but Jase, Bill, and Pete seemed genuinely glad to see him.

"Hey buddy, over here." Jase flagged him down in the cafeteria. "How you feelin' man?"

Ray shrugged, sat down. "Still a little sore, I guess," he said.

"I'll bet," said Bill. "You go to the doctor?"

He sighed. "Yeah, my mom made me."

"So what's the verdict?" asked Pete. "You going to be able to have kids, or what?"

Ray laughed. "Yeah, I guess so. He said they were like, bruised? But there shouldn't be any, you know, permanent damage."

"Shit," said Jase. "That sucks man. That must have been like . . ." He waved a hand. "Ahh, I don't even want to think about it."

"I can't believe those guys just got a month suspension," said Pete.

"You just know, if they weren't on the football team, and if Elmdale wasn't winning in the district, they'd have been kicked out for the rest of the semester."

"Yeah," chorused Jase and Bill.

"Yeah, well, that's how it goes," said Ray.

"Listen to him!" said Jase. "Mr. Fucking Philosophical. They nailed you in the nads, man, and you don't even want revenge. Hey, wait a minute." He peered closely at Ray, then turned to the others. "The boy's got kinda a glow."

"Yeah, they're called bruises," said Ray.

"Naw, naw, you're right Jase, there's definitely a . . . a glow," said Pete.

Jase grinned. "That Wendy chick. You and her are doing it, aren't you?"

Not quite, not yet, thought Ray, though he had distinct hopes. But what was he going to say? All this newfound macho shit his friends were investing him with would wash away in an instant if he said no. "Hey, that stuff's between me and her, dude, and if you go spreading rumors around about her reputation, you're going to need stitches next."

Jase sat back. "Whoa, chill Lone Ranger, we'll be cool."

"Yeah, man, we won't say anything," said Pete. "I must say though, I never figured you to be so old school. Protecting your girl, defending her honor. I guess that shit really does work. You're an inspiration to us all, dude." He clapped Ray on the shoulder.

CHAPTER

15

"What would you do if you could start the whole world over again?" asked Wendy. It was high summer in Kennedy Park, the grass gold as a savanna, the sky above so clear and blue you could believe it was the first day of creation.

They sat back-to-back under their tree, Wendy writing in her journal, Ray drawing a picture of a lion in full chase, a herd of zebra scattering in the distance, their stripes shimmering like a heat mirage. The warm pressure of her back was a constant reminder of the unanticipated goodness of this world, just the way it was. After all, school was out, Ray was earning a steady paycheck at Glickman Hardware and all his free time he spent with Wendy, talking and drawing and fooling around. Pretty damn ideal. Still . . . He added some gold to the lion's mane, and looked up. "I'd give everybody something that they loved to do, and were great at, and then I'd give them the inalienable right to do it."

He felt her take a deep breath and wiggle a little. "Oh, that's good." He felt as well as heard her, her voice rumbling through their backs. "That's really good. It goes right along with the first laws. You know, life and love? I mean, all life has an instinct to fulfill its function. Birds fly, trees grow, cats contemplate eternity. Rays draw and Wendys write. And that's a kind of love, when you're doing something you love, don't you think? I mean, it feels that way to me."

"Me too," he said, marveling once more at how she could put words to such things. "What about you? What would you do?"

She sighed and tilted her head back to rest against his shoulder. "I'd make it so there was no such thing as being ugly. Everyone would be beautiful in their own way."

Ray almost said he'd make it so fuckwads like Kyle Denreddy would be born with their heads shoved up their asses, but he thought it would kind of kill the mood. "I'd make it so that when you hurt someone, it hurts you three times as much as it does them."

"Goddess! You are so good at this!" She scrambled around to face him and grabbed his hands. "What would you do about world hunger?"

Ray shook his head. "No, no, it's your turn. What would you do?"

She scrunched her face up in thought. "I don't know. Oh yes I do. I'd make it so there was no greed. The idea of wanting more than you need would just never occur to anyone. And if you did have more than you needed, you'd automatically, *instinctively,* give it away."

"That's good." He liked this game. "I'd make it so that if you drank too much, you'd just fall asleep, instead of acting like a jerk."

"I'd make it so that instead of going to school, we could just read books."

"I'd make it so there was no money, and no bill collectors!"

"I'd make it so there was no disease, and no one ever got old or died."

"I'd make it so everyone had a really cool computer."

"I'd make it so that Brussels sprouts tasted like cotton candy."

"I'd make it so that we had wings that could fold out from our backs, and we could fly."

"Cool. I'd make it so we grew fur in the winter, and didn't need coats!"

They both burst out laughing, and he grabbed her, wrapped his arms around her and they rolled together on the ground, giggling and wrestling and kissing, enfolded in the warmth and goodness of the summer and each other.

"I'd make it so we could be together forever," said Wendy, her head resting on the ground, her eyes burnished to gold by the sunlight.

"Me too," said Ray.

One Saturday afternoon, as he and Wendy wandered the Strip, the sign for the Clock caught his eye. "Hey," he said, jiggling her hand. "You hungry?"

She shrugged. "Yeah, kinda."

"There's this place you've got to see. It's like totally frozen in time, it's got this really mean waitress, and I think it's a front for some gangsters. Good hamburgers, though."

Wendy laughed and swung her hand in his. "Sounds great."

Inside they took a booth across the room from the one the gangsters had used. Flo looked really put out as she brought them menus. Ray had the distinct impression that she hadn't had a real customer since the last time he was in. She handed the plastic coated menus over with a sigh and stood there waiting for their order. "Cheeseburger, fries, and a Coke," Ray said promptly.

"Uh, same for me," said Wendy, panicking.

After Flo left, Wendy leaned over the table and whispered, "I think she hates us."

Ray nodded. "It's probably the first time she's had to come out from behind the counter in twenty years."

Wendy's giggle was cut short by the entrance of the curly-haired guy from the last time. He glanced at them, and took a seat in the corner booth. "That's him," whispered Ray.

"Him? Really?" Wendy seemed skeptical, but about halfway through their meal, the old guy showed up. "Now *he* looks like a gangster," she muttered through a full mouth.

Again Ray couldn't make out what the two men were saying, but just looking at them, he knew it was something clandestine.

"Maybe they're black market ferret dealers," said Wendy as they walked down the street afterward. "Or they could be smuggling toilets. You know how the ones they make nowadays are all low-flow, and nobody likes them? Oh no, I know. They're the remnants of the Purple Gang."

"The Purple Gang?" They passed the Salvation Army, and just as he said it, he caught sight of a purple ceramic pig in the window.

"Yeah," Wendy nodded. "Back in the twenties, during Prohibition, there was a gang that ran moonshine over from Canada. They were Jewish, and they called themselves the Purple Gang."

"Jewish mobsters? That's insane," said Ray.

When he got home, Ray's mom met him in the living room, her eyes bright, her cheeks glowing pink. She was wearing her new yellow-and-white striped blouse and had on perfume. Ray blinked. "Mom. What's up?"

She grabbed his hands and squeezed them, barely able to contain her excitement. "Oh Raybeam, I've got a surprise for you!" She glanced behind her toward the kitchen, and he heard something, the faint tinkling of ice cubes in a glass, and he knew. He just knew, even before his father came out into the living room to stand beside his mom, his hand on her shoulder. He looked older, his hair was starting to go gray, and the frown lines in his forehead were deeper, but the most striking thing was how much he, Ray, had grown to resemble him.

Ray freed his hands from his mother's and stood back, staring.

"Isn't it wonderful?" she beamed. "He's stationed in town again, and we bumped into each other at the grocery store. I didn't want to tell you, not until we were sure, but we've been talking a lot and . . ."

With a grin that turned Ray's insides to water, his father leaned forward and clamped his free hand onto his shoulder. "We're going to be a family again, son."

They had dinner together. Ray's mom made his dad's favorite, fried chicken. And his dad set the table. Ray stood in the doorway of the kitchen staring as the man set each knife, fork, and spoon down with care. He looked closely at his father's face. His brow was smooth. A light smile played across his lips and widened as Ray's mom handed him a bowl of salad. He set it down on the table and pulled her into his arms. Embarrassment swamped Ray as they kissed. Keeping his red face averted, he fetched the paper napkins from the cupboard by the sink.

Nobody said much of anything over dinner, but it was a pleasant silence, punctuated by murmurs of appreciation at the chicken and mashed potatoes and corn. Ray couldn't seem to stop staring at his dad, and each time he caught him at it, the man just smiled, chewing contentedly, his eyes clear and happy. This was a different person than the one he'd known before. His mother's joy at their reunion, at first alien and incomprehensible to Ray, began gradually to seep into him, and he found himself smiling back at his father, and asking him to pass the gravy.

After dinner his mom and dad settled on the couch together and turned on the TV. They sat close, hands touching, amiably discussing what was on that night. When his dad suggested *Law & Order,* and lifted a hand to pull a stray curl from his mother's face, Ray reddened. Shaking, he turned away and went to his room. He sat on his bed, his back against one wall, staring at the other. For the first time in four years, the things he liked about his dad came trickling back to him. The impish gleam in his eyes when he made a joke, the way he used to give Ray a sip of his beer, the time they were at the mall and his dad took him to the Swiss Army knife shop. He told Ray to pick out one of the thirty-dollar models and when he turned thirteen, he'd buy it for him. The way he'd looked at him then, with pride, it made Ray's heart stretch to think of it. And then his heart clenched like a fist, because his dad hadn't bought him the damn knife, had he?

No. On Ray's birthday he'd been out drinking. He got home late and got into an argument with Mom about some credit card bill that culminated with him smashing the remains of Ray's birthday cake into the wall beneath the kitchen clock. No pocketknife had ever materialized. Smart move, old man, thought Ray. That way I can't stick it in your back.

Ray took a deep breath and unclenched his fists. He didn't need this. He had Wendy, and he and Wendy had their own world. He didn't need his dad, for sure, and he didn't need his mom either, if she was so dead set on getting back with him. He'd move out. Yeah. He'd ask Mr. Glickman for more hours, he'd go full time, drop out of school if he had to, and he'd get his own place, and then he and Wendy could live together, and everything would be all right. He didn't have to do this.

He pulled his sketchbook out of his backpack and lost himself for a time drawing aimless doodles with black Magic Marker.

There was a knock on his door. Ray shoved his sketchbook under the bed. "Yeah?"

The door opened, and his dad popped his head in. "Ray, you got a minute?" The tentative look on his face was startling.

Ray blinked and eyed him cautiously. "Uh, sure."

His dad came in and sat down gingerly on the edge of the bed. He held his hands clasped between his knees. "I wanted to talk to you."

Ray shifted nervously. "Okay."

His dad nodded and chewed on his lower lip. "I just wanted to say, you know . . . I know I haven't always been a very good father to you. Or a very good husband to Jane, for that matter."

Ray held his breath. Was this . . . was he actually apologizing?

"I'm sorry for all the time I missed and all the time I was here but not . . ." He took a deep breath. "Not here for you." He stared at his son evenly. "I know I did wrong, and you deserved better. I know I don't have the right to ask this, but . . . I want to make up for it. And I need your help."

Ray swallowed hard. His heart was stretching again. He couldn't believe he was hearing this. "My help?"

His dad nodded. "I can't do anything if you hold me at a distance. I'm a better man now, Ray. And I can be a better father, if you'll let me."

Ray's heart thudded in his chest, clenching and opening, clenching and opening. He'd apologized. And now he was looking at his son with hope and remorse, with respect and pride. It was intoxicating, that look in his father's eyes. He knew he'd been wrong. And he'd come back for them. Ray was important enough for him to come back for him, important enough for him to apologize, and then ask, actually ask, for another chance. Mesmerized, Ray nodded his head, and heard himself mumble, "Okay."

His father wrapped his arms around him and held him in a crushing hug that mashed Ray's face up against his blue work shirt.

Are you sure about this, Ray?" Wendy hung back at the front door.

"Yeah, yeah." He tugged on her arm. "I know. I was skeptical at first, too, but he really has changed. He's really nice now, you'll see. He even asked me to draw him a picture of an F-4 Phantom jet. He wants to take it to the base and hang it over his workbench."

Wendy raised her eyebrows. "Wow."

"See? That's what I'm saying. Come on."

Reluctantly Wendy followed Ray into the den where his mom and dad sat watching TV. Upon seeing them, Ray's mom shot up off the couch, wringing her hands anxiously. Wendy always felt sorry for her. She reminded her of a frightened bird.

Ray's dad grinned and stood. Wendy took a deep breath. He really did look like an older version of Ray. Thick dark hair shot with gray, pale blue eyes. Wendy searched his face for some sign of the fury she knew he possessed, but all she could see was his charming grin, the rakish way his hair hung over his broad forehead. Almost involuntarily, she smiled.

"Wendy," he said, offering his hand. "I've heard a lot about you."

His hand engulfed hers, holding it briefly in a warm embrace, and then he released her. "It's nice to meet you," she said, embarrassed to find the words coming out in a meek whisper.

"Aw, isn't that sweet?" He looked at his wife. "She's shy."

In shock, Wendy took a step back. No one had ever said she was shy before. Beside her, Ray strangled a snort of laughter. "Dad," he groaned, and she didn't even have to look to know he was rolling his eyes.

As if a storm cloud passed over his face, Carl Mackie's expression darkened. His grin grew fixed and the look he shot Ray was piercing. "What?" There was an edge to his voice that he swiftly masked with laughter. "What?" He swept his hands out to his sides and his expression softened again. "I'm being nice here," he cried, all joking now, though as long as she lived she would never forget the look he'd shot Ray, like a hawk sighting on a rabbit.

Jane giggled. "Sit down everybody. I'll get you something to drink." She turned to the kitchen. "We're having smothered chicken," she called over her back. "I hope that's okay."

Wendy sat down beside Ray on the sofa. He looked at her and smiled, pretending not to have noticed anything, but if she had caught his father's look, she was sure he hadn't missed it. But still he smiled, and made small talk with his dad, working hard to keep everything on an even keel. She'd only been here a few minutes, and already it was exhausting, this constant maneuvering, this carefulness. How could they stand it, any of them? And yet Ray seemed to want this—what?—normal facade so badly. She found she wanted that for him, too. She wanted to help him prolong the illusion, and she squeezed his hand and grinned right along with him.

Ray stood at the picture window in the living room and watched Wendy drive off. That went well, he thought with satisfaction, and turned to go into the kitchen to help with the dishes.

His father stood in front of him, blocking his way. He held a drink in his hand. "Don't you ever do anything like that to me again!" he growled.

Ray jerked back as if burned. "What?"

His father's face twisted into a sneer. "Trot that stuck-up little bitch over here so the two of you can smirk and whisper about me!"

Ray felt the blood rising to his cheeks. "Wendy's not stuck-up, and she's not a bitch."

"Christ," said his father, throwing back the rest of his whiskey. "I shake her hand and she acts like she's gonna catch something from it."

Ray's guts knotted, but he fought to keep his tone light. "Oh that, well she was just surprised. I mean, if you really knew Wendy, you'd never say she was shy. She was just nervous about meeting you."

He narrowed his eyes. "What have you been telling her about me?"

"What? Nothing!" Inside, Ray's heart was clenching again. Idiot, he thought, how could you have fallen for it? How could you think he'd ever really change?

Ray's dad stepped closer, his voice rising to a roar. "What filthy lies have you been telling her?"

Ray tightened his jaw. "They're not lies, are they, Dad?"

He grimaced and threw his empty glass across the room. It hit the coffee table and shattered.

His mom came in from the kitchen. "Ray, why don't you go back to your room for a little while," she said, glancing between them nervously.

"Uh-uh. I don't think so," said Ray, his fists clenched at his sides.

His father shot him a dark look. "Do as your mother says, Ray."

"Or what?" Ray demanded, advancing on him. "Are you going to hit me?"

"Your father's just tired, Ray," said his mother. "He didn't mean anything."

"Bullshit!" shouted Ray, suddenly every bit as angry with her as with him. "You always do this. Make excuses for him, when he's really just a mean old drunk." He turned to stare at his father. "A total loser."

His mother bit her lips and shook her head, tears standing in her eyes.

His father clenched his jaw. "How dare you speak to me like that in my own house?"

"Your house?" Ray laughed. "Who's made the payments on this place the past four years? Not you. Her. Her and me. This isn't your house, it's ours. It's more mine than yours."

"Oh, so you think you're all grown up now do you? Well I'm here to tell you I'm still your father, and I'm gonna teach you a lesson you won't soon forget."

Ray's blood sang with rage. He knew he should back down, but he just didn't care. It was like that day in the park with Kyle, only more so. In a few brief moments his father had destroyed the dream Ray had worked so hard to believe in, the dream he'd finally allowed himself to admit he desperately wanted. Now Ray wanted to hurt *him*, to make him feel pain. He didn't care what else happened. "Then bring it on, old man. I'm not some little kid you can scare into silence anymore."

"Stop it! Both of you stop it!" screamed his mother.

"Shut up!" shouted his father, shoving her aside.

"Leave her alone!" yelled Ray, lunging at him. His fist connected with his father's midsection. It felt good. Even better was to hear his dad's gasp of shock as the breath went out of him. His mother was still screaming for him to stop, but he didn't care, didn't really care about her at all, or about anything except hurting his dad.

His father backhanded him across the face, and it snapped his head to the side, but the next second Ray launched himself at him, punching him in the face and again in the gut. His dad stumbled back, bumped into the coffee table and fell, splayed across it. Ray was about to throw himself on him again, lift him up and smash his stupid head through the table, but his mother grabbed him by the shoulder. "Honey, enough."

He whirled on her, his hand raised to slap her silly, and he just stopped himself in time. But he still saw the look of fear in her eyes, the same look he'd seen her give his dad so many times, and over her shoulder, in the mirror on the wall, he saw himself. There was blood trickling from the corner of his mouth, his eyes glowed blue and savage and he was breathing hard, red-faced, a vein standing out in his forehead. It was like seeing a younger version of his father. Which is exactly what he was. He stared back at the man picking himself up off the coffee table, and then at his mother, staring uncertainly between them. He grabbed his jacket from the rack by the door, and he got the hell out of there.

———

He just walked around for hours, down to the Strip, past the Clock, where the lights were still on despite the late hour, until at last his footsteps carried him to Kennedy Park. He sat under the elm tree. The night was chilly, the ground cold and hard. He shifted and pulled his jacket closer around him.

What on earth was he going to do? If he stayed in that house a day longer, he was going to become his father for sure. He'd lose everything; Wendy, himself, the world they'd created together. He had to do something to protect all that, to save it from his father . . . from himself? Christ, he almost hit his mom tonight. He'd rather chew his arm off than chance that happening.

So he had to get out, by any means necessary. He thought about going to Wendy's house and throwing himself on her parents' mercy. They were nice people. They'd probably try to help him. But Wendy had been so skeptical about his dad's new leaf, and she'd been so right, as it turned out. He was embarrassed, and besides, what would he say? Ray tried to imagine himself telling good, kind, decent Paul Chrenko that he had to leave home because he was afraid he was going to hit his mother. "Oh and by the way, Paul, I'm in love with your daughter," he muttered. No. He'd find a way to handle this himself.

He stayed out until very late, and then snuck back into the house while his mom and dad slept. The next day, at the hardware store, he approached his boss, Mr. Glickman.

"Uh," said Ray, tapping lightly at the open door of the back office. Mr. Glickman looked up from a stack of invoices. He was in his sixties, and had once been powerfully built. Now he had a soft, sort of deflated look, his slack muscles hanging from his large frame like sheets of damp laundry. He smiled. "Hey, Ray, what can I do for you?" He looked back down at the stack of invoices and marked something off against the spreadsheet on the computer screen.

"Well, uh, I was wondering if I could get more hours. Full-time, hopefully."

Mr. Glickman sat back and bit his upper lip, still staring at the screen. "You'll be going back to school soon."

"No, uh, probably not. Look, Mr. Glickman, I need—I need to find my own place, like, right away."

He sighed and turned to face Ray, a weary and disappointed expression in his eyes. "You get your girl in trouble?"

"No." Ray shook his head. "No, it's not that. It's—It's my dad, Mr. Glickman. He moved back this summer. He left us way back when, but now he's back and I can't stay there anymore. I just can't."

Mr. Glickman tilted his head and rubbed his jaw with one hand. He gazed at Ray, anger and regret mixed in his eyes. "My advice to you is suck it up and stay in school. There's no future for you here in any case. I'm sorry Ray. You're a good worker, and I'd like to help you out, but business isn't good. I'm barely staying afloat as it is, and now with Renovation Station coming to town, my days are numbered. I'm looking at closing this place pretty soon, retiring—"

"Renovation Station?"

"Yeah, they bought the Kennedy Park land from the city last week. They'll be putting up one of those big stores of theirs. With their distribution network and warehouse space, I just can't compete. They're going to drive me right out of business."

COMING SOON: RENOVATION STATION. TOOLS, HOME FIXTURES, HARDWARE AND MORE. EVERYTHING FOR THE HOUSE AND GARDEN, read the sign on the chain-link fence surrounding Kennedy Park. Beyond the fence lay the blasted remains of their private world. Ray and Wendy stood on the sidewalk, holding hands, watching as dump trucks and earth movers churned up the muddy field, their massive tires obliterating the grass far more thoroughly than Ray ever could with his nervous plucking.

The swings and the picnic table were gone, along with most of the trees. At the far end of the park stood their elm, or what was left of it. They had cut off all but its largest branches, and those stood out now, stark and obscene, like raw bones. Men in hard hats and climbing harnesses crawled about it like a fatal pestilence. The roar of chain saws filled the air, and as they watched, another limb was severed and lowered to the ground by a crane.

Ray squeezed Wendy's hand. "C'mon. Let's go. We don't have to watch this," he said.

She shook her head. Her face was red and puffy from crying. "No. You can go if you want to. I'm not."

So he stayed with her, watching them dismantle their tree. When they sawed through the trunk there was a cracking noise like the heart of the world breaking, and its fall made the ground beneath their feet tremble.

"It's like they're destroying our world," said Wendy. "The one we built together."

He held her tight. "No. That can only happen if we let it. As long as we're together, our world will exist."

After seeing Wendy home, Ray went over to the Clock. The two guys were there again, deep in conversation in their corner booth. "I'm telling you, Jacky," said the old one. "The drop box is full. We've got to get moving before it's too late."

Jacky, the guy in the overcoat, shook his head. "I can't go back to Pricemart, they know me there now."

"Then go someplace else!" the old man put his hands out in a pleading gesture. "Why not just hit the jewelers? I'm telling you, Jacky, that stuff never goes out of style. Diamonds are forever, boychickle."

Jacky shrugged. "Yeah, but I can't do 'em all. We've got, like, five to use, not counting the—"

They broke off as Ray walked up to the counter. He pretended not to have heard anything. Not that what he had heard really told him anything. He just knew. He'd thought it the last two times, but today, he knew. There was gangster shit going on in this place.

He ordered another cheeseburger and did his best to act really, really cool. When Flo came back with his Coke he amazed himself by saying, in a perfectly level voice, "You need any help around here? Busboy, cook?"

Flo gave him a jaded look and turned to refill a napkin holder, but Jacky cast him a speculative glance and there was a murmured conference between him and the old man. "Hey kid, come here."

Ray turned on the stool and stood. It was like he was in a movie. He could practically hear theme music as he walked down the aisle for his interview.

"Have a seat, kid," said Jacky. "What's your name?"

"Ray." He sat down, leaning forward with his elbows on the table.

"Ray. Nice to meet you, Ray. Hey Flo, bring Ray's food over here, will ya?" He stuck out a hand and shook Ray's with an encompassing grip. "I'm Jacky. This here's my uncle Sol."

The old man put down his paper and smiled, nodding.

"You been in here a few times before, haven't you, Ray?"

Ray nodded.

"Yeah, well you got good taste." He and Sol laughed, casting glances Flo's way. She glared at them.

"So, what kind of job are you looking for?" asked Jacky.

Ray shrugged. "Doesn't matter. I'm adaptable." He rested his chin on his hands and glanced between the two of them.

"Oh yeah?" Jacky raised one eyebrow and flicked a look at Uncle Sol. "You think you're pretty smart, don't you? How old are you kid?"

"Eighteen," Ray lied.

Jacky snickered. "Sixteen, more like."

"Seventeen," Ray asserted.

"I don't know, Solly," said Jacky, eyeing Ray speculatively. "You think he can be responsible? Can he use his head?"

"Well, try him out on something simple first, see how it goes."

Ray knitted his brows, wondering for the first time exactly what they wanted to hire him for. "Uh, I don't want to kill anyone," he said.

For a moment Sol and Jacky stared at him in silence, and then they both burst out laughing. "Okay, okay Solly. We'll hire him," said Jacky, wiping tears from his eyes. "Congratulations . . ." His voice dissolved in giggling.

While Ray finished his cheeseburger, Jacky left "to run a few errands." He came back with a stack of mail. He opened an envelope and took out a brand-spanking-new credit card. It had a picture of a tropical beach, with a palm tree and a big full moon. "Isn't it beautiful?" asked Jacky.

Ray nodded.

"Now Ray, this card has a five thousand dollar credit limit. Do you think you can spend that much, this afternoon, and bring all the stuff back here by nine P.M.?"

Ray's eyes widened, goggling at the card. The name on it was Steve Wagner. "But it's not my card."

Jacky handed Ray a pen and slid the card toward him. "Sign the back with the name on the front," he said.

Ray did it, scrawling the unfamiliar name on the little strip provided.

"Now it's your card," said Jacky. "Just be sure to sign the same name on the charge slip."

"So Raymond," said Sol. "What would you buy, if you had five thousand dollars to spend in one afternoon? Jewelry?"

"Electronics?" interjected Jacky.

Sol shot him a glance. "A nice ring or a heavy gold bracelet, maybe?"

"A cellular phone, or maybe a computer," said Jacky.

"A computer?" Ray brightened. "Man, I'd love a computer."

"Oh, so you like computers," said Jacky. "Tell me, what's the hottest selling model nowadays, do you know?"

"Well, my friend Jase has a Cybernautics TS5 with voice recognition, expandable RAM slot, and a flat-screen monitor. He's got a cable modem for it, too. It's really sweet, but the best-selling computer nowadays is probably still the Greatway 7800. It's got a huge processor, and it comes with a bunch of RAM, so you don't need so many extra cards. You get a lot of power for not so much money, you know?"

Jacky and Sol exchanged glances. "And a complete setup, with a monitor and a printer and all that, how much would that run?" asked Jacky, leaning across the table.

Ray scrunched up his face. "Probably about three grand, with everything."

"Then that's what I want you to buy, Ray."

Ray blinked.

"Not for you to keep of course," added Sol.

"No, of course not," said Jacky. "At least not right away. Today you'll get a commission, a percentage of the value of the goods you purchase. But if you do a good job, and bring it all back here, with the receipts, then it won't be long before you can afford that cherry system your friend has, or one even better. Now after the computer, I want you to concentrate on cell phones, but go to a few different stores, okay? Remember Ray, max out the card, and bring everything back here. Come in the back door, okay?"

———

Ray, what is going on?" demanded Wendy as they drove to Computer Empire in her mother's station wagon.

"I told you, we're going shopping."

"For a new computer? You can't afford that."

"Not now, but soon I will. I'm going to get my own place, too, real soon. Anyway, it's not for me, it's for someone else. It's this new job I got today."

"You got a job? What are you doing?"

"Well, just buying stuff, right now, but I'm thinking later, there'll be more."

She shook her head. "I don't get it, you're getting equipment for your new job?"

"Not exactly. Um. I'm working for those guys from the Clock."

"Those Purple Gang guys?"

"Yeah, them. They're running some kind of credit card scam, and from what I can tell, they've got all these phony cards, and they're shorthanded. I was asking Flo for a job at the time, and they heard me, so they asked me to take this card and spend it. Here, check it out." He dug the card out of his pocket and handed it to her.

"So you're Steve Wagner?" she asked.

"Just for tonight. I imagine I'll be somebody else next time."

She sighed. "Isn't this illegal?"

"Well, yeah," he said. "But don't worry, this Steve guy won't have to pay for the stuff. There's a law says you're not liable for more than fifty bucks on any unauthorized charges. The only one losing money is the bank."

"Oh." She seemed mollified by this, but still, her whole attitude during the shopping spree was pretty somber. It was bringing him down. Here he was, let loose with five thousand dollars to spend on computer stuff, and she was getting all *Judge Judy* on him about it. Okay, so he couldn't keep any of it, still, he'd get paid, and then some of what he bought today he could buy again, legitimately, for himself, once he had his own place.

When they were looking at cell phones, he asked her which color she liked.

"What difference does it make? It's not like I'm keeping it."

"But I bet I'll be able to buy you one after tonight. Or pretty soon anyway."

"Ray, I don't want a cell phone. I'm not sure you should get mixed up with these people. It could be dangerous."

His frustration got the better of him. "Goddammit, Wendy, I need the money! I need my own place. I've got to get out of that house like, now, before something really bad happens. What do you know? Your parents are all like, lovey-dovey and shit. You don't have to cope with someone like my dad. You have no idea."

She nodded silently, her eyes wide. She was quiet the rest of the time, and Ray did his best to enjoy the spending, but it wasn't the same anymore. Instead of playing the big spender, showing off for his girl, he felt somehow meager, like all of this was something less than stocking shelves in a hardware store.

He dropped Wendy off at home and drove over to the Clock with the stuff. He knocked on the backdoor and a guy he didn't know opened it. He was tall, broad-chested, in a blue serge suit, his black wavy hair gleaming blue in the fluorescent light from within. "So you're the new kid, huh?" He sniffed and wiped his nose with the side of his hand. "S'Bob."

Ray had a feeling Bob wasn't impressed with the new hire, but he let him in anyway. Ray followed him downstairs to a large room filled with desks, computers, telephones, Xerox machines, and laser printers of astounding variety, most of them top of the line. Pale blue indoor-outdoor carpeting covered the floor, buckling where cables ran underneath it, and fluorescent lights behind plastic panels in the dropped ceiling lent the place an unearthly hue.

Jacky lounged against a desk, browsing through a sheaf of papers. He spotted Ray and sauntered over. "So Ray, you got the stuff?"

Ray nodded. "It's in the car."

"Bob, help Ray unload, put it all in Sol's office," said Jacky.

They carried the boxes to a small room paneled in imitation wood-grain fiberboard. The walls were covered with old photographs of men smoking cigars and kids in knickers and caps. On the desk sat a baseball signed by Hank Greenberg. Jacky came in, still holding the papers, and set them down on the desk to inspect the merchandise.

He nodded judiciously. "You did good, Ray," he said, and pulled a cigar box out of the bottom drawer of the desk. He opened it and pulled out a wad of bills. He counted off five hundred dollars and handed it to Ray.

"Thanks," said Ray, the money lovely and thick in his hand. His eyes strayed to the sheaf of papers on the desk.

"Credit reports, Ray," said Jacky, following his gaze. He picked up a sheet and showed it to him. "See, it's got their names, birth dates, social security numbers, everything we need to establish accounts in their names."

"Like the card you gave me?"

Jacky nodded. "Yeah, we charge stuff and then sell it. Sometimes we take out loans; sometimes we buy gift certificates, use 'em for something just a little bit more than the amount of the certificate, so the receipt shows a cash sale, and then return the stuff. We file temporary change of address forms for people, funneling their mail to one of our drops, then we use preapproved credit card applications to establish more accounts. There's a million different ways to make money in the world, Ray." Jacky took him by the shoulders. "You want to make money, don't you?"

"Well, yeah."

"Of course you do!" Jacky gave him a friendly little shake. "You're a smart man. And being a smart man, Ray, would you rather work fifty hours or ten hours, for the same amount of money?"

"Uh, ten hours, I guess."

"Ten hours! Exactly! So what would you say if I told you you could make twenty-five grand in one week, instead of twelve months?"

Ray laughed. "You got to be kidding me."

"Not at all Ray, not at all," said Jacky.

"But-but it's illegal, isn't it?" he asked, though of course he'd known all along that it was.

Jacky tilted his head to one side. "Rules. You know what rules are, don't you, Ray?"

He shook his head.

"Rules are how the banks, the big corporations and the government make sure that people like you and me never win. Rules are for losers, Ray."

CHAPTER

16

Wendy was never sure exactly what had made her first notice Lorca. On the very first day of women's studies class her freshman year in college, a tall, gangly blond woman, her arms laden with books, slipped through the door and scurried to a seat in the back. Perhaps it was some subliminal clue, some flicker in her eyes as she glanced at Wendy and then away, something in the hunch of her shoulders or the stiff, self-conscious expression on her face. Something told Wendy, right away, that here was a sister, a fellow survivor of the same childhood gulag.

That's why she decided to go up to her when she saw her in the student union a few weeks later. Lorca sat with her head bent over her books, her squiggly hair hanging down over her face. The union was crowded, and that was the only excuse Wendy needed. "Excuse me," she said, laying a hand on the empty chair across from Lorca. "Do you mind if I sit here?"

Lorca glanced up from her reading, a glimmer of recognition in her eyes. "Sure," and for a moment Wendy thought she might say something else, but instead her gaze retreated to the safety of her open book.

Feeling awkward, Wendy stirred sugar into her coffee. She took a deep breath and plunged in. "How do you like the class?"

Lorca looked up, apparently shocked at being spoken to. She shrugged. "It's hard, but really interesting. Um, Dr. Prinh does a good job describing the more complex data configurations."

Wendy drew her brows together in puzzlement, then spotted the title of the book she was reading, *Advanced Data Structures*.

"Oh sorry, no. I meant the women's studies class. We're in it together."

Lorca sat back, looking at her warily. Wendy was certain that this obviously dedicated student was hoping she would leave her alone so she could get back to her work. But then Lorca smiled. "Oh yeah. Well, it should be an easy 'A,' and God knows I need one this term."

Wendy nodded, at a loss. She sipped her coffee. Lorca went back to reading her book and something about that just pissed Wendy off. "But what about what the teacher said, about women doing two-thirds of the world's work and only owning one-third of the property. Doesn't that bother you?"

Lorca's eyes went wide, and she stared at Wendy as if perhaps she had a dangerous lunatic on her hands. "Well sure, I guess. I mean I feel sorry for those women, but it doesn't really have anything to do with me. I'm in a technical field."

"And you think that's going to protect you? That survey she quoted was for all professions. What will you do, when you find out you're not making as much as your male colleagues?"

Lorca shrugged. "Ask for a raise, I guess. Look, I'm just taking the course because I needed another humanities class and it was either that or art appreciation. I really haven't experienced any sexism, so I just don't know that much about it."

Wendy shook her head. "Haven't experienced any sexism? But you're a woman."

"Well, yeah, but . . . I've just been lucky I guess."

Wendy nodded blankly.

Lorca bit her lip. "Sorry, is that your major?"

"No. You can only minor in it. I'm not sure what my major's gonna be yet. Sociology or history maybe. I don't know."

Lorca's lips quirked.

"What?"

"Have fun getting a job when you graduate."

Wendy shrugged. She was hoping that if she played her cards right, she could go to school indefinitely. "So what's your major?"

"Computer engineering."

"Wow. I bet you'll get a good job."

Lorca shrugged. "Yeah, probably. This school has a good program. The big corps send recruiters around all the time."

"Are there a lot of women in your program?"

"No." Lorca shook her head, then caught Wendy's look. "But that could just be because not as many women are interested in computers."

Wendy grinned and leaned forward, resting her elbows on the table. "And why is that?" Lorca looked panicky now. But the class had filled Wendy with righteous outrage and she just couldn't contain herself. "I'll tell you why," she continued. "Because boys hog the computers in the elementary school classrooms, and all the games are made for them."

Lorca gave her a long, thoughtful look. "Um. I've got to go." Frantically she gathered up her books and fled, nearly overturning her chair in her haste.

However, the next day in class Lorca took the seat beside Wendy and offered her a tentative smile. After class she leaned across the aisle, proffering a disk. "Um, this is a game I wrote a long time ago, back in high school. See, uh, I was thinking about what you said yesterday. I used to play a lot of computer games, and the truth is, it always bugged me, too, how they're all made for boys—all the violence, not to mention the bimbos with enormous breasts. So I wrote my own. I don't know if you're into that, but I thought . . . I just thought you might like to see it." She dropped the disk on Wendy's desk, and turned to gather her books.

"Wow!" said Wendy, picking up the disk. "You wrote a computer game? In high school? That's really cool. Thanks."

"Oh"—Lorca turned—"it doesn't have any graphics or anything. I didn't know how to do graphics then. It's just a text game."

"Still. Thanks. I can't wait to try it out."

"Oh." In her surprise Lorca gave a broad, brilliant smile. "Okay."

"Hey, do you have another class right now?" asked Wendy.

Lorca shook her head.

"Want to go get a coffee?"

Lorca smiled again, that broad, brilliant unguarded smile. "Sure."

———

They went to the student union, where they sat at one of the numerous round little tables scattered about the food court, sipping coffee from Styrofoam cups.

"Yeah," said Lorca, "even though I was thin as a rail, they called me Orca the Killer Whale all through junior high and high school. It was so stupid. I wasn't even fat. Those kids were awful. Not that the teachers were much better."

"Oh, I know!" said Wendy. "Sometimes, I swear, they were on the side of the bullies, don't you think?"

Lorca laughed. "Could be. We had this sadistic English teacher in seventh grade. She made us read writing assignments out loud in front of the class, can you imagine?"

Wendy nodded and sipped her coffee. "Did the kids write stories about you?"

Lorca stared at her dumbfounded. "How did you know?"

"It happened to me, too."

"Oh my God. Wasn't that like the worst thing? These two boys, Frank Wickam and Terry Benetti, they hated me. I swear, they lived to make my life miserable. Anyway, they wrote a two-part story about Orca the Killer Whale, and it was full of all these inside jokes about me. Everybody in class knew it was about me, they were laughing so hard they practically peed their pants, but the teacher pretended that she didn't know what was going on. She knew. She only heard them call me that about a million times."

Wendy nodded. "See, now how can you say you've never experienced sexism, with what you went through in junior high?"

Lorca sat back. "But that wasn't because I was a girl, it was—"

"Because you didn't act like a girl." Wendy held her gaze steadily, brooking no argument. "Think about it. You looked different, you weren't into the same things the other girls were into. You didn't play the game. You refused your role in a sexist society that wanted you to pin everything on your looks and your ability to please men."

Lorca frowned. "I didn't have any looks to pin anything on, and I didn't like boys. I didn't have much of a choice."

"You had a choice. You know you did."

Wendy was shocked at her own harsh, almost accusatory tone, but Lorca nodded softly. "I guess you're right." She laughed. "I remember how it all started, how I wound up an outcast. It was my former best friend. I was at her house one afternoon, and her brother had DeathGlut 2000. He'd always say, 'You can play after I lose,' but he never lost. And I'd just hang around for hours, waiting, you know? Anyway, he'd just gotten up, and I was just starting to play when my friend Cici comes in and says, 'Amanda and I are watching *Full House*.' And she stands there staring at me like I'm supposed to just drop everything and go with her. And I didn't. I kept playing. Anyway, she got really mad at me, said I was weird and stuff. After that she started making trouble for me."

"So you see my point."

"Which was?"

"That you have experienced sexism."

Lorca stared at her for a long time, then she glanced around her, as if seeing the university student union, as if seeing the world, for the first time. "Well, I never thought about it like that before, but . . . yeah. It would explain a lot of stuff that I never understood at the time. Yeah, I guess you're right. I have."

Lorca Polly Danes. How Ray rued the day he first heard that name. He was at home, sitting at his hot new Cybernautics TS7 computer, scanning credit reports for Jacky and Sol. He had his own place now, a loft space in a converted factory downtown. He'd furnished it lavishly with all the latest stuff: brushed stainless steel table in the kitchen, state-of-the-art home entertainment system, leather chairs and couches, and an antique crystal chandelier that had prompted Wendy to dub his home Stately Ray Manor.

He had a sweet red Lexus convertible, too. And he'd bought Wendy a car over her protestations. She'd moved in, finally, after graduating from high school. Now she was enrolled at Holbrook University. She worked really hard. He didn't get it. He could afford to support both of them in style, but she said school was important to her. She'd never liked it before, but now, she was all about school. He tried to be supportive.

The door of the freight elevator opened and Wendy came breezing in, looking for all the world like Mary Tyler Moore. He swore, if she had a beret, she'd flip it. He smiled to see her, stood up, hugged and kissed her.

"Guess what?" she said, pulling back, her eyes shining.

"What?" he asked, glancing back at the screen. The first report was for Yves Urich, who had excellent credit, but far too distinctive a name.

"I met this cool woman today," Wendy continued, throwing her coat over the back of the couch and sitting down. "She sits across from me in women's studies. Her name's Lorca. Lorca Polly Danes. Isn't that a cool name?"

Again, too distinctive, plus it reminded him of a bad movie. He laughed. "I guess," he said, sitting back down at the computer and scrolling to the next credit report. Michael Robert. Perfect.

"What do you mean?" There was an edge to her voice, a warning, if he'd bothered to listen.

Ray looked up from the computer screen. "Well, it sounds kind of goofy to me. Like orca, the killer whale."

She gave him a beady-eyed stare, like she was getting him in her sights. "Do you want to hear about my day at all?" she complained. "Do you even give a shit?"

"Yes! I'm sorry. You met this girl."

"Woman. Goddess, Ray, I can't believe you."

Sudden frustration made his jaw clench. "Well, I can't believe you. Christ, you're not in the door five seconds, I say like two things, and you're jumping down my throat already! What is the right thing to say? Why don't you just tell me, 'cause if I knew I'd say it!" He slammed his fist down on the table, making the keyboard and his coffee jump. He stared at his fist and slowly unclenched it. No. No, he wasn't going to do this.

Wendy sighed, sounding quite put upon. "I just wanted to tell you about this cool woman. Her name—Her name is Lorca." She shot him a defiant glare.

Relieved that she still wanted to talk, that he hadn't destroyed everything, Ray got up and sat beside her. "Okay. Tell me. Tell me what happened."

"Well . . . you sure you want to hear about it?" Wendy gazed at him from beneath her eyebrows.

"Yes, yes I'm sure. Tell me."

Her expression brightened. "Well, she's in my women's studies class, but she's just taking it to fill a requirement. Anyway, it turns out she had the same kind of junior high experience I did. I'm just excited because I think we can be friends. It's been a long time since I've had a real girl-friend, you know?" She gave him a challenging look.

Ray nodded. "That's great. I'm happy for you." He smiled, but what he really felt was relief that their argument hadn't gotten worse, that he'd been able to avert disaster. Not sure what else to say, he retreated to his computer once more.

Wendy sighed and stood up. "Oh yeah, Ray? Did you remember to pick up condoms?"

Dammit. "Oh, uh, no, I forgot, sorry."

"Shit, Ray!"

"I'm sorry," he said defensively. "I got busy. I'll get them later, I prom-ise." He looked at her, but she was already turning away, picking up her books and taking them into the bedroom to study.

A week or so later Wendy brought Lorca home with her. Ray was in the kitchen, chopping up tomatoes for red sauce. Since he'd become a gangster, he felt somehow obligated to learn to make real red sauce. Never mind the guys he was working for were Jewish—General Tso's chicken probably would have ingratiated him more. He heard the freight elevator open and Wendy stepped out followed by a tall, gangly girl with squiggly blond hair and a broad, almost froglike face.

"Ray? This is Lorca," said Wendy with a gleam in her eye. The girl hung back, smiling shyly.

"Oh hi," Ray waved a red-smeared hand. "Want a beer?"

Lorca shook her head and glanced down. "No thanks." Her eyes trav-eled along the floor and then up, taking in the rugs, the entertainment center, the pictures, coming at last to rest upon the crystal chandelier above. Pride warmed him, and Ray braced himself for her reaction.

"Wow, cool place," she said to Wendy.

"Oh thanks, most of the stuff is Ray's."

"Oh." She glanced at him, gave him a nervous little smile, then turned back to Wendy. "So, what did you think of yesterday's assigned reading?"

"*The Apartheid of Sex*? I loved it. It's so true, at birth we're channeled into one of two classes depending on an accident of birth."

" 'Accident'?" asked Ray.

Wendy glanced at him. "What type of genitals we have." She turned back to Lorca. "And one by one she answered every objection to the obliteration of those classes, of male and female."

"Yeah. It made me see things in a whole new light. I—"

"Wait a minute," said Ray. "You can't just get rid of male and female. I mean, you can pretend there's no difference, I guess, but the fact remains that women get pregnant and men don't."

They both stared at him, and then glanced at each other and laughed. "Ray, I believe Lorca was saying something," said Wendy. "Kindly abandon the male prerogative of interrupting a woman any time she's speaking, and let her finish."

She might as well have slapped him. He blushed and returned to his red sauce.

"Well," said Lorca, shooting him a snotty look, "I was saying I love how she answered all the objections to a genderless world one by one. It was very convincing. Segregated public rest rooms, sports, all of it. Once you start acknowledging male and female as two points along a broad spectrum of possible genders, it changes everything."

"Yeah, I loved her bit about the 'bathroom bugaboo.' You know, there is no reason 'persons with penises,' as she puts it, can't sit down to pee like the rest of us, and then I'm sure there'd be adequate facilities for all, 'cause you know men won't put up with waiting in line."

Ray looked up. The two had moved over to the couch and were sitting together, their heads bent close. Jealousy flared inside him, and he remembered how Wendy and he used to talk about creating their own world, only neither of them had ever said there wouldn't be such a thing as men or women in it. He felt edged out, obsolete, like a tyrannosaur at a mammal convention.

The rest of the evening, Ray might as well not have been there. Lorca and Wendy talked the entire time about their women's studies class.

"Have you ever played Titania?" Ray tried at one point when the conversation had finally veered off from the evil male patriarchy to

Lorca's plans to write computer games. "You play the Queen of Faerie, and you have to defeat the Dark Lord Hern."

"Oh yeah, I know that one," Lorca said, barely glancing at him. "But it's really a misrepresentation of ancient European goddess religions," she said to Wendy, smiling. "Hern is really the god of the hunt, the goddess's consort."

"He was demonized by the Christian missionaries," agreed Wendy. "They turned him into the devil, and obviously the makers of the game bought into the lie." They both sat there staring at him like he was some sort of backward child.

The beep of his cell phone saved him from further embarrassment. Ray went to where his coat hung by the freight elevator and fished the phone out of the pocket. "Hello?"

"Ray, Jacky. Baby, that info you got us was solid gold. We've got an overflow situation here now. Can you come down and collect some cards, take 'em out for a spin tonight before they get stale?"

What a relief, thought Ray. "Sure, be happy to."

He hung up and took his jacket from the hook on the wall. "That was work," he called over his shoulder as he opened the door. "I've got to go in."

Okay, today we're discussing the ancient Sumerian Inanna myth cycle. Everyone open their books to page ninety-seven, please. We're starting with 'The Huluppu Tree' story," said the ancient lit professor, Dr. Duane. She was in her sixties and somehow formidable and kindly all at once. She wore her hair in a long silver braid down her back and her eyes crinkled when she smiled.

Wendy opened her book and followed along as Dr. Duane read aloud, "In the early days, the very earliest days, in the early nights, the very earliest nights . . ." The language was beautiful. It had such a soothing, stately cadence to it. Wendy had been up all night studying for her geology exam, and she was starting to nod off when Dr. Duane read, "Then the Serpent That Knows No Charm wound itself about the base of the huluppu tree. The Anzu bird nested among the leaves of the tree. And Belili, the laughing maid, came to live in the trunk of the tree."

Startled, Wendy turned the page to catch up and there beside the text was a photograph of a carving depicting a woman with large wings, a snake coiled at her feet.

The sight of it combined with those words just about lifted Wendy out of her chair. She gasped aloud, and Dr. Duane fell silent. The whole class was staring at her. "Sorry," she mumbled.

Dr. Duane peered at her with bemused concern. "Are you okay?"

Wendy nodded. A funny tingling spread from her scalp to the tips of her fingers and toes. She felt as if her face were vibrating, her whole body filling with an energy she could barely contain; a flame that seemed to consume her from within. Lili, her Lili was real. Sometime back in the childhood of human civilization she had existed, and ever afterward people had written about her. She had never been forgotten, not even by those who thought they were inventing her. She looked at Dr. Duane, her mouth working, but no words came out.

"Are you sure?"

Wendy shook herself and made an effort to focus. "Yes. I'm fine. Really. I just . . ." she faltered, the tale of Lili eager on her tongue, but everyone would think she was a loon, and more than anything, she just wanted to hear the rest of the story. "I really like this class."

She heard snickers around her, but Dr. Duane smiled at her indulgently. "Well, there'll be time for discussion afterwards."

When she finished reading, Wendy was the first person with her hand up. "Who are Belili and the Serpent That Knows No Charm?"

"Ah yes, Belili and the snake. They're interesting, aren't they?" The fire inside Wendy was answered by the flickering embers in Dr. Duane's gaze. "Belili is Sumerian for Lilith. Or rather Lilith is Hebrew for Belili, since this story predates her appearance as the first woman, prior to Eve, in Hebrew legend surrounding the Fall. In fact, some scholars, and I happen to be one of them, think that the story of the Garden of Eden in the Bible is based on 'The Huluppu Tree.' "

"There was a woman before Eve?"

"That's right, not in the written text, but according to Hebrew legend she was created from the same material God made Adam from, and therefore considered herself equal to him. When she refused to do his bidding, Adam complained to God, who banished her."

"Wow. The first feminist."

Dr. Duane grinned at her. "You could say that."

Wendy licked her lips. "So are Belili and the snake in any of the other Sumerian stories?"

Dr. Duane shook her head. "Only marginally. The snake, not specifically the Serpent That Knows No Charm, but basically the same time-honored figure of mankind's downfall, reappears in *Gilgamesh*. It steals the elixir of life Gilgamesh worked so hard to acquire. As for Belili, there is mention of an Old Belili in 'The Descent of Inanna.' She helps Dumuzi when he is fleeing from the demons Inanna has set on him to drag him back to the underworld. It's difficult to discern the underlying sociopolitical meaning of her appearance in this context, but it is my belief that she and the snake and bird who are her companions are the deities of a rival cult to the worship of Inanna. That is the real reason Inanna cuts down the huluppu tree and drives Belili and her companions away, and it is the reason Old Belili thwarts Inanna's design in 'The Descent.' "

Wendy looked at the picture in her textbook. Belili's eyes were dark and mesmerizing. As if she was looking back at her across centuries, daring her to believe that she was real, now as then. When Wendy looked up again, all the other students were leaving. Class was over. She fumbled her books into her backpack and managed to walk out without dropping anything or bursting into flames.

Surprise! Happy birthday!" called Ray as he struggled in the front door of his folks' house with the big, brightly wrapped box. From the living room he heard the TV playing. His mom liked to watch the afternoon talk shows. He'd carefully planned this visit for a time when she'd be home, but his dad wouldn't.

The TV went silent, and he heard his mother's footsteps. "Ray?" She beamed when she saw him. "Oh my God, Ray! You remembered!" She rushed over to hug him, and he just had time to deposit the box on the couch before she wrapped her thin arms around him. "Oh honey, I've missed you so much!" She kissed him on the cheek and stood back to look at him. "You look good!" she said, almost sounding surprised. "Sit down, sit down. Tell me how your job is going."

Ray sat on the couch in front of the picture window. In the living room. Like company. "Fine, Mom. Just fine." He'd told her he was in sales for a credit card company. "Uh. How are you?"

"Oh, I'm fine," she said, in a dismissive tone that did little to comfort him. As she sat down in the green velour armchair across from him, Ray studied her closely. There was a shadow on her left cheek. His heart sank, but he decided not to mention it for now. "Here," he said, proffering the box. "This is for you."

She gasped in delight, her eyes wide. "Oh Raybeam, you didn't need to get me anything."

He shrugged. "Yeah, well, I couldn't afford anything nice last year, so this makes up for it."

She held the box in her lap and leaned around it. "Oh, but I loved the hand-painted note cards you made me."

"Ah," he waved off her compliment but couldn't prevent a little spark of pride from igniting within him. It had been a while since he'd drawn anything. He'd been too busy. "Go on, open it."

She carefully peeled back the tape from the package, neatly removing the wrapping paper in one piece. "An espresso machine!" she cried. "Oh but Raybeam, this must have been expensive!"

"Hey, I can afford it, and I know you like your coffee, so . . ."

She set the box on the floor and hugged him again. "So how's Wendy?"

"She's fine. Busy with school, you know."

"And your job is okay."

"Oh it's great. It's fun and the commission's really high."

"Well I guess it must be, if you can afford your own place"—she craned her neck to peer out the picture window behind him—"and a new car *and* an espresso machine."

"I can afford a lot more than that now, Mom. That's the other reason I came here today. I wanted to talk to you."

She still smiled, but a little worry line creased her forehead. "Hmm?"

Ray leaned forward. "I want to get you your own place, so you can get out of here, so you can get away from him. I mean it, Mom."

Her smile grew wary, and she gave a little shake of her head. "Honey—"

"I'll buy you a new place. I can afford it, honest."

She sighed. "You don't understand. Even if you could afford it, it wouldn't be right. You have your own life to live. And even if it weren't for that, honey, I can't leave him."

"Why?" blurted Ray, his voice sounding harsher than he'd meant it to. "And I *can* afford it, by the way."

She raised her hands. "All right, all right, you can afford it, and you're a dear, sweet boy to ask. But no. I won't leave him, Ray, no way."

He shook his head in bewilderment.

She leaned forward, her hands on her knees. "Honey, I love your father. I always have."

"But he yells at you and hits you. He's done it again, I can see." He pointed at the fading bruise on her cheek. "He's mean and you deserve better."

She laughed as if she knew some secret he could never comprehend. "If we're lucky, we don't get what we really deserve in life." Her tone became light, even cheerful. "And your father's much better lately, really, he is. He's trying very hard."

"But he still hits you."

She blushed and looked down at the floor, as if she had something to be ashamed of.

"Is he still drinking?"

She tilted her head to one side. "Sometimes, not as much as he used to."

Ray stared at her. "I don't get it."

"He needs me, Ray."

"Yeah, but what about you?"

She shrugged. "Maybe I need him to need me."

Outside he heard a car come down the street, and her eyes darted over his shoulder, her face suddenly a mask of tension. Ray turned around, but it wasn't his dad's car. It was a blue Suburban and it continued on down the street. They both relaxed, and she made some chitchat about her office, but pretty soon he got up and made his excuses to leave.

"Remember what I said, Mom," he told her, hugging her good-bye. "The offer is open, any time you change your mind."

"Okay, honey." She kissed him, and stood at the door waving as he drove away.

Wendy flung open the door of the freight elevator and ran over to the computer alcove where Ray was playing a game. "Ray! Ray! Check this out, I can't believe it."

Ray paused mid-slaughter and gave her a quizzical look. "What? What's wrong?"

"Nothing! Nothing's wrong, but check this out!" She showed him the picture of Belili and read the text aloud.

"Oh," he said, still looking puzzled, distracted, but trying to humor her. "That's nice."

"Nice? Nice? Don't you remember? From my journal? I wrote about them. They're Hister and Lili, remember? The creation story about the girl and the snake, writing the rules? Remember?"

He smiled at her. "Of course I remember. That's cool." He glanced at the screen, wondering, no doubt, if it was safe for him to go back to his game.

She shook her head, staring at the book again. "But what does it mean? I created Lili out of my imagination, but she already existed. Five thousand years ago, someone else wrote her story. I—Maybe I was in touch with something really primeval that day when I quote-unquote invented her. Maybe I was guided by her, because she's always been there." She looked at Ray again, searching his face for some confirmation of this unshakable conviction that had seized her the moment she heard those words and saw that picture.

"Well," said Ray, "it's probably just a coincidence, you know? Lili and Belili, they're not that close, and snakes and trees are common elements of creation stories. You yourself modeled yours after the Garden of Eden, the author of this story probably did the same."

"No! No, this story is from ancient Sumeria. It's older than the Garden of Eden."

"Really?"

"Yeah." She stared at Ray, suddenly furious with him for not seeing what she saw, for not understanding the power of this discovery. "But then I guess this isn't interesting to you, is it? Just because I've found out something profound about my beliefs, my personal mythology. You don't really care. You're just waiting for me to go away so you can get back to your game."

He sighed, a certain here-we-go-again look on his face. "That's not true. I'm happy for you."

She put her hands on her hips. "Happy for me? But it has nothing to do with you, does it?"

He shook his head, bewildered. She could see him trying to figure out the right thing to say. "I don't understand."

"Well . . ." And suddenly she was at a loss for words, her elation turned to despair in the face of Ray's incomprehension.

Maybe she was wrong, maybe this wasn't the cosmic revelation she'd thought it was. Maybe he was right, maybe it was just a coincidence, and the world had no soul after all. Rage shook her. If that were true, then that time she had long dreamed of, before evil entered the world, when human beings were innocent and joy was the law of the land had never existed. Lili was not its envoy. Tears blinded her. She ran back into the bedroom and flung herself down on the bed, feeling desolate, like she had back in junior high when her mother, uncomprehending, had called her by that hated nickname Kyle Denreddy had made up for her.

Wendy found Lorca at their usual table in the student union. She dumped her books dramatically on the table and sat down, grabbing Lorca's hands and pulling her away from the printout she was reading. "You are not going to believe this."

Lorca shook her head, eyes already alighting with anticipation. "What?"

Wendy took a deep breath. "Okay. You remember me telling you about how I got through junior high? Lili and Hister?"

She looked puzzled. "Yeah."

"Okay, read this." Wendy grabbed her Sumerian text and fumbled through the pages. She thrust the book at Lorca. "The eighth stanza."

Lorca read it. She was silent awhile, and Wendy started to get nervous. Maybe Ray was right. Maybe she was just a freak. But when Lorca lifted her head, her eyes were wide. "Oh my God, it's them."

Wendy nodded vigorously. The tingling feeling started up in her scalp and her fingers again, like it had in class.

"So what do you think this means?" asked Lorca in a hushed tone.

Wendy shook her head. "I don't know. But I'm going to find out." As she spoke her determination grew in her, like a tree carefully planted. "I'm going to major in ancient lit, and I'm going to study these texts, and go to graduate school. I'm going to uncover Lili's story. I'm going to prove that there once was a time when human beings lived in harmony with each other and the world."

CHAPTER

17

"Hey, I can't have coffee today," said Lorca one day on their way out of class. "I'm going to a guest lecture."

"What kind of lecture?" asked Wendy, shouldering her backpack.

Lorca handed her a flyer.

The University of Holbrook Computer and Information Science Department, in conjunction with the Department of Biology and Life Sciences present "Neural Profiling: The Ultimate Human–Computer Interface," a lecture by Zazula Von Sach, Ph.D., professor of biocomputing at Cornell University.

"Wow, this looks pretty whacked out."

Lorca grinned. "Yeah, I've heard of this Dr. Von Sach. She's supposed to be great. Hey, you wanna come?"

Wendy shrugged. "Why not? Lit's not until three."

The lecture was held in the Chelsea Auditorium, on the other side of campus. By the time they got there the lights were already dimming. They grabbed seats near the back just as a woman in a tailored linen pantsuit stepped up and arranged her notes. Her pale silver-gold hair was bobbed at chin length and a fine gold chain winked from between the folds of her ivory blouse.

"Good afternoon and thank you all for attending," she said in a faint Eastern European accent. "Today I'm going to talk about the interface between human beings and computers. The most powerful computer in the world is useless without a means of communicating its calculations to human beings. For years we've had a visual interface with computers through video display monitors, and now a verbal interface has become, if not common, at least widespread. Also the crude beginnings of a virtual reality interface using visors and gloves have been developed.

"But what if we could communicate directly with computers? Organic brain to silicon brain, so to speak. Such an interface would allow for a sophistication and nuance in computer–human communications previously unheralded and would open up the possibility of a seamless, richly detailed virtual reality almost indistinguishable to the user from actual sense perception. The key to achieving this technology lies not with the silicon brain, the computer, but with the organic one.

"Currently Dr. M.A.L. Nicolelis has developed high density electrode ensembles that can be implanted in the brain for extended periods of time and used to record neural activity at a level of detail previously unknown. Further advancement of this technology may allow computers to actually send signals directly to the centers of the brain corresponding to various sense and cognitive activity, such as the calcarine sulcus for vision, the superior temporal gyrus for hearing, the primary somatosensory cortex for touch, and the pyriform lobe for smell.

"By first recording the user's neural activity in these centers, a computer could develop a library of profiles for the neural activity patterns for each sensation. Such a library could then be used to produce the same patterns produced by the real stimuli and the user would receive the same sensation.

"Of course currently such an approach faces several major obstacles including the requirement of extensive brain surgery for implantation of the electrode arrays. However, advancements in electrode technology and some promising research on the effect of powerful electromagnetic fields on brain activity may point the way for a viable interface technology that in essence eradicates the computer–human divide. The consequences of such technology promise to challenge our very notions of what is real."

"That was absolutely amazing!" said Lorca on their way out of the auditorium. Her eyes were wide and bright, her hands gesturing animatedly. "Just think, you could create your own virtual world. Make it anything you wanted it to be. Goddess!"

Wendy grimaced. "Yeah, but you'd have to let a computer into your brain to do it. I mean, who in their right mind would do that?"

Goddess Lili, bless this circle of women. Join us now and every day. Let us know your strength, that is our strength, your wisdom, that is our wisdom, your love, that is our love," Wendy intoned.

Five women sat cross-legged in a circle in the middle of Ray and Wendy's loft: in addition to Wendy and Lorca there were Veronica, a wiccan nursing student they'd met at the campus women's center and Dev and Irene, two friends of Veronica's from her goddess study group. The women's faces were lit by the amber glow of candles set around the red and black batik altar cloth in the center of their circle. The air was thick with the smell of the patchouli incense they'd lit to welcome the element of air to their ritual. Also on the cloth sat a stone from the lake where Lorca's parents had a cottage. It was there to represent earth. A plastic goldfish provided by Veronica represented water and of course, the candles were for fire.

A brass statue of the goddess Kali stood in the center of the cloth, bedecked with beads, ribbons, and flowers. Wendy had tried to find a statue of Lilith for the occasion, but her search of secondhand shops, occult bookstores, and online merchants had come up empty, so they used this figure of Veronica's instead. "It doesn't matter," Veronica had assured her. "All goddesses are one goddess."

Wendy's breathing was deep and even, lulled by the peaceful faces of her coven sisters and the repetitive cadence of her chant. When she finished her invocation, they all clasped hands and spoke in unison, "The circle is cast, we are between the worlds, in all the worlds."

One by one they went around the circle, each woman making a declaration of intention, stating something she planned to do, committing herself to that goal.

Veronica's brown, shoulder-length hair gleamed in the candlelight as she lifted her smiling face, and closed her eyes. "I will love myself, today and always, even if I fail organic chemistry again," she said.

Dev, a skinny black woman with gray starting at her temples, scrunched up her face with determination and said, "I will make time, *make* time, to volunteer at the AIDS Outreach Project. Once a week, goddess, once a week."

"I will write something every day," said Irene, and then nodded, her dark curls bobbing over her pale round face.

Lorca gripped Wendy's hand tightly, swallowed and said in a soft, hesitant voice, "I will honor the goddess in myself and all women."

It was Wendy's turn. "I will make it my life's work to study the goddess and uncover her secret past. I will find proof of a woman-loving culture before the advent of the patriarchy, and through that knowledge, what once was may yet be again."

With that they all stood, and moving slowly in a clockwise circle they began to chant, "Like a seed, let it be planted, like a dream, let it fly free, like a star, let it shine brightly, what I say, so mote it be."

As the chant picked up in tempo, so did their movements. They released each other's hands and began to clap in time to the chant. Irene had a beautiful bass voice and Dev's was high and sweet. Together they turned the chant into a song. Veronica's skirt whirled about her legs as she spun and danced; a flashing purple whirlwind.

Wendy felt herself swept along by the rhythm, intoxicated with the smell of patchouli and candle wax, joyous at the beauty of her sisters. She twirled in her progression about the altar, raised her arms over her head and let out a series of high-pitched yips that would have humiliated her at any other time, but that now proved to be the very thing to build the energy they were raising higher. Lorca, who'd been chanting softly under the other voices, suddenly burst out with a full-throated "Like a dream, let it fly free!" Her voice reverberated with raw, jagged emotion and then steadied, deepened, and lifted them higher.

It was close now. Wendy felt it. They all had their arms above their heads, their bodies twirling and swaying. She felt the energy flowing up through her feet. She felt it tingling up her arms to her fingers, seeking release. With a great mutual shout they all leapt into the air, sending the energy up and out, to weave their will into the fabric of the world.

Ray pulled open the door of the freight elevator and threw his keys on the dining table. Blown out candles stood about the living room area, and the air was thick with patchouli incense. "Wendy?" he called, but there was no answer. He heard voices from the bedroom.

"So of course he draws you naked, how typical," Lorca was saying. She and Wendy and Veronica and a couple of other women he didn't know were all in there, standing around with glasses of wine in their hands, looking at his pictures on the walls. Wendy had insisted that they hang up his artwork in the loft. He'd talked her into putting it in the bedroom, but obviously it didn't matter. His jaw clenched.

"And what about this one?" Lorca pointed to the picture of the first day of the world. "Is that like a huge vagina, about to swallow those two guys? I mean, how Freudian can you get?"

Wendy was opening her mouth to say something when she glanced over and saw him standing there. "Oh Ray," she said, in a guilty, surprised kind of way. "We were just . . ."

He nodded, feeling cold inside. "Don't let me stop you," he said, and turned on his heel. He scooped his keys up from the dining table and left.

Raymond, how are you?" said Sol the next morning as Ray eased himself into the corner booth at the Clock. "Jacky should be along soon. Are you hungry? Order something to eat."

"No thanks, I'm not hungry." His head was still throbbing from the Jägermeister he'd had the night before.

"What's the matter? Don't you feel well?"

Ray shrugged. "Just a little hungover, that's all."

"So how's Wendy?" Sol clasped his hands and grinned. He'd only met her once, but Sol had taken an instant and indelible shine to her.

"She's fine, I guess."

Sol frowned. "What's the matter?"

"Huh? Nothing. We had a fight, sort of, that's all."

He shook his head. "Make up with her, Ray. You'll feel better. And ask her to marry you already."

Ray barked harsh laughter. "Oh yeah, that's a good idea."

Sol shook his head in consternation. "Look, don't be a fool. A girl like that you don't just shack up with until something better comes along. She is the something better, Raychickle. Don't let her get away. Marry the girl, for crying out loud! Do her parents know she's living with you?"

"Yeah, they know."

"They don't mind?"

Ray shrugged. "What difference does it make if they do?"

Sol was shocked. "What difference? They're her family!" he said, as if this should be self-explanatory.

Jacky came in, interrupting Sol's lecture. "Hey, Solly, Ray," he said, sitting down next to Ray. He looked at Sol. "You tell him yet?"

"No, I didn't tell him. I was waiting for you!"

"Tell me what?" asked Ray.

"We've been really pleased with the information you've been gathering online for us," said Jacky. "Anybody can front us buying merchandise. It's a waste having you do it. From now on we want you in charge of data collection, full time. And we're upping your percentage."

Ray decided to take Sol's advice. At least the making up part. Really, Wendy should apologize to him, but his promotion had put him in a good mood, and he didn't want to ruin it by thinking too much about what had happened the night before. On the way home he stopped at the grocery store and picked up a bottle of wine to celebrate his new position.

When he got home Wendy was standing at the brushed stainless steel table, furiously chopping onions. At first he thought it was the onions making her nose red and her eyes water, but then she sobbed and he knew it was real crying.

"What's the matter?" He walked across the kitchen to her, the wine bottle dangling from his hand like a damp, dead goose. He set it on the counter, took the knife from her hands, and held her close. "What is it?"

She twisted and thrashed in his arms, abandoned herself to sobbing once more, and finally managed to babble, "I'm p-p-pregnant!"

The words turned him to stone; cold all over, his body immobile as his mind launched into an argument with reality. The kind of argument he always lost.

No, this is not happening.

Yes, it is.

I'm not standing here in the kitchen holding Wendy in my arms.

Yes, you are.

She's not pregnant.

"How do you know?" he said out loud.

"It's been two months!" She'd stopped crying. She went and sat on the couch, looking forlorn. "With exams and everything, I lost track. So I went to the clinic today, and got tested . . ." Her face crumpled in on itself, a terrible thing to see, and she hid it in her hands. "It was positive."

Oh yes she is.

He was speechless, remembering when they had run out of condoms, and he'd forgotten to buy more. His words came back to damn him. "I'm sure we can get away without it, one time."

God, how could he have been so stupid? He looked at her. She didn't say anything, but he knew she was thinking of the same night. To hide his shame he turned and busied himself with opening the wine bottle. He took a long drink from it and carried it with him to the couch, where he sat beside her. Now what? On to the next question, he supposed. "What do you want to do about it?"

"I don't know." She broke down crying again.

He held her for a long time, humming softly to soothe her. Unbidden, the tune grew words, became a song his mother had sung to quiet him after his father's rages. "Daisy, Daisy, give me your answer true. I'm half crazy, all o'er the love of you. It won't be a stylish marriage, I can't afford a carriage, but you'll look sweet, upon the seat of a bicycle built for two." He sang it over and over until she fell asleep, and still he held her, and drank the rest of the wine.

I t was about a week later that the bottom really dropped out of his world. Ray was playing HornQuest when the phone rang.

"Ray? It's Jacky. The jig is up. Sol's been arrested."

Ray's heart shuddered and his throat tightened. "Arrested? How?" he croaked.

"Crappy luck. He got pulled over for a burnt-out headlight and the cop saw some credit cards on the dashboard. He noticed the names weren't the same as Solly's."

"Shit. What are we going to do?"

"I'll tell you what we're going to do. Destroy all the evidence and get out of town. Luckily Bob just bought a bunch of paper shredders. I was going to sell 'em, but now . . . Listen, can you get over here? We need to make this whole operation disappear, tonight."

"Yeah, sure, okay. I'll be right over."

It took them until two o'clock in the morning to shred all the paperwork and load what they could of the equipment into Jacky's SUV.

"So, uh, where are you going?" asked Ray as he hauled the last garbage bag of shredded paper out and threw it on top of the mountain beside the Dumpster.

"I'm not telling you." Jacky slammed the rear gate of his truck shut. "And you're not telling me where you're going either. We don't know each other anymore after today."

Ray shook his head. "What do you mean, where I'm going? I'm not moving."

Jacky laughed. "Then you're going to jail, kid. Take your pick. I mean they got Sol, and Sol knows everything. Besides, he's old. He doesn't want to do time. He's going to try to bargain himself out of a stint in the joint. Mark my words, he'll finger us."

Ray staggered. Jacky was right. His loft, his wonderful loft with all his stuff . . . his home. He had to leave it.

He felt bereft. This was worse than all the moves they'd made with his father. He thought of his crystal chandelier, hanging in his loft like an inverted tree of light. When he'd hoisted it up there he'd paused at the top of the ladder, surveying the wide-open factory floor, thinking, This is my kingdom.

But, no more. He took a deep breath. The apartment, his stuff, those were just things. Wendy was his real home. As long as she was with him, he'd be fine.

When he got in around two-thirty, she was still sitting up, reading. Stalling, Ray went into the kitchen and got himself a beer.

"Where were you, Ray?" she asked without looking up from her book. By her tone he could tell this was more than just a I-didn't-know-where-you-were mad. This was a you-fucker-how-could-you mad. All of a sudden it came back to him. She'd had that appointment with the counselor this afternoon, about whether or not to get an abortion, and he was supposed to go with her. Crap. Well, at least he had the mother of all excuses.

"I'm sorry honey, you won't believe what happened today." He came over and sat next to her on the couch. "I just got back from the Clock right now. I've got bad news. Sol got arrested. We have to move." His eyes strayed around the place, calculating how much of the stuff they could take with them. "We can go anywhere you want."

"What?" Wendy stared at him, wide-eyed. "Are you kidding? I can't move, it's the middle of the term! And now I have to take a makeup for the test I missed in women's studies, because of that appointment we had today with the counselor at the student health clinic. Remember that, Ray? You were supposed to go with me, but you were nowhere to be found. Where the fuck were you?"

"I know, I'm sorry. Jacky called and I forgot all about it. We've got to get out of town, I'm telling you. They're cracking down on identity crime these days. I could be looking at five years. I'm sorry about the thing with the counselor, but what do we need counseling for anyway? We both know what you're going to do." He knew it was the wrong thing to say as soon as it was out of his mouth.

Her eyes took on a hard, closed look. "Oh we do, do we? You just assume I'm going to have an abortion. What if I don't? What if I keep it?"

Ray lifted his eyebrows. "Is that what you want?"

"No. Maybe. I don't know. That's why I made the appointment. Goddammit Ray, why, today of all days, did you have to skip out on me?"

Anger stabbed at his heart. "I didn't skip out on you! I told you, Sol got arrested. I had to help Jacky and Bob clear out the office. I'm sorry I didn't call you, but I forgot about the thing today. Christ, why are you being such a bitch about this?"

She bared her teeth at him. "Because I knew. I knew this would happen some day. Fuck, Ray, what did you expect? Now you're talking about skipping town! What about me? What am I supposed to do?"

"Come with me! I mean get real. I'm sorry you'll miss school, but would you rather have me in jail? Come with me and as soon as we get where we're going, we'll take care of this pregnancy thing, however you want to take care of it. I've got plenty of cash. We'll be all right."

She laughed bitterly. "You just assume I'm going to drop everything and go with you. What about my life, Ray? What about my career?"

"You're a student."

"So? That means nothing to you, doesn't it? You can't see the value in anything besides turning a fast buck. Goddess, Ray. I don't even know you anymore. Who are you?"

He glowered. "I'm still me."

"No, you're not." She looked sad now. "You've changed. This credit scam stuff has changed you. You used to like to talk about stuff; politics, religion, changing the world. Now all you care about is money."

"Yeah, well what about you?" His voice shook. "You've changed, too. You changed the rules on me, you and your feminist friends. I can't do anything right anymore. And stuff that was supposed to be private, just between us, you show them so they can ridicule it!"

Wendy shook her head. "Ray that was—"

But self-righteousness filled him and he couldn't stop. "My own home feels like some kind of battlefield, where I'm always the target. Lorca's taught you to hate men."

She rolled her eyes in annoyance. "Oh come off it Ray. You know I don't hate men. Not that I'm so crazy about *your* friends. Jacky, Bob. They treat women like socks. No wonder none of them are married. Aw, Ray, why'd you have to get mixed up with them? Why'd you have to quit school?"

Ray clenched his teeth. "Oh, don't start on that again! Not everyone has to go to school to be successful, you know."

Wendy folded her arms. "Oh yeah, and this whole crime thing has worked out great for you, hasn't it?"

Ray sprang from the couch and paced. "Goddammit, would you get off my back? If I don't get out of here I'm looking at some serious jail time."

Wendy's face was set, her eyes hard. "Well, don't let me stop you, Ray."

He spun to face her. "What?"

"You heard me. You have to go, go. Don't let me hold you back."

His heart twisted. "You mean you—"

"That's right Ray. That's what I've been saying. I'm not going with you."

He came back to the couch and sat down again. "I don't know how long I'll be gone."

"Don't bother coming back. It's over. I can't live like this anymore. Never knowing when the cops might be at our door, not being able to tell my friends what you actually do for a living—"

"Oh, so you're ashamed of me, is that it?"

"Well, frankly, yes."

Her remark cut him to the bone. He stood up. "Well fuck you, then! I guess this apartment, the TV, the DVD, the car I bought you, none of that means anything to you then."

She just sat there on the couch, looking up at him. "Not really, no. It was always you I loved, but you're not you anymore. I don't know where the Ray I loved went, but he's gone now. I guess I just didn't want to admit it. Besides, all we seem to do anymore is fight." She started to cry, her tears a more bitter accusation than any of her words.

Ray felt cold inside, and oddly disconnected, as if this were happening to somebody else. "So that's it, then. You're really breaking up with me?"

Wendy took a deep breath, and looked at him. "Yes."

Inside, his heart screamed "No!" but anger and pride silenced the word. "Fine then! You're always talking about being independent, a free woman. Guess you'll get to find out what it's like, being a student, without the financial backing of your hood boyfriend." He went to the computer nook and grabbed an empty paper carton and started throwing things into it, not paying much attention to what he took. "Keep the rest of this stuff if you want it," he said when the box was full. "I don't." Maybe she could pawn the TV and the DVD, if she had to.

Driving to the airport, he remembered his dad that last day before he left, when he picked Ray up from school. He remembered how he'd stared out through the windshield, past the street and the suburb, like he was staring down their common destiny. And he had been. Just like he was right about what he said out at the airfield. "Love doesn't last. You go with love, you'll wind up with nothing."

CHAPTER

18

They pulled up to the clinic in Lorca's blue Toyota. A group of protesters circled the parking lot, waving hand-lettered signs and posters of fetuses. As they negotiated the driveway, the protestors clustered around them, shouting and crying. A woman plastered herself against the passenger-side window, screaming, "Don't kill your baby!" On the other side, an elderly man held up a picture of a late-term fetus, cute and gooey and pink. "Your child deserves life!" he cried, his voice muffled by the window.

"Oh my goddess," said Lorca as she eased the car through the mob and into a parking space. "Can you believe this?"

Fear and desperation clawed at Wendy's stomach. "How are we going to get in? How are we even going to get out of the car? They're blocking the doors."

"Stay put," said Lorca, her face set. "I'll get you out."

Lorca wedged open the car door and slid out, pushing through the protesters to get to Wendy's side of the car. She got it open, and Wendy crawled out, wishing she still had her junior high knack of being invisible. But no dice. A woman with blond braids crammed herself between Wendy and Lorca, a baby in her arms. "All life is precious!" she blurted, spraying Wendy with spittle. "Look at this beautiful baby, this could be yours!"

Her face was desperate, sincere. Wendy wanted to hate her but she couldn't, instead she shook her head, trying to get around her. "I can't. You don't understand."

The man with the fetus poster threw himself to his knees before her.

"The Lord is my shepherd, I shall not want . . ." As she sidestepped around him he grabbed her sleeve.

"Hey, leave her alone!" yelled Lorca. "What's the matter with you people?"

The blond woman's baby started to cry. "Here," she said, thrusting the squalling infant in Wendy's face. "Hold her, you'll see. You'll never forgive yourself if you do this!"

Wendy twisted away, tried to pry the man's hands off her sleeve. She lost sight of Lorca, and panic bubbled in her stomach. Out of the corner of her eye she caught sight of a burly figure in an orange vest moving toward her through the crowd. She flashed on an image of a thirteen-year-old girl in pigtails body slamming Kyle Denreddy in the schoolyard of West Junior High. "Get back, get back," came the throaty alto as she cut through the mob to Wendy's side. Instead of pigtails, a bandanna held back her abundant dark hair. She was taller, and time had mellowed her scowl. "Don't look at them, don't talk to them," she told Wendy, taking her elbow and steering her through the throng, warding off protestors with a firm but gentle arm. Lorca reappeared on Wendy's other side, and together the two of them got her through the doors.

"I'm so sorry," Robin said once they were all safely inside the clinic foyer. "We didn't expect you for another fifteen minutes."

Wendy turned to her. "Robin? Don't you know me? It's Wendy."

For the first time, she focused on Wendy's face, her own face lighting up with amazement. "Oh my god. Wendy Chrenko!" She swept Wendy up in a bear hug; a brief moment of delirious safety, wrapped in those strong arms, pillowed against that broad bosom. Robin set her down again, staring at her. "So how are you, anyway? Oh, I'm sorry, that's really stupid."

"It's okay." Suddenly at a loss for words, Wendy glanced about the foyer; a table piled with pamphlets, a chair, an ashtray, and a plastic plant. Lorca stood by the door to the reception area, looking kind of wild-eyed. "Oh Lorca, this is Robin, my friend from junior high."

"Actually, it's Raven now. Nice to meet you, Lorca."

"Same here. You really saved our butts out there. I thought they were going to tie us to a couple of stakes or something."

"Yeah. It's sick, isn't it? They talk about compassion all the time, but those people wouldn't know compassion if it hit them over the head with a two-by-four. I've been volunteering as a patient escort here for about three months now, and believe it or not, what you saw out there today is mild."

"Wow, I can't get over running into you like this," said Wendy. "So your name is Raven now, that's cool."

"Yeah. After I left home, I wanted to start a new life, and I did. New life, new name."

"I heard you ran away. What happened?"

"My stepfather was hitting on me," she said lightly, but the dark look in her eyes betrayed her offhand manner. Then a wry, self-satisfied grin spread across her lips. "So I stole my brother's motorcycle and went to California. I was out there for a couple of years. I came out, had a torrid affair with a married woman, met another woman and moved to Indiana with her." She sighed. "That broke up about a year ago and I decided to come back here. I'm a bouncer now at Club Indigo, a dyke bar over on Georgia Avenue." She glanced between them, checking for their reaction.

Lorca looked surprised, but she didn't say anything. Wendy smiled. "I can't tell you how good it is to see you again. As usual, you're protecting me from bullies."

Raven grinned. "Yeah, I guess it's my calling." She glanced at the door. "Well, I guess you better sign in. Here"—she picked up a pamphlet on vasectomies and scrawled her name and number on it—"call me later. I mean it."

Wendy took the pamphlet from her. "Okay, I will."

The doctor gave Wendy a pill and explained that within two days her uterus would expel the nascent zygote. "Stay at home, and be prepared for a lot of bleeding," she said. "And schedule a follow-up appointment on your way out today. We'll want to check that everything went okay."

Raven helped them back to their car. As Lorca pulled out of the parking lot she paused to watch Wendy's old friend walking back to the clinic. "So Raven's a lesbian, then," she said, a speculative note in her voice.

"Evidently," said Wendy, wondering if she'd feel any less numb when the pill took effect and blood was pouring out of her body.

"Huh," said Lorca.

———

The tiny bathroom in Raven's apartment was filled with candles; on the back of the toilet, on the edge of the sink, on the windowsill. Their flames were reflected in the mirror and in the warm water in the tub where Wendy crouched. She was naked but for an old nightgown she wore to keep her upper body warm. The thin, sodden flannel floated about her calves and thighs, like pale pink seaweed. Lorca sat on the toilet next to the tub, holding her hand. Raven sat on the floor at Lorca's feet, and Veronica stood at the foot of the tub.

The ritual had been Veronica's idea. Wendy had just wanted to hole up in the loft until the pill did its job, but then Veronica had explained to her how in Japan there were special sections of the Shinto shrines dedicated to "water babies" where women who had abortions could grieve their loss in a publicly sanctioned way that did not call into question the validity of their decision to terminate a pregnancy. Hearing this, and reflecting upon what she'd gone through at the clinic, Wendy decided to take her friend up on her offer.

Now Veronica placed her brass statue of Kali upon the edge of the sink and said, "The goddess is threefold: maiden, mother and crone. The maiden watches over all our new endeavors. She is the ungerminated seed, the beginning of all life. The mother gives life, and nurtures us as she nurtures our projects, our dreams, our goals. The crone brings death, it is she who teaches us the painful lesson of parting, it is she who demands that we relinquish the past to make room for the future. The dark of the moon is her time, a time of farewell, a time of reflection before the quickening of the new moon.

"We are here together on this night, in the dark of the moon, to support our sister Wendy in her decision to terminate her pregnancy. In doing so she closes one door, one possibility for her future. But because the goddess is threefold, because nature always seeks balance, in closing this door she opens another. The wise crone understands this, and tonight we invoke her wisdom.

"Great goddess Kali, mother of life, bringer of death, let your truth be a comfort to Wendy as she steps through that door and into the future she has chosen. Welcome with loving arms the potential life that returns to you this night, harbor it safely until the proper time for it to manifest in this world has come."

Wendy closed her eyes and pressed her palms to her already spasming belly. In a voice at first soft and tentative, she chanted, "You might have been strong, you might have been smart, you might have been kind, you might have been wise . . ." As she went on, naming all the potentialities of the zygote her aching uterus labored to expel, a vision pierced her heart—Ray smiling at a baby cradled in his arms—dispelling the numbness that had enveloped her since the clinic. Her voice became a ragged sob, "You might have been mine, you might have been ours . . ." and then dissolved completely and all she could do was wail out her grief and loss.

Lorca, Raven, and Veronica surrounded her, holding her in their arms and rocking her, smoothing her hair, and chanting, "You are strong, you are smart, you are kind, you are wise . . ." Pain tore through her abdomen, worse than the worst menstrual cramps she'd ever had, and the water around her trembling thighs bloomed red. "You are ours, we are yours, you are home, you are home."

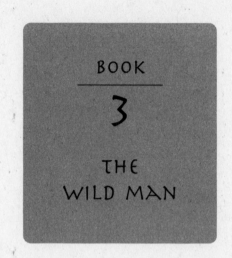

BOOK

3

THE
WILD MAN

CHAPTER
19

Wendy hunched over her desk in her bedroom in the apartment she shared with Lorca and Raven, working on the outline for her Ph.D. dissertation, *Remnants of Matriarchy in the Ancient Sumerian Inanna Cycle.* She rubbed at her sore eyes. Her hand trembled. She was shaky with exhaustion and hunger, but still she kept working.

Tonight she was reading Samuel Noah Kramer's translation of a text concerning social reforms instituted in the Sumerian city of Lagash during the reign of King Urukagina around 2350 B.C. Tantalizingly, these reforms were referred to as "Return to the Mother."

The official who kept the reserve food stores dared not trespass into the widow's garden, dared not cut down her trees or take away the fruit. If a poor man constructed a fishery, the rich man dared not take the fish for himself.

In previous times, women took more than one husband, but now, if a woman tries to marry two men, she is stoned with rocks upon which her crime is written. A woman who says to a man . . . [Unfortunately this portion of the text is indecipherable.] will have her teeth crushed with bricks upon which her crime is engraved, the bricks will be displayed at the city gate so all will know of her crime.

Wendy sighed and sat back, swiveling her chair to face the wall across the room from where she had her desk and her bed. When she first moved in she had covered it with pictures; images of goddesses, drawings, photographs of herself and her friends. She let her eyes stray across the multitude of faces as she struggled against despair.

It was always like this; for every tidbit she found that seemed to point to a matriarchal, or at least egalitarian prehistory, she encountered two or more irrefutable earmarks of patriarchy. It was maddening. The Sumerians had a bicameral congress made up of citizens that reached decisions concerning the fate of their city through consensus, and they had kings. Goddesses were prevalent, and so was polygamy and arranged marriage. Property was inherited through the male line, but temple harlots preserved matrilineal inheritance by obscuring the paternity of their children. Slavery was widespread, a woman found to be a witch had her nose cut off, and in the city of Kish a woman who owned a tavern became king and founded a dynasty that ruled for five hundred years.

The door to the room opened. "Knock, knock," said Lorca, leaning there, dressed in jeans and a short-waisted velvet jacket: going out clothes. She had a worried look on her face. Wendy had been getting that look from Lorca a lot lately, and a couple of times Lorca had let her know that she thought Wendy was working too hard. Coming from Lorca, that was worth paying attention to, but what could she do? The deadline for her dissertation outline was just weeks away, and she still wasn't ready. She had too much to do. She couldn't stop.

"Hey, Raven and I are going out," said Lorca. "Bitch and Animal are playing at the Lavender Rose Café tonight. Why don't you take a break and come with us?"

Wendy shook her head sadly. "Wish I could, but I've got too much work to do."

"Still working on the outline?"

"Yeah."

"How come you have to write a paper describing what you're going to do and what arguments you're going to use for your dissertation? Why can't you just do the dissertation?"

"Well, they want to know ahead of time. That's just how it is."

Lorca sighed and Raven appeared behind her, the chains on her leather jacket jingling softly as she wrapped her arms around Lorca and hugged her. Wendy tried to ignore the jealous clutch in her guts as Lorca smiled blissfully and leaned her head back onto her lover's ample bosom.

"Maybe between the two of us we can haul her out of here bodily," said Lorca.

"Can't pry the hermit crab out of her shell, eh?" rumbled Raven. She looked at Wendy, eyes narrowed and mouth pursed in a mockery of her trademark scowl. "It'll still be here when you get back, you know."

"I want to go with you, honest, but I can't." Wendy waved her hands at the stacks of books, journals, and papers heaped on and around her desk. At the same time that she desperately wanted her friends to talk her into going out with them, she just as desperately wanted them to take their seven-years-of-romantic-bliss-and-counting selves out of her sight.

It wasn't that she wanted to take Raven's place with Lorca, or Lorca's place with Raven, for that matter. They were her best friends, she loved them with all her heart, but she wasn't *in* love with either of them. She was just jealous of what they had together. Blindly jealous with a growing resentment that both shamed and alarmed her. It was too much to deal with. It was easier to stay in and search ancient Sumeria for signs of a matriarchal past.

"Damn, woman," said Raven, releasing Lorca and stepping through the doorway to take a seat on the bed. "You've barely left this room for the past three months."

"I go to classes," said Wendy defensively. "And there's my job."

"Ah yes, waiting tables at the Nugget Diner. What a fulfilling experience. Pouring coffee and smiling for the sake of the tip through every stupid joke, every rude comment and clumsy come-on," said Lorca, joining Raven on the bed.

Crap, obviously neither of them were going anywhere any time soon. Why did they have to choose this moment to lecture her on the dreariness of her life? "Oh, it's not so bad," she muttered, glancing wistfully at her papers and books. Even the paradoxes and frustrations of ancient Sumerian society were better than this.

"Yeah, but where's the fun, Wendy?" said Raven. "I mean, don't you ever want to cut loose? Don't you ever just want to—I don't know—bring somebody home and fuck the daylights out of 'em?" Raven bounced on the bed, wiggling her eyebrows suggestively.

Wendy grimaced. Why did Raven always have to be so damned blunt? "The last thing I need right now is a relationship," she asserted.

Raven furrowed her brow. "Who's talking about a relationship? I'm talking about meaningless, hot, mind-blowing sex. Come with us to the concert tonight. Afterwards we'll take you to a bar—a *straight* bar—and find someone for you."

Lorca shook her head. "Wendy doesn't have that kind of sex, Raven."

Wendy stood up and folded her arms across her chest. "I beg your pardon?"

Lorca shrugged. "Well, you don't. I mean look at that one guy, Scott, Steve . . ."

"Seth?"

"Yeah, him. You said yourself he was good in bed, but you took that to mean all kinds of other things."

Wendy tossed her head. "Oh, like that he was a whole human being that I could have a meaningful exchange of thoughts and feelings with?"

Lorca pointed her finger at her. "Exactly. You couldn't value the sex just for its own sake."

"Yeah," Raven added thoughtfully. "He was an idiot, but even I have to admit he was fine. You should have just used him."

Wendy threw her hands up. "Okay, that's enough. I can't believe I'm hearing this from you two, the official poster kids for committed lesbian monogamy. Tell you what." As she spoke she advanced on them. "Let me finish my goddamn prospectus so all the work I've done for the past seven years isn't completely wasted, and then we can have a big what's-wrong-with-Wendy party and you can give me the benefit of your keen insights into the mysteries of heterosexual relationships, okay?"

Eyes wide, Raven and Lorca stood up and retreated to the hallway.

"Now, if you'll excuse me, I have work to do," said Wendy, shutting the door on them.

The Ziploc baggie that held Wendy's makeup rattled as she tossed it into the worn porcelain sink of the Nugget Diner's ladies' room. She stared at her bleak reflection in the mirror. Goddess, she looked like crap; dark smudges under her eyes, her mouth a colorless slash, all life bled from her sallow skin by too many late nights studying, too many long days waiting tables. Better paint on a big ol' smile if she wanted any tips today, she thought ruefully as she opened the powder-smudged baggie and fished out her lipstick.

She didn't get it. Last night she'd finally found the documentation she needed to support the hypothesis of her dissertation: that the figure of Belili in the Inanna myth cycle is a prior goddess who was supplanted by Inanna. Now she could finish her prospectus, hand it in to her review committee and with any luck, she'd get their approval and start work on her dissertation by next semester. So why wasn't she happy? Why, instead, did she feel mostly relieved, and a bit weary at the thought of the nights of work yet to come?

She rubbed her now red lips together, blotted them on a paper towel and went to work on her eyes. The makeup was a pain in the ass, but she'd learned very quickly that it paid for her to adhere as closely as possible to the prevailing beauty standard, and to smile, and to pretend to like the people she was serving.

Wendy gathered her makeup back into the baggie, shoved it in her purse and went out into the din and clatter of the lunch rush.

This isn't what I ordered," said the woman at table nine. There was something familiar about her, but Wendy couldn't place it. She had a faint European accent. She was in her early sixties maybe, and was way too elegantly dressed for this place. Her silver-blond hair was swept up in a French twist and small gold knots adorned her earlobes. She was reading a professional journal of some kind, barely glancing up as she spoke.

It made Wendy feel even more invisible than she usually did at this job. That was what she hated most about waitressing; more than the long hours on her feet, more than the irate customers looking for an easy target to take out their frustrations on. She hated the anonymity that washed over her every day when she put on that apron.

It didn't have to be that way. Some waitresses made good tips by charming their patrons with their outgoing personalities, but it never really worked for her, and she'd found it was easier to blend into the background. She wondered what Ray would think, if he knew how far she had fallen from her high school ideals, if he knew she had become every bit the faceless drudge she had exhorted him not to be. She pushed the thought from her mind and fumbled for her pad. "You ordered the club sandwich?" she said to her customer, flipping to the order in question.

"Yes, but I said no mayo, and I wanted wheat bread, not white." She turned a page of her journal and read on.

Wendy whisked the offending sandwich away. "I'm sorry, I'll get you a new one."

"And hurry will you?" she said without looking up. "I have work to get back to."

"Of course." Wendy headed for the kitchen, but before she could get there, the guys at table twelve stopped her.

"More coffee here Wen-dala," said George, one of the regulars. He'd been calling her that ever since he found out she was studying ancient goddesses. He thought "Wen-dala" was funny because it rhymed with "mandala"—to him all religions besides Christianity were the same. Wendy wished she'd never told him, but he'd asked her about her school-work and she'd been flattered that he wanted to know more about her.

"And we need more ketchup," said his buddy Jeff, pointing to his plate of fries already drowning in the stuff.

"Sure," she said, reaching for the empty bottle he held outstretched. Just before her fingers closed around the neck he jerked it away from her. "Ah! Gotcha!" He laughed.

Grimacing inside, she put one fist to her hip and shot him a stern-yet-amused look she'd designed for such occasions.

"Just keeping you on your toes," he said leaning forward, his eyes level with her chest as he made a big show of proffering the ketchup bottle in an open hand.

Enduring his smirk, she took the bottle from him and managed not to roll her eyes until her back was turned to them.

She took the sandwich back, put a rush on a new one, grabbed a coffeepot and a fresh bottle of ketchup, took care of the guys at table twelve and gave them their check. A couple of college students sat down at table ten, and she brought them their menus and their waters. By then table eight—a couple of young mothers with five boisterous kids between them—was ready to order.

"Okay, Courtney, what do you want?" One of the women, a harried blonde about Wendy's age, addressed a toddler who was busy gumming her menu.

The menu, now damp and dented, slipped from between Courtney's cherub lips. "Hot dog!" she shouted.

"I don't know if they have hot dogs, honey."

Courtney began to wail and a little boy about four years old knocked over his water. "Stephen!" cried the other mother. "What are you doing?" Two older kids, maybe seven, were fighting over the sugar packets and the baby in the high chair shrieked and threw a half-eaten saltine to the floor.

"We do have hot dogs," Wendy said, mopping up the water with a paper napkin.

"Okay, a hot dog for her, then," said Courtney's mother.

"I want a hot dog! Mom! Mom! I want a hot dog!" shouted Stephen.

"All right, all right," said his mother, fishing another saltine out of her bulging purse and handing it to the baby.

"Two hot dogs," continued the blond woman. "Paul and Gloria, what do you want? Come on, hurry up. What are you doing?"

"Mom, Paul won't let me have the blue sugar. I want the blue sugar," whined Gloria.

"It's not sugar, it's Equal, and you're not having any of it," said her mother, snatching the packets away from the kids. "Now what do you want, a hamburger?"

When Wendy finally got their orders she dashed back to the kitchen for table nine's club sandwich. As she returned with it, she saw the woman standing up and putting on her coat.

"I'm so sorry! Here's your club sandwich," said Wendy, hopefully proffering the plate.

The woman shook her head. "It's too late. I'll take it to go."

"Of course, I'm so sorry," Wendy said again, though she knew there was no hope of salvaging a tip out of this one. She couldn't help staring at the woman. Where did she know her from?

The woman sighed and glanced at the booth behind her where Courtney and Stephen were now engaged in a battle of wills over the salt shaker. Apparently whoever screamed the loudest got to keep it. "I'll be glad to get out of here. Little monsters like that should be kept in cages."

Courtney's mother gasped and stared at her.

Biting her lip to keep from smiling Wendy gave the older woman her check and took the sandwich back to box it up before a fight broke out.

The woman was already at the cash register by the time Wendy was through. Back at table eight, the mothers were glaring at the older woman, but she paid them no mind and handed Joani, the cashier, her credit card. Wendy set the Styrofoam carton on the counter and glanced at the card as Joani ran it through the scanner.

Zazula Von Sach. Her face finally clicked into context: looking up from notes at a podium in the Chelsea Auditorium. She'd given that talk Lorca had taken her to, back in their freshman year.

"Oh, are you at the university?" blurted Wendy.

Zazula Von Sach focused on her for perhaps the very first time. "Yes, why do you ask?"

"Oh, I'm a student there. A friend of mine and I saw your guest lecture a few years ago. She's a big fan of your work."

The woman smiled, and it lit her eyes with a warmth Wendy never would have suspected of her. "Well, you'll have to bring her by to meet me, then."

She won't be there," Lorca protested as they climbed to the third floor of the computer science building. "They keep office hours, and we don't know what hers are."

"Would you stop worrying?" said Wendy. "If she's there you'll tell her how much you admire her work, and if she's not, we'll leave."

"But she's probably busy," Lorca persisted.

"You're just assuming you'll be a nuisance to her. You're not valuing yourself because you're a woman."

"I'm not valuing myself because I don't have a Ph.D." She gave Wendy a pointed look.

Wendy huffed and narrowed her eyes at her. "Anyway, here we are." She rapped sharply on the door of Dr. Von Sach's office.

"Come in," said a muffled voice.

Wendy opened the door.

Zazula Von Sach looked up from her desk. Her eyes were bright blue; wide and round as porcelain dinner plates. For a split second Wendy had the irrational feeling that she was under a microscope, and then the professor smiled warmly, and her whole face lit up, just as it had at the Nugget. "Oh hello," she said, coming around from behind the desk. "Come in. I'm so glad you came by. This must be your friend."

The office was cramped, two sets of shelves overflowing with books and papers barely left room for the desk, itself overburdened with computer equipment. Lorca hung back in the doorway, but Wendy hauled her in, pushing her toward Dr. Von Sach.

"I'm Wendy Chrenko, and this is Lorca Danes. She's a programmer at Ninsega."

Dr. Von Sach pumped Lorca's hand enthusiastically. "So good to meet you."

"Nice to meet you," Lorca wavered. "Um—I liked your talk."

"Thank you, it's nice to know someone out there is listening." She clasped her hands in front of her. Wendy noticed a large sapphire ring on her right middle finger. "But refresh my memory, what was I talking about?"

"The human–computer interface," said Lorca, sounding like she was getting her bearings a bit, relaxing in the warmth of Dr. Von Sach's reception. "I thought your strategy for stimulating the sense centers of the brain was fascinating."

"Oh yes." Dr. Von Sach leaned on the edge of her desk. "You know that's come quite a long way since I gave that talk. Back then it was all speculation, but now direct sensory experience of a computer generated environment is quite feasible. Of course, I haven't had a chance to do a proper field test, but it's very promising."

"Really?" Lorca's eyes were aglow.

Dr. Von Sach smiled and nodded, her eyes sparkling like that ring on her finger. "I just need to try it out on a guinea pig, so to speak."

"I'd love to hear all about it, doctor," said Lorca.

"Oh, for heaven's sake." She waved her hands in the air. "Call me Zazula. I'm almost finished here. Maybe you'd like to have lunch together and we can continue our discussion."

———

Y|ou see, what we take to be seamless reality probably isn't," said Zazula over her tuna fish sandwich at the nearby deli, Cold Cut and Run. "We take in certain cues—visual, tactile, aural—and our minds fill in the rest. Right now, looking at me, you're maybe getting an eye, part of my lips, my nose, and your mind is filling in the rest based on previous experience and context. So it isn't necessary to provide a subject in virtual reality with complete sensory input. Just like in real life, they can fill in the gaps. With electrodes being as sophisticated as they are nowadays, it's really not that big a deal to stimulate various sense centers." She paused and looked intently at them. "So Lorca, Wendy, tell me about yourselves."

"Wendy's a grad student and I work for Ninsega," said Lorca, beaming under Zazula's attentive gaze.

"Computer games!" Suddenly childlike, Zazula clapped her hands together. "How marvelous! Tell me about some of the games you've written, Lorca!"

"Well"—Lorca shyly pushed her chicken salad croissant around on the paper plate—"mostly I've just done support graphics, you know, landscapes, surface textures, stuff like that . . ."

"Yeah, but tell her about your new project," said Wendy.

Zazula's eyes flicked to Wendy and then fastened onto Lorca again. "Please do."

"Oh well," Lorca shrugged, then beamed. "I get to write my own game, the whole scenario, everything."

"But that's fantastic, Lorca! You must be so excited!"

"I am. It's going to be an adventure role-playing game for women based on the ancient Sumerian myth cycle of the goddess Inanna."

Zazula leaned forward. "Better and better. It's about time someone wrote some computer entertainment for women. So much of it seems to be just for adolescent boys."

"Yeah, exactly."

"So I'm guessing it's no accident that the game is based on the legends of Inanna, then."

"Right," Lorca nodded, her smile so wide it seemed like her face was about to split in half. "Wendy is a scholar of ancient Sumeria. She's preparing for her Ph.D."

"Really! What is your dissertation about, Wendy?"

"It's entitled *Remnants of Matriarchy in the Ancient Sumerian Inanna Cycle.*"

Zazula pursed her lips. "Oooh. That must be fascinating. I'd love to read it, when you finish."

Wendy found herself really liking Zazula. She was so smart, and open, so friendly, not at all the way she'd seemed when Wendy had waited on her. Caught up in Zazula's enthusiasm, Wendy found herself remembering what had turned her on about her dissertation topic in the first place. "See, there's this other figure, the laughing maid, Belili. I think she's a goddess of a rival cult, one that the Inanna cult supplanted in and around the city-state of Erech in the protoliterate period. There's this fascinating story, 'The Huluppu Tree.' It has some striking similarities to the story of the Garden of Eden, and I think Belili and the Serpent That Knows No Charm are the keys to a matriarchal culture prior to the Sumerians."

Zazula drew in a deep breath, her eyes narrowed, then widened, flashing with amazement.

"Wendy turned me on to feminism when we met as undergrads," interjected Lorca. "Then we both got into goddess spirituality."

Zazula blinked and shook her head, a bemused smile on her lips. "See, and so many women of my generation say the younger women coming up these days have no feminist consciousness. Just goes to show how wrong they are. The two of you are doing such important work for women everywhere. You know, I'm so glad you both stopped by to see me. Believe me, in my field I don't get that many opportunities to talk about things like this, things that are important to me as a woman. You two are a breath of fresh air."

"Wow," said Lorca.

"Thanks," said Wendy.

Zazula looked off to the distance wistfully. "I've always loved the goddesses." She looked back at them with a conspiratorial grin and leaned forward. "When I was a little girl, I used to pretend I was Diana."

Wendy sat back. "No way!"

"Oh yes," Zazula nodded, sat back and took a sip of iced tea. "My family had an estate outside Vienna, and I'd run around in the woods with a bow and arrow." Her smile became wry, self-deprecating. "The great huntress."

CHAPTER

20

Zazula soon became an integral member of their circle of friends, blending in so effortlessly that Raven, Veronica, Wendy, and Lorca felt as if she'd always been among them. When Lorca announced that her computer game was almost finished, it was Zazula's idea to prepare a special dinner for her in celebration.

The walls of Wendy, Raven, and Lorca's kitchen were painted red. The ceiling was yellow. Wendy stood at Raven's grandmother's ornately carved oak dining table, chopping vegetables and imagining what Ray might have painted on those walls.

Green vines and blue flowers twined up between the stove and the refrigerator as the clatter of cooking and conversation washed over her. Streaked with yellow, the leaves curled up around the white cabinets. Blue birds flew in a circle around the utilitarian white glass light fixture in the center of the ceiling. Wendy caught herself staring up at the round light, her knife stilled.

"That woman was back today, broken collarbone this time," said Veronica. She stood at the kitchen sink rinsing broccoli. Her eyes were steady, focused on what her hands were doing, but the rigid set of her face and a slight tremor in her voice betrayed her.

"Goddess," swore Wendy, refocusing. She inserted the tip of her knife into a head of cabbage and rocked it, splitting it in half.

"Is she going back to her boyfriend again?" asked Raven, pulling plates out of the cupboard beside the stove.

Veronica nodded. "Yeah. I talked to her again, gave her the phone number and address of a women's shelter. But she says she can't leave him."

"I don't understand," said Zazula, sitting at the opposite end of the table from Wendy, a glass of white wine in her hand. "If somebody hit me, I'd be out of there so fast it'd make your head swing." She took a sip of wine. "And that's if I was feeling charitable. Bastard'd be lucky if I didn't kill him in his sleep."

"Yeah, but you gotta understand," said Raven, stacking the plates on the table and turning to the silverware drawer next to the fridge. "Abuse is a gradual process. It starts with the abuser isolating the victim from family and friends and belittling her, eroding her confidence in herself. By the time things become physically violent, she's trapped in a web of depression and low self-esteem that can be very hard to get out of."

"That's right," said Wendy, chopping the cabbage into thin shreds. "Look at Ray's mom. He tried to get her to leave his father. He tried so hard. Offered to get her her own place, pay her bills, everything. She wouldn't do it." And what had Wendy done to help? Nothing. Oh, she'd been supportive, she supposed, as long as it didn't interfere with her own all-important self-actualization. The knife slipped, nicking Wendy's left index finger. "Shit!" She dropped the knife, and hurried to the sink.

"Are you okay?" said Veronica, relinquishing her spot to let Wendy plunge her hand under the running water.

"It's just a nick," said Wendy, peering at the tiny cut in her finger. "No big."

"Well, be careful," growled Raven. "This is supposed to be a vegetarian meal. Do you need a Band-Aid?"

"Nah," said Wendy, pressing her cut finger into the palm of her right hand. "It'll stop bleeding in a second."

"Well, I think you should put her right out of your mind, Veronica," said Zazula. "Women like that are a lost cause, and they just suck energy from the rest of us. Weak women are every bit as dangerous to women like us as men are."

"How can you say that?" Veronica turned to face her. "What's the point in being a feminist if we don't help other women?"

Zazula blinked and took another sip of wine. "Of course, so focus your time and energy on the countless women who want help. Volunteer at that shelter you mentioned, then you'll be helping women who are actively engaged in saving *themselves*. Your time and energy are valuable resources, don't waste them, that's all I'm saying."

Veronica nodded and passed the broccoli over to Wendy for chopping. "I know, you're right, it's just so frustrating, to see that going on and not be able to do anything about it."

"When will Lorca be home?" asked Zazula.

"Pretty soon now, I think," said Wendy, separating broccoli florets from their stem with the tip of her knife. "She called this afternoon to say that she'd be a little late because marketing had made a few changes to the game and she had to double-check them. But that's okay, it gives us time to get everything ready. So how's your work going, Z?"

Zazula made a face. "Well, everything would be just hanky-dory if that damned Christofsen would give me the authorization I need to take things to the next level. But he hates me. We knew each other back at Cornell. We were undergrads together. He wanted me to sleep with him and I told him to go screw himself, and he's never forgiven me. He's always spreading rumors about me, making things that should be simple incredibly difficult."

"What a wad!" said Wendy.

"Mmm," she agreed, "He's a pervert, too; likes little girls."

"Oh my gods," said Veronica, who was now peeling carrots. "And he's still at the university?"

Zazula sighed and gave them a pained smile. "Politics. Beware, Wendy, academia is the worst for politics."

"Oh, believe me, I know. Selecting my dissertation committee was a nightmare. Especially since my study's interdisciplinary. No matter who I picked, I knew some of them would be looking very closely for excuses to deny me, and it's well known that the head of the anthropology department is hostile to feminist scholarship. But my defense was last Thursday, and it went really smoothly. I was shocked."

"When do you find out if they're approving it or not?" asked Raven.

"Next week."

They heard Lorca's key in the lock, and Raven abandoned the paper napkins she'd been folding and went to greet her lover, the rest of them trailing after her. Their cheers and shouts of congratulations died on their lips when they saw Lorca standing there, her shoulders slumped, her mouth a bitter slash, her blue eyes radiating disillusionment. "They ruined it," she said.

They got her fed first, Raven taking her coat and carefully arranging her at the kitchen table, Veronica spooning rice and stir-fry onto her plate before inviting everyone else to help themselves.

It was a silent, hasty meal and then, when Raven was scraping the plates into the garbage, Zazula said, "Come Lorca, is it really so bad? Show us."

They all filed into the living room, and Lorca put the DVD containing the game demo into the player.

At first the screen was black. "In the first days, when the world was young and human culture was in its infancy, there lived a woman whose life became legend," intoned a male voice-over. "A woman unlike any other. A woman whose destiny was to become an immortal, a goddess." At this a sword blade slashed through the blank screen to reveal its wielder, a woman with long blond hair, a gold crown, a studded leather skirt, and a brass bra. Her breasts were huge, impossibly proportioned to her tiny waist and ridiculously long legs. Two men advanced on her and she fought them as the voice-over continued, "Desired by many, possessed by only one." The image cut to the woman wrapped in the arms of a man wearing a crown, and again to two armies charging across a field. "The fate of a nation will be determined by the sword of Inanna!"

Again they were shown the parody of feminine beauty poised with her legs spread wide, her sword held before her. At the bottom of the screen appeared the words, "The Sword of Inanna: A Legend 5,000 Years in the Making."

There was a stunned silence after the screen went blank. Lorca sat very still, as if hoping to sink into the couch and disappear. Wendy was the first to speak. "Well." She cleared her throat. "That was . . ."

"An abomination?" said Lorca, suddenly shooting up off the couch, her eyes flashing. "I swear, that's not how I wrote it. I can't believe they did this to me!"

"I'm so sorry, Lorca," said Zazula. "And I wish I could say I'm surprised, but I'm not."

"Yeah," said Raven. "A pillar of patriarchal society like Ninsega isn't going to put out a game about the Goddess without turning her into another boobular boy toy."

"This is so typical of the male corporate establishment mind set," said Zazula. "You're not the only one, Lorca. My virtual reality interface has incredible potential, but can I get funding, or even authorization to conduct experiments? No. They're so shortsighted. It's all about the bottom line and the status quo."

Lorca didn't seem to be listening. She stared at the blank screen, anger and disappointment written in her scowl. "She's blond," she muttered. "There were no blond Sumerians."

"If only there were some way we could each do our own work, without all this interference from the outside world," mused Zazula.

A thought occurred to Wendy. "You can," she said.

They all looked at her.

"Oh come on." She stood up and stretched her hands out, palms up. "It's staring you right in the face. You work together, developing the interface and the software to play on it. Form your own company. You'll make a million, and Ninsega and Dr. Christofsen will never be able to tell you what to do again."

Lorca shook her head skeptically. "Yeah, but a start-up like that would cost a lot of money. Just for starters, we'd have to support ourselves without paychecks for at least a year, not to mention all the equipment."

"Actually," said Zazula, suddenly blushing bright pink, "I have a considerable sum that I've been wanting to move out of tech stocks."

"Really?" said Wendy.

Zazula nodded. "I didn't want to mention it before because, well, I didn't want you to think I was just some rich bitch on a second-youth fling or something. I don't know." She shrugged and looked around at them all, hesitantly.

"I knew you had money, Zazula," said Raven.

"I didn't," said Veronica, "but I certainly won't hold it against you."

Lorca cracked a grin, her stoic mask breaking apart to reveal fresh hope. "Really? Are you serious?"

Zazula laughed and nodded. "Yes! Yes! Oh," she cried, jumping up and sweeping Wendy into a hug. "Thank you! What a marvelous idea!" She clapped her hands and turned to Lorca, grinning.

Lorca, too, stood up, her despair now utterly banished. "We can do this." She laughed. "We can do this."

"There's just one thing," said Zazula.

Lorca's face froze. "What?"

"What are we going to do for our first simulation?"

Four days later, Wendy waited in a small conference room for her dissertation committee to show up. The air was chilly, but sweat collected on her arms and face all the same. When Drs. Teasley, Westmoreland, Duane, and Rusch came in, her stomach sank. They were frowning, all but Dr. Duane, who cast her a sad smile. They sat down, and she couldn't prevent herself from leaning forward in anticipation of what they would say.

Dr. Teasley, from the anthropology department, took off his glasses and shook his head disapprovingly. "Let me guess," he said. "You decided to go into ancient literature after reading *The Language of the Goddess* or *Ancient Mirrors of Womanhood* or *The Women's Encyclopedia of Myths and Secrets,* and you were so inspired, you just had to find out more for yourself."

Numbly, Wendy nodded. "Y-yes, I read all those books," she stammered.

Dr. Teasley and Dr. Westmoreland exchanged knowing glances. "Every couple years, we get one like you," said Westmoreland. "Not as many as we once did, thank God, but still, your type surfaces with depressing regularity. The books you've read have misled you. There's never been any real proof of ancient matriarchies."

"These so-called feminist scholars draw all kinds of unfounded conclusions," said Teasley, warming to the subject, "drawing comparisons between things that are in no way related. Just because one culture has a female deity with a name similar to that of another culture's they say the two groups worshipped the same goddess. It's preposterous!"

Wendy knew she shouldn't say anything. She'd already defended her prospectus last week. This was her committee's final decision, the time to persuade them was past. Anything she said now could only make things worse for her, but she was so angry. "Are you saying that my scholarship is inadequate?"

"It's not a question of the adequacy of your scholarship, it's a question of the reputation of this university," said Westmoreland.

"In today's conservative academic climate we simply can't afford to foster the perception that Holbrook is a haven for feminist wish-fulfillment masquerading as research," added Dr. Rusch.

"What about the perception that Holbrook is a haven for free thought?" Wendy retorted.

"I'm sorry Wendy," said Dr. Duane. "I've gone on record concerning my dissent with the rest of the committee. I'm very disappointed in my colleagues."

Westmoreland gave her a withering glance. "Nevertheless, that is this committee's decision. Your dissertation prospectus is rejected."

Wendy felt as if the floor had opened up beneath her and she was falling, falling into the black abyss of her future. As though from a great distance, she watched her advisers file out of the room, and one thought kept spiraling around and around in her brain. I gave Ray up for this, and I failed. And that was maybe the worst part of all, the sudden searing longing that finally broke free from the place where she'd buried it with books and papers.

Dr. Duane was waiting for her outside in the hallway. "Wendy, I'm so sorry." Looking concerned, she put a hand to Wendy's shoulder. "Do you feel all right? Do you need to sit down?"

Wendy shook her head. "I-I'm okay."

Dr. Duane gave her a sympathetic smile. "I've filed a letter disputing my colleagues' decision with the dean, but there's not much more that I can do."

"Oh thank you, Dr. Duane," said Wendy, shaking her head slowly. "I just can't believe it. How can they do this? At the defense they acted like everything was okay. They knew they were going to reject it anyway, didn't they? Just because of the topic."

Dr. Duane nodded. "Teasley and Westmoreland are opposed to any theory that supports prehistoric matriarchies."

"But how can they ignore all the archaeological evidence? All those goddess figures, all over the world—doesn't that mean anything to them?"

Dr. Duane tilted her head to one side. "Well, those figures in and of themselves don't necessarily indicate a matriarchy."

Wendy gaped at her. Not you, too, she thought. "But they're female images."

"Yes, and so are the photos of barely clad models that our culture uses to sell everything from carbonated sugar water to motor oil. Do those images inspire reverence for women? Do they exalt us? No, I'm afraid the only way we could ever be absolutely certain that the matriarchies existed would be if we could go back in time and see for ourselves."

Lorca sat on the couch in their apartment, watching Wendy pace the floor. "I've spent six years of my life for nothing!" Wendy cried, "Fuck! What am I going to do? Everything! Everything I planned. All that work! All those nights I stayed up, alone, working, reading, researching." She stopped suddenly and looked at Lorca. Her eyes were very large. "I distanced myself from my friends. Oh Lorca, how many times I wanted to go out with you and Raven! How many times Veronica called and wanted to do something? And I told her no, because I had to work. I could have been out, having a life, meeting people, who knows, even dating. I wanted to enjoy life, I wanted to *have* a life, maybe even someone to share it with, but I thought—" She broke off and shook her head, her fists clenched at her sides. "God— godde—." She took a breath. "God damn me, I thought this was more important."

She raised her fists and threw them down, then lifted her hands, palms upwards, toward Lorca, her face beseeching. "What an idiot."

Lorca shook her head. "You're not an idiot, Wendy."

"Yes I am," she said bitterly, sinking into the chair and resting her arms on her knees. "In every way that's really important, I'm a total fucking idiot." She looked at her friend again. "I set myself up for this, Lorca."

"That's ridiculous."

Wendy shook her head. "No. No. I did. I knew how the head of the history department felt about feminist research. I knew my topic was interdisciplinary. I could have done something in ancient literature, and it would have been fine. But I had to do this. I thought the strength of my passion for the subject was enough to overcome all obstacles. I treated the academic process like my personal garden, where I could let my own thoughts grow wild. I treated it like something it wasn't, and now I'm crying because reality caught me up short."

Lorca closed her eyes and sighed, feeling tired in the face of Wendy's determined self-recrimination. "Listen to you. Blaming yourself. Did you fail to prepare your prospectus properly? No. You *know* your scholarship was solid. They're rejecting it for political reasons."

"But I should have known that they would."

Aaargh. Wendy could be so damned stubborn. "And that makes the line of inquiry unworthy of investigation?"

"It'll never see the light of day."

"Oh, so, since some thoughts are not permitted, we shouldn't have them, then, is that it?" Lorca knew she was right, and that gave her the strength to meet Wendy's glare with her own, staring her down. "Since certain institutions say some ideas are inappropriate, we shouldn't have such ideas. We should just think what academia and movies and prime-time television tell us to think, I guess." She paused and bent over, peering at her friend. "Sorry, who are you?"

Wendy bared her teeth. "I wasted seven years of my life."

One thing Lorca had always loved about Wendy was that she didn't give up easily, but this really *was* pissing her off. "Wasted? Wasted? You met *me* in college, Wendy. You met Veronica and Raven. Your closest friends. The people who love you most in this world. How dare you? How dare you say you wasted your life?"

The thought that she'd hurt her friend's feelings made Wendy immediately cave. "I'm sorry. I didn't mean—I just mean that you have Raven, and Veronica has her boyfriend, and me—what do I have? I just had this, and now I have nothing."

Lorca sighed. She couldn't really stay mad at Wendy under any circumstances, and right now, well, she was just being so pathetic. Lorca walked over to her and put her hands to the sides of Wendy's face, tipping her head back as she pressed her lips to Wendy's forehead. "You have us," she said, her smile belying her stern tone. "And don't you ever forget it."

Wendy swallowed, and nodded. "You're right," she admitted. "You're right, of course, I just—" She stopped and stared into space.

"You're just very upset right now," said Lorca, but she wondered at the haunted look in her friend's eyes. "Is this just because of the dissertation? I mean, not that that's not more than enough. Just, is there something else bothering you?"

Wendy shook her head but wouldn't quite meet her eyes as she said, "No, there's nothing else."

Lorca sighed. If Wendy didn't want to talk about it, there was no drawing her out. She knew that from experience.

Wendy went into her room and lay down on the bed. She rolled onto her side, staring dully at the opposite wall. It was covered with pictures of ancient Sumerian carvings, the one of Belili with spread wings taking pride of place in the center, and off, up in one corner, near the ceiling, a portrait in pastels of a boy who looked like a snake, with trees in his eyes.

She couldn't tell Lorca, or anyone else, for that matter, how much she missed Ray. It was insane, but what seemed to bother her the most about her prospectus failing, what kept running through her mind, was how she'd broken up with Ray because she wanted to stay in school. She'd done it for this. For this, and she'd failed. She'd given him up for nothing.

She got up and went to her desk, woke up her computer and went online. Not thinking about what she was doing, as if in a trance, she started pulling up Internet yellow pages.

Eight hours later she got up, rubbed her red-rimmed eyes and fell back into bed. Of course she couldn't find him. Ray probably hadn't been Ray for years. There was no going back.

Or was there? She thought of Dr. Duane's words: *The only way we could ever be absolutely certain that the matriarchies existed would be if we could go back in time and see for ourselves.*

Ray was lost to her forever, that was certain, but with the technology Lorca and Zazula were working on, there might be a way to prove that the kind of world she and Ray had dreamed of back in high school *had* once existed. And if it had existed once, then it could again . . .

CHAPTER

21

"So they had donkeys, cattle, and pigs, but not horses?" said Lorca as she typed code at the computer in her bedroom. It had been three months since the Inanna game debacle and the rejection of Wendy's dissertation topic, and they'd been working on the simulation nonstop ever since.

"Right," Wendy got up from the bed and leaned over the back of Lorca's chair, peering at the incomprehensible lines of the program. "Horses didn't come along until the Ur III Dynasty, around 2000 B.C., and we're setting this around 2300 B.C."

Lorca nodded. "During the reign of Lugal-zagesi in Lagash. Did you ever find out what an apputtum looks like?"

"No, but let's just assume it's a braid at the top of the head, surrounded by a shaved circle. The important part is that it's a way of identifying slaves. You know, before we started this, I thought I knew everything about this period, but now . . . there's still a lot of gaps."

"I don't know, being the one who has to code in all these details, I think you know plenty. Now what about food, what were they eating?"

Down the hall, they heard the door to their apartment open. Zazula came into the room with a brown paper shopping bag and a huge grin. "I finished it!"

Wendy went to her, hugged her and peeked in the bag. Lying at the bottom was a black coiled something. "Is that it?"

She nodded, setting the bag down on the bed and taking off her coat. Lorca hit SAVE and came over to stand by Wendy. With ceremony, Zazula opened the bag and withdrew the VR interface. It was jointed, and ridged like human vertebrae, with electrodes to tap into the neural paths of the spinal column. At the top was a round . . . head, with more spines on that, and two curving prongs on either side of it.

"Gah!" cried Lorca. "It looks like the Tingler!"

Wendy shook her head. The prongs were just for bracing it against the shoulders. "It looks like a snake," she said.

"I brought the demo program with me," said Zazula, hoisting the apparatus by the round part at the top, the rest of it spiraling down just like a real snake. "So, who wants to go first?"

"I do," said Lorca. She glanced at Wendy, pleading with her eyes.

"Is it really safe?" said Wendy.

Zazula stared at her with a look of surprise. "Of course, don't worry," she said hastily. "I've tried it myself. If you want to wait in the other room, I'll call you when we're through."

Wendy shook her head.

"I have complete confidence in Dr. Von Sach," said Lorca. She glanced at Zazula, who beamed.

"You see?" said Zazula. "The subject is willing, even eager. This is just a test, a formality, no?"

Lorca disrobed and lay on her stomach on the bed. From the same grocery bag, Zazula took a cable and an adapter, and plugged them into the back of the computer. She inserted the disk and tapped a few keys, took the snake and fit it over Lorca's shoulders and arranged it down her spine. "It taps into the neurons with very fine needles, like acupuncture, only even finer. She ran her fingers down the spines. "Each of the nodes taps into a different neural pathway, to handle different sensations and cognitive centers in the brain," she said. "You'll experience a moment of disorientation, then a blankness, and then the sim should start. You'll be hang gliding. Are you ready?"

"Ready," said Lorca, her voice muffled by the pillow.

Starting at the bottom of the snake and working her way up, Zazula pressed in the spines. Each one clicked as it locked into place.

"Does it hurt?" asked Wendy, about halfway through.

"She can't answer you now," said Zazula.

"Oh." Wendy knelt down beside the bed, peering at Lorca's face, which was blank, peaceful in repose.

With the last of the spines in place, Zazula returned to the computer and started up the sim program.

As far as Wendy could tell, nothing happened. Lorca just lay there, and they stood around for about ten minutes, at which time the computer beeped and a message informed them that the program had finished. Zazula released the spines, starting from the top and working down, and lifted the snake from Lorca's back. Wendy examined her spine, looking for needle holes, but couldn't find any.

"Mmmff," Lorca muttered, rolled over and sat up. She shook her head and stared at them owlishly.

"Well?" pressed Wendy. "What was it like?"

A smile played at her lips and blossomed into a grin. "It was fantastic! Just like I was really flying. And I felt the wind, saw . . . saw some incredible scenery. I could even smell the pines!"

They set up for the Sumerian experiment in Zazula's grand colonial villa in Belle Heights. When Zazula bought the place, she'd had all the interior walls on the third floor removed, and she'd outfitted it as a lab so she could work on her VR interface when she wasn't at the college lab. It was a perfect space for their purposes, open and airy, with lots of light from the rows of arched windows lining the front and the back of the house. Over the years a fair amount of equipment had gathered in the space, but there was still more than enough room for the isolation chamber, Lorca's computers, and the medical equipment they'd need to monitor Wendy's physical stats while she was in the simulation.

"See," Wendy told Veronica as they stood around the eight-foot-long gleaming black ovoid of the isolation chamber, her portal to ancient Sumeria, "we'll fill it with salt water and I'll float, so you don't have to worry about me getting bedsores."

Veronica nodded gravely. From the start she'd been concerned about the idea of Wendy staying in the simulation for the weeks and probably months required to fully explore ancient Sumeria and delve into the secrets of its past.

"And here is where you'll be monitoring my respiration, heart rate and brain wave activity," Wendy continued, showing her friend the bank of monitors beside the chamber. "You can check on me as often as you want, and if anything goes wrong, Zazula and Lorca will just take me out."

Veronica pursed her lips and took a deep breath. "You'll need to be fed intravenously—"

"Zazula's taking care of that. She has excellent contacts with a hospital supply company."

"Not to mention getting fitted with a catheter."

"Joy of joys." Wendy gave her a wry grin, and heaved a sigh of relief when Veronica returned it.

The other woman shrugged in resignation. "You're going to do this no matter what I do or say. At least I can be around to make sure you come through all right."

Wendy grinned, took Veronica's hand and dragged her over to Lorca and Zazula's workstation, a conglomeration of computers and monitors spanning three desks and a folding table. "Vonnie's on board!" she cried.

The other two looked up from the monitor they'd been staring at, and smiled. "Wonderful!" cried Zazula. "This calls for a celebration. I'll order Chinese, and there's a bottle of Asti in the refrigerator."

"Cool," said Lorca. "I was just going to suggest we break for tonight anyway."

Veronica shook her head and pulled free of Wendy. "I can't stay. I'm sorry. My shift starts in half an hour."

"Drag." Wendy gave her friend a big hug. "But I'm so glad you're going to be involved in this."

Veronica hugged Wendy back hard, and then released her. "I should know better than to try and talk you out of anything," she said. "And it *is* nice to see you happy again."

So how much longer before we're ready, do you think?" asked Wendy around a mouthful of eggroll. She and Lorca and Zazula sat on the tan couch that was pushed up under one of the windows in the lab. A number of overturned cardboard boxes served as tables, supporting cartons of chicken subgum chow mein, egg foo young, and Singapore rice noodles. A bottle of Asti sat half-empty on the floor.

"We're really close," said Lorca. "Probably just another month."

Wendy's stomach gave a lurch of excitement. It had been six months. Nothing compared to all the years she'd been in college, but still, somehow, an eternity. She'd spent hours lying on this couch with the snake on her back, running through sections of the simulation, calling out to Lorca what she saw and felt and tasted, so Lorca could adjust the code accordingly. And still the ten-foot-tall purple naditum priestess who smelled of goat cheese haunted her dreams. Despite that and other less disturbing bugs, Wendy was captivated by what she'd seen. It was incredible, exactly like walking through the ancient city of Erech come to life. From the moment she'd sat on the city wall, looking out at the plain of the Euphrates, she'd longed for the time when she would immerse herself completely in that world.

"We're just finishing the mythic subroutines," said Zazula. "In fact, Gilgamesh is almost done." She gave a deep, contented sigh. "Just imagine, you'll be entering a dialogue with the ancient past, picking out its secrets. And Belili, the Serpent That Knows No Charm, Utnapishtim, they all hold keys to the time that came before written history." She clapped her hands and grinned. "They'll be like co-conspirators in an espionage of the mythstream!"

Wendy grinned. "I like that." She leaned over and picked up the Asti and took a good solid swallow. In her mind's eye she saw the huluppu tree garden. How she longed to meet Belili. The need to know that she was real burned down her throat along with the bubbling wine and surrounded her heart with a buzzing warmth. But doubt soon seeped through her euphoria. How could she be sure? She wanted so desperately to prove that Belili was the goddess of a previous matriarchal culture. How could she be sure that she wouldn't interpret what she saw in ways that supported her hypothesis? Even subconsciously.

Her doubt must have shown on her face, because Lorca gave her a quizzical look. "What?"

Wendy shrugged. "Well, I mean, no matter how complete the simulation is—and it's good, it's really good," she hastened to add at the sight of Lorca's gathering scowl. "But, how can we be sure that I won't just find what I want to find?"

Lorca nodded. "Yeah, Zazula and I were talking about this just yesterday. Hey, Zazula, tell Wendy your idea."

"You mean about the persona?" Zazula waved her chopsticks in the air and chewed hastily. "Well, one way around the baggage of your own viewpoint would be to develop a persona for you to take on while you're in the sim." She swallowed. "A contemporary of the culture. And then we just put a temporary block on your memory, so you will basically take on this role, and experience ancient Sumeria and its mythic past from *their* point of view."

Wendy brightened. "Yes, that's a great idea. Somebody who would have a comprehensive understanding of the culture."

"Someone of low status then," said Lorca.

"Low status?" Zazula arched her brows in surprise.

"Survival mechanism," said Lorca.

"Right," said Wendy, meeting Lorca's eyes. "Nobody understands the structure of a society better than a slave."

Naked, Wendy stepped into the isolation chamber and lay down in the salt water, which was body temperature. It really did feel like floating in nothingness. Veronica looked down at her. "Are you sure about this?"

Wendy nodded. "Surer than I've been about anything in a long time."

Veronica nodded and took her arm, inserting the IV needle—a cold prickle—and taping it down. Her eyes brimming, she kissed Wendy. "Go with the goddess," she whispered.

Over her shoulder, Wendy saw Lorca and Raven standing together. She waved them over. "Good luck," said Raven, her voice hoarse.

"Thanks."

Lorca grabbed her hand and squeezed it hard. "You'll be fine. We'll be monitoring you the whole time. You'll be fine."

Wendy smiled, nodded. "Of course I will be. Don't worry. I know you won't let anything happen to me."

Lorca's gaze faltered, but she nodded, squeezed Wendy's hand one more time, and retreated.

Next Zazula hove into her view, a gleam of excitement in her eyes. "Are you ready?"

Wendy grinned. "I'm ready. Bring it on."

At the click of the first node sliding into place, Wendy's body went numb, at the second, she became deaf, at the third the world was replaced by a blank gray wall, and by the fifth, she wasn't Wendy anymore.

Shula sat on the wall of Erech, gutting fish and watching the world be born . . .

CHAPTER

22

Ray slouched at the desk in the corner of his living room and opened the top right drawer, staring glumly at the jumble of driver's licenses inside. Almost all the states were represented, plus a few for foreign countries. All different colors, different styles, and all with his face staring up at him. It was like seeing fifty different versions of himself, different lives he'd led.

When he'd first arrived in L.A., Ray set himself up as Lawrence Hocking, some professor with a lot of inherited wealth he'd picked up off his favorite modern convenience, the Creditcheck web site. In Lawrence's name he rented an apartment, set up several credit accounts and bought a green MG roadster. For about a month he lived in style in L.A., cruising, going to restaurants, getting royally drunk, and screwing a bunch of women who were just this side of being prostitutes.

But as soon as he had Lawrence set up, he started developing the next identity, forging a driver's license and birth certificate, so that when it was time to make the jump, his new identity would be ready.

And that's how it was: every few months a new name, a new city, a new life. It was better this way, he told himself, glancing around his sparsely furnished apartment. A black leather recliner sat in the middle of the living room, in front of the flat-screen, picture-frame TV. A DVD player and stereo components sat in a glass-and-laminate case beneath the TV, flanked on either side by towering Bose speakers. An upended cardboard box, the one his new computer had come in, sat beside the chair and served as a side table. He slept on a futon in one of the two bedrooms, and other than the desk where he kept his computer, that was the extent of the furnishings.

For a while he'd done each new place up with great care, choosing a style that he thought went along with the new identity. Pictures on the walls, knickknacks, couches and chairs and dining tables, a brand new wardrobe, the whole schmear. But gradually he'd slacked off on that. It hardly seemed worth the trouble. It all got left behind each time he moved, anyway. Now he just stuck to the basics. The only consistent possession in his life was the box of stuff he'd brought with him from the loft he'd shared with Wendy. He never opened it, and every time he moved, he toyed with the idea of leaving it behind, but inevitably, the box would wind up in his new digs, shoved in the corner of a closet or a spare bedroom, ignored but not forgotten.

Ray sighed and turned off his computer, where he'd been researching his next identity. Time to go out, he decided, taking his leather jacket from where it hung on the doorknob and shrugging it on. He went out into the warm summer evening, the sky just starting to purple with dusk at nine P.M.

He hopped into his forest green Land Rover and drove to Calloway's, a bar he'd found about a week ago that served killer buffalo wings and a wide selection of local craft beers.

He sat at the bar with a plate of wings and a mug of Harry's Hardass Lager, telling himself, for the umpteenth time, that everything he needed to be happy was right in front of him, with no worries or attachments to mess stuff up. He tossed a bare bone onto his plate and took a deep swallow of beer. Setting the mug back down he smelled perfume, and turned to see a woman standing beside him, trying to get the bartender's attention. She had long, dark, wavy hair, full red lips, and a shapely nose. For a moment Ray sat there paralyzed, gaping, his heart pounding as if it could break free from the cage of his ribs and fly, all sensible admonitions concerning the simple life forgotten, to its desire. And then she turned, and he saw that it wasn't her, of course. Of course not. How could it be? How stupid of him. But she *was* beautiful, heartbreakingly so, in fact.

"Hey, Buck," Ray called out to the bartender, who was chatting with a customer at the other end of the bar. "Someone's dying of thirst over here."

She smiled and looked at him. She had large, dark eyes. "Thanks. I don't know what it is, I can never get their attention." She had a soft, mellow voice, like aged bourbon, and she smelled like Easter lilies.

"Oh, you're just too nice about it, that's all." Ray propped one elbow on the bar and rested his chin against it. "You have to be more assertive."

Her smile quirked up at one edge. "Is that so?"

"Yeah." Ray felt himself blushing. He couldn't think of anything good to say. God how he hated this. He felt like such an ass.

The bartender came up, and she asked for a scotch and soda while he was fumbling around for the right words to link together to ask her what she wanted to drink. Well, that's it, he thought as Buck turned away to fix her drink. I've blown it.

"You come here often?" she asked.

He remembered to breathe. "Yeah, now I do. I just discovered the place last week. Good wings." He gestured at his half-demolished plateful and decided against offering her one. That was probably gross. "I'm new in town," he said instead.

"Really? What made you decide to move here?"

He shrugged. "Business."

"Oh, what do you do?"

"I'm in sales."

"Ah, sales," she nodded sagely. "Me, too. I'm Linda." She stuck out a hand.

"Ray," he said, without thinking, and then wondered how long it had been since he'd told anyone his real name. He took her cool hand in his and they shook. She had a firm grip. Buck showed up with her scotch and soda and she pulled her hand back and reached for her purse, sitting on the bar.

"Hey, Linda, why don't I get that?"

She blinked. "Oh, oh, you know, some other time I'd love that but"— she glanced over her shoulder, her forehead suddenly creased with worry—"I'm sort of . . . waiting for someone." She pulled some bills out of her purse and placed them on the bar.

"Oh, well, if you're waiting for him, maybe he's not worth the wait," said Ray. Christ, that sounded stupid, he thought.

But she smiled again, and pushed her hair back behind her ear. Was that a bruise on her jaw, or just a shadow? She turned to face him again and he couldn't tell.

"Maybe not, but . . ." She shrugged. "Anyway"—she touched his arm lightly—"it was nice meeting you Ray. 'Bye." And she took her drink and walked away.

He watched her sit down at a table and then stand up again, waving eagerly to a short, musclebound guy just coming in the door. He was balding and he wore a goatee. He had a thick neck and walked with a kind of bowlegged swagger you sometimes saw with those overly muscled types. Ray grimaced and turned away, consoling himself with the remainder of his chicken wings and a succession of refills on his beer.

A few hours later, he lurched out of Calloway's and headed to his Land Rover, thinking maybe he'd go online when he got home and play some PrismQuest before going to bed. He had his keys out and he was just about to unlock the car door when he heard yelling.

"Get in the car!" It was a man's voice, rough as gravel.

"No! I don't want to!" Even raised in fear, he recognized Linda's smooth contralto. His stomach tightening, he stepped out from between the cars and spotted them a few yards away. It was full dark now, but the light of a half-moon and the neon blare of the Calloway's sign illuminated them. The guy who Linda had been waiting for had her by the arm, and he was dragging her toward a beat-up Toyota, license plate number 827 URB. She struggled in his grip. "Please Jimmy, let me go, you're hurting me!"

"I'm hurting you? Bitch, you're going to find out what pain is if you don't *get—in—the—fucking—car!*" Jimmy swung her around and shoved her toward the Toyota. Linda staggered and fell and he advanced on her as she lay cowering on the pavement.

"Hey," said Ray, coming up behind him. Jimmy whirled around and Ray threw his fist at him. It landed in the middle of his face with a satisfying smack that sent a jolt of pain through Ray's knuckles and up his arm.

But it was worse for Jimmy. "Fuck!" he screamed, staggering back against the Toyota, his hands to his nose.

Linda glanced up at him, and then at Ray, and her eyes widened. She scrambled to her feet and ran to him. "Please," she said, gripping his jacket. "You've got to help me."

Ray nodded, but for now he kept his eyes on Jimmy, who had lowered his hands to reveal a trickle of blood, gleaming black in the moonlight, coming from his left nostril. He glared at them from beneath his brows, and Linda wisely got behind Ray.

"Who the fuck are you?"

"I'm the guy that's going to see she gets home safe," said Ray.

Jimmy scowled, but he didn't come any closer, and there was uncertainty in his gaze as he looked back and forth between them. "Fuck you! Mind your own business! Linda, who is this?"

"I don't know, Jimmy. I don't know him."

Ray started backing up, one arm behind him, guiding Linda along. "Come on," he said to her, risking a glance over his shoulder. "My car's over there."

When he looked back, Jimmy was kicking the already dented side of the Toyota in frustration. "Fuck!" he yelled a few more times as they made their way to the Land Rover.

As Ray opened the passenger side door for her, they heard the sound of tires screeching, and turned to see the Toyota backing up swiftly toward them. "Shit," Ray muttered. "Hurry." Linda scrambled inside and he got the door shut. "Lock it!" he said, and turned to face Jimmy again.

But he just hung out the window of the car. "You both better watch your backs. Next time you won't get the drop on me, and I'll fucking kill you!" And with that, he peeled out of the parking lot.

Ray got in the car, locked it, and heaved a great sigh. In the passenger seat, Linda was all jitter and moonlight; trembling, crying, fumbling in her purse for tissues.

"Hey," he said, reaching a tentative hand to her shoulder. "It's okay. It's okay, he's gone."

She nodded, holding a wadded tissue to one eye, and a little whimper escaped her lips. "Th-thank you. If you hadn't come along, I don't—I don't know what—"

"Hey, don't think about that. I did come along, and you're all right now. You're going to be all right."

She took a deep, shuddery breath and nodded again. "He's just—He gets crazy sometimes, you know? When he's been drinking?"

"Yeah."

"He can be really sweet, too, but—" She shook her head and fell silent.

"He's never going to change, you know," said Ray.

She nodded. "I know, I know you're right. I have to leave him. I'm afraid, but I have to do it." She swallowed, and looked at Ray, and suddenly she was in his arms, her tears slick against his neck, clutching his shoulders and sobbing.

"Shh," said Ray, stroking her dark hair. "It's all right." He held her tighter than he probably should have, considering. "It's all right," he said again, as she quieted down. "I'll take you home. Okay?"

"No!" She pulled back. "No, I—I live, lived with him. I can't go there."

"Oh, then a friend's house, or a family member?"

She sniffled and shook her head. "No, I just moved here. I don't know anyone in this town." She swallowed and looked up at him, her eyes enormous and ringed with smudged mascara. "Nobody but you, Ray."

So he took her back to his place, and they drank a little more, and they talked. Pretty soon they got onto the subject of Ray's father, and Ray drank a lot more, and talked a lot more. Linda's dark eyes drank in his confession of helplessness and rage, obliterating it just as the bourbon Ray drank obliterated his judgment, his reserve, and his isolation.

He had meant to put fresh sheets on the futon for her and bed himself down in his easy chair, but somehow that's not what happened. Somehow they wound up in bed together and Ray awoke late the next morning with the muddled memory of her mouth on his, wet and open and tasting of bourbon. He sighed and smiled and rolled over, relishing the lazy satedness of his body. He reached a hand out, but found only empty bed beside him.

Ray sat up, looking owlishly about him and listening for the sound of the shower. No shower sound. The first rumblings of a hangover grumbled in his brain, like gathering thunderclouds. "Linda?" he called. Getting up he pulled on the jeans that lay beside the bed. He hoped she wasn't trying to fix breakfast. He hadn't shopped for food in weeks and anything that was in the fridge was bound to be—

He stood in the hallway, staring at his living room, which was bare, empty, absolutely devoid of all furnishings. The headache that had been threatening ever since he'd opened his eyes bore down upon him with all the fury of a summer storm. Everything, the computer, the chair, the TV, DVD, stereo, the *desk,* all of it was gone.

Ray blinked, and then a thought sent him running into the spare bedroom, his guts turning to ice water. The door to the closet where he'd shoved his box of stuff from his time with Wendy stood open. *Oh no.* The closet was empty. *Oh yes, that, too.*

Sudden rage gripped him. He was going to find that bitch. He was going to get his stuff back. He stumbled back into his bedroom, searching for his wallet, his keys, but of course they were gone, too, and the desk, where all his other I.D.s had been. Shit. He went to the window in the living room and looked out. Of course, the Land Rover was gone. How else could she have hauled all his shit away? Fuck. He was screwed. No money, no I.D., no way of getting a new I.D. or more money. And no idea where this Linda bitch had gone to. If that was even her real name. Had she ever told him her last name? No, of course not. But he did have the license plate number for her boyfriend's car.

Ray walked up the street of decaying town houses, looking for number 301. He'd been walking all day, it seemed like. First two miles to the library to use their Internet access to run down the license plate number of the Toyota—it was registered to a James Houks residing at 301 South Boulevard—and then five more miles to this run-down seedy neighborhood tucked between the river and the spikey towers of an oil refinery. He didn't even know for sure that this Jimmy guy was in on it. Had it been a set up from the start, or had Linda just taken advantage of the opportunity? Or maybe, a reproachful little voice in his head said, Jimmy had put her up to it, forced her to do it. Maybe it wasn't her fault at all.

He saw his Land Rover before he saw the address. It stood parked in the driveway next to a two-story brick-and-wood town house. The place was just as run-down as the rest of the street, the white paint on its trim peeling like dead skin.

Ray glanced in the window of the Land Rover just in case they'd left the keys inside, but no dice, and the door was locked when he tried the handle, so he went on back to the tiny, weed-choked yard behind the town house. There was a porch and above it, a second-story balcony. In the distant past, some ambitious resident had nailed a trellis to the side of the porch and the balcony and attempted to grow some vine or other up it. Dusty stalks like bones protruded from the little patch of dirt at the base, testimony to long-dead aspirations.

Nervous, Ray licked his lips and rubbed his hands together. His palms were sweating and he hoped that would make them stickier, somehow. He crouched and leapt at the trellis, grabbing at the brittle slats. The splintering wood tore his palms but he managed to get a toehold—he was thankful for the relative flexibility of his high-tops—and launch himself up and grab at the wrought-iron railing of the balcony. His breath came like a ragged wind as he clung there, his feet bumping at the trellis, which gave way at the pressure, withholding further support. His arms started to tremble, and with a desperate heave he swung his legs first in and then out and up to the side and he managed to catch the edge of the gutter with one toe. He pulled his other leg up and got it beneath him, and surged up and over the railing. He crouched there beside the window, caught his breath, and peered inside.

An empty room. Well, hallelujah. Ray wiped his hands on his jeans and tried pushing the edge of the window frame up. It was locked. The caulk around the glass was dry and cracked. He pried his thumbnail under it and a chunk came loose like an old scab. Sweating, watching through the window for Jimmy or Linda to show up at any moment, he scraped the rest of the caulk away from the glass and slid the pane free from the frame.

He heard a stereo playing downstairs. In fact, he recognized the CD. It was one of his. He crept into the hallway and down the stairs, which opened onto a short hallway. Through a doorway to the right he saw Linda sitting on a brown velour couch smoothing her nails with a metal nail file. The small, dark-paneled room was crammed full of his stuff. The flat screen stood propped against a window, and his computer monitor sat beside it, its screen blank, pouting at this indignity. But they'd set up his stereo, on top of his desk, which hulked beside a peeling vinyl recliner. On the coffee table next to the couch his I.D.s lay scattered and his wallet curled forlornly in the shadow of a dusty jar of potpourri.

"Hey, Linda," said Ray warmly, stepping into the room.

She looked at him, eyes very wide, and her mouth opened. Her hand holding the nail file froze in midair.

"Honey, I missed you this morning," he went on, sitting down next to her on the couch in what he hoped was a relaxed manner. "I was going to make French toast."

The expression on her face abruptly closed, taking on a pinched and hungry look, and he would have sworn this could not be the woman he'd met the night before. "What do you want?" Her voice was guttural, harsh.

"I want my stuff back," he said.

She looked him up and down, noted the absence of any obvious weapon and cocked her head to one side, allowing just enough of the tenderness she'd shown him the night before into her eyes to tease him. "If you know what's good for you, you'll get the fuck out of here. Right now." Her eyes darted to the front door. "Jimmy'll be back soon."

"Well, obviously I don't know what's good for me, or I wouldn't be here," said Ray, noting the many levels on which that statement was true. He swallowed. "I tried to help you, and this is what you do? You stole everything from me—my whole life. How could you do that?"

She lifted one eyebrow and a wry smile curved the harsh line of her mouth. "Yeah, well, what about you, *Ray*? You're not exactly what you seem to be either." She waved a hand at his I.D.s. "I mean, which one of these is really you?"

He blinked and jerked his eyes back to hers. "That's different. I don't hurt anybody."

She shrugged. "Neither do we. It's just stuff, right? So maybe we get our hands a little dirtier than you do, maybe we're a little more direct about it. But it's still just stealing, isn't it?"

He stood up and walked around the coffee table, trying to keep an eye on her as he scanned the room for the cardboard box. Almost as an afterthought he picked his wallet up from the coffee table and leaned forward to scoop up his I.D.s. As his left hand dragged the skittery pieces of plastic across the table, her nail file flashed down like a bolt of lightning, straight through the back of his hand.

Ray screamed and lifted up his hand. The nail file stuck out of the back of it. It had gone right between the tendons and nearly out the other side. Pain froze his fingers into claws, and as he watched, blood welled up around the wound and dripped onto the carpet. With an odd buzzing sensation in his head, he dragged his eyes away from the spectacle of his hand to stare at Linda. She stood between the coffee table and the couch, pointing a gun at him. Her eyes were a perfect match for the black hole of its barrel, and Ray saw his death looking out from all three of them. He was never going to see Wendy again.

"Get out, motherfucker."

He did as she suggested, and found himself standing on the front walk of the house, cradling his injured hand, somehow, miraculously, still alive. The nail file still stuck out of the back of his hand, and he pulled it out with a jerk and a fresh spurt of pain and blood. He tossed the nail file aside and staggered down the walk.

Ahead of him, a pile of garbage stood by the curb. Among the bags and cans he saw the corner of a cardboard box. He stumbled over and pulled it out. It was his box. He pulled the lid off. His stuff was still there: a bunch of computer game disks, a Swiss Army knife, a purple ceramic pig, a sketch pad, a battered brown folio, and a spiral notebook, its blue cover worn almost white. Gratefully he picked up the box, using the wrist of his injured hand to brace it against his chest, and walked home.

One day last week I came home to find Ray cooking spaghetti sauce, wearing boxer shorts, work boots, and that ridiculous apron Aunt Jessica gave me for my birthday last year. It's pink checks with a lot of white eyelet lace around the edges. And seeing that image, my faith was renewed. My faith in us, in myself, in my dream of a world where such sights are commonplace, a world where the divisions between men and women are gone, where each of us is free to be exactly who we are. And I was so happy, because I'd been thinking lately that it was impossible. That we'd never understand one another, and that if we, two people who love each other, can't bridge that gap, then what hope is there for the rest of the world?

But now I know it can be done. I have proof and I won't give up until everyone can experience the joy and freedom of expression I've been blessed with in my life. So I'm flying high for a few days. Ray and I are getting along great, it's like all the fights we've had just evaporated. And then comes Friday. Ray rents some DVDs. One of them is *The Pit and the Pendulum,* and it just strikes me that this film is incredibly misogynist. The imagery of the pit, the villain's obsession with his wife. So I say so. And in an eyeblink it's all over. We argue. Ray insists that the film is not sexist. He gets really mad, saying I won't let him talk. But I am, I'm just not agreeing with him. We're both angry for days, sniping at each other; nasty, barbed attacks. So now I think, how could I have been so naive? I thought I could be free, and with Ray. I thought we could do it together. But now I know. That world is still out there, still possible, but Ray is not a part of it. He doesn't want to be. And I'm sad because I love him. Sad because I'll miss him.

His hands shook and he put down the notebook, brought his trembling hands up to his trembling face to catch the hot river of emotion pouring from his eyes.

He remembered. He remembered that day he wore the apron, because all his clothes were dirty and he needed something to protect him from the splatter of spaghetti sauce. He remembered how she called him Bettina and chased him around the loft with a spatula. She'd pinned him down on the sofa and ravished him like an eighteenth-century nobleman having his way with a serving wench. God, it had been exquisite.

And he remembered the fight the following weekend. One of their worst, and one of the most petty, or so he thought at the time. He realized with grim satisfaction that he'd been right when he'd said that she blamed him for everything men did. They weren't just Ray and Wendy to her. They were Man and Woman, a proving ground for the validity of heterosexual relationships. If they failed, then the whole world failed.

But in spite of all that, in spite of all her impossible expectations, or maybe because of them, he'd felt and been and thought and done more in the three years they were together than he had in the seven years since. He'd known who he was then, or at least who he wanted to be. The Wild Man, the one who played outside the game.

And he'd gone about it all wrong. He could see that now. He thought he was beating the system by defrauding credit card companies, but really he was just getting into a new game. A game that he ultimately lost, that beat him first when he lost Wendy, and that he didn't have enough sense to stop playing, so it clocked him again and again; by sapping him of all identity, and then mutilating his hand and robbing him blind.

He sat with his back against the wall of his empty apartment, his knees up. The detritus of his relationship with Wendy was scattered around him in a small circle on the vast rug. He looked around the bare walls and felt adrift, like a shipwreck victim grasping at the splintered remains of the boat, clinging for dear life.

Because after seven years and several brief relationships that never set so much as a ripple across the still, deep waters of his heart, he could not forget her. Or rather he could not forget the dream of what they could have been together. A dream that had been her dream, and that he had forgotten he shared until just now, reading her words. Because despite all his quibbling over how she chose to describe it, despite her doubts of his ability to imagine it, he knew it well. He had no words of his own to describe it, but he knew how it felt. He knew it like a favorite T-shirt, by feel. A life they could have together, a life of mutual joy.

It was like that summer they'd spent before college, when they made their own world out of the streets of Elmdale. It was, he knew now, the only world in which he could be happy, and out of fear, he'd abandoned it.

CHAPTER
23

Years of scamming off of other people's credit had left Ray's own remarkably pristine, and since he had rented his old loft in his own name, and bought his first car that way, too, he wasn't burdened with a total lack of credit history. So it was no trick for Ray to scam himself, and open a line of credit in his own name. Of course, he'd have to pay up eventually. That's why he traveled by bus back to Elmdale, and rented the cheapest car he could find, and booked a room at the cheapest hotel in town.

That would be the Rialto, the logical conclusion to a progression of decrepitude over the past few blocks of North Boulevard. It was white, or mostly white, with an air of genteel decay about it; the geometric arch over the entrance a nod to the heyday of Art Deco. Paint peeled from its pillars to reveal the light yellow of happier days.

He checked in—signing his own name—and dumped his suitcase on the bed. Its white, chenille-draped bulk shuddered and squeaked in protest. He turned on the air-conditioning and went down to the coffeeshop on the corner.

Ray sat in a corner booth and ordered coffee. He gazed out the window at the cloudy afternoon, the soft gray sky brushed by the tops of trees, like her eyes with her hair hanging over them.

The feeling that she was here in town washed over him, and he foolishly wallowed in it. His hands, unbidden, took his wallet from his breast pocket and withdrew the small, folded piece of paper on which he'd written Wendy's phone number and address. The creases were already wearing out, from being unfolded and refolded so many times. Might as well get it over with, he thought, and he paid the waitress and retreated to the privacy of his hotel room to make the inevitable phone call.

It had been six years since she'd moved in there. She wouldn't be there anymore. He steeled himself for the three-toned shriek of an out-of-service number, but instead someone picked it up on the third ring. "Hello?" It wasn't Wendy. He would know her voice.

"Yes. Can I speak to Wendy, please?"

There was a pause. "She's not in right now. Can I take a message?"

He thought about it. She might not want to talk to him. His best bet was probably to surprise her. "No, that's okay. I'll just call again later. Do you know when she might be back?"

"I honestly have no idea," said the woman.

"Oh. Okay, then," said Ray, and hung up. The moment the receiver hit the hook, he was filled with a wild elation. She still lived there.

So what if she wasn't there now? She would be, and he'd keep calling. He'd go there if necessary, camp out on her doorstep. In fact, maybe it was just as well she wasn't there tonight. It gave him time to think of the right thing to say.

He pulled her journal out of his flight bag and opened it at random. He read:

Morality is strictly a human characteristic, and consequently, humans are the only things capable of behaving morally, which makes it all the more imperative that we do so. We're the only ones who have a choice. Far from abandoning moral behavior, separating it from the concept of a moral structure to the universe, from god, if you will, actually strengthens the need for moral action, and places the responsibility for it right where it belongs, not with god, but with ourselves.

And I do think that every human being, unless damaged in some way, knows the difference between right and wrong. Not according to some rules put down in a book somewhere, but on a case-by-case basis. You know, when you're in that situation, whether you're doing right or wrong. It's called a conscience, and I believe it is an instinct, a moral instinct that humans possess, and I think that if you listen to that instinct, pay attention to it, you can develop it sufficiently to where you are not blinded by the letters of laws, but can see before you the truth of the matter.

So I guess I'm some sort of moral anarchist. Unfortunately, I don't think enough people pay attention to their moral instinct to make real anarchy a pleasant proposition.

Ray put the journal down and walked to the window. He stared out at the pet shop across the street. B'WANA DON'S read the sign, its letters painted to resemble pieces of bamboo. Sticking with the whole jungle theme, a monkey peered out from the hole in the "o," inexplicably licking its lips with a faded red tongue. He turned away and stared at the phone. No, it was too soon. He grabbed his wallet and went downstairs to the liquor store next to the coffeeshop. He bought a six-pack of Bud and went back to the room, opened a can, and picked up Wendy's journal again.

If there is a moral structure to the universe, it is one in which the values are aesthetic. The proper balance of symmetry and disorder, to create a pattern, a beautiful pattern, like a fractal. Only we who are inside the pattern can only see occasional cross-sections of the overall pattern. We do our best to try and decipher what that pattern is, and we call our theory god.

Problem is, some people think they're right.

He mulled that over for a while, finished one beer and opened another. He tried calling Wendy again.

Again the same woman answered. "She can't come to the phone right now. Can I take a message?" she said.

"No, that's all right, I'll try again later. When would be a good time?"

"I don't know," the woman said impatiently. "Why don't you leave your number and she can call you back?"

"Uh, sure." Ray fumbled with the phone, picking it up to squint at the number under the little plastic strip above the keys. He read it to her.

"And your name?"

"Oh, my name."

"Yes."

"It's—" Panicking, he started hissing into the receiver while pounding the phone against the bedside table. He made crackling noises with a crumpled piece of newspaper, and then said "Hello? Hel—" and hung up.

Surprisingly enough, she didn't call back, though Ray spent that night and the next day in the hotel room, watching TV and living off take-out from the coffeeshop.

He stretched out on his belly across the bed, and picked up Wendy's journal again. He ran his hand over its worn cover, wondering if this was as close as he'd ever get to touching her again.

One day Hister and Lili were walking along in the forest and they heard the sound of laughter. But not good laughter, not laughter that comes from joy. This was the bad kind; mean laughter.

Going toward the noise Hister and Lili found a group of grugs tormenting a beautiful bird. The grugs stood in a circle around the bird, pointing at it and laughing. "Ha!" said the tallest grug. "Blue feathers! Who ever heard of blue feathers?!!" And the bird looked sadly at the beautiful blue feathers in its tail, and tears rolled from its eyes, and the feathers turned a dull, drab gray and fell to the ground.

Pointing at the brilliant spray of green and yellow plumage on the bird's head, one of the other grugs said, "Ha! Look at that stupid hat!" The bird sadly watched as these feathers, too, turned gray and fell to the ground.

Hister and Lili saw all this and said, "We have to do something to help this bird."

So they climbed up the tall tree in the middle of the forest, where the moon sleeps during the day, and they woke her.

Now not very many people know this, but the moon is also a mirror. When you look at her, you see yourself. So Lili and Hister told the moon about the bird, and she agreed to help them.

So Hister and Lili and the moon crept up on the grugs, who were still harassing the bird. By now almost all its feathers were gone, and it looked like a plucked chicken.

"Oh, what a pretty flower!" said Lili in a loud voice.

"Yes," said the snake. "Look at all the pretty colors it has! The petals are pink, and in the center it's yellow!"

"It's not like any other flower I've ever seen before," said Lili.

The grugs were getting bored with the bird by now because its beautiful plumage was all gone, and it was gray and small, and there was nothing for them to make fun of anymore. So hearing this, they ran over to see what Hister and Lili were looking at so they could ridicule it and rob it of all its unique beauty. But when they got to where Hister and Lili were standing, there was no flower. What they saw instead was the moon.

And looking at the moon they saw themselves, only they didn't know it was a reflection. "Look at those ugly creatures!" cried the head grug.

"They're ridiculous!" cried one of the other grugs. "They have ears on both sides of their heads!"

"And noses in the middle of their faces," chimed in the third.

"These are the silliest creatures I've ever seen!" said the head grug. "Look at how they laugh and point!"

The grugs were so busy ridiculing their own reflections that they didn't realize that with every word they spoke they got smaller.

"They have teeth in their mouths. That's so stupid!" said one of the grugs, and their teeth fell out.

"They have two arms and two legs," cried another, and their arms and legs fell off.

"Listen!" cried the third grug. "They're talking. Don't their voices sound funny?"

And with that their mouths sealed up and they couldn't talk anymore. And they realized that their arms and legs were gone, and their bodies were small, gray and shapeless, and in terror, they burrowed under a log and disappeared.

Hister and Lili thanked the moon for her help, and she went back to her tree to finish her nap. And Hister and Lili found the bird, who was still perched on a branch, weeping for its lost plumage.

"We took care of the grugs," said Lili proudly. "They won't bother you anymore."

"Thank you," said the bird, "but what am I going to do? My feathers are all gone and I can't fly."

"They'll grow back," Hister told the bird, "and until they do, you can stay with us."

And so the bird did. And when its plumage grew back, twice as brilliant and luxurious as before, the bird told all its friends and relatives of their kindness, and that's how Hister and Lili became friends with all the birds in the forest.

The End.

Ray put the journal down, rolled onto his back and stared up at the ceiling. She'd written that when she was fourteen. Back then she'd been the bird, denuded of her inner beauty by Kyle Denreddy and the other grugs. But it could just as easily be about him now, only his case was more severe. He hadn't just lost his feathers, he'd convinced himself he didn't want them. He'd sided against himself by abandoning his own identity.

Ray heaved a sigh, sat up and pulled the cardboard box closer. He took off the lid and fished out the worn brown folio. He sat with it unopened in his lap for a moment. Then he reached back into the box, pulled out his sketch pad and pencils, and turned to a blank page.

Later that night, he tried Wendy one more time.

"Hello?" This was a different woman from before, her voice was vaguely familiar, but it still wasn't Wendy.

"Uh, is Wendy there?" asked Ray, wincing at the pleading waver in his voice.

"No." There was a pause. "Who is this?" she asked sharply.

"Um. I'm an old friend of hers."

More silence. Then, "This is Ray, isn't it?"

He finally placed the voice. It was Lorca. Shit, if there was one person on this earth who'd make sure he never saw Wendy again, it would be Lorca. What could he say? She obviously recognized his voice. Best to just downplay the whole thing. "Yeah, I'm in town and I just wanted to say hi."

"Well hi, Ray, how's it going?"

"Fine."

"Great, glad to hear it. Now what's up?"

"What do you mean?"

"It's been seven years and we never heard from you."

We. Ray's blood went hot with jealousy, but Lorca wasn't through.

"All of a sudden you call, and you have to talk to Wendy like it's life or death."

"It's not. I just happened to be in town and I thought I'd look her up, that's all."

"Well, if it were as casual as all that, you wouldn't be calling three times a day and bashing your phone against a table to avoid leaving your name. Why are you so desperate to reach her, now, after seven years? What do you want?"

"I—" Ray found himself incapable of answering that question, truthfully or otherwise. "Look, will you just tell her I called? I'm at the Rialto on North Bouleva—"

"Listen, Ray, even if Wendy could come to the phone she wouldn't want to. You ran out on her when she needed you most, you abdicated your responsibility. She's made it clear to me in the past that she never wants to speak to you, so you can call as many times as you want to, but you won't talk to Wendy."

"You said even if she could. Is something wrong? Is she okay?"

Lorca didn't quite disguise a sigh. "She's fine. We don't need your help, just leave us alone," she said and hung up.

Immediately Ray called back, but he got a busy signal. She'd taken the phone off the hook.

Suddenly frightened, Ray sat on the edge of the bed, the forgotten receiver in his hand bleeping a counterpoint to his racing heart.

Lorca was lying. Wendy was not fine. Something was wrong, he could tell by the way the steam went out of her as soon as he asked that. And she'd said they didn't need his help. Two things were fishy about that; Lorca never admitted that Wendy needed help of any kind, and Ray had never actually offered any.

Though he would have. He hung up the phone to silence its tonal recriminations. He'd learned a long time ago that helping Wendy was worth it. Only he'd forgotten. He was stupid like that, a slow learner.

The next day he was down on the corner of 135th and Sixth, across the street from Wendy's apartment building. He got himself a seat by the window in the café there, lingering over coffee until the collective glares of the staff behind the counter drove him back out into the street. There was a public phone on the corner. He went over to it, picked up the receiver and pretended to be having a conversation with someone, all the while keeping an eye on who went in and out of the building. He hadn't seen Wendy yet.

A woman in a paisley flowered skirt struggled up the steps with two plastic shopping bags. He wasn't sure, but it might be Veronica. Two boys in jeans and flannel shirts with the sleeves cut off came out, jouncing down the steps and ambling up the street, shoving each other cheerfully.

As Ray chattered nonsense to the phone's "If you would like to make a call . . ." the sun inched toward the top of the buildings. "I can't Thursday, I have to pick up the elephant," said Ray as an elderly lady passed by, walking a herd of poodles. A man with an aged porkpie hat slouched over his forehead walked up the steps, his hands thrust into the pockets of his rumpled gray suit coat.

The woman in the paisley skirt reappeared, walking down the steps and up the street with a brisk gait. This time he was certain it was Veronica. Great. He hadn't seen hide nor hair of Lorca. Maybe she didn't live here, maybe she was at work. At any rate, he'd never have a better opportunity than this, so he hung up the phone and went across the street to the foyer of the apartment building. Scanning the apartment numbers, he saw a name he recognized: Danes, L., 305. So Lorca was living there after all. He went back out to the street, and around to the alley in back.

Standing there, scanning the back wall for a way in, he suddenly felt foolish. Was he really going to break in? What did he hope to accomplish here? But then, the waver in Lorca's voice when she told him, "We don't need your help, just leave us alone," spurred him on.

It was an old building, brick, with cornices on the windows, and a fire escape to boot. He went up to the third floor, and taking a wild guess, went over to a pair of French windows. The curtains were drawn, no information there. He tried the latch, it was locked. Was there an alarm system? he wondered. Only one way to find out, he thought, and throwing subtlety to the wind, kicked at the seam where the two windows met. They popped inward, and Ray drew aside the drapes and climbed inside.

The place was decorated in early Pier 1, all kinds of primitive statues, batiks, cushions. A monstrously ugly orange velour couch squatted in the middle of the room. The place was quiet. He was fairly certain no one was home. Directly across from him was the TV, the corner to the left of it dominated by shelves overflowing with books, plants, and more statues. That would be a good resource, if he had time for it. To the right of the TV was the front door, to the right of that a kitchen, separated from the living room by a counter. A door to the left of the French windows led to a bathroom filled with scattered towels, bottles of lotion and soap, and several pairs of pantyhose drying on the towel rack—no help there. He shut the door again and turned around. On the other side of the room a short hallway led to four other doors.

The first one he opened was a closet: sheets, blankets, that kind of stuff. Ray opened the second door. It was a bedroom. Clothes lay in piles about the floor, there was a bed, a desk with a computer, a dresser. The wall opposite the bed was covered with pictures of ancient carvings, goddesses. With a start and a lurch in his heart, he saw his old self-portrait up there. So this *was* Wendy's room, and she hadn't forgotten him entirely.

On top of the dresser were more photographs. Wendy, Lorca, Veronica, and a woman Ray didn't know, all dressed in black with peaked hats at some party; Lorca and Veronica at a lake somewhere; a wedding picture of Wendy's mom and dad; and toward the back, half-turned to the wall, a picture of Wendy and him on his mother's front lawn, all done up for the junior prom.

Unbidden, his hands reached for it, his fingers tracing those happy faces, as if he could grasp what had been lost and pull it into the present by sheer force. He opened the top drawer of the dresser; socks and underwear. Embarrassed, he stopped himself. He didn't break in here just to rummage around in her underwear drawer.

He glanced around the room again. Sitting on the bedside table was a spiral-bound notebook. He went over and picked it up, opening it at random.

I'm so glad I crossed paths with Zazula Von Sach. To think that if I hadn't waited on her that day at the Nugget, this plan never would never have come about. I'm so excited, Lili. Zazula and Lorca both say it won't be much longer now. It feels like it's been forever already. Oh, and Zazula had a great idea about how to deal with the—

"What the fuck do you think you're doing?" said someone behind him. Ray spun around to see Veronica charging at him with a brass, multi-armed statue in her hand. It was definitely Veronica. Ray had time to notice that she looked older, yet still somehow girlish in her print skirt and concert T-shirt. She lifted the statue and coshed him on the forehead with it. That was about the same time she recognized him.

"Shit! Ow!" yelled Ray, dropping the notebook and reeling back against the wall.

"Crap! Ray? Ray! I'm sorry! Fuck, what are you doing here?" Apology and outrage warred in her voice.

"Uhh." Ray let himself sink to the floor, his right hand over the gash she'd carved in his forehead. Blood poured over his fingers.

Veronica knelt at his side. "Are you okay?"

"Um." There were so many ways in which he was not okay, Ray didn't know where to begin. "Yeah, I guess."

"Tsk. Let me see." She peeled back his fingers and probed the gash. "Oh, I think I just grazed you. Head wounds always bleed like a moth-erfucker. Can you get up?" She stood and offered him a hand.

Ray struggled to his feet and let her lead him back to the couch in the living room.

"Have a seat," said Veronica. She noticed his bandaged left hand. He must have reopened the wound climbing up the fire escape. Blood seeped through the strips of T-shirt he'd bound it with. "What happened there?" she asked, pointing at it, her hands on her hips.

"Um, long story," he said. "It's a puncture wound. I keep pouring hydrogen peroxide on it, and it seems to be doing okay." At least his hand hadn't turned black and fallen off, so far.

She gave him a pained sigh. "Puncture wounds are some of the most dangerous. Let me see." She unwrapped his hand and looked at the wound critically. "Not bad, but you should have gone to a doctor." She stood and went into the bathroom, returning with a washcloth, a roll of gauze, and some Band-Aids. "You know you scared the crap out of me," she said as she redressed his hand and cleaned the cut on his forehead. "I thought you were a burglar or a rapist or something." She looked at him speculatively. "You're not are you? Here to rob or murder or rape somebody?"

"God, no! Nothing like that! I was just—"

"Breaking in," she finished for him.

Ray shrugged.

"So it *was* you who's been calling." Veronica went into the kitchen and returned with a couple of cans of Coke. She handed him one and sat down in the wicker chair on the other side of the wooden chest that served as a coffee table. She shook her head sadly. "Stalker city, man. What did you hope to accomplish here today, Ray?"

He shook his head and opened his pop. Of all of Wendy's college girlfriends Veronica had always seemed the most well-balanced. She never vilified him as a representative of all mankind, she never joined in when the others tried to put him on the spot. Therefore her well-founded exasperation stung all the more. How could he tell her about the dead end he'd hit? About how he realized he'd made the biggest mistake of his life breaking up with Wendy. That she was the love of his life, and there would never be another.

As it turned out, he didn't have the chance, because she was talking again. "Is it the power thing?" she asked, popping the tab on her pop and lifting it for a long, slurping swallow. "You have low self-esteem, so you're trying to assert yourself by controlling her?"

Ray laughed, which made his head ache. Lifting his hand to the Band-Aids, he said, "Does it look like I'm in control of anything? Jesus, I can't even talk to her. Where is she anyway?"

Veronica sighed and stared at him wearily. "That's really none of your business, now is it?"

"I'm just concerned about her. I want to make sure she's all right."

Veronica tilted her head in irritation. "And why wouldn't she be all right? Because she's a woman? Because without a man in her life she can't possibly be okay, better than okay, even?"

Ray raised his eyebrows. "There's no man in her life?"

Veronica stared at him and took a long pull on her drink.

"Oh. Oh Jesus God!" He lifted his pop can to his forehead, having forgotten opening it, and dribbled cola on the rug. "So she's gay now, then?"

Veronica rolled her eyes and stared at the ceiling. For a moment she appeared to be in prayer. She took a deep breath, exhaled, and then, eyes still fixed on the immutable, said, "Wendy is fine. We're all fine. She doesn't need your help, she can—" She stopped, looking at him. "She can take care of herself."

Ray nodded, drank what was left of his pop and stared at the wax rings on the coffee table for a little while, desperately trying to maintain. If she was a lesbian now—and he could just see Lorca talking her into it—then there was no hope for him. He'd been trumped by the all-time, ironclad foolproof brush-off of the modern age. With an effort he collected himself. "Yeah. I know her, and I know that's true. But whatever trouble she's in—"

"I didn't say she was in trouble," retorted Veronica.

Ray looked at her. He had his opening, and he went for it. "You said she could take care of herself, implying that there's some situation or person she has to take care of herself from."

"If there's anyone she has to take care of herself from, it's you." Veronica's gaze was level, measuring.

"I just want to help," said Ray.

"Well," and she looked away. "There's nothing for you to help with."

Bingo. She was lying. She couldn't look him in the eye and tell him nothing was going on. He was just about to ask her who Zazula Von Sach was, when the front door opened and Lorca came in.

She wore a worn brown corduroy blazer, jeans, and a diaphanous yellow scarf bunched around her throat. "Oh," she said, looking past Veronica to where Ray still sat on the couch. Her eyes widened and then hardened to a brilliant shine. "Well, if it isn't Ray! How you doing, Ray?"

She stalked toward him, and he shifted with fear. "Hello, Lorca," he said. "How've you been?"

Lorca sneered at him. "What are you doing here, Ray?"

He shrugged. "I came to see Wendy."

"Wendy's not here."

"Yeah, well, so I hear."

"Yeah, 'cause that's what we've been telling you every time you call. How'd you get in, anyway?" She cast a glance at Veronica.

"He broke in," Veronica told her.

Lorca turned to her. "Do you mean to say this guy broke in here, and you're letting him sit on our couch drinking Coke?"

"It's empty," said Ray, upending the can to prove it.

Veronica shrugged. "I guess I felt sorry for him."

Lorca snorted. "Only you could feel sorry for a stalker."

"I'm not a stalker," Ray protested.

Lorca laughed. "Oh, please. The incessant phone calls, now you break in; it's textbook. We should call the cops, slap a restraining order on you."

"Oh yeah, well why don't you?" Ray stood, which made his head throb. He thought better of it and sat down again. He glanced at Veronica. "I notice that you didn't even think of it, though that would be the logical response if you came home and found an intruder. Instead you took matters into your own hands and bashed me with some Hindu deity." He waved his hand at the gash on his forehead.

"You clocked him with Kali?" said Lorca. "Cool."

Veronica gave her a little smile.

"I'll tell you why you won't call the cops," said Ray. "You're afraid."

"Afraid?" Lorca and Veronica said in unison. A glance passed between them. Lorca laughed again, but this time it seemed forced. "That's ridiculous," she said.

"Okay." Ray nodded. "Then you won't mind telling me who Zazula Von Sach is."

Veronica gave a little gasp. Lorca's smile faltered, and she struggled to regain it. "She's a researcher," she said lightly, though her eyes were boring holes through his skull. "A colleague of mine."

"Oh, a colleague of yours. And this plan?"

Lorca's eyes widened, but she managed to keep the smile. Beside her Veronica had gone stone-faced and was watching them both closely. "What plan?"

"The one Wendy mentions in her journal," he nodded toward the bedrooms.

Lorca curled her lip. "You read her journal? Ew. Did you paw through her underwear drawer, too? This is disgusting." She looked to Veronica, who nodded and looked at him with an expression of stinging disappointment.

Ray nodded. He definitely had them off balance. Lorca was changing the subject, but it gave him a chance to make his Big Bid for Sympathy. "Yeah, you're right. I am desperate, but not in the way you think." He swallowed. "See, recently I had a really, really close brush with death and—" He shook his head and stared at his feet. "I realized what a terrible thing I'd done, for me as well as her. I decided to get out of, you know . . . the business, and try to make amends. I don't know if she *can* forgive me, but I had to at least apologize, and tell her how much—" This was getting to him. He was trying to get their sympathy, sure, but as he spoke he found the words coming from a place that had nothing to do with deception. "How much she meant to me, how much she still does." He looked up from under his eyebrows to see if this was having any effect. It didn't seem to be. "So I came back to talk to her, and you ladies give me the runaround. Every time I call, Wendy's out, or she's busy, she can't come to the phone. I think, I'm not a complete idiot, these women are lying to me. Wendy's there, they just won't give her my calls, or another distinct possibility, she's telling them to say these things because she doesn't want to talk to me—"

"That was what we were shooting for," agreed Veronica. "The second one."

"Yeah well, whatever. The point is I need to talk to her. I realized that for the last seven years of my life I've been asleep, and now I've woken up, and . . ." He gasped for breath. His head was swimming. "I don't know what I'll do if I can't f-f-find her." He was hyperventilating. He lowered his head between his legs, struggling to control his breathing.

"Jeez, dude," he faintly heard Veronica say over the blood pounding in his ears. He forced himself to take long deep breaths, but the thought that he had lost Wendy forever kept catching at his lungs, making them spasm in panic. Eventually he got over it by thinking about these women, Lorca and Veronica, the other one who'd answered the phone, how much they hated him, how hard it was going to be to get their cooperation. And he *had* to get their cooperation, because Wendy was . . . because.

He waited until his vision cleared, until he was breathing normally again, and then he sat up. Veronica and Lorca were looking at him with stunned expressions. Silent, awaiting the next development. "Think what you want of me," he said, "but I care about Wendy, and if she's in some kind of trouble because of this plan of yours—"

"Fuck you!" shouted Veronica, suddenly standing up, stepping over the coffee table toward him, knocking down candles and pop cans as she went. "I was willing to give you a chance, despite everything Wendy told me, I thought you might be okay, but you're just another shit-for-brains cowboy who thinks he knows everything. You don't know anything at all. Get the fuck out of here, cowboy."

This wasn't good. Veronica, who'd always seemed so mild-tempered, was glowering at him with a murderous gleam in her eye. Lorca was all cold and logical, like always, but beneath all that egghead professional shit, she plainly hated his guts, and he could see it in the way she looked at him. Retreat was clearly indicated. Besides, by their behavior they'd already told him more than he expected there was to know. This was no innocent group of career girls sharing an apartment. These women were into something deep. He realized that in all this time they hadn't called the cops, and it sure wasn't because they didn't want him in jail. He needed to do some checking on this Von Sach person, but first he needed to get out of here. He glanced at Veronica. She was still his best bet. "I just wanted to tell Wendy how sorry I was. And I guess I screwed everything up. I'm sorry." He looked at Lorca. It took a lot out of him, but he told her he was sorry, and then he said, "Tell Wendy I'm sorry. I won't bother you again. I can't anyway. I have a flight out tomorrow." That last part was a lie, but he thought it might put their minds at ease.

The three of them looked at each other. Finally, Lorca stepped aside and pointed to the door.

He nodded, edging past her. And then he was out in the hallway, making tracks for the stairs before they changed their minds and made him the star sacrifice in one of their arcane rituals.

CHAPTER
24

There she was again. A big, tough-looking woman in a leather biker jacket standing on the corner next to the dry cleaners. Ray dropped the curtain and turned from the window of his room in the Rialto. She'd shown up last night about two hours after he left Wendy's apartment and she'd been there again this morning, talking on a cellular phone. Except for a break around twelve, presumably for lunch, she'd been there all day, staring at the hotel entrance, watching out for him. It made him feel all warm and goopy inside.

He left the window and went to the phone, dialing a local pizza place. He ordered a small pepperoni and promised a big tip if they'd stop by a liquor store and pick up a six-pack on the way.

He went to the dresser and stared at himself in the mirror. What was he doing here? He'd come to find Wendy, to apologize, to do whatever it took to get back together with her, but was that really the answer to his problem? Wendy had shown him who he really was, and he thought getting her back would bring him back to himself, but was that right? Who was he, if he couldn't be himself when he was alone? Was it wrong, maybe, to want to get that from her? Like he was using her? Did he want to get back with her because he loved her, or because he thought she could do something for him?

On the table by the dresser, his laptop beeped. The first of his background checks on Zazula Von Sach had arrived. Just as he was turning toward the computer, there was a knock on the door. "Pizza," called a voice on the other side. Ray got his wallet from the nightstand, hoping fervently they'd brought the beer. He opened the door. The guy wore a blue jacket and cap, both emblazoned with the logo of Pizza Pete. A six-pack of Miller sat atop the pizza box in his hands.

"Oh hey, thanks man," said Ray, pulling an extra twenty from his wallet. What the hell, might as well spend the money while he could. Besides, he could use all the friends he could buy. "Hey, what's your name?"

"Mike."

"Mike. Thanks again." Ray handed him the money.

Mike glanced at the money in his hand, and back up at Ray. "No problem man. Any time."

Ray set the pizza down next to the laptop, opened a beer and started paging through Zazula's report. She was currently residing at 81 Franklin Avenue in Belle Heights. She drove a pink Jaguar, license plate number 809-FGD. Obviously she was rolling in dough. She was currently employed by Holbrook University. He also got six previous addresses, and the roommates she'd had at three of them. She'd been born in Austria, married Leopold Von Sach at the age of sixteen and became a U.S. citizen when she was forty-five.

According to *Who's Who of Women Scientists in America,* she was one of the leading lights in biocomputing. Her profile in that worthy publication also stated that she'd attended the St. Vivian School For Girls in Bern, Switzerland, and that at the age of twenty-five she received twin master's degrees in biology and computing from Yale University. She then went to Cornell, where she began to combine these two disciplines while studying for her doctorate. Her Ph.D. dissertation, *Perception, Organization, and Recall Strategies of the Human Brain and Their Implications for Computing,* was published in several prominent journals in both fields, and won the Calvin G. Harkness Award for Innovation in Information Technology. Following her Ph.D., she continued her research at Cornell, where she also taught courses in biocomputing. At that point the profile broke off, merely stating that she was currently in the department of computer science at Holbrook University. The entry was two years old.

He did some checking on Leopold Von Sach and found out that he was a wealthy industrialist who owned several factories in Austria. He was thirty years older than his bride. He also found a death record for

Mr. Von Sach, dated three years after their marriage. The cause of death was listed as a heart attack. "Serves him right," Ray muttered.

So Zazula had been a child-bride, and from the sound of it, she'd left St. Vivian's before graduating. Which made her advent as "one of the leading lights in biocomputing" all the more remarkable. Obviously not a woman to let a little thing like the death of a husband too old for her get her down. He did some more checking in the tax records of Leopold's holdings and discovered that yes, indeed, she inherited everything. And sold the factories about a year after she arrived in the States. Man, she really *was* rolling in dough. Made him wonder why she even bothered with a job, but then, what would a leading light in biocomputing do without a high profile university research position?

Still, the convenient death of her husband aside, there was nothing here to indicate what she might be up to with Wendy. After all, men in their late forties with young wives and high-pressure jobs were known to have heart attacks upon occasion. Especially in Vienna, he speculated—all those rich pastries.

According to Cornell's records, she'd left that fine institution of higher learning twelve years ago. And according to her credit report, she hadn't started at Holbrook until five years after that. So she hadn't jumped from Cornell straight to the position at Holbrook University. Then why did she leave Cornell, when everything seemed to be going so well there? And what happened in that five year gap, anyway?

He ran checks on her roommates from the time she was at Cornell to when she resurfaced at Holbrook. And the death certificate of Georgina Hughs leapt out at him like a bloody dagger. A fellow faculty member, she'd been Zazula's roommate during the time leading up to her departure from Cornell. The cause of death was listed as atropine poisoning, and was deemed accidental. On a hunch Ray checked Zazula's insurance records for that time period. Bingo, a lengthy stay at the Bonaventure Psychiatric Clinic. Pay dirt. If only he could get into her psychiatrist's records.

He found the doctor's name—Herda Boshcroft—on the insurance report, tracked down her social security number and her birth date. As luck would have it she was still practicing at the same institution, so there was a chance she'd have records of Zazula's case on file in their system—if he could get in.

He did an email search, and found her home email address. He got a node number for her ISP, logged off, reconfigured his modem software to use Dr. Boshcroft's user name, and took a stab at what her password might be. He tried her birth date first, and got it on the second try: Dr. Boshcroft used the European notation. He rifled through her email to see if she'd sent herself anything from work, funny downloads, work files, anything. Luckily she never deleted her messages. He had to go back two months, but eventually he found a grocery list she'd composed when at work, and mailed to herself. He swiped her work email, located the institute's LAN number, and logged on.

According to Dr. Boshcroft, Zazula had some deep-seated problems. Her father, a self-styled behaviorist, treated his children and his wife like an experiment in natural science, taking notes on their behavior and maintaining a detached attitude toward them. Boshcroft diagnosed Zazula as a borderline sociopath, with a strong identification with her father. Go figure. Included among the psychiatrist's notes were transcripts of her school records from St. Vivian's. Reading them was like watching a photograph develop, the pattern of her life emerging through details.

At the age of nine, Zazula was caught keeping six kittens in her room. At eleven she stole some lab mice. They were discovered in a makeshift maze in her room. At twelve she stole some frogs from the senior biology class and dissected one of them. At fourteen she won first prize in the school science fair for an experiment demonstrating the relative effects of sugar in the diet of lab rats. At fifteen her roommate had to be hospitalized after consuming twenty-five cups of coffee at a single sitting. The girl later told school administrators that Zazula had suggested she do it, "to see what would happen."

His hands shaking, Ray saved all this stuff to a file on his desktop and logged back on using one of his regular I.D.s. He looked up atropine on a medical database, and found out it was a derivative of belladonna, a plant used for centuries as a cure for digestive problems and in larger doses, as a deadly poison. It turned out atropine also blocks reception of the neurotransmitter acetylcholine, associated with the function of memory. Abnormally low levels of acetylcholine were associated with Alzheimer's disease.

He switched back to *Who's Who*, and scanned the listing of Zazula's publications. In the same year that Georgina Hughs died of atropine poisoning, Zazula had published a paper in the *Journal of Neural Physiology* entitled "The Role of Atropine in Memory Manipulation."

He switched off the laptop and sat there, his third beer forgotten beside him. It didn't matter what his motivations were anymore. Wendy was in trouble. He could wallow in a sea of self-recrimination later, after he made sure she was safe.

Suddenly he shot up from his chair, knocking the empty pizza box off the table, and grabbed the phone. He put it back down again. After that scene at Wendy's apartment, not even Veronica would listen to him. They'd think he'd made it all up, or the fact that he'd gone to such lengths to pry Zazula's secrets loose from the past would just confirm their worst opinions of him.

But what *was* he going to do? He had She-Zilla outside just waiting to follow his next move, and he still didn't know where Wendy was, though the first place he wanted to check was Zazula Von Sach's residence.

Ray paced the floor. His foot crunched on something and he looked down and saw that he'd stepped on the pizza box. He looked at the Pizza Pete logo blankly for a moment, and then he picked up the phone again.

Pizza Pete," came the voice from the other side of the door. Good, thought Ray, it was the same guy. He recognized the voice. He took a deep breath. Okay, this was it. He had one chance, and one chance only. He opened the door.

The guy was standing there like before. "Okay, how much is it?" asked Ray, pretending to look for his wallet.

"Ten sixty-five," said the guy.

"Where's my wallet?" mumbled Ray. "Oh, you can set the pizza on the desk," he said as he pretended to search the bedside table. The guy came in and set the pizza down next to the computer. "Oh, yeah, I left it in the bathroom. Just a sec." Instead of going into the bathroom, Ray shut the door to the room and slid the security bar into place.

When he turned around the pizza guy was staring at him. "Uh-oh," he said.

"Now it's not as bad as you might think," said Ray, standing in front of the door. "I don't want your money and I'm not going to hurt you. I just need your help. Take a look out the window."

"Look, pal, just pay me and let me go okay?"

"I will, Mike." Ray opened his wallet, which had been in his pocket the whole time. "In fact, I'll do a lot better than that. I gave you a good tip before, didn't I? Just do me a favor and look out the window." He pulled a wad of bills out.

Mike looked at him uneasily, and then at the money, then back at Ray, more appraisingly. They were both the same size, both, apparently, thankfully, unarmed. It was a toss-up who'd win if it came to a fight. His eyes did a skittery little dance around the room, found nothing particularly alarming and then he backed slowly toward the window and glanced out it.

"See that fat chick down there in the leather jacket?"

He looked back at Ray. "So what?"

"She's part of a feminist biker gang, Mike."

He laughed. "Very funny. I gotta go." He stepped toward Ray, his hand outstretched.

"She's watching me," said Ray, slowly counting off twenties, watching Mike's face. "She and her friends are holding my girlfriend, and I've got to help her, but I can't leave here without being followed." As he counted out the twenty-fifth bill he noticed a sharpening of interest in Mike's eyes. He held up the money. "That's where you come in, Mike, and all you have to do is lend me your clothes—just your pants, jacket, and hat. So I can get out of here without being noticed. They won't know it's me, see? They'll think I'm you, and I can get to the bottom of what's going on here. 'Cause these bitches are into some deep shit, Wendy's really in trouble. I know it sounds crazy, but if you knew these women—real hardcore lesbian feminist man-haters—you'd understand. And Wendy, that's my girlfriend, she's just too kindhearted for her own good. She's gotten mixed up with these psycho-bitches, and now they won't let me see her, talk to her on the phone, nothing. It's some kind of cult thing, Mike. I've got to help her, but as long as they're watching me, I can't do anything."

Mike stared at him. "That's a pretty wild story—are you on something?"

"No, couple beers is all. Look Mike, I know it sounds crazy, but think of your situation. If I'd wanted to maul you, or kill you, or rob you, wouldn't I have done it already? Why would I make something like this up? What good would it do me?"

Mike shrugged and looked out the window again. "So these bitches are really on your ass, huh?"

"Like white on rice. And they hate men, Mike. They don't want me to see Wendy. They're purposely keeping us apart, even though she still loves me, I know she does." It felt good to say that last part, even if it wasn't true. "Mike, if you help me out with this, not only will you be making a stand for men everywhere against the mounting tide of political correctness, but I'll give you two thousand bucks just for sitting around here for an hour or two, while I go take care of Wendy."

Mike took off his hat and looked at it. "Make it four and you've got a deal."

"If you throw in your car keys it's a deal."

The guy laughed. "Sure, the shit heap's not worth two."

Ray walked out of the hotel in Mike's pizza delivery uniform, got into his car and drove off. The biker chick never batted an eye.

The wrought-iron gate to Zazula Von Sach's residence stood open, but Ray drove past it to park in someone else's driveway about a quarter mile down the road. He took the brown folio—now bulging with both Wendy's journal and his sketchbook—from the passenger's seat, got out of the car and walked back to the gate to Zazula's place. He kept close to the bushes along the side of the drive until he came into view of the house. It was a neoclassical, wedding-cake type of affair; white pillars, ornate cornices and window copings, the works. The gravel driveway swelled into a circle in front of the house. No cars there, but another driveway led off to one side of the place. He followed it to a garage. Ray peeked in the side door. No cars there, either. That was a good sign. Maybe nobody was home.

Ray opened a wrought-iron gate beside the garage and entered an im-maculately ordered English-style garden blooming with roses and bor-dered by box hedges. There was a back terrace. Ray glanced around for security cameras. He didn't see any, but of course with all these hedges, they could be anywhere. Screw it, he decided and walked up the steps. If this Zazula was half as paranoid as Lorca and Veronica were, she wouldn't call the cops either.

The rear entrance consisted of a large set of French doors, streaked with moisture and the shadowy leaves of plants. Just for the heck of it, he tried the handle. It turned. Ray tried to push the door open but something blocked it. He pushed harder and heard the clatter of pottery hitting a tile floor. He stepped through the opening and over the large potted palm he had overturned. Around him stood masses of potted plants; on the floor, on tables and chairs and several metal instrument stands that looked like they'd been conscripted from some laboratory or other. Ray picked his way around a grouping of cactus to the large oval pool in the center of the room. Glass panels in the ceiling above let light in to play upon the surface of the water, breaking the mosaic at its bottom into undulating blotches of color which intermittently resolved into a coat of arms: a big bird clutching a lamb in its talons. Yikes.

Ray walked around the pool to another set of doors that led out into a hallway with a black-and-white checkered floor. Ray listened intently for a few minutes, ready to duck back inside and hide behind a fern or something, but the house was silent. Ray followed the hallway past a huge ballroom equipped with a chandelier and a parlor that looked like something out of Versailles. A staircase led up and he took it, the stairs creaking at every step. He glanced nervously over his shoulder, but he didn't see anyone. Evidently no one was home. The second floor seemed to be mostly bedrooms. There was an office and a library, both of which might bear checking out, but he was looking for the big prize. A freak like Zazula just had to have a laboratory around here someplace.

And he was right. It was on the third floor. Actually, it *was* the third floor. She'd torn all the interior walls out, so that it was just one vast, white-tiled expanse of computers, lab tables, and weird contraptions. Ray wandered about the place, at a loss as to where to begin. He noticed a lot of the stuff seemed to be in disuse, and he zeroed in on an area where coffee cups, plates, and a Harlequin romance novel seemed to indicate that someone had been there recently. It was a computer workstation.

Ray stepped closer and peered at the screen. The screen saver was a hideous picture of a cat with the bright, gleaming red lips of some beach bunny soda shill pasted across its mouth. As he watched, its lips puckered and it made kissy noises at him. He took an involuntary step back, then grabbed the mouse to bring up the desktop.

He sat down on the black leather swivel chair and set his folio down on the desk next to the monitor. It had been silly of him to bring it, he realized. He'd thought that if Wendy was here, if he actually got to see her, then maybe showing her his recent drawings, or pointing out what he'd read in her journal might help somehow. Stupid.

He turned his attention back to the computer screen and checked the recent applications. He found a solitaire game, a word processor, and a program that, when he opened its help files, turned out to be a compiler for PDX, a programming language popular for coding simulations. In fact, it was running something right then. Ray pulled it up and was greeted by a stream of meaningless numbers. Spying a view menu at the top of the screen, Ray opened it and found that it was currently set to data. He selected graphic instead, and the numbers vanished, replaced by an undulating fractal, a many-hued, snakelike thing, twisting across the screen. He checked the view menu again, and found that his other options were algorithm and setup. He picked algorithm, and was equally baffled by the instructions listed there.

A thick cable ran out of the back of the CPU and trailed off behind a stack of crates. Ray followed it to a large, shiny black oval squatting in the middle of the floor. It was roughly eight feet long and came up to about his waist. The cable went into it at one end, and there were other tubes and wires as well. With a shock of horror Ray saw an IV stand beside it, fluid dripping. Until that moment, a part of him had been willing to believe he was overreacting. That this whole nightmarish scenario he'd come up with was just that, a nightmare. But now he knew it was true. With shaking hands he felt around the black oval for the seam of a lid, and found it and the latch also. His breath came in great, shaky gusts as he gripped the lid and raised it up. And what he saw almost made him drop it again. Wendy, naked and floating, wires trailing among her hair, electrodes all over her body. But what frightened him most, what really sent a spike of panic through his gut, were her eyes. Her eyes were open, but she stared right through him. And then she muttered something in a foreign language and cringed as if in pain.

Quickly Ray lowered the lid again. "Crap, crap, crap," he muttered, turning away, turning back again, putting his hands to the lid again and then turning away again. His whole body was shaking now, breaking out in sweat. What was he going to do?

A distant rumble interrupted his panic. It grew louder; the roar of a motorcycle. He had to call the cops, he thought. The people who did this to Wendy were coming back and he didn't know what had been done to her, or how to undo it, or what just yanking her out of that contraption might do to her. He glanced around for a phone, but couldn't find one. He remembered seeing one in the hallway downstairs, however.

He ran for it as the motorcycle reached a deafening crescendo and then, just as he reached the stairs, cut off. His guts twisted and he plunged down the stairs. There was no time, no time. He got to the front hall and saw the phone, one of those fancy French types sitting on a gilt table under a mirror. He lunged for it. The receiver was in his hand. It felt like a miracle.

"So I said, 'Move your sorry ass out of my way or I'll cut off your dick and feed it to you,' " said the biker woman from outside his hotel as she stepped through the door. She saw Ray and stopped dead in her tracks.

"Fantastic, good for you. It's about time men started being scared of us for a change," said an elegantly dressed older woman, coming in behind her. She followed the biker's gaze. "Oh."

Ray frantically jabbed at the keypad but before he could make the connection the biker barreled into him, knocking him to the ground. The phone went with him, crashing with a startled ring. She wrested the receiver from his hands and dragged him up by the collar. They did a little dance across the checkerboard tile in which his impersonation of Ginger Rogers failed miserably. "What the fuck do you think you're doing?" said his dance partner.

The older woman poked her head up beside hers. "Ooh, he looks scared," she chirped in delight. There was a gleam in her eyes wholly at odds with her refined appearance. Zazula, he thought.

"He better be scared," snarled the biker, " 'cause in a minute I'm going to take him outside and see how much I can get him to look like dirt."

"Now, now, Raven," said Zazula. "There's no need for that. I'm sure we can sit down over a cup of tea and settle this nonsense." She smiled at him, and Ray was suddenly reminded of the screen saver on the computer upstairs.

Raven twisted Ray's arm up behind his back and hustled him into the Louis XIV parlor. "Grab some pantyhose, Zazula," she shouted over her shoulder.

Ray struggled in Raven's grasp, and got a firm twist to the shoulder for his trouble. "Let me go," he gritted.

"No chance, dickhead," Raven spoke softly in his ear. "Wendy told me all about you. In fact, I met her at the abortion clinic."

Something went out of him then: his self-righteous anger, fleeing on his outgoing breath.

So, I understand you are most anxious to speak with Wendy," said Zazula, pouring tea from a hand-painted ceramic pot.

Ray sat securely bound to an ornately carved gilt chair. After tying him up, Raven had gone upstairs to check on Wendy, and now it was just him and Zazula, who sat across from him on a pink velvet couch.

"What have you done to Wendy?" he asked, his hands gripping the chair arms.

Zazula raised an eyebrow. "Nobody's done anything to Wendy."

"Bullshit!" he yelled, straining at his bonds. "I saw her up there in that-that thing! She was all, staring, and her face—She was in pain. What have you done to her?"

Zazula set down the teapot and waved her hand dismissively. "It's just a little experiment," she said. "Wendy's in no danger. In fact, she's getting to live out a long-cherished dream. She's exploring a virtual reality ancient Sumeria for signs of prehistoric matriarchies. Now, does that sound so bad?"

It sounded like something Wendy would eagerly involve herself in, at least. Supposing of course that Zazula was telling him the truth.

"Though to say virtual reality is really an injustice," Zazula went on.

"It's nothing like the kind you're familiar with; clunky animation, no smell or touch sensation, nothing like real reality." She dropped a lump of sugar into one of the cups and brought it over to him. "You must excuse our precautions," she said, indicating his bonds. "But I wouldn't want you to think I'm inhospitable. Sip." She held the cup to his lips. He didn't seem to have much choice. He took a drink of the hot, fragrant liquid. He was thirsty, he suddenly realized.

"You know, if all you wanted was a reconciliation, you've handled things very badly. A gentleman does not intrude when a lady is indisposed."

"I-I was afraid for her," he said, quite honestly.

She gave him a small, enigmatic smile, and offered the cup to him again. He drank. "You really do love her, don't you?"

Ray's fingers and toes tingled. Probably the pantyhose cutting off his circulation. He nodded.

"You would do anything to be with her again, wouldn't you?" Again the cup hovered before his lips.

"Yes," said Ray and he drank again.

Zazula sighed and set the cup back down, sinking onto the couch once more. "It's so romantic! After all this time, you come looking for her, only to discover that she's in another world . . ." Her face was growing fuzzy, as if she were being photographed through gauze. She rested her chin in her hands and gazed at him, her face now a blur, her voice coming to him as if from a great distance. "How I do hate to keep lovers apart. And it will be interesting, don't you think? To see what happens?"

CHAPTER

25

The crowd, the bloody ground, the sounds of the cane and Shula's own miserable moaning faded from her awareness until there was nothing but the burning of her body, like an unquenchable fire, an unstoppable force, pushing her forward. But to what? Why had she been chosen, if it was only to suffer and die? Had the goddess ever wanted anything of her but this, the agony of her flesh?

And then she saw her, Inanna, standing before her, clearer, more distinct than even the pain. And then the pain, too, was gone, the crowd was gone, the ropes that tied her were gone. Inanna held out her hand, and Shula took it.

They were in the same room where Inanna had prepared for her wedding. Shula was dressed once again in the robes of a naditum. There was no blood, no pain, and in the corner of her eye she saw the luminous, undulating form of the Serpent That Knows No Charm.

Inanna, sitting on her dais, said, "From the great above, I turn my ear to the great below. I, Queen of Heaven, turn my ear to the underworld. In the earliest days, An took for himself the heavens, Enlil took for himself the earth. Enki divided the waters and took them for his own. My older sister, Ereshkigal, took the underworld for her domain. But what of me? What of the maid, the Star of Dawn? What is to be my domain?"

"Lady," said Shula, bowing before her. "You are the ruler of all Erech. You are the Queen of Heaven, the Dawn Star. No light shines that does not burn with your fire. You have brought the mé, the sacred laws, to your city and your people. We in Erech worship you. Why do you turn your ear to the underworld? Why do you think of leaving your people? Is it because that is where I'll learn who you really are? Is that where I'll learn your true stories?"

Inanna said, "I am Queen of the Great Above, but my sister has a throne in the underworld. As long as she sits upon it, I cannot rest."

Shula tried to hide her consternation. In her ear the snake whispered, "Half of creation is not enough for her?"

"Attend me," said Inanna. "We will go to the underworld. My minister, Ninshubur, will wait for our return. If in three days I do not return to the land of the living, she will send up a cry of lament. She will tear her clothing, she will rend her breast, she will beat the drum in the public square, she will go to Nippur, to Enlil's bright house, and beg him to save his granddaughter, his precious lapis jewel."

"All very well for Inanna, but what of you?" asked the snake. Enlil would not be moved to rescue a mortal such as she, whose fate was death now or later. In the eyes of a god, her life span, shorter or longer, was too brief for concern.

Misconstruing her expression of doubt, Inanna continued, "If Enlil will not save me, Ninshubur will go to Ur. In the temple of Nanna, the God of the Moon, she will cry out, 'Do not let your daughter, your vessel of fine boxwood, be broken, do not let your shining jewel be buried in the dust of the underworld!' "

Still no word of Ninshubur intervening with the gods on behalf of Shula, Inanna's servant.

"If Nanna will not listen, Ninshubur will go to Eridu. She will weep in the house of Enki. She will say, 'Do not let your granddaughter be put to death in the underworld.'

"Father Enki is wiser than all the gods. He knows how to make the bread of life, he knows where to find the water of life. He will save me, surely."

Shula had her doubts on this. After all, hadn't Inanna taken advantage of his drunken generosity, carrying away the mé to Erech before the god had sobered and changed his mind? And what of her? She had carried away a mé, too, and lost it.

"Come now. I must prepare for the journey." Inanna rose. She went to the room where the mé were stored and took up seven in her hands.

"The mé of high priesthood, the mé of kingship, the mé of godhead, the mé of war, the mé of descent to the underworld, the mé of ascent from the underworld, the mé of truth."

"Watch out for that last one," the snake whispered to Shula. "It'll get you every time."

"These I will take with me to the underworld, they will be as seven armies about me," continued Inanna. "Come." And she waved Shula after her as she swept off to her bedchamber.

Shula lifted Inanna's palla robe over her head, and fastened over it the breastplate that drew men to her. She put on her wrist the gold bracelet and painted her eyes with kohl.

"Arrange my hair in locks across my forehead," Inanna told her. Shula barely completed that task before Inanna pointed to a beaded headband adorned with charms of gold, the very crown she wore that first day at the river. "Place the Shugurra, the crown of the steppe on my head."

Shula did so, and then placed the lapis measuring rod and line in her hand.

"Bring my lapis beads. No, the long ones," said Inanna. "Oh wait, I'll wear them both."

As they sailed down the river, the landscape became increasingly desolate. After a few days they came to a flat, featureless plain through which the river cut straight as Inanna's measuring rod. In the distance a series of tall white arches pointed up to the leaden sky, toward a mountain standing alone in the flat landscape.

As they approached the first arch, Shula spotted a white hillock to one side of the river. As they neared it, it resolved into the massive skull of some long-dead creature, and then she noticed the white humps of neck bones pushing up through the ground, leading like a series of weathered pillars to the arching ribs of the beast.

"Tiamat's bones," the snake whispered in her ear.

"Who is Tiamat?" she asked.

"She was the goddess, the primal source of life. Her son Marduk cut her in half, and made one half the sky and the other half the earth. Presumably this is the second half."

"I've never heard that story," said Shula.

"That's because no one has told it yet."

As they passed through the skeleton of the sundered behemoth, Shula saw birds flying in the lofty spaces between her upturned ribs. Her tail-bones lay toppled on the other bank of the river, and they nearly ran aground on her submerged pelvis.

As they left the remains behind them, Shula focused on the mountain, which was now visible as a huge pile of bones; skulls and spines apparent among the myriad splintered fragments on the near slope.

The river flowed into the mountain, but their way was blocked by a sluice gate. A tall figure in a vulture helmet and armor woven of hair and fingernails stood on a ledge beside the gate, a boat hook in his hand. With it he brought the boat to a stop. Inanna and Shula climbed onto the landing.

"Open the gate, Neti," cried Inanna. "I would enter."

"Who are you?" challenged the gatekeeper.

"I am Inanna, Queen of Heaven, on my way to the east."

The gatekeeper cocked his head to one side. "If you are truly Inanna, Queen of Heaven, on your way to the east, why has your heart led you on the journey from which none return?"

"Because . . ." and Inanna glanced at Shula. "Because of my elder sister, Ereshkigal. Her husband Gugalanna, the Bull of Heaven, has died. I come for his funeral, and to console my sister."

There was a rattling sound, and Shula looked just in time to see a small stone, fallen from Inanna's hand, skitter across the landing and fall into the water with a splash.

"So much for the truth," said the snake.

Shula glanced at the gatekeeper, who, if he noticed Inanna's lie, gave no sign of it. "Wait here, I will give the Queen of the Underworld your message."

When he had gone through the small door beside the sluice gate, shutting and locking it behind him, Shula turned to Inanna. "Oh Holy Inanna, great and awesome is your power, but I fear the consequences of your lie."

Inanna shrugged, and adjusted the crown on her forehead. "Don't be silly. If I told him the real reason, he never would have let me in."

Shula sighed. "I don't think he was fooled."

"Nonsense, here he is now."

The door opened, and the gatekeeper, Neti, said, "Enter."

As soon as Inanna stepped through the door, Neti removed the Shu-gurra from her head.

"What is this?" she protested.

"This is the way of the underworld," said Neti. "When you enter here, you leave all that you possessed in the living world behind you."

Inanna bit her lip. "Very well, you may take my crown, but you cannot have my lapis beads. Those I will keep."

Shula stood in one corner of the dim room, not moving, making no noise, hoping to be overlooked. But Neti's eyes were sharp, and accustomed to the dark. He turned to her, and after gazing at her for some time, said, "It seems the living world has already taken all that you possessed. You may enter freely."

"Hmm, you are welcome in the underworld," the snake said in her ear. "That's never a good sign."

The hallway was long, arching up into darkness above their heads. In the flickering light of the candle, Shula caught glimpses of bones in the walls: fingers, toes, and occasionally teeth. They came to another door, tall and clad in iron. Neti selected a key from the ring at his waist, and unlocked it. He admitted them, but as soon as they were through the door, he took the short strand of lapis beads from Inanna's neck.

"What is this?" she protested.

"It is the law of the underworld, you must leave all worldly things behind you."

Inanna gave a little stamp of her foot, but seeing that Neti was unmoved, she sighed. "Very well. You may take my short strand of lapis beads, but I will keep the long ones."

At the third gate, Neti admitted them, but once inside, he took the long strands of lapis beads from about Inanna's neck.

"What are you doing?" she said angrily.

"I told you," he said impatiently. "When you enter the underworld, you must leave behind all that was precious to you in life."

"Well, you can have my beads, but I will keep my shining breastplate that no man can resist."

Neti gave her a little smile, and they walked on.

Before they had walked in silence, but now Shula heard moaning and whispering, though she could not make out what was being said. Also, there was a growing stench of rotting flesh. Out of the corner of her eye she caught movement, and to her horror, saw a face partially buried in the wall. It blinked at her, and said, "Soon you will be as I."

Shula hurried after Inanna and Neti, those words echoing behind her, "Soon, soon . . ."

At the fourth gate, Neti removed Inanna's breastplate and again she protested.

"If you would enter, you must leave it behind," said Neti, who apparently was the one man who could resist it.

"Very well," said Inanna, "but I will keep my gold bracelet."

Wearily, Neti led the way. Again Shula heard noises, high-pitched and tittering. Risking a glance up she saw bats hanging from the beams of the ceiling. She relaxed. It was just bats. As they waited for Neti to open the fifth gate, one of them flew at her on silent wings. She ducked and twisted out of the way and sank to the floor crying. She'd caught a glimpse of its face, its wizened little human face.

Neti opened the door and Shula ran in before them. This section of the passageway was narrower than the others. It twisted and turned, branching in multiple directions. There were voices here, too, soft but distinct.

"You should have taken the herbs Enheduanna gave you . . . You should have stayed in Eridu . . . You should have run away from the temple, at least then you would have your child, now you have nothing . . . You should have left Inanna's birds in the garden and accepted your beating. How much better off you would be if you had. Your punishment has only been worse for being delayed . . . If only you had not dropped the birds in the first place . . . If only you had never met Inanna . . ."

Shula turned around and around, bewildered by the voices. These were not the whisperings of the Serpent That Knows No Charm. In fact, she had not seen the snake's glow in the periphery of her vision since she had entered the first gate. Now she could not see Inanna and Neti either, and from where she stood numerous passages branched off. She could not be sure which one she'd come down.

"If only you'd gotten pregnant sooner. You'd be a wife now, with a baby and a roof over your head . . . If only you hadn't come here . . ."

Shula stopped turning, and walked down the passageway in front of her. It was dark, but there was a glow coming from up ahead, around a bend in the passageway. When Shula rounded it she saw an alcove in one side of the passage. It was brightly lit with candles, and carved to look like the kitchen of Ur-Neattu's house. A woman knelt at the hearth, children played on the floor nearby. As she turned to put the stew pot on the table, Pada-Sin came in the door, and she smiled at her husband. She had Shula's face.

There were more of these alcoves. One showed Shula in the temple, scribing. Not copying from an older text, but writing her own words. Beside her on the table sat a small stone, her mé.

"Oh," said Shula, stepping toward her other self, but her double did not look at her, or give any other sign that she knew she was there.

These tableaux ranged from the sublime—herself resting in Belili's lap under the huluppu tree, the moon smiling down upon them, to the downright earthy—she and the shepherd boy locked together in a passionate embrace in the temple of the harlots.

The meaning of the last one was unclear to her. In it she sat in a room of startlingly sharp angles. She was moving her hands across a tray on the table, her face bathed in the flickering light coming from an opening in a box before her.

Shula shook her head and turned to an opening in the passageway that led to a large, dark hall, Ereshkigal's throne room, for there she sat on the dais at the far end. She was pregnant, dressed in black, with a crown of gnarled roots upon her head. She stared with eyes like bottomless pits of darkness at a figure before her. With a start, Shula realized it was Inanna, naked and bowed before the Queen of the Underworld. She had given up everything—robe, bracelet, measuring rod—after all.

From behind Ereshkigal's throne stepped seven tall figures, their faces hidden behind hideous grimacing masks. They came down the dais, to stand before Inanna.

"Behold my sister, Queen of Heaven, bowed before you seven judges, naked as a beggar," said Ereshkigal. "She has come here under false pretenses, claiming to mourn my husband's death, when really she wanted to steal my throne. Speak now, what is your judgment on her?"

The middle of the seven judges spoke. "The laws of the underworld are clear. None that enter here may leave. Our sentence is death."

"No!" protested Inanna, rising to her feet. "Let me go. I will leave you in peace."

"You should have thought of that before," said Ereshkigal. "Now it's too late."

The judges surrounded Inanna. She broke past them, leaping upon the dais and grasping Ereshkigal by the hair. Inanna pulled Ereshkigal from the throne.

With a shout of anger, Ereshkigal struck Inanna across the face and she fell. She was surrounded again by the judges, who carried her off the dais, and stood around her in a circle. One at a time, the judges pronounced their sentence, "Death," and fastened upon her a fatal gaze.

Shula looked away for fear of being stricken herself. When she looked back again, the judges were lifting Inanna's lifeless body, which they hung from a hook on the wall, like a piece of meat.

Seeing her queen, once so proud and bold, now dead and desecrated, Shula wept. For though Inanna had been thoughtless of her, and had gotten her into trouble many times, she had also led her to witness marvels and miracles, had soothed her like a sister, and looked on her with love.

"Who is that?" said Ereshkigal, who had resumed her throne. "Who is crying?"

Shula choked back her tears and was silent, holding her breath for fear that Inanna's fate would soon be her own.

"Be not afraid. Step forward so I may look upon you," said Ereshkigal. Already her judges were drifting toward Shula. She could come forward on her own or they would drag her before the Queen of the Underworld. Reluctantly, Shula stepped forth.

Leaning forward, Ereshkigal peered at her with eyes shadowed by sleeplessness. "Who are you?"

Shula sank to her knees, and bowed her head before the goddess. "I am Shula, the maidservant of Inanna, chosen by her own hand when I was but a slave. She wanted me to discover who she really was. Can you tell me?"

"Oh mortal, your queen is dead."

Shula nodded, looking sideways at Inanna's corpse hanging limply from the hook.

"You are in my hands now."

Shula trembled and looked at Ereshkigal, expecting at any moment to be struck dead like her mistress. But the look Ereshkigal returned held more pity than vengeance.

"You have already sent me one to stay here in your place," said the goddess, putting her hand to her distended belly. "You may leave here if you will be parted from your mistress's side."

Shula glanced again at Inanna's lifeless body. "My Queen is stricken, my Queen is dead," she said. "Once she was the glory of all Sumer, her face blazing forth like a thousand armies. Now she hangs from a hook like a piece of meat, with no cloth to cover her, no voice but mine to sing her dirge. I would sit vigil by her, if I may."

"Very well," said Ereshkigal. "Truly you are a loyal servant."

For three days and three nights, Shula sat vigil by Inanna's body. Occasionally, Ereshkigal spoke to her. "I, too, have lost one that I love. No more do his hands touch me, no more does the Wild Bull of Heaven station himself at my loins. I miss my man, oh mortal, I miss my man."

Shula nodded and bowed her head. "Great Lady, I am sorry for your loss."

"Sorry for my loss! You have lost two!" cried Ereshkigal, and Shula looked up to see her clutching her belly. "This one that I carry was yours."

Shula gasped and leaned forward, her hand unwittingly reaching for the child in Ereshkigal's belly.

The queen started, her face suddenly absent with pain. Shula realized that she was quite young. Only her gaunt cheeks and shadowed eyes made her appear old. "It has begun," she told Shula. "My labor has begun."

The pain passed, for the moment, and Ereshkigal refocused on Shula, as if she had just remembered she was there.

"I do not think you passed through all seven of the gates. Which hall brought you to my chamber?"

Shula thought of the twisting passageway, the whispering voices, and the glimpses of what might have been. "The Hall of Regrets," she told her.

"Ah, of course. You lost a child growing inside you, and you wonder, What if she had been born?"

Shula nodded, sudden tears rolling down her cheeks.

"But you must know that if that had happened, the child would soon have joined me anyway. You would have been thrown out on the streets, with no money, no family, no house to dwell in. Your baby would have starved."

Shula gulped, nodding her head again. "I'm sure that's true, but since none of that happened, I cannot feel as if it did. I can only know the sorrow that is mine. The sorrow of losing something before I even knew what it might be."

"And now you must witness the birth of your child in the underworld, where she will dwell forevermore."

"No!" cried Shula getting to her feet. "Let me have my child!"

Ereshkigal waved her off. "That cannot be, though you will recover something else you have lost."

Shula would have run at Ereshkigal, thrown herself at her feet, and taken her hem in her hands, but just then the goddess was wracked with another pain. "Oooh!" she cried, clutching her belly. "I am widening, like a door!"

When the pain subsided, Shula said, "In the Hall of Regrets, I saw many things. Most were clear in their meaning. My life as Pada-Sin's wife, for example, but there was one I could not understand."

"That is the one that has secured your passage from this place."

"I don't understand."

"No, but you did once, and you will again."

Not long after that, Ereshkigal's labor began in earnest. She trembled and wailed. Shaken by a vast pain, she threw off her robes, and rolled, naked and moaning, upon her dais. A pair of flies, buzzing, hovered over her. Where they came from, Shula could not say.

"Help me," cried the Queen of the Underworld, looking at Shula.

Alarmed, Shula sat up. "Don't you have a midwife? Is there no one else here who can assist you?"

Grimacing, Ereshkigal closed her eyes. "You are here."

In a nearby room, Shula found a pitcher of water and a basin. She brought them, and soaking a cloth in the water, lay it across the goddess's brow. She let Ereshkigal squeeze her hand when the next pain came.

"Oh, oh, my insides!" cried the Queen of the Underworld, and in answer came two voices, echoing her own: "Oh, oh, your insides!"

Shula looked around the room, but could not spot the source of these voices. All she saw were the two flies, which had lit upon the goddess's throne.

"Oh, oh, my womb!" cried Ereshkigal, and again came the echoing voices, "Oh, oh, your womb!"

Shula tried to remember what the midwife had done when Abpahar gave birth to Ilshubur. She held the queen's hand, and told her to breathe deeply. The queen, her face twisted in agony, drew breath in long ragged gasps. She crouched, straining to push the child from her wracked loins, and each time she cried out, a pair of voices answered her.

Her torment went on for hours, and Shula did what she could for her, giving her water to drink, wiping the sweat from her brow. At long last, she spied the curve of a bloody head emerging from the taut flesh of the queen's vulva. Ereshkigal screamed as her flesh tore from the force of the coming child. Shula reached out, catching the infant as it slid from her body.

It was a shriveled, wailing thing, covered in blood and a white, grainy substance. Instinctively, Shula lifted her shawl to put the babe to her own breast.

"Bite . . . the . . . cord . . ." panted Ereshkigal, taking the child from her arms before Shula could attempt nursing it.

Shula did, chewing through the ropy umbilicus that connected the infant to her formless, sustentative twin, the placenta. Looking up, she saw with sorrow that the queen had already brought the child to her breast, and was feeding her.

"Please," she began, but Ereshkigal ignored her. Her attention was focused on two figures who had emerged from the shadows.

"Who are you?" she asked.

As they approached, Shula recognized them. They were Zimsi and Yimsi, Enki's neuter servants.

"Who are you," repeated Ereshkigal, "who cried out with me in my pain? If you are gods, I will bless you. If you are mortals, I will grant you a boon. I will give you the river-gift, the waters in their fullness."

"We do not want it," said Zimsi and Yimsi.

"I will give you the harvest-gift, the grain of the fields."

"We do not want it," repeated Zimsi and Yimsi.

Ereshkigal tossed her head, and her tone became sharp with impatience. "Then speak! Tell me what you wish."

Zimsi and Yimsi looked at each other and then at Inanna's body hanging from the hook. "We want only that corpse there, hanging on the wall."

Ereshkigal shook her head. "It belongs to Inanna."

"Whether it belongs to our queen, whether it belongs to our king, it is what we wish."

"I offer you the bounty of the field, the fullness of the river, and you refuse them. Instead you ask for that dead thing hanging from a hook. So be it. The body of Inanna is yours."

In an instant, Zimsi and Yimsi had Inanna's body down from the wall and they laid it out upon the floor. Zimsi produced a pouch and sprinkled its contents over the corpse. Yimsi produced a vial and sprinkled its contents over the corpse.

Shula, with hesitant steps, approached them. They looked up. "We know you," they said. "You are her servant."

She nodded, and then said, "What are you doing?"

"When Inanna did not return from the underworld, her minister, Ninshubur, sent up a cry in the temple of Enlil, begging the Lord of the Air to aid her, but he said the goddess was too proud, that she had brought this upon herself, and he refused," said Zimsi.

"Then Ninshubur went to the house of Nanna and sent up a cry there also, but the God of the Moon said Inanna was too ambitious, that this calamity was all her fault, and he would not help her either," added Yimsi.

"But then Ninshubur came to the house of our lord, where she sent up a wail bemoaning Inanna's fate in the underworld," said Zimsi.

"Lord Enki has always had a fondness for Inanna. Even though she stole his holy mé."

"He gave me the food of life," said Zimsi.

"He gave me the water of life," said Yimsi.

"He turned us into flies, so we could pass through the gates as swiftly as a worried man's thoughts. He sent us here," they finished in unison.

Shula looked down, and saw that Inanna's eyes, vacant in death, now blinked, and stared up at her with life anew. Inanna coughed and sat up. She looked at the three of them, then raised her arms impatiently. "Help me up," she said, and when they had helped her stand, "Let us leave this place."

"Not so fast," said Ereshkigal, clutching the babe to her breast. She stood flanked by her seven judges, and as she spoke, the shadows in the room began to coalesce. "The law of the underworld is clear. None who enter here can leave again. If you wish to go, you must send another back to take your place."

The shadows, which had become twisted, grotesque forms—parodies of men and women—began to gibber.

"These are the gulla," said Ereshkigal. "They eat no food, they drink no beer, they accept no offerings. They do not know the joy of lovemaking, they have no children to hold dear. They tear the wife from the husband's side, they rip the child from the mother's arms, they have no mercy, and no remorse."

The gulla, small ones with bodies like twisted sticks, large ones like upturned kettles, attached themselves to Inanna with claws and jaws.

"They will accompany you to the world above," said the judges. "You will be free of them only when you name the one to take your place."

Inanna, beleaguered by the demons, turned to leave the presence of the Queen of the Underworld. Shula, her eyes still on the babe in Ereshkigal's arms, stopped her. "My Queen, you may be free of these gulla now. Name me. I will take your place here in the underworld."

Inanna hesitated, but shook her head, and the limbs of the gulla attached to her hair rattled. "No. You have served me faithfully, I will not leave you here in my place."

"But—" Shula turned to Ereshkigal. She threw herself on the ground at her feet and took her hem in her hands. "Please, oh please Queen, if my child must dwell here, let me stay, too. Let me rear my child in the underworld."

Ereshkigal looked at her long and hard. "Would you really be glad of that sacrifice? I think not. When this child was in you"—she nodded at the infant asleep in her arms—"you did not want it. You prayed day and night that I would take her from you, and I did. Now she is mine. You will return to the land of the living."

"Oh Goddess," cried Shula, awakening her child, who echoed her with heartrending wails. "Your words are harsh. Have pity on me."

"My words are true, and I have pitied you already."

Shula sat up, and swallowed her tears. "Please, Goddess," she said, looking into Ereshkigal's face. "I am at your mercy."

Ereshkigal smiled faintly, and adjusted the wailing infant in her arms. "Then you are mistaken. I have no mercy."

Shula reached for her child, but Ereshkigal struck her with her free hand, knocking her to the floor. The Queen of the Underworld threw a small stone at her, and said, "That is all you will take with you. Now go!"

Shula, lying on the floor, saw the pebble resting beside her, saw the carvings on its surface, and picked it up.

All the way through the seven gates of the underworld, Shula heard the wailing of her child. Her cry echoed over the plain as they sailed back down the river, and at night, over the chittering of the gulla, it echoed across the hills.

CHAPTER
26

As they approached Erech, the largest of the gulla walked before Inanna, the second largest walked behind her. The people of the city gathered on the walls and at the gate to watch them pass. Shula followed Inanna and her entourage of gulla up the broad avenue to the temple. The ramp to the temple entrance was lined with priests and priestesses. Shula spotted the ensi and the high priestess. Their faces were dark with worry. "That one there," said the ensi, pointing at the gulla who walked before Inanna. "He carries a scepter, but he is no minister."

The high priestess nodded her head. "And the one who follows her," she said, nodding to the gulla behind Inanna. "He carries a mace, yet he is no warrior."

Before the entrance to the temple stood Ninshubur, dressed in filthy rags. As they approached, she threw herself at Inanna's feet.

"Walk on, Inanna," said the gulla who was not a warrior. "We will take your minister in your place."

Ninshubur rolled her eyes in fear of the demons, but she did not flee.

"No!" said Inanna. "Ninshubur has been my constant friend and adviser. She wears rags in mourning for me. She sent up a cry for me in the house of Enki, she beat the drum for me in the market square. We have been companions in peace and in battle. I will never let you have Ninshubur."

"Walk on, then," said the gulla who was not a minister.

They entered Inanna's holy house, her temple. In the main hall a boy dressed in sackcloth cried out at the sight of them, and fell, weeping, at the feet of the goddess.

"Walk on, Inanna," said the gulla. "We will take this boy in your place."

"You will not! This is Shara, my youngest son. He soothes me with sweet hymns, he trims my nails, he combs my hair. He is the delight of my eyes. I will never give Shara to you!"

"Walk on, then."

They went to the hall where the accounts are kept. A young man, haggard, with doleful eyes, sat frowning over a tablet. When Inanna entered he cried out, and threw himself at her feet. "Mother! We thought you dead. I wished my days to pass quickly, that I might join you."

Inanna knelt and took her elder son in her arms. "I have returned."

The largest gulla grunted. "We will take this one then. Walk on, Inanna."

"No!" cried Inanna. "This is my son, my eldest son. He is a brave warrior, a responsible man. Loyal to me in my absence, he has kept the accounts. I will never let you have Lula."

"Very well then, we will walk on," said the gulla.

They entered the holy bedchamber, but it was empty. "Where is my husband, Dumuzi?" mused Inanna.

They entered the gardens. The gardens were empty. They went to the assembly hall, the pillared hall, and there on the throne sat Dumuzi, dressed in the shining robes of kingship. In his hand he held the scepter of sovereignty over all the land. At his side a musician played a reed pipe for the enjoyment of the King and his guests. Platters of food and jars of beer sat around in various states of consumption.

When Inanna entered, Dumuzi did not rise. He did not tear his fine clothing at the sight of his wife bedeviled by the gulla. He did not weep.

Inanna's face blackened with rage. "You! You who hold the kingship only by virtue of being my husband. You! Whom I gave sons, Erech, the bounty of the land, the crown of kingship, you dare to revel while I sojourn in the land of the dead! Oh, my heart. My wicked and treacherous heart, that could make me love such a one as you!" She turned to the gulla. "Take him!"

The gulla released Inanna and flew, chattering, like a storm of dead leaves, to attach themselves to Dumuzi. The larger gulla overturned the beer jars. The gulla with the scepter struck the flute from the shepherd's hands and smashed it with his foot.

The gulla beat Dumuzi and he howled. "How can you do this to me? I am your husband!"

Inanna did not answer. She stared in silence as the gulla tore the shining garments from Dumuzi's body and laid open his flesh with their knives.

Dumuzi screamed and blood ran down his face. Terrified, Shula cowered behind one of the pillars. When she'd seen Dumuzi, resplendent on the throne of Erech, she'd sympathized with Inanna. But now, seeing the form Inanna's vengeance took, she quaked with the agony of the Shepherd King. His friends, advisers, and servants had fled. He was in the hands of the gulla, who know no mercy.

"Why? Why do you curse me so?" cried Dumuzi, as the gulla twisted his arms, as they tore out his hair.

"Because you did not love me enough," said Inanna, and her words struck a chord in Shula, disturbing the slumber of some memory from deep in her unknown past. "You preferred the occupations of a king over the duties of a husband. Where are your friends? Where are your counselors? They have fled, they stand at your side no more. You cared more for them, for your throne, than you did for me, but you would be a shepherd still if I had not taken you to my bed."

"O" cried Dumuzi. "O Utu, my brother-in-law, God of the Sun, I brought food to the holy house, I kissed the holy lips. Have pity on me, the husband of your sister! For all the days we hunted together in good fellowship, turn my hands into the hands of a gazelle, turn my feet into the feet of a gazelle, let me flee this place!"

The sun came forth from the clouds. The sun came down from the sky in Erech. The demons torturing Dumuzi were blinded by the light. Shula was blinded by the light. Even Inanna, the Queen of Heaven, was blinded by the sun. And when the light faded, when the sun returned to the sky, it was no longer a man who stood surrounded by the demons of death, but a gazelle, agile and quick-limbed. The gulla could not hold it and the beast bounded from the hall.

The small gulla flew to Inanna. They attached themselves to her with claws and jaws. The larger gulla surrounded her, and readied the stock for her neck. "Come, Inanna. Your husband has fled, you must return with us," said the gulla who was not a minister.

"No! We will find Dumuzi. We will go to his sheepfold, we will go to his friend's house, we will go to his sister's house. We will find him, and he will return with you."

Shula, wishing for feet like a gazelle, attempted to slip from the hall unnoticed, but it was not to be. "My maidservant will assist you," said Inanna. "Shula!"

Shula turned, her stomach churning. "You will go to the sheepfold to look for Dumuzi."

"But the girl will run away," said the largest gulla.

"Then send some of the gulla with her," said Inanna. "I cannot escape even half your number, and you'll need only two or three for her."

"Very well," agreed the chief gulla. "You will come with us to the home of Dumuzi's friend, and Bilbul, Picpic, and Hothot will go with your servant to the sheepfold."

Three little demons, with wizened faces like malevolent babies, flew from Inanna's side, straight at Shula. "We'll fix her," said Picpic.

"If she doesn't take us to the sheepfold, we'll twist her arms in knots," said Hothot.

"We'll pour pitch in her vulva," enthused Bilbul.

As they dived at her, Shula screamed, throwing up her hands to cover her face. They fastened themselves into her hair, drawing it up from her head as they hovered around her, beating their batlike wings.

"You'll take us to the sheepfold, and nowhere else, understand, wench?" bullied Hothot.

"Yes," said Shula, her voice but a whisper. She bowed her head, the motion tugging at the roots of her hair, and directed her steps out of the temple.

"She's a worthless creature," said Bilbul conversationally. "Aren't you?" he pulled on Shula's hair to make her nod her head.

"See?" he said, fluttering madly in her face. He dragged one gruesome clawed finger across her cheek. "She cries."

"Oh yes, brother," chirped Picpic. "She's as doleful as an ox."

"Go on, ox. Ha!" yelled Hothot, lashing her neck with his tail.

Shula sobbed wordlessly and directed her steps out of the temple. She would not be rid of these, she knew, until Dumuzi was found.

The demons drove Shula out of the city and across marsh and field. As they topped the crest of a hillock, she staggered, her feet cut and bruised, and sank to her knees on the ground.

"Aw, she's tired. Should we let her rest?" cried Picpic.

"We could," said Bilbul, swooping down to nestle himself in her folded arms. "I can rest here," he said, making horrifying sucking noises as he nuzzled her breast. "Will you be my mama?"

Shula sobbed anew and pushed the thing from her arms. He growled and snarled, biting at her breast. Hothot and Picpic tugged sharply on her hair. "Never! Never will she rest, not until her bones have ground through her flesh with walking, not until the skin on her feet is worn away."

They tormented her until she struggled to her feet and started off again. Hours later, when Shula did feel as though her feet were raw and her muscles flayed, they came to a broad field with a gentle slope, and in its center the tumbledown sheepfold. Dumuzi's flock was scattered; only a few old rams and ewes remained. They pawed the ground at their approach.

The sheepfold was desolate. Water had been poured on the hearth and the butter churn lay broken. As Shula and the gulla attached to her crossed the threshold, the drinking cup fell from its peg and smashed upon the ground.

"Dumuzi is gone," she said, and felt horror and relief tear at her like the claws of these gulla. She did not want to turn any creature over to these demons, but she did not want to stay with them either. In distraction, she fingered the stone Ereshkigal had given her. Suddenly she remembered her night in the garden with Belili, when she asked her to be her guardian spirit, and she said she would, if Shula would remember that she was not always a slave. Well, she was a slave no longer, though she'd served Inanna as if she were. And what had it gotten her? Inanna had turned these gulla on her, as if she were just an extension of the goddess's own body and will. Shula squeezed her eyes shut, and she prayed to her guardian to deliver her from these demons.

Bilbul was busily sniffing the chair and the posts of the sheepfold. "I have it. I have the smell of him. Come, let us follow it. It will take us to him." And they were off, running again across the countryside, running until the breath tore through Shula's chest like a sword. They entered a wood, and stumbling over roots and through bushes, Shula and her escorts came to a small house in the forest.

When they reached the door, Picpic pounded on it. "Let us in! Let us in! We are the gulla from the land of the dead. We know no mercy, we know no joy. We will destroy your house if you do not open the door for us!"

The door opened and an old woman stood there. Shula recognized her at once, though the last time she'd seen her, she was a young girl. A young girl with long black hair and large black wings.

"Old Belili, we seek the king, Dumuzi," said Hothot.

"There is no place that he can hide from us, not even here," added Picpic.

"You may enter," said Belili to Shula.

Prodded by demons, Shula stepped through the doorway into the little house. A man, naked, his body covered with cuts and bruises, crouched by the fireplace. When he saw them enter, he cried out and stood up, and Shula saw that it was Dumuzi. "Old Belili, you are older than Inanna, older even than Erech. Help me. These gulla will take me to the underworld. They will dress me in thorns, they will beat me with sticks."

But already the gulla had flown from Shula's side, and they surrounded him, grasping him with their gnarled hands. Belili blinked, and muttering, threw something onto the fire. The air was filled with a sweet, smoky haze, and instead of Dumuzi standing there as a man, there was a snake on the floor. The gulla could not hold him and he slithered away. Furious, spitting bile and gnashing their teeth, the gulla flew at Shula once more, but Belili raised her arms and lifted her wings. "Enough!" she cried out. "Leave this one with me. You know you will find Dumuzi anyway. As you said, there is no place he can hide now that you have his scent. You do not need her."

The gulla chittered with frustration, but they did not advance on Belili, who stood in front of Shula, her wings spread protectively around her. With a single cry they swept from the house like dry, dead leaves rattling across the doorstep.

Belili sighed, and closed the door behind them. "They will find him, of course, out in the wilderness, and they will take him back to the underworld. But his sister will go after him, and half the year, she will take his place in the land of the dead."

"How do you know?" asked Shula.

"I read it somewhere. Are you hungry?"

Belili fed Shula, and bathed her, and gave her clean clothes to wear. Shula slept in a soft cot beside the fire, and when her feet healed, she went out into the woods and the marshes, gathering wood and sweet grasses for Belili's hearth. She loved the feel of the cool air moving through her hair, taking the past away with it. She loved the clean smell of the air, which scrubbed away the stench of the underworld.

One morning, as she neared the reed beds surrounding a small stream, she heard a voice raised in a song of mourning, a desolate sound, like the wind blowing across broken reeds. Following the sound, Shula crept to the top of a hillock and peered over it.

There she saw Inanna, crouching among the reeds at the side of the stream. The hem of her skirt was torn, her face was gaunt. "My heart is a reed piping in wilderness," she cried. "My heart is an instrument of grief, piping in the wilderness. The Wild Bull lies dead, the Shepherd, the Wild Bull is dead. Dumuzi lives no more. The jackal lies in his bed, the raven roosts in his sheepfold. His reed pipe is silent, only the wind can play it now. His sweet songs are no more to be heard, only the wind can sing them now."

Shula watched in wonder as the goddess smeared mud upon her face, as she piled dirt upon her head and beat upon her chest. How could she mourn him, whom she herself had condemned? Despite everything, Shula felt pity for the goddess, but she remained hidden behind the hillock. She would not go to her. Her guardian was Belili, who lived without fear. Inanna was powerful, yes, but she was not free. She walked in fear of the Sky God An. She betrayed her sister, Ereshkigal, and she could not bear the presence of a free spirit in her garden.

Inanna had asked Shula to discover who she really was, and watching her now, Shula thought she knew. Reckless and imperious, spoiled and capricious, she was an example to all the people of Erech; a reason for them to be grateful that they were ruled by a king and not a queen. A reason to make every man hold fast to dominion over his wives and daughters. She was an all-powerful god's uneasy dream of what a goddess would be, a cautionary tale of destructive female power.

Silently, Shula crept back down the hill and returned to Belili's cabin, leaving Inanna to her grief.

The next morning, Shula awoke with her back aflame, as if a bed of coals rested there. She lifted her head blearily to find that she was back in her cell in the temple prison. But she was not alone. A woman stroked her hair, and murmured soft words of encouragement. Craning her neck, Shula saw that it was the harlot priestess, Bilah. "What—" She struggled to sit up, but the pain stopped her.

"Shh," said Bilah. "It's all right, you're all right now. You lost the child, but you survived the ordeal. Here"—she pushed a cup of something steaming and bitter under Shula's nose—"drink this and rest."

When Shula awoke again, the pain had receded to a dull throb, and it occurred to her to wonder why she was still at the temple, why they hadn't thrown her out into the street by now. Bilah was still there, too, curled up beside her on the floor. Had they imprisoned her, too, for some reason?

At her stirrings, Bilah opened her eyes, and Shula asked her these questions.

"No, I haven't been arrested," she said, sitting up and rubbing the sleep from her eyes. "I'm here to look after you. As for why you're still here, when it became clear that the flogging would not kill you, Shapar consulted the oracle as to what your fate should be. The portents foretold that you would work yet another miracle, if you were permitted to join the harlot priestesses."

The door to the cell opened, and Urhulli stepped through. At the sight of her, tears sprang to Shula's eyes. She could not speak, but held out her hands to welcome her friend. Urhulli came to her, strong clean hands gripping her own. "You're awake. How do you feel?"

"Not as well as I could, but better than I have. At least I don't have to fend for myself in the public square, Bilah told me. I'm to be a harlot priestess now."

"Yes." Urhulli gripped her hands all the tighter. "I will miss you, but at least you are still alive, and you will be safe now."

"Until the next miracle," observed Bilah.

CHAPTER

27

One day a man came to the temple, a farmer's son from a far village. Shula attended him, gave him the holy rite, and afterward, as they drank beer together, he told her a fantastic story.

"In the wilderness beyond my father's lands, there lives a man who is not a man. A man who is wild. He runs naked with the beasts, he cuts not his hair, he grooms not his beard. He kneels at the side of the stream to drink, like a lion. He eats berries and leaves, like a deer. But for his ignorance, he is a man still, for his fingers know our knots, and he unties the cords that hold the game in our snares."

The man's eyes took on a speculative gleam. "We want him off our lands. We have tried driving him away with torches and clubs, but the man runs faster than a deer, and cannot be trapped, as I told you. But perhaps he can be civilized.

"This man is ignorant of women. Maybe if you show him the joys that are known to civilized men, he will gladly learn to be one. And then he can come to the city and find work, and we will be rid of him."

Shula considered this. The man was only mildly drunk, not Enki-drunk. He did not seem to be speaking flippantly, and she got the feeling he would pay her quite a few coins if she could get the wild man away from his father's lands. And this wild man was without knowledge of women—an innocent. It was a tantalizing offer.

She drank her beer and tried not to look too interested. "I'm sure I could turn him to civilization," she boasted, "but what will you pay me?"

"Five thousand mina, if you succeed."

"Give me half of that before I ever set foot from Erech, and I will do it."

The man sighed and shook his head. "It is impossible, I have traveled far to this city. I could not carry all that gold."

"You don't have it," Shula observed.

"No, no. My father, Shipullar, has many fields, many sheep and oxen. He is a wealthy man. He will be able to pay you handsomely."

Shula shook her head.

"To prove it to you, I will bring you tomorrow a goat of pure white, a goat as only a man with a herd of ten thousand would have. You will see. You can sacrifice it to Inanna, to bless your journey."

Shula stood, capped the man's empty beer jar, and handed it to him. "If you arrive tomorrow with such a goat, I will go with you," she said, laughing, and showed him the door.

To her amazement the man returned the next day, while she was mending some clothes. She had forgotten about his outrageous story, until he stepped through the door leading a goat of pure white. Without a word to him, she left her sewing and examined the animal from nose to tail. She couldn't find a single hair darker than the moon. Even its hooves were white, and its eyes were the color of blood. Kneeling beside the animal, she looked up at him. "I will go with you," she said.

Shula slaughtered the goat, offering its blood and a portion of the meat to Inanna, for this was her temple, and though Shula held Belili in her heart as her goddess, appearances had to be kept up. The rest of the meat she cut into strips and dried for the journey.

Saddle-sore and weary, Shula dismounted at the gate to Shipullar's farm. They had traveled three days. Shipullar's younger son, Nunna Sin, took the donkeys, and the old man welcomed her inside the house. He gave her broth to drink, and a place to sleep near the fire.

The next day the sun broke through the clouds and a warm breeze blew across the fields, scented with tales of the forest and the wild things that roamed there, and Shula knew it was time to seek out the wild man.

She took food and extra clothing in a basket, as well as a knife, oil for dressing the hair, sandals, and a man's tunic and skirt given to her by the farmers. She walked off across the fields where Shipullar and his sons broke up the soil for planting.

The trees of the forest were close set, the underbrush thick between them. Thorns tugged at her skirt and shawl, roots and fallen limbs tripped her, twice causing her to stumble and spill the contents of her basket. Her first days in the forest, she saw nothing but the plants and an occasional bird. The other creatures of the wood kept their distance from her, though she felt their presence, just past the edge of her vision, watching her from the shadows between the trees.

Maybe the wild man was among them, she thought as she sat on a fallen log, eating bread and pickled figs. All around her the forest seemed to be breathing, and she imagined it was his breath, hot in her ear. A wild man. What would he look like, she wondered, and imagined a hairy beast with long yellow teeth and lips stained red from the blood of some prey he had just eaten. She shivered and stood up, and gathering her things, set off once more through the trees. She came to a stream and she sat on its bank, dangling her legs in the cool water, letting it rinse the dirt from her weary feet. She refilled her water skin and left it on the bank beside her basket. She took off her skirt and shawl, and stepped into the stream to bathe.

Rising from the water, her sopping wet hair dripping rivulets down her face, she had the distinct feeling that something was watching her, but when she glanced at the banks of the stream, all she saw were trees and bushes.

Until she spoke it, he had no name; until she clothed him, he knew not nakedness. When the woman came, that's when he became a man.

He awoke one morning in a glade, the sun warming his eyelids, birdsong rousing his ears. He sat up and discovered he was thirsty. He followed the sound of running water until he found a stream. He knelt on its bank, lowering his face to the cool water to drink.

A she-wolf appeared on the opposite bank, her pups tumbling about her. She showed no fear at the sight of him, and he did not fear her. When she and her family had drunk their fill and disappeared into the forest once more, he crossed the water and followed them.

A little ways from the stream he found a bush with red berries on it. Awakening to his hunger he ate them, and foraged for more. He moved through thicket and glade, disturbing neither the spider's web nor the rabbit's burrow. The larks sang to him and the lion greeted him like a brother, washing the berry juice from his cheeks with his raspy tongue. As the sun neared the tops of the trees he heard a rustling sound, and following it, found a young buck, his hind leg caught in a loop of woven fibers. He quieted the deer with a gentle touch, with a soft, wordless whisper, and freed its foot. The buck regarded him calmly with large brown eyes and they were like brothers, and they ran through the woods together.

He spent his days with the deer, nuzzling with the foals at their mothers' teats when he was hungry, drinking at the stream, foraging for berries and sweet grasses. His brothers and sisters shied away from the smell of the lion and the wolf, but he often lingered where these beasts had passed, and he became their friend, too, though he never shared the meat they killed. For sport he wrestled with the lions, their tawny bodies twined around his.

Occasionally, most often at the edge of the forest that faced the morning sun, he found a beast or bird (once a snake), entangled in a loop of woven fibers, and he freed it. He did not know that hands just like his own had woven these snares. He did not know what men were, or that they hunted beasts with traps. He only knew the rush of the wind across his body as he ran with the deer, the smell of rabbits nesting in the night, the light of the stars, the warmth of the sun, and the sweetness of berries.

One day as he was drinking at the stream, his deer brothers and sisters fled from the bank, leaving him alone to lift his face and gaze upon the creature on the opposite bank.

He had never seen a creature like this one before, with hands and feet like his, legs and arms like his, but hairless on the face, so that the lips seemed very large, and looking at them gave him a strange feeling he'd never had before.

Shula slept in a hollow made soft with fallen leaves. She dreamed she was falling out of a blue sky, toward a city on the coast of a vast sea.

The city was huge, buildings and roads stretching out across the land as far as she could see. The buildings were tall, their spires reaching up toward her like fingers to drag her down. Carts moved along the roads at dizzying speeds, with no oxen or donkeys to drag them. As she fell, the noise of the city rose up around her, shrill trumpets and bells, and growling noises, like the rumblings of beasts. She had lost sight of the sea, her bewildered eyes taking in the shining metalwork atop the buildings; spires and great round sieves, and then she was past the tops of the buildings, falling between their sheer sides, to the road below. The buildings were unimaginably tall, their sides lined with windows that reflected the sun. This was not Erech, she knew. Mighty as it was, Erech was but an anthill compared to this city. The god of this city must be very powerful, greater than all the Anunna gods put together, for the people who lived here had done impossible feats of building to honor their god, to make visible to all in the land the greatness of his power.

And then she didn't think anything else, for the ground was rushing up to meet her, bringing with it incomprehensible sights and smells and sounds: bright colors, people dressed in strange clothes, voices calling out in an unintelligible language, and always the rumble and roar that she now realized came from the carts, which hid their beasts of burden in shining, brightly colored cases.

She plummeted head first toward the paving stones, revealed to be impeccably smooth in the moment before her impact.

Shula sat up, wide-eyed, panting, feeling with relief the softness of her leaf bed. And then she saw him, crouching in the shadow of a hawthorn bush, staring at her with eyes she knew.

He was covered with dirt, his beard was long and bedraggled, his hair wild and snarled with leaves and twigs. But his eyes. She knew his eyes. They were the eyes of her first lover, the one who was all she could remember of the time before she was a slave.

"Ré," she whispered, and opened her arms to him, but still he did not know her. He backed away, retreating to the shelter of the hawthorn, his eyes gleaming warily from among the branches.

Shula looked away, and slowly lowered her arms. Sitting very still, not alarming him with her gaze, she attempted to become part of the scenery, so he would not be afraid, so he would not flee, for she wanted nothing more than to hold him in her arms. They ached for him, as much as they had for her unborn child. She knew him. He was the father of the child she *would* have.

Having ascertained with a flick of her eyes that the wild man had settled down to watch her from the safety of the bush, she disciplined herself to go quietly about her business, unpacking food from her basket, bread and cheese and dried goat meat. She drank from her water skin, and casually placed it some distance from herself, in the direction of the bush. As she ate she began to hum soft noises of a reassuring nature for his benefit.

She heard rustling from the direction of the bush, but did not turn to look, even when she heard him pick up the water skin, squeeze it experimentally several times, and at last drink from it. She just kept on singing, softly, until he crept closer and reached out one hand to touch her hair. She turned her head then, to look at him again. This close there was no mistake, and Shula felt something breaking inside her, the fragments shifting, changing the shape of her heart. She remembered. She remembered Ray, who wore jeans and flannel shirts, who kissed her in Kennedy Park and fought to protect her and her notebook. Ray who had loved her. Her. Wendy.

With a jolt she returned to Shula, sitting in the forest with a wild man inches from her face, and as Wendy, she grabbed onto him like she was drowning.

They didn't speak. For her part, there were no words to describe the confusion, fear, and joy she felt. And as for Ré, she did not think he remembered speech.

Other things, if forgotten, were swiftly remembered, however. He buried his face in the hollow between her neck and shoulder, and began to kiss and bite the flesh there. She sighed, and breathed in deep the smell of him, that altogether known smell that roused both memory and desire. She ran her hands over his back. The fine soft down that covered his back felt like a miracle, like the first time she'd felt it, the first time they made love. Her mouth sought his, reaching inside him as though he were the only safe haven. She found herself sobbing as he suckled her breasts, his penis erect and pressed against her thigh, and then there was nothing more to remember for a while.

———

Looking at Ré sleeping, curled on the ground beside her, Shula was overwhelmed by a feeling of protectiveness for him. The shifting light of the sun through the trees reminded her of lying with him beneath the elm tree at Kennedy Park. They had just been reinventing the world. The other world. The one she came from. And what world was that? And how had she come from that one to this one?

She focused on the memory of the summer sun dappling her and Ré with patches of light, the feel of his skin, always warm, like sunshine, the cool liquid blue of his eyes as he gazed calmly into hers, sharing something they both understood, but could not express. They had been talking about what they would do, if the world were starting over again, and they could make up its laws, and like most things at that time, the conversation had evolved into them kissing and fondling each other, reveling in the goodness of summer and love and sunshine. Her vulva pulsed with the recollection, and she leaned over and brushed her hand across Ré's chest. He turned to gaze at her with those same liquid blue eyes, eyes that held another world inside them, not this one, and only sometimes the one they came from.

And then she remembered sitting on the wall of Erech, hope flying up out of her like a bird into the dawn sky. How had she come to be here then, if she was really a woman of the . . . twenty-first century? What was here, if she was from . . . Elmdale?

Had she ever really been captured and enslaved? The earliest thing she could remember was sitting on the wall of Erech the morning of the day she met Inanna. And before that? A feeling of floating in darkness. But more than that, a sense of almost unbearable excitement, and beneath that sadness, disillusionment, loneliness. As if the anticipation of—what?—were like a canvas tarp stretched tight over a gaping hole. She shook her head as the faces of Urhulli and Bilah and Badtibri flashed before her. But they weren't Urhulli, Bilah, and Badtibri, were they? Lorca, Veronica, and Raven. Her friends. Wendy's friends.

Taking a sudden deep breath she sat up, and ran her hands over her clothes. A rough-spun wool shawl and skirt. But she had not always worn clothes like these, had she?

Nope. There had been a particular pair of jeans she had just adored her first year in grad school. Her fingers remembered the soft feel of them, worn and faded from being washed so frequently. Imagine, the most Shula part of her thought, washing machines!

Yes. Washing machines, and cars, and buildings unspeakably tall, though none of that had occurred to her at the time. The miracles she had wandered among, all unaware. Wonders beyond the imagining of an ancient Sumerian slave girl.

Ancient Sumeria! That's right! That's where she was. She was in ancient Sumeria, but how? Had she traveled in time? No. No, it was something else. A plan. They'd had a plan. The loneliness returned, and the disillusionment and anger and passion and a longing, a longing for something she had lost. An afternoon when the world was brand-new, and could be anything she wanted it to be. She suddenly remembered the artificial chill of air-conditioning in a tiny conference room, and a sense of fury boiling up over hopelessness as her . . . dissertation topic . . . was denied. And then the project. The computer simulation and the isolation tank. The darkness and the floating, the anticipation of coming to this place, of finally finding out—what?

Ré stirred, shifted, and opened eyes still blurred with dreams. She leaned over and kissed him again. She couldn't get enough of kissing him; he was her elixir of life, the font of her memories. But what of his?

Did he have memories? She thought of Urhulli and Bilah and Badtibri, or rather Lorca, Veronica, and Raven. And she remembered the project they'd created together: a virtual reality simulation. But her friends were not in the simulation with her. Urhulli and Bilah and Badtibri were representations of them. Virtual constructs, nothing more. Like henna seeping through damp linen, her real life had bled into this . . . this dream, this nightmare. That was what Ré was, too, she realized, suddenly feeling more lost than she ever had with Inanna, more lost than she had her first day as a priestess, following a shepherd boy through the temple of the harlots. She had always been seeking him, throughout Shula's abrupt and tumbled life, and now—well, now she knew. This was all of him that was left to her, this fragment, this dream or nightmare.

The woman took him out of the forest, to a place where people lived like bees in a hive. As she led him along the narrow stone passages of the place, the noise and stink of all the people frightened him, and he longed for the forest.

They came to an open area where people were exchanging small shiny stones for all kinds of things, cloth like the woman had dressed him in, things that grew in the soil, the carcasses of dead animals, and so forth. In a large red tent at one end of the square someone was screaming and crying. His blood quickened, his eyesight sharpened, as in the old days when hearing the cry of a snared deer. "What is that? What's happening in there?" he asked the woman.

"It is the bridal tent. The king has sex with the brides before they join their new husbands."

"But how can he do that? Why is it permitted?"

She sighed. "He is the king, it is his right, if he chooses to exercise it. Besides, who can stop him?"

"I will stop him," he said, and charged into the tent. There, on a pile of rugs a man with curly hair crouched over a girl who looked little more than a child. The man held her arms down and she tossed her tear-streaked face in fear.

Ré ran to them and seized the man by his hair. Tangling his fingers in the dark curls, he hauled his head up and punched him in the face, using the momentum of his blow to shove the man off the girl.

The king went sprawling into the side of the tent, which billowed out, and cushioned his fall. It was but a moment before he'd regained his feet, and crouching low, launched himself at Ré. The king caught him in the midsection, and they fell to the ground, rolling and grappling with one another. The king grasped the back of Ré's head and pushed his face into the dirt. Ré tasted grit and blood. He reached behind him and grabbed the king's hand, pulling his thumb back against the joint. The king gasped and pulled his hand away, and Ré leapt to his feet and charged him, knocking him into the tent pole. Red cloth rained down upon them, and they struggled toward each other as if through a sea of blood.

Half-smothered by the cloth, Ré found strong arms encircling him, squeezing him. He reared back and brought his forehead down on the king's nose and they fell together, rolled over one another, hopelessly tangled. His head swam, and he scrabbled at the cloth, but couldn't find his way free. At last there was a tearing sound, and daylight and fresh air flooded in. He stood, blinking, to find the king standing there, the torn red cloth in his hands. A crowd stood watching them. He spotted the girl, who must have fled when the fight started, in her mother's arms.

Ré looked to the king, bracing for a new onslaught, but the man grinned and held his hands out, open. Laughing, the king embraced him, and then stood back, his hands upon Ré's shoulders. "Never have I, King Gilgamesh, met a man who was a match for me. Friend, you are the one foretold to me in a dream. You are the star from heaven, the man who is my equal."

"It is wrong for you to lie with these girls against their will," said Ré, stepping back.

"You are right, in that you are above me. But I promise you this, if it disturbs you, I will not do it. Be my friend, and help me to be a better man." Gilgamesh reached out his hand.

Ré found that his outrage had fled. He tried to get it back but it escaped him. He could do nothing but laugh and take the man's hand in friendship. Gilgamesh wrapped an arm around his shoulder and led him up the street. "What do they call you?"

The only name he had was the one the woman gave him. "Ré."

"Ré? What kind of a name is that?" scoffed Gilgamesh. "It is not even a word. It's just a syllable. No. I will call you Enkidu, the star from the sky."

Enkidu. Shula knew that name. There was a story about a wild man named Enkidu who was befriended by Gilgamesh. She had transcribed it for Enheduanna back at the temple. How had it gone? She searched her memory, sifting through fragments like a gleaner searching for stray grain in the dirt of a culled field. There had been something about a forest. A forest of cedars sacred to Inanna. And Gilgamesh had desecrated that forest, he and his companion Enkidu slew the guardian of that forest, and . . . and . . . Inanna had killed Enkidu in punishment for their deed.

Sudden panic filled her and she tried to force her way through the crowd surrounding Ré and the king. "Stop!" she cried. "Stop, Ré, don't go with him! Come back!" But her words were swallowed in the surrounding hubbub. Jumping up, she was just able to glimpse the tops of their heads, moving away up the avenue toward the palace. She managed to fight her way through the press of bodies only to find guards with swords and spears holding back the crowd. "Ré!" she screamed and tried to dodge around one of the guards. He shoved her across the face with the shaft of his spear and she fell back, her eyes watering from the pain. "Ré!" she screamed until she was hoarse, but the people around her held her arms and would not let her try to dodge the guards again.

After the king had left and the crowd dispersed, Shula sat on the ground in the middle of the street, weeping and pouring dust on her head. He was gone, again. And he would die, or this figment of him would, and here she was trapped in this place and was she Wendy, or was she Shula, and what was the difference and what was the reason for any of it?

"You there! Move or my oxen will trample you!"

Shula looked up to see a wagon full of dried dung cakes lurching down the road toward her. Two things that had been bouncing about in her mind suddenly collided. The mé and the game she and Ray had played, back in high school. The first day of the world. She scrambled out of the way of the dung cart and untied her mé from her skirt and looked at it. If this was a simulated world, one she and her friends had created, if they, in fact, had decided the rules, then maybe this was . . .

The mé of making mé," said Enheduanna, handing her back the stone. "I won't even ask how you came by it."

Shula shrugged and gave her teacher a wry smile. "Some miracle or other."

They sat in Enheduanna's study. The afternoon sun slanted through her skylight to glitter upon the mosaic on the floor, making the fish sparkle as if leaping from the sea. Enheduanna leaned forward and poured a little more wine in Shula's cup. "Truly, you have been afflicted," she said.

Shula sighed and examined the date she had been nibbling upon. "It would seem I have no one to blame but myself." She looked back at Enheduanna. "Do you recall the transcription I assisted you with?"

"Of course. I hope to be remembered for it for many generations to come."

"And do you still have the original tablets for the story of Gilgamesh?"

Enheduanna frowned. "Ye-es."

Shula bit her lip. Enheduanna's inflection suddenly didn't seem so . . . well, Sumerian. What a Wendy thing to think, she thought, and shook herself, and took a drink of wine. "How does that story end?"

"Well, Gilgamesh and Enkidu kill the monster Humbaba, who guards the sacred cedars, and in wrath over their act of sacrilege, Inanna strikes Enkidu dead. She can't kill Gilgamesh, you see, because—"

"She kills Enkidu?" Shula struck her chest with her fist and moaned. "I knew it. I knew."

Enheduanna looked at her strangely. "Yes, well. In his grief Gilgamesh seeks out Utnapishtim, who was alive before the flood, because he knows the spring where flows the water of life."

"The water of life? To bring Enkidu back to life." Hope stirred in her feebly, like a fledgling bird.

"Yes, you see? You remember. Gilgamesh takes some of the water to revive Enkidu with, but on the way home he stops to bathe in a pool, and the snake steals back the elixir."

"The snake? The Serpent That Knows No Charm?"

"Who else? The perennial envoy of natural law. You see the story is really about the futility of humans trying to transcend death. It is immutable. We all die, and not even a king can change that."

Shula leaned forward, and picked her mé up from the table. She held it firmly in her hand, and looked back at Enheduanna. "Not a king, no. But a goddess can."

CHAPTER
28

"We will drink to Enkidu," cried Gilgamesh when the beer arrived. He had brought him back to the palace and introduced him to his ministers. "My friend, my brother, the one who was foretold in my dreams, who matches me strength for strength."

Ré, or Enkidu, as he now knew himself, sat on a cushion at Gilgamesh's right side. He drank the beer, but his eyes were still wild, gazing about him blankly like a beast discovering it is in a cage, like an animal learning that he is a man.

"There is a grove of cedars, holy to Inanna," said Gilgamesh. "These trees are taller than any I've ever seen, as tall as the walls of Erech. If we could cut them, they would yield lumber enough to build a thousand thrones. They would bring riches to the city. Merchants would come from afar to exchange goods for our fine lumber."

"I know the trees you speak of," said Enkidu. "But they are guarded by a monster, Humbaba. He is larger than ten houses. His head is as broad as the plain of the Euphrates, his teeth are more terrible than a thousand swords, his eyes cause the fiercest of creatures to quail at their sight. When I was an animal I knew nothing, yet I knew to stay away from that grove."

Gilgamesh scoffed at his friend's fears. "There is nothing that the two of us cannot accomplish together. We will slay Humbaba, and then the riches of the cedar grove will be ours."

Enkidu shook his head. "His breath is a fire that lays waste to everything around him. He hears all, even the breathing of an insect at the edge of the forest. Do you think he will not hear us?"

Gilgamesh, who was not really listening, shrugged and said, "Only the gods live forever. I will go ahead of you, and if I die, at least I will have the honor of dying in battle. What of your strength that equaled mine, where is it now?"

"I feel weak," sighed Enkidu. "Weak and sick with fear at this thing you plan to do."

"It is Humbaba who has stolen your strength. We must slay him and end his evil influence over you."

"No," cried Enkidu, "it is this journey that will bring us death." But no matter what he said of Humbaba's prowess—that his cry was so fierce as to strike deaf all who heard it, that his footstep shook the ground— Gilgamesh would not listen.

"Why are you afraid?" he complained. "We will be together, there is nothing that can overcome us."

Shula ran her hands over the tablets laying before her on the tamarisk-plank table, feeling the textures of the words. Her eyes drank in the sight of these symbols, her Sumerian suddenly more halting than before, suddenly a foreign language to decipher. She found the section where Inanna strikes Enkidu dead, and those marks somehow seemed sharper, biting into her fingertips as she took the mé in her other hand and pressed it to the bottom right corner of the tablet.

Behind her she heard Enheduanna gasp as the mé sank into the tablet as easily as if it were fresh, soft clay. Indeed, the entire tablet was now as it had been when first inscribed, before drying and becoming permanent.

Shula ran her fingers across the line that read, "Inanna fixed her eye upon Enkidu and dealt him his death." She pressed the edge of her thumb into the word "Enkidu," obliterating it. From a jar on the table she took soft clay and smeared it into the depression, removing all trace of the symbols. And then she took a reed stylus, and she wrote the name "Gil-gamesh" in its place.

—————

The house of the elders was arumble with argument. Enkidu, still unused to the sound of so many voices, found a corner of the room to retreat to, as Gilgamesh approached the council.

"We need lumber," shouted a young man in a brown skirt and shawl. "The builders cannot build because they have no beams to support ceilings."

"Sadunna is right," said a heavyset man with gray in his beard. "I know where there's a whole forest of cedar, ripe for cutting. Beautiful tall trees, gurs and gurs of lumber, and it could be ours if not for—"

"Oh not Humbaba again," grumbled the oldest man present. His face was gaunt, his head bald and spotted. "I tell you Ur-Neattu, you are new to the congress, but this comes up every year."

"Old Hagarra, wise Hagarra, let the words of a young man touch your ears. I tell you that forest has more trees than the ensi has sheep. Why can't we have some of them?" said Sadunna.

"Because they are forbidden," said Hagarra.

"But we would only use them for the glory of Inanna, to make her city the tallest in all Sumeria. To raise high her mighty walls for all the land to see," said Ur-Neattu.

"Oh come now. Everyone here knows you are a builder," said Hagarra.

"That may be, but I tell you I am not the only one whose business has suffered."

"Besides, if the walls are not repaired soon, our enemies will overrun us," said a fourth man. "I think Ur-Neattu is right, we need those trees."

"But Humbaba, he is too mighty. He kills all who come near the trees," said a fifth man.

"I don't want to hear any more about Humbaba," cried Gilgamesh, striding to the center of the floor. "I will prove to you he is not the unvanquishable monster you think he is. I will prove to you that the laws of the gods are not unassailable."

There was silence in the hall, during which Enkidu heard the elders' breath quicken, saw the blush spreading across their cheeks. They were taken up with recollections of the battles of their youth. A sick, twisted feeling came over Enkidu's guts. He felt weak, as if he couldn't raise his arms. He saw what was happening. Gilgamesh would convince them. The elders of the city of Erech would support his foolish venture, and he, Enkidu, because he was Gilgamesh's friend, would accompany him.

"You see?" said Gilgamesh, after the elders, to a one, had supported the plan to kill Humbaba. "The wise ones have overruled you."

Amid the elders' prayers to An, Utu, and Shamash, to protect their king (they did not mention Enkidu) and bring him success, the armorer was brought forth. He brought Gilgamesh his bow and arrow, his ax, and his sword, and likewise weapons for Enkidu. The ax felt heavy in his hand; he could not lift it. His insides were leaden with dread, but following Gilgamesh's footsteps, he left the city, and they set off together for the sacred forest.

In the wild lands, Enkidu, who knew their trails, led the way. They came at last to a part of the forest where the trees were old, and nothing but silence dwelled among them. A gate, wrought of gold, stood between two of the trees, and Gilgamesh said, "It is the gate to Humbaba's forest."

The top of the gate was lined with points sharper than an eagle's talons. In the center of the gate, where the two doors met, was a face of gold, grimacing horribly. Hands grasping the bars of the gate formed handles.

Enkidu reached out, and took hold of one of the handles. It made his skin tingle and he pulled open the gate. At the moment that the door swung away from its mate, the hand Enkidu grasped came alive, and twisting, grabbed his wrist.

Enkidu cried out, and tried to pull his hand away, but the gold hand held him fast, gripping his wrist so tightly he felt his hand go hot and then cold, and then lose feeling altogether.

With a shout Gilgamesh raised his ax, and swung it hard, and Enkidu, thinking he would chop his hand off, yet unable to move, screamed.

With a ring like a bell, the ax struck the gold hand just above the wrist. Enkidu lifted his hand to stare at the gold one still wrapped about his wrist. As he watched, it turned to stone and crumbled away. He flexed his fingers, but still there was no feeling in them.

"My hand," he said to Gilgamesh. "I can't feel anything."

"It will pass, my friend," said Gilgamesh. "Come, I will lead the way from here."

Still shaking his numb hand, Enkidu followed Gilgamesh through the sundered gate. They followed a trail trampled in the dirt. Enkidu glimpsed crescent-shaped impressions, left from the hooves of some impossibly huge beast. It grew dark, and Gilgamesh said, "We will stop here for the night."

Enkidu, troubled by his hand, found little sleep, and beside him, Gilgamesh tossed with dreams. Sometime in the night, his friend the king awoke. "I had a dream. We were standing beneath a cliff, like insects compared to its height, and a rock slide obliterated us. Then a man came and pulled me out from beneath the rocks, and gave me water to drink."

"Your dream means that you will be victorious over Humbaba," said Enkidu, and he trembled, for no one had saved *him* from the rock slide. But he did not say this to Gilgamesh, and soon his friend slept once more.

In the morning Gilgamesh said, "Why should we seek out the monster? We are here among his trees. If we fell one, he will come to us."

And so the king wielded his mighty ax, and when he struck the trunk of a tall cedar, it rang like a bell, sounding out across the land. The tree cracked and groaned under the blows from Gilgamesh's ax, and with a sound like the heart of the world breaking, the cedar crashed to the ground.

In the aftermath of the tree's fall, the ground continued to tremble, reverberating with the footsteps of a huge beast. There was a sound like the rising of a flood, coming to their ears from all directions at once, increasing in volume until it obliterated all other sounds of the forest.

And then Humbaba appeared, coming down the path toward them, a creature whose form was a mockery of men and animals both. His head was broad, crowned with the crescent horns of a water buffalo. He had four legs, massive as trees, and where the neck and head would have been on an ordinary ox jutted a torso like a man's but grotesque in its size and sporting four arms, which waved clumsily as it walked.

Enkidu, robbed of thought and speech by the sight of this creature, could only watch as it bore down upon them, its mouth open in a howl like the wind at the end of the world, its teeth flashing like a thousand knives.

Humbaba reared back, and swung one mighty fist, striking Enkidu across the back. The blow took his breath from him, and left him cold, crumpled on the ground like a dead leaf.

He rolled over and saw Gilgamesh standing by the fallen tree as if paralyzed, his mouth gaping open. Enkidu would have shouted at him to help. This whole foolish venture was his doing, after all, but there was no time. Humbaba reared up to deliver the blow that would send Enkidu forever from the land of the living. He scrambled to his feet, and his anger at his friend gave strength to his arm as he drove his sword toward the chest of the monster.

The blade sank deep and Humbaba howled; a cry like the wailing of all the dead in the underworld. His cloven hooves stumbled in the dust, he swayed, and fell onto his side with a crash that shook the world.

The impact roused Gilgamesh from his stupor, and he raised his ax over his head to deal Humbaba his death.

"Please," the monster wailed, his hands clasped in supplication. "I will serve you as I have served the gods. I will build houses for you from their trees. Let me live, O King, I will put all the world at your feet."

For a moment the ax hung in the air over Humbaba, and Enkidu saw hesitation in Gilgamesh's eyes. "Don't believe him," cried Enkidu. "He lies to you!" And Gilgamesh raised his ax higher and brought it down on the neck of the monster.

The reek of blood filled the air, and Gilgamesh hoisted up the head of Humbaba. "Behold," he said. "The monster is dead."

Enkidu helped his friend tie a rope to Humbaba's horns, and they hung the head from a tree, but he felt none of the king's elation at their victory. Looking at the headless corpse of the guardian of Inanna's trees, he thought, Something has been broken that will never mend.

The marketplace was crowded, and there was a note of anticipation in the voices of the people there.

"I was at the Moon Gate this morning. And I heard a boy say that the king was returning," said a merchant selling onions.

"So he survived the battle with Humbaba," said the woman picking over his stock. "Was he victorious?"

"Yes. The boy said a shepherd passed him on the road. He is on his way back to Erech with the monster's head."

"What of the man who went with him?" asked Shula, pretending to examine an onion. "The one they call Enkidu. Did he survive?"

"I don't know. The boy did not mention him."

A ripple of excitement went through the crowd, and Shula heard someone say, "The king is coming." People jostled one another for a better view of the street. Shula climbed onto the roof of a nearby house, and from there she saw two figures dressed in armor, approaching the square.

Gilgamesh strode into the center of the marketplace and held the head of Humbaba aloft. "Behold, people of Erech," he cried. "I bring you the head of your oppressor!"

Everyone cheered, their voices rising up to heaven, except for Shula and except for Enkidu, who stood beside Gilgamesh, looking around him with a worried frown.

In the midst of the celebration the sky was split by a clap of thunder, and Inanna appeared.

"What have you done?" she cried, wresting the head of Humbaba from Gilgamesh's hands. "My servant, my loyal servant. You have slain him, and yet in your arrogance, you return to Erech like a hero. You will be punished for this. I fasten my gaze upon you, I fix you with the eye of death."

"No!" Enkidu threw himself before Gilgamesh, and her gaze flickered, resting upon him for a moment. But a moment was enough. Enkidu fell to the ground and was still.

"No!" cried Shula, running to his side. She put her hand to his lifeless chest and pulled it back as if burned. It hadn't worked. She'd changed the story, but fate had obliterated her change. She glared up at Inanna. "You!" She stood up and advanced on Inanna. "Look what you've done!"

Inanna's eyes widened, but her gaze, once terrible as a thousand armies, could not command Shula now. "My servant," said Inanna. "It is my servant Shula, who accompanied me to the underworld, who assisted me in all that I asked. Why do you speak so to your goddess?"

"You are not my goddess, and I will serve you no longer. What a fool I was, to follow you." It was as if a whirlwind possessed her, her words came out like winds to whip at the goddess. "You set the gulla upon me. You dragged me to the underworld with you on your misbegotten adventure. Why did you try to usurp Ereshkigal's throne? Is not half of all creation enough for you?"

To her amazement, Inanna burst into tears at this, but there was no stopping the howling wind of fury that issued from Shula's mouth. "I was a slave once, but a queen in my master's household compared to how you have used me. You let the temple guards flog me. You made me a naditum when I should have been a harlot. My child is dead. She is Ereshkigal's daughter now, to be raised in the underworld and never to see the sun. And now, now you have taken from me the one that I loved."

Wind whipped through the marketplace, lifting Inanna's hair and ruffling her clothing, but it left Shula untouched. In her hand, the mé of making mé grew hot, but still she clutched it. "You said you wanted me to discover who you really are," she continued, "to tell your true stories. Well, now I can tell you who you really are. You are a spoiled child."

The wind blew harder and Inanna began to unravel, as if she were a skein of wool. The wind teased loose a thin strip starting at the goddess's left foot and winding up and around to the top of her head. It peeled away and flew off into the sky. "You do as you wish, and you care not for the consequences to mortals or your own kin." And another strip flew off from the goddess, as fast as the words blew from Shula's mouth. "You are vain and imperious." *Snap!* Another strip of the goddess blew off into the clouds. "Goddess of love and war, you confuse the two. You mistake fear for devotion, you are a sham of women's real power. You loved the farmer, but threw him over for the one your parents favored. In a fit of temper you sent your husband to the underworld, you set the gullas upon him and they rent his flesh, and then you had the gall to mourn him!"

There was hardly anything left of Inanna now, a last few strands of hair and lips and lapis crown. "Worst of all, you turned against your own sister. You cut down the huluppu tree, a thing of beauty, the tree of life. You drove Belili off because she was a free spirit, because she was not afraid of the Sky God An, and because you were jealous of her. Oh Goddess, you are a mockery of women, an invention of kings, your behavior an excuse to vilify us all!"

And with that the final strands that had been Inanna blew away like streamers loosed into the sky.

The marketplace was empty but for Shula, Gilgamesh, and the corpse of Enkidu. As she started toward the body, Gilgamesh backed up hastily. "I will revive him. Lady, I will revive him. I will sail across the sea of death to the island where Utnapishtim dwells. He was alive before the flood, and he knows where to find the elixir of life. I will bring Enkidu back to life, I promise you."

"You will fail," she told him bitterly. "The snake will steal your precious elixir, and he will still be dead. No matter what anyone does, he will still be dead." She glanced behind her, to the spot where Inanna had stood. "You should have married her. You match her in arrogance and selfishness. But I will accompany you to Utnapishtim's island anyway. If he was alive before the flood, then I should talk to him."

CHAPTER

29

They set off across the broad alluvial plain, traveling first by boat, and then, when they reached the mountains, by donkey. After days and days of riding they came to a mountain whose peaks breached the shores of heaven. After the mountain was the sea, vast as death, and they were very small, in their little boat, following the stars to an island they could not see.

When they reached the island, they took the path up from the beach to a little house perched upon a bluff. The old man, Utnapishtim, whose beard was long and white, greeted them at the door and welcomed them inside.

"Utnapishtim," said Shula after the man had served them a meal of barley and goat cheese. "You were alive before the flood. You remember farther back than any person now living. Tell me, what was it like back then, before Enki raised the waters, before kingship came down from heaven?"

"Well," said the old man, resting his cup of beer on the table. "I don't know if I can remember. There were no kings of course . . . and no writing to record what the people did then."

"Were there cities?"

"Oh, there were cities. At least I think there were."

"Were there slaves?"

"No, there were no slaves."

"What about women?"

"Well, there were women . . . ."

"I mean did they run things? Were there queens, or did men and women live as equals?"

"Mmm." Utnapishtim shook his head and plucked a stray grain of barley from his beard. "Mostly I remember being a child, and playing with other children, and my mother's smiling face. Those memories hold a mystery and a power that I am at a loss to explain. Perhaps that is true for everyone. Sometimes I think that when people talk about a time when there was no war, when the world was young and giants walked the earth, it is their own childhood they are remembering; a time when the world *was* new, because we were new. A time before we were required to join the civilization of humankind and learn to care about things that do not matter to us." The old man smiled, and shrugged. "But perhaps I am wrong. I'm sorry, if you really want to know what it was like, you're going to have to go and find out for yourself."

She caught her breath. "Go? Go where? How?"

"Come with me." The old man led the way to a small door at the back of the house. He opened it to reveal a staircase, spiraling down into the darkness.

She descended the staircase, quickly losing count of the steps she took, or how long she'd been there. Far below she saw not light, but a swirling miasma of darkness.

She did not know when she got there, to the time before the flood, or how long she stayed, but it was not what she expected.

There was nothing there. No cities, no people, not even land or water or sky, just the chaos of darkness, the whirl of nonbeing. And in the midst of this, the snake came to her, flickering before her vision like an animated fractal, which is exactly what it was, the seam of this world in which she lived.

"That's it," she told it. "I can't do any more."

The snake opened its mouth and swallowed her whole.

CHAPTER

30

There was a roaring in her ears, like the ocean speaking, and then a brilliant light, and cold. She was shivering, and her world was gone.

"Is she all right?" someone said.

"What do we do now?" asked someone else. She thought she knew their voices, Urhulli and Bilah, but how had she gotten back to the temple? And why was she so cold? Why couldn't she see? That last was easily enough answered. Her eyes were closed, she realized. She opened them, but was blinded by the brightness of the world around her. Bilah and Urhulli were supporting her. She could not move her arms and legs. "Wha-what ha-ha-happened?" she croaked, her voice rough as if she had not used it for many months.

"It's all right, you're out now," said Bilah.

Someone was holding her hand, and they laid her down on a bed of exquisite softness. "I missed you," she rasped.

Eventually her eyesight cleared enough to see that she was not in the temple at Erech. She was in Zazula Von Sach's laboratory, and it was Lorca and Veronica, not Urhulli and Bilah, who had spoken.

She lay wrapped in blankets on the couch tucked up against one wall of the large third-floor laboratory. They stood around her, their hovering faces like four moons in the sky. Raven looked relieved, Veronica scared, Lorca's eyes shone with hope, and Zazula grinned.

"Are you all right?" asked Veronica.

Wendy nodded, goggling at the windows, the tables, the equipment. Everything had such sharp edges, such straight lines. She took a deep breath and struggled to sit up. Her muscles were stiff, her joints barely able to obey. Raven and Veronica grabbed her by the arms and helped her up, then sat beside her.

Lorca just couldn't contain herself any longer. "What was it like? Did you find the matriarchies? Did you find the goddess?"

Wendy shook her head stiffly. "I was a slave, and Inanna treated me as one. Belili helped me, but when I got to the time before the flood, there was nothing there." She shivered. "Why was there nothing there?"

Lorca shook her head, her eyes, dancing only a moment ago, brimmed with tears. "The stories . . . the stories didn't work?"

"That's right, it didn't work." Wendy shrugged and tried to keep the bitterness she felt out of her face. "Where are my clothes?"

Sagging visibly, Lorca pulled a neatly folded stack from under the couch—jeans and a Bitch and Animal T-shirt—and brought them to her, head bowed. As Wendy began to dress, Lorca sat on the edge of the couch next to Veronica. "I thought for sure . . ." She looked up suddenly. "Did you access the deeper levels, the mythic subroutines?" she asked, in a tone almost accusatory.

"Oh yeah." Wendy nodded, struggling to get her awkward arms through the holes of the T-shirt. "I traipsed all over the landscape with Inanna. I was there for all the stories; 'The Huluppu Tree,' 'Inanna and the God of Wisdom,' 'The Descent of Inanna'—that was a treat, I can tell you—even 'Gilgamesh.' "

Wendy paused with her jeans pulled up to her knees, trembling at the mention of Gilgamesh, thinking of Enkidu, whom she had not saved. "I think we made a mistake with the memory thing." She stood to pull her jeans on the rest of the way, and swayed, her head swimming, her vision fizzing around the edges. She zipped up and sat back down again. "It worked too well," she went on. "I had no idea what I was supposed to be doing most of the time I was there. It wasn't until Gilgamesh, when I met Enkidu, that I started to remember who I was." Again the knowledge of what she had lost when she let Ray go swamped her. She'd gone to another world to avoid it, and it had followed her all the way there and back.

Zazula darted forward and knelt at her feet. "So it worked then? You didn't know who you were at all?"

"Oh, I knew who I was," said Wendy. "I was the slave girl Shula. But I had no past and no recollection of being . . . me . . . Wendy." It was strange, like waking from a dream in which she remembered everything, from the start of the sim at the city wall to the moment at the foot of Utnapishtim's tower when she finally saw the snake for what it was. But in a way, it had all happened to somebody else. Shula was a part played by Wendy, and thinking of her, Wendy was suffused with both pity and longing. She missed her. She actually missed her. Who was Shula, now that she was Wendy? Where was Shula, now that Wendy was here?

Zazula grinned. "Excellent. Then my theory about the selective release of atropine into the memory centers of the brain was correct! It worked!"

Wendy shook her head. "No. Weren't you listening? It didn't work. I didn't know who I was, but I also didn't know why I was there, what I was supposed to be doing. I wasted all this time. Inanna is a patriarchal figurehead, at least that's what she'd become by the time her stories were written down, but I couldn't see that. I thought I was supposed to serve her, and I did, but she didn't lead me to any ancient matriarchies. All she did was bring me sorrow. Now Belili, she might have been able to tell me something, but I didn't have the wit to ask. I thought I was betraying Inanna just by talking to her. I blew it, because I didn't know why I was there."

Zazula waved a hand. "That's okay. We learned a lot about memory function and the operation of sense centers in the brain. This will be very helpful when I set up my next experiment. I only wish I could publish this one. The results are spectacular."

"Spectacular?" Wendy stood up, nearly knocking Zazula backward. "Spectacular? Are you nuts? I went in there to find proof of a better world, not to learn about brain function. I was flogged to within an inch of my life. I went to the underworld. I was attacked by gullas. I got pregnant and lost the child. I fell in love with Enkidu and watched him die! And for what?" She stopped, panting, her heart beating hard, like a fist pounding at her chest.

They all stared at her. Wendy couldn't bear their various looks of sadness, disappointment, and poorly disguised glee. She staggered past them, through a maze of instrument stands to the isolation chamber. And stopped. Next to the gleaming black carapace stood another I.C., older, more utilitarian, rather like an enormous ice chest. Its grainy white surface was marred with scuffs and streaks. Woozily, she braced her hands on it, her legs trembling. "What's this?" she asked over her shoulder.

"Oh, I had to borrow that from the behavioral sciences department," said Zazula, trailing after her. "It's okay. They weren't using it."

Wendy took in the IV stand, the tubes running in and out of the chamber. "Who's in there?" She turned to face Zazula, and saw that the others had joined them. Over Zazula's shoulder, Veronica was trying to catch her eye.

"Well, you had a visitor while you were out," said Zazula.

"Intruder, more like," said Raven. "He broke in at the apartment, and then here."

"He thought he was going to 'rescue' you," said Lorca. "You know, that white knight crap of his?"

Frustration, hope, and a gnawing fear almost silenced Wendy. "Who?" she grated.

Veronica broke out from between Raven and Zazula and came to her, taking her hand. "Ray," she whispered urgently. "It's Ray. He wanted to get back with you. He said he was sorry. She put him in the chamber. She said she had to do it but—"

"Yes, he was most insistent," said Zazula, stepping forward. "He wanted to pull you out of the simulation. He would have ruined everything. We tried to make him go away, but he kept coming back. Finally I put him in the chamber with the hang-gliding demo, just to keep him out of our hair until the experiment was over."

Wendy felt cold inside, remembering Enkidu—no, Ré—whom she had not saved. Staring at Zazula's calm, reasonable face, she felt dizzy as her world shifted into some nightmare version of all her hopes and dreams. "No," she said lowly. "No, that's not what you did." Wasn't it? Maybe Ré really was just like Urhulli and Bilah and Badtibri, a role filled in by her latent memory to resemble somebody she knew. She glanced at Veronica, who was glancing warily between herself and Zazula, shaking her head ever so slightly. But Urhulli had not brought her back to herself, Bilah had not reminded Shula that she was Wendy. Ré had. "Lorca, do me a favor," she said, never taking her eyes from Zazula. "Check what sim is running on his snake."

With a worried glance at the two of them, Lorca went to a computer set up on an instrument stand next to the white isolation chamber. She tapped a few keys. "The file name is 'Hang-gliding demo 2.5,' " she said, and then there was a pause, and a low whistle. "But the file is huge. Way too big for . . ."

As Wendy stared at Zazula a lot of little things started falling into place, fitting together with their own cold, internal logic. The way she'd acted when Wendy waited on her at the Nugget. Her words, *I just need to try it out on a guinea pig, so to speak,* and *You see? The subject is willing.* Most of all, her reaction when Wendy told them that the experiment had failed. She'd been utterly unfazed by Wendy's failure to find evidence of ancient matriarchies. All she'd cared about was that the memory block had been successful. She gripped Zazula tightly by the shoulders. "You put him in the Sumerian simulation. You made him Enkidu, the wild man, didn't you?"

"What? Wendy, what are you saying?" said Lorca, aghast, leaving the computer and trying to interpose herself between Wendy and Zazula.

Veronica stepped in to block her. "Let her answer, Lorca."

They all looked at Zazula, who rolled her eyes and sighed. "Oh, all right. Yes. I put him in the Sumerian simulation. But I'm sorry, it was just too rich an opportunity to pass up. I mean look at the results! Despite the atropine regimen, encountering someone you knew brought your memory back to you, right Wendy? That's what you said, wasn't it?" She shrugged in Wendy's grip and waved her hands impatiently. "Oh, I'll have to do a full interview with you and record the entire experience. But for now, tell me, did he ever remember who he was?"

In mute horror, Wendy shook her head.

"No? See, that's probably because I had him at a higher dosage." Zazula paused, suddenly aware that they were all staring at her, appalled. "What? Oh, I'm sorry about my little fib. But it was to protect you all, don't you see? I mean, this latest development *was* a little over the line, and in the unfortunate event that the authorities should become involved, I wanted you all to be able to say that I acted alone."

"Not because we would have stopped you?" asked Veronica.

A glare seeped through Zazula's rational facade. "Well, that, too, I suppose, especially with you. You were always going on about 'Is it safe? Is it safe?' when we were getting things ready for Wendy. I knew you wouldn't like this."

"You know how the story goes," said Wendy. "Enkidu dies. What happens? What happens to a person when their persona in the simulation dies?"

Zazula grinned. "That's one of the things I'm hoping to find out. And now that you're out, we can hook up the monitors we were using for you, and see what's happened."

"Oh my god," said Lorca. "I can't believe this."

Zazula gave her a look of concern. "What's wrong?"

Lorca shook her head in bewilderment. "You—you really don't know, do you?"

"She knows," said Veronica darkly. "She just doesn't care. She's putting on a show for us."

Zazula drew herself up. "Are we not all sisters here? Are we going to let a man come between us, after all we've been through together? With all we stand to gain? Are you really going to let the small matter of a bad ex-boyfriend get in your way? How *conventional* of you. How disappointing. Lorca, I thought at least you, and Raven . . . ."

Raven shook her head slowly, hurt and anger brimming in her eyes. "I helped. I tied him up for you . . . I helped you get him into the tank," she whispered, stepping up behind Zazula and gripping the older woman's upper arms, holding her in place.

"That's really not necessary, Raven," said Zazula neutrally. "You're tired, Wendy. You're jumping to all kinds of conclusions. We don't know what's happened. For all we know, Ray is perfectly fine."

Wendy looked at the others. Fear and anger warred in Veronica's face. Lorca and Raven wore nearly identical expressions of hurt and bewilderment. And Zazula's face was a serene mask, marred only by her eyes, which darted between Wendy, Veronica, and Lorca.

"Veronica, can you set up the monitors without her help?" asked Wendy.

"Yes," she answered firmly. "Yes, I can."

Wendy bit her lips, a part of her still unable to accept what she was about to say. "Raven, Lorca, could you two take Zazula to one of the second-floor bedrooms and just . . . keep her there, for now?"

Zazula's face changed. Panic broke through her proud mask, and her eyes, venomous, fixed upon Wendy. "I should have known you'd be like this," she spat. "Weak. Afraid of your power. All this fuss about remembering the past. The past is gone. It's best forgotten. Don't you understand?"

Raven tightened her grip on Zazula's arms and started to steer her toward the stairs. "Wait, wait," cried Zazula. "At least let me see what the monitors show us."

"We'll let you know the results, Zazula," said Wendy. "I'll come down and tell you myself as soon as I know anything."

The moment they'd left, Wendy and Veronica pried open the lid of Ray's isolation chamber. It was heavy. Their arms trembled as they stared down at his naked, motionless form. "Oh god, oh god," whispered Wendy.

"Help me get this lid the rest of the way off," said Veronica sharply, and Wendy obeyed, helping her lower it to the floor. "I checked him three days ago, he was all right then," said Veronica as she pressed her fingers to his neck. "Do you know how long ago his persona died?"

Wendy was transfixed by the sight of him, pale and still, just like he'd been in the market square. She heard her own words as if they came from someone else. "A day, maybe two."

"There's a pulse," said Veronica. Wendy looked up and Veronica gave her an encouraging smile. "It's faint, but it's there. Help me get the monitors over here so we can hook him up."

Ray was alive. Wendy held that fact close to her heart, cherishing it. The rest of the news was not so good. After seemingly endless hours of running tests, Veronica explained to her that Ray was in a deep coma, that what little brainwave activity he still exhibited was falling off, and taking him out of the simulation would likely be fatal.

"What can we do?" She paced the floor beside the isolation chamber. "Do we call the hospital?"

Veronica tilted her head. "We could. And ordinarily I'd say 'hell yes,' but in this case—the doctors will do everything they can for him with the tools they have—but we may have other tools that are more suited to this particular situation. Tools that will be unavailable to us the second they disconnect him from the simulation, which is probably the first thing they'll do."

Lorca came up and stood gravely beside the isolation chamber, staring at the EKG. She had a long red scratch on her cheek, and her eyes were red and puffy.

"How are things downstairs?" asked Veronica.

She swallowed. "All right. We've got her tied to a chair with her own pantyhose. She started getting pretty wiggy for a bit there, but now she's calmed down again."

"Gods," uttered Veronica.

"I know," said Lorca. "I feel like such a tool. I mean, I had no idea." She looked at Wendy. "You've got to know, just because Ray was a scumbag, doesn't mean I wanted him dead."

Wendy felt her frown deepen. "He isn't a scumbag, and he's not dead yet. What if his persona within the simulation comes back to life?" Wendy looked between Lorca and Veronica. "Would his body respond in kind?"

"For what it's worth, I asked Zazula the same thing, and she said that was probably his only chance," said Lorca.

"If we can believe anything she says," said Veronica.

"True, but just the same." Wendy looked at Lorca. "I'm sure you and Raven are anxious to hand Zazula over to the cops as soon as possible, but I think we better hang on to her until we get Ray out of this."

"Agreed," said Lorca.

"Hey, what if you reprogram the simulation, so that his persona is alive again?" asked Veronica.

Lorca shook her head. "It would have to be recompiled. That's probably as bad or worse than disconnecting him from the sim outright." She bit her thumbnail.

"We've got to do something, and soon," said Wendy, pacing again.

"Oh, you might want to see this," said Veronica. She went to the far end of the room and reached behind a dusty, disused bank of file cabinets and drew out a brown folio. Wendy wasn't sure at first, but when Veronica placed the worn cardboard envelope in her hands, there was no mistaking it. "Oh," she breathed, slipping free the elastic band that held it shut.

"I found it here just after Zazula put Ray in the sim. I don't know, I thought you might want to see it. I thought he might have brought it for you or something, and I didn't trust Zazula anymore, so I hid it." She caught Lorca's look and dropped her eyes.

Wendy went over to the couch and sat down. She drew out the sketchbook and opened it. A cubist depiction of a man falling through the air, his outstretched hand pierced by a silver bolt of lightning, his mouth stretched wide in shock and pain as all around him these brightly colored squares—she peered closer, they *were* credit cards—morphed into birds and flew away.

Lorca and Veronica came and sat on either side of her, looking over her shoulders.

Wendy turned to the next page. It was a realistic rendering of a block of North Boulevard just past the Strip. She recognized the bright yellow B'WANA DON'S sign . . . and the menacing figure standing on the corner. She turned another page. This one was just a sketch. He obviously hadn't had time to finish it, but even in its rough state there was no mistaking the two faces that filled the page, gazing upon one another with such depth of feeling. Wendy wondered if he'd had a picture of her, or if he really just remembered her that well. She wasn't sure when she'd started crying, but this was when she noticed the cool, silent rivulets rolling down her cheeks.

She shut the sketchbook and wiped her face on her sleeve. "We don't have time for this now," she said. "Ray doesn't have time for this. We'll go through it all later, when he's here and we can *tell* him how awesome his new stuff is." She sniffed, and opened the folio to put the sketchbook back. That's when she saw her old notebook from high school. Her hand touched it, bringing back to her the memory of that afternoon at Kennedy Park when she'd given him her creation story to read. She'd thought she'd lost it when she moved from the loft, but he'd had it this whole time.

Veronica put a hand on her shoulder. "Something happened to you when you were in there didn't it? When you met Enkidu. I mean besides getting your memory back."

Wendy nodded. "I still love him. Even if he'll never be a feminist, even if he'll never embrace the goddess, even if he's a patriarchal stooge for the rest of his life. I don't care. I was wrong, thinking that the world I wanted to live in could have no Ray in it. I was wrong."

Lorca looked shocked. "How can you say that? After what he did to you?"

Wendy shook her head. "It wasn't all him. He wanted me to come with him. If I'd wanted to keep the baby, he would have raised her with me. I wouldn't go."

"He wanted you to drop everything, school, your whole life. I can't believe you can just forget all that," said Lorca.

"That doesn't matter now." She picked up the folio. "Here. If you really want to understand, look at his pictures, Lorca. I mean just look at them, don't judge, and read my journal. Read the story I wrote for him, read whatever you want, but first . . ." She took Lorca's hand and Veronica's each in one of hers. "First you have to put me back in the simulation. But no atropine this time. I can't spend another three months farting around cleaning fish and following Inanna. As misplaced as Ray's intentions might have been, he meant to rescue me. Now I'm going to rescue him."

CHAPTER
31

She sat on the wall of Erech, gutting fish and watching the world be born. But she wasn't a slave girl named Shula, she was Wendy, and she had a mission to accomplish. She ran to the square where Ray was slain. His body lay there still, only the people had erected a pyre, and were levering him atop it.

"Wait! Wait! Do not light the pyre," she cried. "I will soon return with the elixir of life and restore this man!"

"And who are you, to make so grand a claim? A slave girl, a harlot?" inquired a big-bellied man of dubious hygiene. "We must dispose of this body, it has rotted here long enough. It drives away the customers. If Gilgamesh the king could not accomplish the feat you describe, what makes you think you can?"

Wendy stood her ground, and held up the mé of making mé. "I am a goddess." And she looked upon it, and said, "Take me to the pool where the serpent dwells."

The forest was quiet, peaceful, green. The voice of the stream that fed the pool was light and sweet. Wendy crouched on the bank and peered among the bushes. "Hello . . . Hister?" she whispered. "It is I, Wendy, who was Shula." She didn't have to wait long. The snake uncoiled from the branches of a ginkgo tree, descending its trunk in a lazy spiral. Hister slithered to where she sat, and lifting his head, rested it upon her knee.

"So you know who you are now. That's a start. And do you know now your purpose in coming here?"

She nodded and lifted tentative fingers to stroke the snake's head. "But

I have a new purpose now, and I come to ask a boon of you."

The serpent blinked. "But what of the time before? Don't you want to know what it was like?"

"I went there, there was nothing."

"Ssss," the snake hissed in laughter. "You accept failure so readily, for one who has endured so much. It is a pity, you were so close."

Wendy shook her head. "That's not important now, Hister. I came back because of a man—"

The snake slid from her knee and retreated in disgust. "Haven't you learned anything?"

"I love him. He was the wild man, Hister. He is dead in this world, in the other world his mind sleeps and cannot wake. It is because of me that this has happened, and I must revive him."

The snake turned to face her again. "Oh, the wild man, well perhaps that makes it different. I know what you wish of me, the elixir, but it will avail you not. The laws of this world still say the wild man must die. You cannot change that unless you change the laws. You have the power to do this, why don't you use it?"

"But I did," she protested. "I did use the mé, and it didn't work."

"No, you changed the outcome of one story only. It was not enough. You must start at the beginning."

"At the beginning?"

"Yes." Hister coiled about her feet briefly, and then slithered toward the pond. "Fulfill your purpose, and the wild man may yet live," he muttered as he slid into the water and disappeared.

The little boat still sat upon the shore where Gilgamesh had abandoned it. Wendy pushed it into the water and climbed in. She rowed across the gray swells of the sea, the slosh of the waves slapping against the hull and the drips of the water falling from her oars the only accompaniment to her heartbeat. In the mutable depths of the sea she fancied she saw shapes, large, indefinable forms rolling over in murky contemplation.

When she arrived at the island she made straight for Utnapishtim's house, rapping sharply on the door.

"Oh," said the wizened old man, peering at her from beneath his overgrown eyebrows. "It's you again. You came back, though not the way you left."

"Grandfather, I'm sorry to bother you but—"

"No, not at all, it is lonely on this island. I welcome your company, brief as it might be. Please, come in." He opened the door to the little house wide. "Enjoy a bowl of soup with me before you continue on your journey."

Seated at Utnapishtim's table, Wendy breathed in the wonderful aromas of his nourishing soup. The old man pulled out a chair, and sat opposite her. "I'm sorry I couldn't be more help to you when you were here before. My memory fails me. We were like children then. It is so hard to distinguish between what was real and what we only fantasized."

Wendy smiled, and thought about that, finishing her soup. "Maybe," she said, "maybe what I seek is not a place in time, but a state of mind. The condition of childhood, terrible and sweet, when all is new, when we know not death, and the world is full of giants and monsters."

Utnapishtim grinned. "You have gained a little wisdom, at least, in all your travels."

It was as it had been before, the stairway leading down in a long spiral, only now the walls were transparent, giving onto the grayness of the sea. Descending, she caught sight again of the shape among the waters, enormous and ovoid, rolling over to coast nearer the tower, to come almost up to its transparency, and stare at her with a minuscule and ancient eye. "Tiamat," she whispered and the behemoth rolled away.

She went on, to the bottom of the stairs, to the heart of the void before time, and she said, "Before there was the earth, before there was a universe, before there was anything, there was a woman, a snake, and a tree."

She stood on a grassy plain. A tree stood tall and solitary on a hill rising gently from the broad, even landscape. She walked toward it. Beneath the tree's bower sat her tablet and stylus, and about its roots twined the snake, in his scales she saw the evanescent seam of the simulation itself, the boundary of this illusion. She picked up the tablet, took the stylus in her hand, and wrote:

The first law is life, and from life comes love.
The second law is to remember the first law.
The third law is failing memory, invent.

And she pressed her mé into the tablet, and stood, and walked out onto the plain, the sky like a bright blue bowl above her. She walked through the high grasses, undulating around her like the waves of an amber sea. The warm earth and the grasses filled her nose with a heady perfume. The breeze was soft on her skin, the sun warm, and as she walked, she told herself this story: "There was a woman, and there was a man, and they loved one another."

On the slope of a far off hill, a ripple appeared among the grasses, and she walked toward it. "The woman and the man played together. They gave each other joy and told each other stories about all the wonderful things they were to each other. They helped each other become the people they wished to be, and together, in their playing, they made the world they wished to live in."

She was closer now, the ripple was no longer visible, but she caught a glimpse of dark hair and long hands, and her heart quickened. "They had forgotten this," she said, "but now they remember." All around her the grasses whispered, and then she spied his face, and he hers. With a mutual cry they were in each other's arms, and the earth was their bed, the sky their canopy.

"There's something familiar about this place," said Ray, after a time.

"Yes," said Wendy, "you drew it. Do you remember?"

"I remember now. The first day of the world." He laughed and rolled onto his back to gaze up at the sky, where the snake had taken flight, filling the blue vault with fractal detail. It was waiting, when they were ready, to take them out of the simulation. "Then I guess this is paradise," he said.

"It is not a time," said Wendy, "but it exists in all times. It is not a place, but it is in all places. It is made up of memory and invention. Yet it is always being remembered, always being invented. We are there when we remember that we are children, beloved by our mother, and resting against her body, find ourselves home."

CHAPTER

32

The first face Ray saw when he came out of the simulation was Lorca's. As he blinked in the shocking radiance of daylight that streamed into the open isolation chamber, she looked down at him with an odd expression somewhere between curiosity and apprehension. "Are you all right?" she asked him.

He took a deep breath, flexed his fingers and toes, nodded, and sat up. He folded his hands over his lap and coughed to clear his throat. "Where's Wendy?"

Lorca gave him a wry smile and stepped to one side so he had a clear view of the other isolation chamber. Its lid was open, too, and Veronica stood beside it, holding a towel. Wendy emerged from the black shell, her hair streaming wet, trailing electrodes as she ignored Veronica's ministrations and clambered over the side. Her eyes found his and they were dark and deep, radiant, wonderful.

Ray scrambled over the side of his chamber to meet her, but when his feet landed, his knees gave way. He sat down abruptly on the cold tile floor with a startled croak.

"Shit!" Wendy cried, and she was there, kneeling beside him, cradling his face in her hands, peering into his eyes, running trembling hands over him. "What's wrong? What's wrong?"

"It's probably just lack of use," said Veronica, crouching on the other side of him, wrapping a towel over Wendy's shoulders. "Remember, when you came out before we had to help you walk at first. Remember?"

Wendy nodded, but her eyes still searched his face. "Do you know who you are?"

He gave her a broad smile. "I do now," he said, but she looked unconvinced, so he told her, "I'm Ray Mackie."

Veronica and Wendy hauled him up by the elbows and helped him over to a couch. Wendy sat beside him and Lorca brought them blankets and towels. Veronica muttered something about fixing some tea and wandered off, but Lorca remained. She perched on a swivel chair, looking uncomfortable.

"Where's Raven?" asked Wendy.

Lorca swallowed and glanced at her hands. "She's with Zazula." She looked back up again, straight at Ray. He noticed a long red scratch on her cheek. "You were right about her. She is dangerous. She put Wendy in danger, and I was too busy hating you to see it."

Ray blinked.

"There's one more thing." Lorca got up, went over to the computer station and came back with a brown folio. She handed it to him and he took it from her with a question in his eyes. "We've all been through it," she said. "Maybe we shouldn't have but we did, and I just wanted to say that . . . your stuff is great. You're very talented and you should pursue it." She nodded, shrugged her shoulders, and started to turn away.

"Where are you going?" asked Wendy.

Lorca stopped and looked over her shoulder. "You two seem to be okay, so I was going to help Raven with Zazula. We're going to take her in to the police, for what she did to Ray."

"You are?" said Ray.

"Yeah. We have to. It's only a matter of time before she tries something like this again. I don't know what will happen. I imagine if there's a trial you'll both have to testify. Hopefully it'll all get over quickly and you can get on with your life together. I know that's what you both want." She dropped her eyes and looked back at Wendy. "I read that, too."

Wendy was very pale. "Wait. Lorca, you're talking like—like this is good-bye or something."

She nodded her head. "Isn't that what you want? You want to be with him."

Ray didn't like the look in Wendy's eyes. He didn't like this diffident, noble attitude of Lorca's. "That's pretty passive-aggressive, isn't it?" he said to her. "You were wrong, so rather than just deal with that, you're going to punish Wendy by leaving? Is that fair?"

Lorca's eyes were wide, her face a mask of restrained anger. "Look," she said, her hands palm out to him. "I don't know what you want from me. I've done all I can. She wants to be with you so just be happy about it."

"Yes," said Wendy. "I do want to be with Ray. That doesn't mean I want to lose my best friend." Anger flashed through her the way it did, like a summer storm, brutal and quick. Wendy leapt from the couch, clutching a blanket around her shoulders with one hand as she pointed at both of them with the other. "What is wrong with you two? Why do you always act like you're in competition with each other? For fuck's sake, I love you both!

"You know, I went to ancient Sumeria for the wrong reason. I wanted to prove the existence of ancient matriarchies. But I've decided that it doesn't matter. I don't care if they existed or not. What I care about is the possibility of a world where everyone is treated fairly, with respect for their individuality. I know that Belili and the Serpent That Knows No Charm existed. I know what Hister and Lili mean to me. And I know that whatever came before, the present belongs to us, and the future belongs to our imagination. It doesn't matter if the world we want has ever existed before. What matters is that we do what we can, now, to create it." She put her hands on her hips. "My world, the one I want to live in, is not ancient Sumeria, it's here, with you. With both of you."

Ray and Lorca both opened their mouths at once.

"No," said Wendy. "Neither of you has a choice in this. You have to find a way to get along—no!—not just get along. You have to find common ground. Right now." She planted her feet, crossed her arms, and looked at them both expectantly.

Ray and Lorca exchanged a panicked look. Well, there it was, thought Ray. Common ground. Both of them were absolutely terrified of Wendy at the moment. "We better do what she says," he said.

Wendy gave them both a curt nod. "I'll go check on Raven and Zazula—give you two some privacy to work this out." She grabbed a pair of jeans and a T-shirt that lay crumpled by the couch, got dressed, and left.

Ray watched her go, and then looked at Lorca. She seemed equally baffled, and for a while they just sat there in silence, racking their brains for some mutual interest upon which they could build—what?—some sort of amicable relationship, he guessed. "Computers?" he asked at last in desperation.

She tilted her head sideways and nodded a little. One corner of her mouth twitched to the side as she said "Yeah," in a tone of doubtful disappointment. Her gaze wandered about the room as she tried to think of something else.

"Well what about Wendy?" he asked.

She shot him a look of irritation. "Yeah, I know. We have to do this for her. I know that."

"No, I mean Wendy is our common ground. We both love her," he admitted, putting his hands out, palm up, as if he could show her. "Do you think that could be enough?"

She stared at him blankly for a moment. Then a look of pleased astonishment broke across her face and she smiled. She actually smiled at him. It made him realize he hardly knew her at all. "You're right, Ray," she said, her voice soft with wonder. And then she laughed. "Oh my. I can't believe I said that. But it's true. You're right." She threw her head back and laughed again, a high whooping sound, like the call of a sea bird. When she looked back at Ray there were tears in her eyes. "Shit," she said, wiping at them. "This hurts."

"Don't worry," he assured her. "I'm sure it won't happen all that often." And they both laughed.

"You know, I hardly know you at all," she said. "Just, well . . . Just all the stuff Wendy told me about your identity fraud and how you two broke up. But then, now that I've helped Zazula perform dangerous, unauthorized experiments I guess I'm not feeling so judgmental anymore."

He shrugged. "*She* forgives us."

EPILOGUE

Wendy sat back from her desk and read what she had so far of the new sim script she'd started.

You are alone in the woods, at night. It is winter, and there is snow upon the ground. Above, the stars are brilliant and sharp, like chips of ice. There are so many of them, blinking against the black sky, that if you look at them long enough, they will resolve into an image, something your eyes make up out of the flickering black and white, like you sometimes can with video snow. There is no moon.

It is very cold. You are wearing a tunic, leggings and a thick hooded cape. The rabbit-skin boots on your feet have a design embroidered on them, and looking at it brings you a memory of a woman sitting beside a hearth fire, stitching them to give you luck on your journey. You also have with you a basket of apples, bread, and cheese; a compass; a comb; two spools of thread; a dagger; and your favorite childhood toy.

The sun has disappeared, and you must find it.

If you go forward, you will come to a cave.

If you go backward, you will return to your village.

If you go left, you will come to a river.

If you go right, you will arrive at the Winter Palace.

The Winter Palace—this is the home of Despair and Bitterness, twin brother and sister. Long ago they were banished to eternal darkness by the moon, but now, Bitterness has kidnapped the sun and locked it in a cage, and Despair sits at the bars of the cage, captivated by its warmth, but unable to enjoy it for fear that it will be taken from her.

The cave—there is a bear sleeping in the cave. The bear has the key to the room in the Winter Palace where the sun is being imprisoned. But the key will only work if the bear willingly gives it to the player. The bear will ask the player a question, and they must answer truthfully in order to receive the key. The question is: What sustains you in your soul's darkest night?

It was a good start. She nodded with satisfaction and saved the file as "The Longest Night." She got up from her new ergonomic chair and wound her way through the piles of boxes clogging her office to go see how Ray was coming along with the mural.

She paused for a moment at the door of her office—her office!—and surveyed the new Huluppu Games, Inc. headquarters. Fifty-three desks in various stages of assembly stood interspersed with cardboard boxes in the wide open room. It seemed crowded and chaotic now, but once everything was set up, it would be an airy, spacious workplace. A bank of glass block windows along the back wall, just under the ceiling, let in plenty of natural light, and the pale yellow walls and the new oatmeal Berber carpeting heightened the effect.

She still couldn't get over the success of their first few inner adventures—crosses between computer games and vision quests, utilizing the full-sensory simulation environment Zazula had invented.

Zazula's lawyers had wasted no time in licensing her invention and offering it up for sale. And since the dangerous aspects of the Sumerian experiment had stemmed from prolonged use and atropine poisoning, Ninsega and the other game companies had gobbled it up. That was four years ago. Now The Snake was the new cause of the downfall of modern youth. The scourge of its day and the delight of its corruptees.

Most of the sims were much the same as the computer games she and Lorca had bemoaned in their college days. But Huluppu Games had gained a valuable foot in the door during the brief period in which they'd been the sole outside source for sim scripts. They had good brand recognition and the market for their personal development approach to computer entertainment was growing.

In fact, it was growing so much that they had to either sell the company or expand it. There'd never really been a question in any of their minds about giving in to Ninsega's admittedly dizzying courtship, but when Ray had the idea of drawing much of their staff from the vocational program at the battered women's shelter where Veronica volunteered, Wendy had gotten that tingling, preordained feeling again.

In the area that would become the sales and marketing department, Lorca, Raven, and several of their new hires were setting up the phone system. Their voices rose in laughter and dismay as they attempted to navigate the intricacies of the call transfer feature, and somehow wound up setting every phone to intercom instead. "Clean up in aisle three," Carlina Booth's ordinarily soft voice boomed out of twenty phones at once. With a squeak of embarrassed delight she hung up with a clunk and dissolved into laughter.

On the back wall, in the middle of the building where the break area would be, Wendy saw that Ray's mural was coming along very well indeed. It was a vivid rendition of the huluppu tree. Its green, fan-shaped leaves spread all the way to the ceiling. The branches were teeming with animals and birds of all shapes and descriptions, and of course there was a dark-haired, winged woman laughing, and a snake coiled about the roots of the tree.

Wendy crossed the room and stood back a little, watching Ray, up on a ladder, dabbing flecks of blue into the plumage of a dark but brilliantly feathered bird. His face held a look of peaceful concentration so pure, so calmly, joyfully content that she felt an answering tide of happiness rise within her.

Ray turned and saw her, and smiled wider. He put his brush down and climbed down from the ladder. He had a streak of red paint on his cheek, and his eyes were bright and clear. He put his warm arms around her and she hugged him back, the dried paint on his T-shirt scratchy against her cheek. "It's gorgeous," she told him.

They released each other and Ray looked at the huluppu tree with evident satisfaction. "Yeah," he said, a blush creeping into his cheeks as he dropped his eyes, bit his lip, and then gave her a sheepish grin. "I really like it." He shrugged. "I mean I love doing the sim visuals, but there's something about actually moving your hand and your arm to create the image. I kind of miss it."

"Hey, it's looking good, Beam," said Lorca, coming up to stand beside them. She wore jeans and a green sweatshirt emblazoned with their company logo—a tree, of course. Her hair was tied back with a rubber band and she had a pen tucked behind one ear. "I especially like the Anzu bird. Is that what you mean by rainbow black?"

"Yes! Exactly," said Ray. "That's what the dragon in "The Knight's Quest" needs. See how the blackness has all those other colors in it? The scales should look like that."

Lorca nodded. "Can I get you in the sim?" She cocked one thumb toward the office next to Wendy's that she and Ray shared. "Now while it's fresh in our minds?"

"Yeah, let's go." Ray gave Wendy a kiss and he was off, trailing behind Lorca through the maze of partially assembled desks. Wendy wandered after them, leaning in the doorway, knowing she had her own work to get back to but indulging herself for a few minutes by watching them work together.

Ray grabbed the Snake from his reclining chair and slid it over his shoulders. He tucked the tail down his shirt and Lorca helped him position it over his spine. The technology had been refined quite a bit. Piezoelectric currents had replaced the electrodes, and the tail was a thin strip of flexible plastic. He leaned back in his chair and closed his eyes. Lorca took a seat at her computer and called up the simulation for "The Knight's Quest."

"Skip to the first appearance of the dragon, when the player is at the peak of the mountain," said Ray. There was a pause while Lorca tapped at the keyboard.

"Yeah, see, I know you love the pebble texture, and that's fine, but there needs to be more gradations of light in the scales, more variation."

Lorca typed some more, and Ray said, "That's better. Now intensify the blues and reds. Yes! Perfect." His nostrils flared. "Only for some reason there's a smell of overcooked cabbage. Not strictly my department, but I thought you'd want to know."

Lorca frowned. "What? There shouldn't be any—Oh, I see, it's the sulfur of the dragon's breath mixing with the wildflowers. How's this?"

"Ah, much better."

"How's this?" Lorca grinned and typed some more.

Ray grimaced. "Oh gross! You've got to stop doing that!"

"Hee-hee."

"You better get some mountain breezes in here or I'm coming out."

"Okay, okay. How's that."

"Good. Now, the sky. I think it should be dramatic. Layers of red, pink, and yellow, with the sun glowing orange through the clouds . . . That's good but the colors need to blend more . . . Great, now how about some purple along the horizon?"

They would go on like this for hours, Wendy knew. She slid from her perch on Ray's desk and padded quietly to the door, pausing at the threshold to look back at her two friends, absorbed in the give and take of their collaborative effort.

That had been the most surprising thing of all: how well they worked together. Wendy had never found out exactly what they said to each other that day in Zazula's lab after she and Ray had extricated themselves from the Sumerian sim, but from that day forward, they'd stopped being adversaries. And what began as neutral respect and courtesy had quickly grown into genuine friendship. Wendy leaned against the doorframe and looked away from Ray and Lorca's quiet little miracle, out into the new world it was creating.

ABOUT THE AUTHOR

Anne Harris won the 1999 Spectrum Award for her novel *Accidental Creatures*. Her previous novel, *The Nature of Smoke*, was praised as "an impressive debut" by *Publishers Weekly* and "fizzing with ideas" by *Kirkus Reviews*. She lives in Royal Oak, Michigan.

Learn more at www.inventingmemory.com.